THE OGRE'S
DAUGHTER

Catherine Bardon

THE OGRE'S DAUGHTER

*Translated from the French
by Tina Kover*

Europa Editions
8 Blackstock Mews
London N4 2BT
www.europaeditions.co.uk

This book is a work of fiction. Any references to historical events,
real people, or real locales are used fictitiously.

Copyright © Éditions Les Escales domaine français,
un département d'Édi8, 2022. Published by special arrangement with Éditions
Les Escales domaine français, un département d'Édi8, in conjunction with their
duly appointed agent 2 Seas Literary Agency
First publication 2025 by Europa Editions

Translation by Tina Kover
Original title: *La fille de l'ogre*
Translation copyright 2024 by Europa Editions

All rights reserved, including the right of reproduction
in whole or in part in any form.

A catalogue record for this title is available from the British Library
ISBN 978-1-78770-598-2

Bardon, Catherine
The Ogre's Daughter

Cover photo © Rights reserved

Cover design by Ginevra Rapisardi

Prepress by Grafica Punto Print – Rome

The authorized representative in the EEA
is Edizioni e/o, via Gabriele Camozzi 1, 00192 Rome, Italy.

Printed and bound in Great Britain by Clays Ltd, Elcograf S.p.A

CONTENTS

The Ogre's Daughter - 13

Image Section - 367

Behind the Scenes of
The Ogre's Daughter - 371

Acknowledgments - 375

Bibliography - 377

Further Reading - 377

About the Author - 379

"Do not be fooled; fate is nothing more than a distillation of childhood."
—RAINER MARIA RILKE, *Duino Elegies*

"To let a bit of light into the opaqueness of beings, in their mystery, their fragility, their wanderings, and to tell what is glimpsed, what is divined, what is revealed."
—GAËLLE JOSSE, *Une femme en contre-jour*

"I told myself it would be a novel, with characters and chapters, but that I would invent nothing that couldn't really have happened."
—MARIO VARGAS LLOSA, on *The Feast of the Goat*

THE OGRE'S DAUGHTER

SAN CRISTÓBAL,
DOMINICAN REPUBLIC
1920

"Flor! Flor de Oro!"

The name is delicate, precious, like the child herself. *Flower of Gold.*

It was her father who picked the name. Her mother isn't sure where it came from, so she always tells the little girl he dreamed it up specially for her, just for the pleasure of seeing her smile.

A made-up name, just for her! Flor de Oro is happy. Her Papi loves her.

"Flor! Flor de Oro!"

Her mother is calling from the far end of the courtyard. The puppies have been born.

Flor takes off running, her mouth full of coconut dulce de leche. There's a funny sort of one-legged hop in her gait that throws her slightly off balance, almost a limp. She stumbles and nearly sprawls in the dirt but manages to catch herself. Aminta pretends not to have seen. The discordant note of Flor's clumsiness makes her smile fondly; clearly, neither she nor her husband have passed on their sense of rhythm to their little girl. Aminta, a humble woman without much education, loves to dance. That's what first brought them together, T and her, she thinks: his hand on the small of her back, her pelvis pressed to his, bodies swaying, molding together, curves fitting into hollows, hips undulating, shoulders brushing. That, and their youth, and San Cristóbal, the place where they were born.

No, her little Flor, aged five, has no rhythm in her bones. Perhaps Julia Genoveva would have had some. Perhaps . . .

Flor de Oro is there in front of her mother now, cheeks

flushed pink from running, rosebud lips parted and shiny with sugar, eyes eager. Aminta nods, resolutely banishing the ghost of her elder daughter. They must never allow the loss to cast a shadow over Flor's childhood. Not ever.

Taking the little girl's hand, Aminta leads her to the doghouse. The animal is lying still on her side in the dimness, eyes closed, patiently enduring the voracious suckling of her four rodent-like newborns. Flor bends down, examining each puppy carefully, then points decisively at a round black lump huddled against the mother dog's haunch.

"That one!"

The child kneels and strokes the puppy timidly with her fingertips, then jerks her hand back; the mother dog has begun to growl softly. Proud of her own daring, Flor raises shining eyes to her Mami's smiling face.

* * *

Papi is home. A few days' leave. Flor has seen him only rarely since he became an army cadet, no more than once or twice every couple of months. He's enrolled in the military academy in Haina, far from San Cristóbal, where American marines train future officers for the Dominican Army. Flor hates Americans. Once, she threw rocks at a passing car with four soldiers inside.

T pats the top of his daughter's head distractedly, running his fingers through her dark curls, wishing their texture wasn't so coarse. He questions her mother. Yes, Aminta says, she's well-behaved. Good marks at school. Fine, he nods. Flor asks her father about the puppy. T reluctantly allows himself to be dragged out to the doghouse, but not before putting a straw hat on his little girl's head. They mustn't allow her complexion to be tanned by the sun; she's already regrettably dark-skinned. Eagerly, Flor points out her chosen puppy. "That one's mine. I'm going to call him Coffee." Her father grimaces. This isn't the sort of thing that inspires affection in him. He heaves a sigh.

"No, *mi amor*. Not that one. It's black, so it's bad, like all blacks. Look, it's already stealing milk from the others."

Hunkered down with her elbows on her knees, Flor watches the dogs closely. Her little chin has begun to tremble, tears welling in her eyes, threatening to spill down her cheeks. She loved Coffee already. But Papi is right; the black puppy is nursing greedily, kicking the one next to him, a little white thing with reddish-brown spots on its paws that remind her of shoes. Her father points at it. "Take that one instead. It's nice and white, and you'll see, if you take good care of it, it'll become a *tiguere*! You can call it Snowball!"

There. Papi has decided, and he's always right. He must never be contradicted or, even worse, disappointed. A little girl must always submit to her father's will, especially if he's a soldier. Her puppy will be Snowball.

Flor has no idea what snow is.

Aminta has observed the scene from a distance, powerless. There's no point in stepping in. She is afraid of this man, her husband. He has always been controlling, quick to anger, inflexible, violent, and it's only gotten worse since he began this military training. He was already known for his savagery years ago, when he and his brother were *cuatreros*,[1] and then when he headed up a gang of criminals known as "the 42," and still later, during the time he was employed as a guard at a sugar cane plantation, the Haitian workers living in terror of his cruelty. Oh yes, the beatings he used to dole out with a bull-tendon cosh or a guava-wood cane remain etched in many memories. And deep in her heart, Aminta, who comes from a good family, has always known she made a mistake in marrying this short, uneducated telegraph operator, who has even spent time in prison. Was it the bad-boy aspect of him or his skill at dancing that made her yield? And on top of everything, he

---

[1] *Cuatreros:* Cattle thieves.

isn't faithful—doesn't even attempt to hide his affairs. *What* a disaster. But a daughter shouldn't have to pay for her mother's mistakes, and so Aminta endures. For Flor de Oro, she grits her teeth and sets about making her husband a *malteada*.[2]

Now that the matter of the puppy has been settled and Papi is content, Flor hopes he'll tie ribbons in her hair and call her "*mi princesa*." Or take off his uniform belt and hand it to her so she can wash it in the river. Or, best of all, that he'll dance with her. She twirls in circles around him while he sips his drink, hopping from one foot to the other, her expression hopeful. And T understands. He's in a good mood today. Setting down his glass, he declaims a few verses of poetry beneath his daughter's admiring gaze, then begins humming a popular tune.

Delicately, he tucks a wayward strand of hair behind Flor's ear, then lifts her as if she weighs no more than a feather and sets her back down so that her little canvas shoes are resting on the tops of his leather boots. He counts off the beats of the merengue, and they whirl together, T holding Flor securely in his arms. "*Baila mi'jita; baila, mueve la cadera!*" What fun it is! This is the only game Papi will play with her, and Flor beams up into his face, wiggling her hips delightedly. Abruptly, though, Papi stops; he's grown tired of swinging her around. Flor is left with arms dangling, both feet firmly back on the floor. Papi stamps his boots to shake off the dust left by her shoes and turns away from Flor without a word—but then, changing his mind, he steps back toward her, digs in his pocket, and hands her a five-peso coin "to buy yourself a toy with," and a little piece of sugar cane that he peels for her. "Thank you, Papi!" Flor sucks on the treat, its sweet juices trickling down her throat. How good it tastes! Today really is a wonderful day.

---

[2] *Malteada:* A very popular drink in the Dominican Republic, made of condensed milk, barley beer, and ice.

* * *

In Flor's childhood, there is the ghost.

The unspoken absence. The intangible void, the emptiness she sees in her mother's face sometimes when she pulls away from Flor, or suddenly lets the little hand she is holding drop for no reason, or suppresses a sigh. Flor never knew the sister who died of a tropical fever, the child lost before she'd reached her first birthday. She doesn't know about the yawning hole in Aminta's heart, or the fury and despair of her father who, despite riding through the night on his old nag, wasn't able to bring the doctor back in time; the Haina had been overflowing its banks, and he'd battled the currents and the rain for hours. By the time he finally made it home, his baby daughter was dead. T had vowed then and there to build a bridge across that cursed river.

Flor doesn't know that she was intended to compensate for the lost angel, that she is the replacement child. But instinctively, she senses the too-large space she is being asked, silently, to fill. And so she does her best. She tries her hardest. In school, in Bible class, at home. She's careful always to be lighthearted, never serious, never sad. She feels she isn't entitled to sadness.

In Flor's childhood, there is the crucial absence of her father, whose military and political rise is meteoric. Imperious, domineering, demanding. He has no time for her. Occasionally, even though she isn't the son he wanted, he softens for a moment toward this child who is so cheerful, so easy, if slightly shy and a bit of a little savage sometimes, who adores him completely and is always so fearful of disappointing him. He allows himself to be charmed by the wide, innocent smile that lights up her sun-bronzed face. But it never lasts. There are too many other, more important things that require his attention.

In Flor's childhood, there is the stain of original sin. A stain she can never wash away. The one, perhaps, that explains everything.

A single drop.

A drop of black blood. Haitian. The thing no one talks about. The thing her father is so ashamed of. The one that, years in the future, will lead El Jefe, who claims aristocratic descent, to powder his skin, to plaster his face with clown-white makeup. The secret betrayed by Flor's unruly curls and less-than-alabaster complexion. It's a remote inheritance, this drop of blood. Passed down from a great-great-grandfather in T's maternal line, a Haitian officer named Joseph Chevallier who came to the country when it was still called Dominicana. The secret that must be kept deeply buried, no matter what the cost. But the more they try to hide it, the louder it proclaims itself in Flor as she matures, that drop of blood.

Maybe Julia Genoveva didn't have it. Maybe she was a perfect baby. Maybe that's why Papi and Mami look at Flor with pity, why they don't love her very much. Because she, Flor, isn't perfect.

That drop of blood will haunt her until the day she dies.

Santo Domingo
June 1924

One Sunday, a catastrophe besets Flor's childhood, already a turbulent one thanks to her father's rapid rise through the military ranks. Recently, with a sense of relief, T attended the departure of the last Marines from the Dominican Republic. He took Flor with him to see them off from the port of Santo Domingo, whispering "At last!" in her ear as the American warships steamed out of the harbor. And then, to celebrate their liberation, he bought her an ice cream.

Now that the *Yanquis* have left the country, T's sights are set firmly on the pinnacle of success: command of the entire army. Nothing and no one will stop, or even hinder, his path to the top. For a few years now, Flor de Oro has seen her father only rarely. Her parents' marriage has disintegrated at the same speed with which T's star has risen. It's been a real disaster. Aminta has refused to follow her husband from posting to posting, and he has all but abandoned the family home. Flor and her mother are living alone in San Cristóbal.

On this particular Sunday, Papi has promised to come and see them. Flor, having gotten up early to arrange her hair carefully and put on a white dress with crisply starched ruffles and a pair of black shoes polished until they shine, is waiting for him with feverish excitement. The sun rises slowly in the sky, and the hottest hours of the day arrive, and still there is no sign of him. The house is stifling and airless. Flor goes out beneath the porch awning. She's tempted to play with Snowball, but Aminta warns her about getting dirty: "You wouldn't want to annoy your father, would you?" So Flor waits, sitting quietly in the *mecedora*. Aminta decides to go ahead and serve lunch. The table is set for three. Flor isn't hungry. She pushes her chicken thigh around her plate with her fork. This is usually her favorite dish, but today she can't swallow a bite of it, or even of the *concon*[3] Mami carefully scraped from the bottom of the pot for her. Flor raises bewildered eyes to her mother's face, noting the sagging corners of her mouth, bracketed by lines of bitterness and disappointment. Tears threaten, but Flor fights them back; Mami looks so sad. The afternoon crawls by. Flor dozes, curled up in the rocking chair. Eventually, Aminta can't bear it any longer.

"He isn't coming," she says. "Something must have held him up. He's so busy. It's not his fault."

But really, it *is* his fault, Aminta thinks. A father shouldn't make empty promises to his child; he's hurt Flor de Oro deeply. Feigning cheerfulness, she helps Flor change out of the pretty white dress and into a linen skirt she sewed herself, for in addition to being an excellent cook and impeccable housekeeper, Aminta is an exceptional seamstress. The little girl runs outside to find Snowball and bury her sorrows in the dog's dusty fur.

* * *

Her father has mistresses. Flor has heard Mami shouting about them. She wonders if they're the same kind of mistress as the one who teaches her at school. She often hears her parents arguing when T is home.

"I've got better things to do than be shrieked at by some harpy!"

"*Sin vergüenza, mujeriego* . . . You humiliate me—you dishonor me! All you've ever done is humiliate me!"

---

[3] *Concon:* Dominican term for the crust of rice that sticks to the bottom of the pot during cooking.

"And all *you* ever do is complain! You should be *proud* of me!"
"Proud!" Aminta laughs bitterly.

When the divorce is finalized and Aminta finds herself alone with a 100-peso monthly allowance to raise Flor, she resigns herself quickly to the new circumstances. Little Flor, though, is devastated. She never imagined that life could be like this—that Papi and Mami would live apart forever, in two different houses. Maybe she hasn't been a good enough girl, or clever enough in school, or obedient enough, and Papi got tired of her. Maybe she'll never see him again. Her love of life becomes a thing of the past. She's quiet now, unsmiling, even pouty. The taste of guilt is bitter.

* * *

T has come to see them today. He's wearing a suit instead of his military uniform, and, despite the dusty roads, his black shoes shine like mirrors. He is terribly elegant. Aminta hangs back, keeping near the door. She's taken off her apron and smoothed her skirts with her palms, regretting that her hair isn't tidier. Sitting down in an armchair, T beckons Flor over. Her soft, rounded little face is exactly level with his, which is stern and hard: his *captain* face. Flor, with the wisdom of all her nine years, is sure that all has been forgiven, that now everything will go back to the way it was. The thought is exhilarating, and, unable to suppress a triumphant smile, she flings her skinny arms around her father's neck.

But she is soon disabused of her happy notions. Papi grasps both her wrists and holds them firmly in his lap. Frowning, he fixes her eyes with his and says solemnly, "I hope you can prove yourself worthy of my hopes for you and the sacrifices I'm making for your education. You're going away to study in France."

Aminta, faced with the fait accompli, wrings her hands. She tries to change T's mind. Flor is too young. The school in San

Cristóbal is perfectly good. There's no need to spend so much money on her education. They've never been separated, and Flor de Oro needs her Mami, especially because T—well, T is never around. Aminta regrets those last words as soon as she says them.

But T, his face like stone, merely shrugs. "I'm an important man now. I'll be running this whole country one day soon. My daughter has to receive the best possible education. She's not learning anything here, and you spoil her, Aminta. This will toughen her up—broaden her horizons—give her a little polish. She needs that. She's going to have to live up to her status."

"Status? What status? And why does it have to be so far away? Why France?"

Because it's Europe. The Old World. Much classier than America. And it's where all the members of the Dominican elite are educated. And T has French ancestors, don't forget.

Haitian, not French! Aminta wants to scream. They're nowhere near the same thing. But she bites back the remark and says nothing. After all, what do the feelings of a mother and child matter, compared to the destiny T is forging for himself?

Distraught and confused, Flor de Oro bows her head, a sacrificial lamb on the altar of her father's ego. If she wants T to love her, she knows, she has no choice but to leave.

The truth is that, in his own way, he *does* love her. She is his only child. He is forever trying to dispel the painful memory of his first daughter, and of his defeated return to the miserable family hut, too late to save her. And there's something about Flor de Oro, too—an impishness, a whimsical quality—that he can't resist. He softens again now, allowing himself another fleeting moment of tenderness.

Flor looks up at her father with enormous, tear-filled brown eyes and murmurs, so softly it's almost a whisper, "I'll be a good student, I promise, Papi. I'll get very good marks. You'll be proud of me."

"The highest marks. You have to get the *very highest* marks."

Flor's heart flutters like hummingbird wings in her chest. T rests a hand on the top of his daughter's head and strokes the frizzy curls. Flor closes her eyes. The weight of Papi's hand on her head is a benediction. She feels suddenly hopeful, ready to face any challenge.

For him. For Papi.

* * *

The die is cast. Aminta has no choice but to soothe and encourage her daughter. For, despite the promise she made to T, Flor doesn't want to leave. Her mother paints an idyllic portrait of France, of the friends Flor will make, the foreign languages she'll learn, the elegant young woman she'll become. But Flor shakes her head, weeps, stomps her feet, pleads. She doesn't want to leave the island. Or her Mami. Or her friends, or her cousins. And what about Snowball?

But T has made up his mind, and there's no changing it.

Aminta has two weeks to pack Flor's bags.

As a final formality before her departure, in order to enroll in the boarding school at Bouffémont, Flor must be baptized. After the death of his first daughter, T had turned his back on the Church and—much to Aminta's dismay—refused to have Flor christened. Now he selected one of his close friends, Dr. Jose Mejia, to be her godfather, and one of Aminta's cousins as godmother. Flor wants to dig a hole in the ground and hide in it forever, so embarrassed is she by being baptized at such an ancient age.

* * *

After all of this, though, Flor puts on a brave face when the dreaded day arrives. She stalwartly holds back her tears as she boards the steamship at the port of Santo Domingo, her stomach in knots. Her mother has dressed her in a beautiful traveling outfit, a blue velvet dress with a matching coat—far too warm for this time of year, but it will be cold in France, Aminta warns her. Flor has on new Mary Jane shoes that pinch her feet, and her hair has been brushed smooth and pulled back from her little face with its domed forehead. On the gangway she misses a step and trips, just managing to grab the handrail clumsily. She looks up at the ship. It's enormous; she's never seen one so big. For the first time in her life, faced with a limitless universe, she feels small.

The ship's horn blares suddenly, startling the seagulls, which scatter, crying out raucously. The gangway is withdrawn, and, despite the heavy velvet coat, Flor begins to shiver with cold. The ship casts off, moving slowly, groaningly, away from the dock. Flor is afraid, but she manages something approximating a smile and looks up at the man who has been sent to accompany her on the ocean crossing. Gripping the rail tightly with one hand, she waves frenetically with the other at the land from which she's being banished.

She'll spend ten long days at sea, looked after by an embassy secretary en route to his posting in Paris. She'll have her own cabin. Like a princess. Her head barely reaching above the railing, the princess smiles bravely, for her mother, with that wide, guileless smile that lights up her whole face and reveals all her teeth, that smile loved so much by Aminta, and even by T, sometimes.

Mami is still standing on the slowly receding dock in the light of the setting sun, a tiny, vanishing silhouette, waving her white handkerchief in farewell. Her father didn't come to say goodbye. Too busy. But he'd made a flying visit the previous evening, kissing her and making her promise, again, that she would earn the highest marks in her class: "I promise, Papi."

Back on the deck of the ship, standing next to Flor's small, fragile figure is the tall, trim one of the man assigned to watch over her during the journey, a task he will devote himself to wholeheartedly. He is a fervent admirer of her father, who has raised himself to power through his own sheer strength and now runs the national police with an iron fist—transforming it into an army, in fact, with the full consent of the elderly President Vásquez.

At last the ship is nothing more than a small black dot on the horizon, a plume of gray smoke rising from it and dissipating in the sky.

Aminta leaves the quayside with dragging steps.

Flor de Oro is gone.

* * *

In the solitude of her cabin, Flor's emotions veer between nervousness and excitement. She's going on a long journey like a grown-up, and, Mami promised, she's going to make lots of new friends. And the gentleman traveling with her is very nice; he calls her Señorita Flor de Oro and speaks to her formally, like she's a grand lady. Pride swells in her little chest. But then, suddenly, she feels the prickle of tears. She tries to hold them back, but an image of Snowball pops into her mind, and the floodgates open. Sobbing, she reaches for Rosita, the rag doll Mami made for her to replace the first Rosita, the one made from sugar cane leaves, the one she'd had back on the plantation in San Cristóbal, that dried up and crumbled to dust long ago. Flor hugs Rosita close, kissing her yarn hairs, and whispers a secret to her. They're going to a wonderful place together, she tells the doll; they're going to live in a castle in the middle of a huge forest, with princesses and maybe even fairies. And then, even though Flor de Oro knows she's too big for it, and Papi has forbidden it, she sticks her thumb in her mouth, humming, and rocks Rosita to sleep.

This exile, this separation, marks the end of her childhood. This loneliness is Flor's first taste of the pain that will often reduce her to silence, lightened by occasional, fleeting moments of happiness. The pain that will never truly leave her again.

Bouffémont
September 1924

It's the Dominican ambassador in Paris who recommended the place. T stated explicitly that he wanted the *very best* school for Flor. Top-ranking, international, and *secular*. No religious schools.

The Bouffémont Boarding School for Girls, newly established in a magnificent complex on the edge of Montmorency Forest, is without a doubt the right place for T's daughter. Highly selective and extremely costly, this prestigious institution prides itself on accepting only young girls from the very best families in France and abroad. Like the great English and American schools, Bouffémont offers a complete range of study and training: classes and individual assignments, sports, artistic and leisure activities. Girls aged eight to twenty are given a solid moral, intellectual, and physical education using the most up-to-date methods, ensuring that they will be worthy representatives of their families and their social class—and even, in the case of the most ambitious young ladies, able to carry out a profession . . . perhaps. That, of course, would be the cherry on the cake.

Virgil, Homer, and Rousseau in the morning; golf or horseback riding in the afternoon; a classical concert each evening—everything T would have liked for himself, but never had. He didn't bat an eyelash when the school's exorbitant fees were revealed: 2,500 francs per term.

* * *

The broad drive cuts through the ample grounds, filled with ancient trees. Flor is a tiny, anxious figure in the wide back seat of the limousine, open-mouthed, her nose pressed to the window. This place doesn't look like a school at all; it's more like a castle, like the ones in the stories Mami told her. Suddenly she's afraid. Everything is so *big*—outsized, even. The chauffeur pulls up beneath the glare of two recumbent lions carved from white stone. A turret-topped staircase leads to a magisterial, pillared building overlooking an immaculate flower bed. This can't be right; the chauffeur must have made a mistake. "Here you are, Señorita." Flor swallows with difficulty around the lump in her throat. So this really is her new school.

A young woman in a severely cut slate-gray suit leads her to the headmistress's office while the chauffeur unloads her trunks. When he bids her goodbye, Flor has to fight back tears. She's all alone now, for good. Too late, she realizes that she forgot to give him the tip provided by the ambassador's wife, and a wave of guilt sweeps over her. What must he think of her? As long as no one tells her father . . .

Madame Pichon—Henriette Pichon, the school's founding headmistress—is moved by this little girl with the anxious face, who speaks exactly five words of French: *bonjour*, *oui Madame*, and *merci beaucoup*. In fact, she's almost disturbed by the distress she can sense in the child, so young, so scrawny, so timid. She tries to put Flor at ease, hesitating for a moment and then—etiquette be damned—taking the girl's hand with a laugh. "Come on, *allons-y*."

"We have three hundred pupils here at Bouffémont. There are three buildings: Castel-Sous-Bois, the Palais Scolaire, and this one, the Manoir de Longpré, where the private rooms are. This is where you'll be living," Madame Pichon says, opening a door.

Flor steps into her room, where a small alcove with a sofa opens out into an immense chamber furnished with a huge bed (a *parents'* bed, she thinks to herself), a wardrobe, a desk, bookcases, two armchairs, and its own bathroom. Tall, dark-curtained windows overlook the grounds. It's spacious, light-filled, elegant. Flor goes to the window. She examines the curtains, touches them—they're thick, of an indeterminate burgundy shade—then looks out the window at the view, a pale, gray and white world with a few touches of green. Nothing like the brilliant colors of home. She wonders where Rosita will sleep.

But soon Henriette is showing her the Palais Scolaire and its "amenities," rattling off Bouffémont's credo in perfect Spanish all the while: "Knowledge, intelligence, distinction, physical and moral beauty." Flor wonders doubtfully if she's good enough to be here. The headmistress is still talking: "This school was designed by Maurice Boutterin, chief government architect and winner of the Grand Prix de Rome in 1909." Flor senses that this is something she should be impressed by, so she nods energetically.

"There are nineteen classrooms," Henriette continues, "a magnificent library with twenty thousand books, a laboratory for science experiments, a sewing room, a laundry and ironing room, several soundproofed rooms for musical study, nine terraces for rest and relaxation, a medical office, a dentist's office, a hair salon, gymnasiums, an auditorium, and—our crowning luxury—a heated indoor swimming pool three hundred meters square."

Winding up this recitation worthy of the best tour guide, Madame Pichon pauses to catch her breath . . . then starts again:

"Ten kilometers of paths for strolling—and there is the large pond, fed with fresh running water, for you to swim in, my dear." Flor shivers at the very thought. For a child of the tropics, it's very cold here. Just as Mami said it would be. " . . . And the lake for canoeing, and tennis courts . . . the golf course and stables . . . "

Madame Pichon goes on and on, detailing everything that promises to make Flor's new life into a fairy tale. The little girl feels dizzy. All she's certain of is that this place is enormous, and she's going to get lost. All she wants is to go back to the room that's hers now, unpack her things, and cuddle Rosita.

* * *

It's time for lunch, and Flor is escorted to the dining room, where she sits down at a table full of other little girls who are already engaged in animated conversation. She can't understand a word they're saying, so she loses herself in contemplation of the multicolored stained glass in the dome overhead, glowing in the sunlight like a precious jewel.

The rest of the day is a blur of unpacking, introductions, and games. Flor meets only one other pupil who speaks Spanish: Celia, an Argentinian girl whose father is in politics, a bit like Flor's. Those are the only two things they have in common. But since there are no other options, they spend much of the afternoon together, and sit next to each other at dinner.

Flor has trouble falling asleep that night, dwarfed by the massive bed. Curling up in a tight ball, she presses her face to Rosita's dress, her yarn hair, breathing in the last faint scents of her island.

BOUFFÉMONT
1924–1927

The first few days don't go very well.

Except for the gardener and a few male service workers whom the pupils rarely see, Bouffémont is an entirely female universe. The outside world has lost its reality. The music of her native language, the childhood stories, the scorching glare of the sun, the soft warmth of the sea, her mother's voice, the sweet taste of mangoes, her father's rages—Flor has lost touch with them all, with everything that made her the happy little girl she used to be. Here the sky is so gray, the sun so pallid, the colors of the trees so drab. And she's cold, always cold. She can't seem to manage to get warm. She never knew it was possible to be so cold. It's cold in the corridors going from classroom to classroom; it's cold in the enormous dining room; it's cold in the Bouffémont Church where she attends services, and in the gymnasium where she has to run around in shorts. She retreats to the second-floor library whenever she can, huddling against the radiators near the study tables.

Why did they send her so far away from everything she's always known?

She misses Mami. Her indulgent smile, the warmth of her arms and the jasmine perfume of her neck, her delicious *sancocho* and the way they used to dance in the garden after school, her goodnight kisses (*"Sueña con los angelitos, mi'jita . . . "*). Even when Mami pulled dreadfully on her hair with the comb to untangle it, or when she made her finish a whole serving of *mangú*—she misses that, too.

And she misses Papi. And Snowball. The sorrow is so great

that Flor cries sometimes, at night, alone in her enormous bedroom. She's begun sucking her thumb again, like a baby. It causes a large, hard bump on her knuckle, a whitish growth she tries to hide from the others. It's ugly, she knows, but she can't break the habit. She's just glad Papi isn't here to see it.

* * *

Despite what her mother claimed—her mother, who has never been to Bouffémont, who has never even left the island—it's not easy to make new friends here. Not at all.

Flor, short and thin, with frizzy hair and legs as gangly as a stork's, is far from the most popular girl in school. Her drop of black blood doesn't help matters, and she comes from a country so tiny that no one can even locate it on a map. They've certainly never read her father's name in the newspapers here. And on top of all that, one glance at her wardrobe is enough to tell that she knows nothing about fashion. And that she's clearly rather poor. Flor feels nonexistent, almost invisible among these girls who are much more well-born than she is, the daughters of wealthy industrialists, heirs and heiresses, aristocrats, highnesses.

There are actual princesses at Bouffémont, not like Flor when she used to play at being queen with her girl cousins. *Real* ones. Illana is Russian, and Maryam and Zana come from Iran, a very big country they show her in the library's atlas. Flor finds her own island with the help of Madame Ponsard, the librarian, and points at the green dot in the middle of a wide blue ocean. "Look, there it is." Maryam makes a little moue of distaste, and Zana wrinkles her aquiline nose and says, with a disdainful sniff, "Goodness, it's *miniscule*." "That's why we've never heard of it," her sister adds dismissively.

Flor is offended. "First of all, it isn't miniscule," she retorts, adding, "and also, it's beautiful—more beautiful than you can imagine," for good measure, hoping she sounds mysterious and intriguing.

And then, all of a sudden, she thinks of the perfect riposte, one that ought to shut up those princesses. They've been studying Julius Caesar in Latin class (which she hates), and it's the emperor who whispers the phrase in her ear: "I would rather be first in a little village than second in Rome."[4]

With those words, she effectively alienates both Iranian princesses.

* * *

Flor experiences her first autumn, then her first winter. She gathers chestnuts, coming home with dirt-encrusted fingernails that she has to scrub clean laboriously. She discovers new smells: dead leaves rotting in damp soil, mushrooms, the wisps of fog that rise from the forest floor. And snow. It's dazzling. Now she understands why her dog is called Snowball; she can explain it to Mami. In the meantime, she tells Rosita all about it. Rosita isn't very well; her cotton stuffing is poking out of little rips in her cloth body. Flor stitches these up in sewing class and gives Rosita pretty button eyes, too. She's very proud of the result.

* * *

Flor has invented a confidante for herself. Yulissa. She's too big truly to believe Yulissa is real, of course, but she's also too little not to need her. Yulissa waits for her in the big bed every night, a secret friend to whom Flor can tell everything. They giggle beneath the down comforter and make fun of the schoolmates who look down on Flor. The princesses especially, with their hooked noses, and their big dark eyes that wander sideways, and their scornful little mouths. Flor tells Yulissa about her Prince Charming. And about her Papi. Especially about him. She hopes so much that he'll be different when she goes

---

[4] Plutarch, *Caesar*.

home, that he'll have a little more time for her, that he'll be proud of her, finally. Sometimes she dreams of a different father altogether. Like a very young child, she imagines that her parents aren't really her parents, that her father isn't really her father. Other girls might wish for fathers that were richer, more important, but Flor wishes hers was someone *less* rich, *less* important. Someone gentle and affectionate. But then she stops herself, because she feels like she's being disloyal to Mami. Then she kneels on the floor next to her too-large bed, clasps her hands beneath her chin, and asks Jesus to protect her Papi and her Mami, and to make her breasts grow.

Flor cocoons herself in this little world. Yulissa and Rosita.

* * *

Flor *must* live up to her father's expectations. So she grits her teeth and forces herself to smile, all the time, until she looks like a fool.

She is a little girl in every way. Small for her age, thin for her height, immature for her years. She who has always been surrounded by family and friends now finds herself alone in an unknown world whose rulebook she hasn't been given. She's never had much of a taste for school—always preferring to run wild outdoors, to swim and fish and play with animals—but now she applies herself to her studies with all the intensity of her nine years. She works with disarming zeal to find her footing in this new environment, to learn the etiquette and ways of the school. She promised to be a model student and bring home top marks, and she must avoid disappointing Papi at all costs. She's determined to learn French as quickly as possible, and English, too. She has no choice, anyway, if she wants to have friends.

Naturally lighthearted and vivacious, Flor tries to show that she can also be good and kind. Little by little, with the innocence of youth, she starts to make friends, but the process is slow and painful. The other girls see their families often. Flor's family, though, is a long ten-day sea voyage away.

The weekends are lonely, a long dark tunnel stretching to Monday morning. Only a handful of pupils remain at the deserted school. They have the lake all to themselves, and the golf course, but not the stables, because the grooms don't work on weekends. There is mass on Sunday morning; and mealtimes, when even the slightest utterance reverberates mournfully in the vast, empty dining room; and game time, when they pretend to be having fun; and long hours of reading. And boredom. Time becomes a soft, shapeless thing, dulling every sense. Flor spends most of hers alone in her room, an open book in her lap to fool the house monitor. She gives herself over to imaginings, flying away to rejoin Mami and her cousins, back to the island with its aromas and colors and warmth, the heat of the sun on her skin, the taste of salt on her lips. She thinks of home so hard that she's almost really there, wallowing in wistful daydreams until she comes back to herself with a start, chastising herself: *Papi wouldn't like this*. And then she applies herself to her book again.

* * *

Flor's room is a vision of princely Art Deco elegance that she secretly refers to as "her apartments." Its immensity and luxury make a deep impression on her child's mind. Gradually, she lets go of Yulissa. She and her new friends have formed a club, "The World's End Girls." Huddling closely together, they tell each other stories about werewolves and witches. There are Prince Charmings, too, always brave and handsome in white uniforms with golden buttons, riding noble steeds.

On some Friday evenings, Flor takes the school's private bus from Bouffémont to its terminus at Porte de Chaillot in the northwestern suburbs of Paris, where a liveried chauffeur awaits her behind the wheel of a limousine. Since they found out her destination—the ambassador's residence—the princesses have begun to look at her differently. Flor doesn't like going there very much, but at least there she can hear her native language, spoken with that mangled Castilian accent unique to Dominicans. And there are other Dominican children, whom she envies because they have their mothers and fathers with them. And the large, impersonal bedroom, the tedious formal dinners, the curtsies. *Gracias, Señor; gracias, Señora.* The fish forks. The tiny glass of port, which she loves. The wine, of which she's allowed a miniscule taste—she has to *learn*, after all—and the snowy white tablecloths, and the servants, and the tips she never forgets to slip them when it's time to return to Bouffémont. All the little things she must be taught so she'll grow into a worldly and sophisticated young lady.

Every Friday, a chauffeur comes to pick up Mathilde de Cadeville, who is the daughter of a Breton duke, and brings her back again on Monday. One weekend, she invites Flor home with her. Mathilde lives in a huge house even more beautiful than Bouffémont, with extensive grounds. Flor makes sure to behave at the dinner table exactly the way she's been taught at the ambassador's residence, and her performance is nearly perfect. Even so, the duke turns up his nose at her without even attempting to conceal it. "She's a sweet little thing, but *common*. Father's one of those two-bit soldiers, isn't he? Banana republic, you know . . ."

The words drift through the half-open door of the smoking room, where the gentlemen have retired after dinner. Are they talking about her? Flor ponders the meaning of the remarks. There are bananas at home, and her Papi is a soldier, yes, but what does "two-bit" mean? And what's a banana republic? She runs into Mathilde's mother in the corridor. The woman smiles at her indulgently and tells her to go back to the playroom.

It bothers Flor that she can't return these invitations, but it isn't like she can invite her new friends to the ambassador's residence. But as a surprise for her birthday, the ambassador's wife organizes an afternoon tea party: "Invite your friends, as many as you like." Ten girls come to celebrate with her. "Tacky," Mathilde murmurs to her as an aside, surveying the embassy décor with a faint grimace of disapproval.

* * *

There is no one Flor can really talk with about her main worries: her lack of breasts and, a bit later on, the growth of new hair on her body, and her first period. The day she feels her belly cramp with a pain different from any she's ever experienced before, she curls up on her bed with a soft groan. Could it be something she ate? No one's explained anything to her. She doesn't have the slightest idea of what's happening. The cramp twists in her middle again, more violently this time, and there's a terrifying spot of crimson blood on her panties. She summons up the courage to visit the nurse, who, surprised at her youth, reassures her with a smile and sends her back to her "apartments."

* * *

When the weekly mail delivery arrives, there is rarely anything in it for Flor. Only the very occasional letter. Her father doesn't phone her. Neither does Mami. With her 100-peso-per-week allowance, Aminta can't afford it. Flor isn't just deeply upset by this—she's ashamed. She doesn't understand. How could her family send her away to a strange country, so far from everything that had made her life what it was, and then never contact her? Still, she's a courageous little girl. After all, she has no choice. She soothes herself to sleep with thoughts of sunny beaches and coconut palms, dreaming of the summer, when she'll see Mami again, and Papi, and Snowball.

Collège féminin de Bouffément
Rafael L. Trujillo
Santo Domingo

Dear Papa,
I've received your answer to the telegram I sent you on your birthday, which made me very happy.
It's been almost three years since I last saw you, and you can't imagine how much I want to see you again.
If I come home in July like you say I can, you'll see how much I've grown and how different I am, and I hope <u>you'll be different, too</u>.
Can I count on it?
All my love and a thousand kisses from your daughter,
Flor de Oro
PS: I got your picture, and I hope you liked the one of me.

Flor entrusts her letter home to the ambassador, and nervously awaits the reply.

* * *

Señorita Flor de Oro Trujillo
Paris
France

Santo Domingo, 20 February 1927
My dear daughter,
How pleased I was to receive your affectionate little card, which you forgot to date! And your photo with it, in which I'm happy to see the positive changes in you after only months away.
I'm eager to be with you again, and I hope to see you here over the upcoming school holidays.
I've noted with pleasure how you are progressing in your

studies, according to what the headmistress tells me. I hope you will continue to apply yourself as you have done so far.
  No more for now, with love from your father,
  Rafael L. Trujillo[5]

---

[5] See the original letters in the Image Section, p. 367.

Santo Domingo
July 1927

Flor's gaze sweeps over the rugged coral rock cliff rising up off the port side of the ship, following the ballet of the pelicans accompanying the vessel on its slow progression toward land. She loves to watch them nosediving into the sea from time to time, swooping up a fish, then soaring skyward again. She blinks, dazzled by the brightness of the sun, the clarity of the light. Her nose twitches as wave after wave of forgotten scents reaches her nostrils like so many caresses: coffee, mangoes, tobacco, palm leaves, salt. She breathes deeply, her whole body seeming to expand, shivers of pure pleasure running up and down her spine. She feels as if she's being reborn, picking up her old life exactly where she left it. But no, she isn't quite the same. She's grown. Changed—a great deal, even. She's not a little girl anymore. Mami will be so surprised. And Papi, so proud.

The deep blue of the seawater gradually turns murkier, brownish, as the ship eases its way into the boggy waters of the Ozama River. After nearly three years away, Flor has come home for the summer holidays, thanks to the lengthy battle waged by her mother to persuade T, who cares little for his first wife's sorrows—or his daughter's—but finally yielded to Aminta's persistence.

Flor has kept the promise she made to her father. In spite of the loneliness, the cold, the anxiety and fear, the *Reyes* passing unmarked by celebrations,[6] the forgotten birthdays—in spite

---

[6] *Reyes*: Epiphany, the holiday that replaces Christmas in the Dominican Republic.

of it all, the little girl has stayed the course. She's earned excellent marks at Bouffémont, and even managed to stop sucking her thumb. Alone in her first-class cabin during the ocean crossing, she often leafed through the pages of her precious school notebook, reading and rereading her teachers' comments: *Flor de Oro is a studious and hard-working pupil. Flor de Oro has a strong work ethic. Despite occasionally being a bit too chatty*—here, Flor nods; she always has so many things to tell her seatmate—*and a difficult start*—she remembers so clearly those first weeks when she couldn't understand a word in class—*Flor de Oro has had a very good year.* Papi will be proud of her, she's sure of it. She's worked so hard, even in the subjects she doesn't like, like calculus and Latin and geometry. She's done it all for him.

Now, after so many long, tedious, seemingly endless days at sea, the port of Santo Domingo comes into view. Flor can feel her heart thumping in her chest. From the deck, she surveys the throng that has come to greet the ship, looking for them. Her parents. Her legs tremble. She looks for them. She descends the gangplank, gripping the railing, looking for them, scanning every face in the crowd. A man in a military uniform approaches her. He inclines his head. "Señorita." He escorts her to a limousine, followed by the porters with her luggage. Flor's disappointment is intense. She fights back bitter tears, curling into a small twelve-year-old ball in the wide back seat of the car, staring blankly at the pennants fluttering proudly from its fenders. She doesn't even know where she's being taken. Eventually the limousine pulls up in front of a house in the residential neighborhood of Gazcue.

Where are her father and mother? Getting out of the car and approaching the house, a pretentious little simulacrum of a colonial palace, Flor stiffens. A woman is standing at the top of the steps, wearing a gaudy flowered dress that looks like it was made from curtains. Flor's never seen her before. The woman's manner is stilted, formal, her lips frozen in a smile, one hand futilely extended.

"Welcome, Flor de Oro. I'm Bienvenida, your . . . " She hesitates for an instant, awkwardly, a pink flush creeping up her neck. " . . . your father's new wife."

There it is. This is precisely what Flor suspected. She forces herself to smile at the woman who has taken her mother's place, despite the lump of bitterness that feels lodged in her chest. She knew T had gotten married again, in Puerto Plata, last March; Aminta had told her about it in a letter that was dignified, uncomplaining, emotionless, merely stating the facts. Flor had wept over the news, out of sorrow for her mother, and also because it told her just how little she counted in her father's mind and heart, when he couldn't even be bothered to tell her himself.

Flor nods at Bienvenida in greeting now; she certainly isn't going to kiss her hello, or even shake her hand. She follows the woman into the house. Bienvenida offers her a lemonade. She isn't *so* young, Flor thinks. She even seems nice, in spite of everything. *Definitely not as pretty as Mami, though, or as cheerful.*

Half an hour passes while Bienvenida struggles to think of things to say. She isn't very successful, only managing a standard pleasantry or two. So Flor has a conversation with Aminta in her mind, instead, supplying both questions and answers, not fully present in this house.

Suddenly there is a commotion outside.

The sound of a horn interrupts Flor's thoughts. A car door slamming. Soldierly footsteps. Her father. Flor rushes out to greet him. "Papi!" T sweeps her into his arms and kisses her, his eyes crinkling with happiness. He seems so pleased to see her. "How *tall* you've gotten, my Flor de Oro! *Amorcito*, you're becoming a real young lady! I have a surprise for you, *querida* . . . "

A second car pulls up. The rear door opens, and Aminta climbs out. Flor flings herself into her mother's embrace, trembling with joy.

This is why they didn't come to the port. So they could surprise her. Flor is silently grateful to her father.

The only thing missing is Snowball. He's waiting for her in San Cristóbal, Aminta reassures Flor; she'll see him when she comes. Unfortunately, Mami can't stay. She's not exactly a welcome guest in Bienvenida's house. Aminta, thrown over for a girl half her age, has to be back home by nightfall.

Flor settles into a large bedroom with pink curtains. Alone, just like at Bouffémont, but minus her friends. She'd much rather have gone with Mami, but no one asked her opinion.

* * *

For these few summertime weeks, Flor divides her time between the little palm-roofed house in San Cristóbal, always kept immaculately neat by Aminta, and the princely residence in the capital. She has fun in San Cristóbal, with her cousins and her childhood friends, going to the local beach and sometimes as far as Najayo, frolicking in the water, fishing, playing in one another's gardens and climbing mango trees, hunting crabs and gathering big pink conch shells, having sleepovers. In Gazcue, despite the plentiful books and the swimming pool, the days are dull. Bienvenida doesn't know how to act around children; she's awkward, clumsy, affected, insincere. And more than anything, she's morose. She's already like a shadow. T is hardly around, and Flor often finds herself dining alone with her stepmother, which isn't very much fun. Aminta chuckles sarcastically when Flor tells her these things. "Another one of her names is Inocencia, you know. Fitting. She comes from a very good family in Montecristi. He's cheating on her too, of course. Always the mistresses . . . "

These aren't confidences to be shared with a twelve-year-old girl. Flor conceals her discomfort by burying her face in Snowball's fur. Aminta, realizing that she's let herself be carried away by her resentment of T, flaps a hand at her daughter. "I'm just in a bad mood, *mi'jita*. It'll pass. Go on out and play with your cousins!"

But Flor is neither blind nor stupid. She understands her mother's bitterness. T gives her barely enough money to live on decently, while spending extravagantly in Santo Domingo. For a man who aspires to the highest office in the land, he's an incredible cheapskate. And Flor knows, too, that Aminta is feeling all the pain of a woman scorned, cast aside for someone younger, richer, more socially acceptable. She's sorry for Mami, and heartbroken on her behalf, and so she tries to show her twice as much affection as before.

Flor is alone with her father only once during the entire vacation, a few days before she goes back to France. He congratulates her on her high marks and, as a reward, takes her horseback riding. Just the two of them. He boosts her up into the saddle and adjusts the height of her stirrups himself. He's an excellent rider, and Flor is proud to be trotting along next to him, seated English-style on her mount; her riding lessons have paid off. Papi has left off his medal-laden uniform for once—he's a lieutenant colonel now, Aminta has explained—and is wearing a simple, well-fitting linen suit and a soft hat, looking like a real father. By the time they break into a gallop, he has let down his defenses and become the Papi he's never known how to be. He compliments Flor, which is rare, and congratulates himself, too; he made the right decision—which he never doubted, of course—in sending her to France. Not only did it take the problem of her education off his hands, but she's clearly thriving. T is so busy patting himself on the back that he doesn't notice the shadow of sadness that passes over Flor's face.

Early August finds the Gazcue household in an uproar. T has been made brigadier general, and, four days after that, the national police is transformed into a military force. This means that

T is now head of the army, a spectacular leap in a seemingly unstoppable upward trajectory. He's set his sights on accomplishing a Dantean task: to turn the country around, make it into a modern state, throwing off the yoke of the *Yanquis*. Nothing else matters to him now, and he devotes himself to the job with uncommon energy, body and soul. He no longer has any time for his private life, putting in only brief token appearances at home, neglecting Bienvenida, forgetting about his daughter completely. Only his mistresses still count, or perhaps a little.

September begins, and Flor's Dominican holidays are nearing their end. Time seems to speed up, like a runaway horse she can't rein in. One last picnic, a final dive into the pool, a walk on the beach, and then she has to pack her bags and say goodbye to her friends and family. It feels as if she hasn't had time to do much of anything, least of all enjoy her father's company.

The steamship is at the dock. The horn sounds, the anchor is weighed. On deck, Flor watches the Dominican coast fade away like a dream without substance, and wonders where her real life is.

* * *

Back at Bouffémont.

Flor has brought a gramophone and some records back in her trunks, along with a few photographs and bunches of mangoes and limoncillos—a bit of her island—for her friends. She's surprised by how happy she is to be back in her big room with its dark curtains, to see her teachers again, and Nina, her favorite mare, and the tall, melancholy trees of shadow-filled Montmorency Forest, and the pale sunlight of the French autumn. And the World's End Girls, of course.

There are new girls at school this year, too. One of them is Lucie Mayer, a German who will become Flor's dear friend.

Bouffémont
1928–1932

1928

Flor stands in one of the changing rooms on either side of the basement gymnasium, examining her torso. Some of her classmates already have bosoms: Lucie, for example, whose breasts jiggle beneath her bathing suit when she laughs. But Flor, to her chagrin, is still as flat-chested as a little girl. "It'll happen," Lucie tells her. "Don't worry. Everyone at their own pace."

On a school trip to the Opéra, Flor discovers Mozart and Rossini. It's magnificent. She never knew people could sing like that. Lucie, whose parents are music lovers—or *mélomanes* in French, a word Flor thinks is beautifully melodious—introduces her to classical music. She finds the Italian composers too light; the Germans are more impressive, more substantial. Flor wants to be a *mélomane*, too. She develops a passion for Brahms. Lucie approves.

Riding, which was such a challenge at first, has become an addiction. Flor, who always rode a mule back home, can now gallop on a purebred and even jump, her skill rapidly exceeding her classmates'. If she can muster up the courage, she'll ask her father to buy her a horse when she returns home. She also looks forward to the weekly cooking lesson, with its chaos of flour, broken eggs, butter, and burnt oil. She and Lucie clown around so much that they get thrown out of class. *That's* one thing she definitely won't be telling Papi about.

The ambassador hands her an envelope stuffed with money for her winter holidays. Her father has remembered her, has, in fact, been generous. The money is his way of showing love. Lucie has invited Flor to St. Moritz. Here she discovers mountains, and skiing—which she isn't very good at, but it's fun. And Lucie's parents, the *mélomanes*, are so nice. Flor learns to speak some basic German.

She doesn't go home the next summer. Armed with a fresh envelope of money, she travels to Biarritz with Mathilde, who is spending the school holidays there with her family. She can tell that everyone pities her a bit for being so alone, but she keeps her chin up and smiles bravely. Everything is fine.

* * *

1929

A four o'clock rendezvous at the central fountain. Lucie's waiting there when Flor arrives. Hand-in-hand, they run through the vast green grounds to the forest and settle, out of breath, on an enormous tree stump they call their bench. Lucie has gotten her hands on a pack of cigarettes. German ones. "We grow tobacco in my country, you know," Flor says, trying to sound knowledgeable.
"Have you ever smoked?" Lucie asks.
"No."
Lucie lights the cigarette. The smoke stings their eyes. "You first," she says to Flor.
"No, you go ahead."
Lucie inhales and coughs, spluttering smoke. Flor laughs. Her turn. She takes the cigarette delicately between her first and middle fingers, like a movie star, and inhales deeply. She coughs. The smoke burns her throat. Lucie giggles. More coughing. Never again.

The next day, they try again. And the day after that. Always in secret. Until it doesn't make them cough any more. Lips puckered, Lucie practices blowing smoke rings. Flor holds the smoke in her lungs and then makes it stream out of her nostrils. They're always looking for ways to make their smoking look more sophisticated. Flor poses, tilting her head slightly and exhaling a long gray ribbon with studied elegance. "You look like Jean Harlow! No—more like Kay Francis!" Well, that's something, at least. Flor still doesn't have a bosom, but she smokes like a Hollywood star. And that makes her feel good. Sneaking off to smoke becomes a ritual for the girls.

Flor has decided to treat herself to a visit to the school's hairdresser with part of her monthly allowance. She has to ask permission first, from Madame Vatel, the bursar, who agrees without hesitation; Flor has a certain cachet at Bouffémont. Her academic fees are paid in cash, with a tidy sum added for the girl's personal expenses.

Flor sits down in the hairdresser's swivel chair. "I'd like my hair to be smooth, like this" (she's brought in a photo of an American actress cut out of a magazine). The hairdresser brushes Flor's hair, which frizzes out wildly around her face, crackling with static electricity. The hairdresser doesn't say anything—one doesn't criticize the pupils at Bouffémont—but thinks to herself that this won't be an easy job. The girl smiles trustingly at her in the mirror. Well, she'll do her best. A great deal of heating, combing, and smoothing later, Flor leaves the chair feeling like a slightly different person. She's happy; she has hair just like the actress's. Well, almost. For at the first hint of rain, tight curls begin dancing the merengue around her face, and the whole process has to be started over from scratch. She becomes a regular at the school's salon. It's her only indulgence.

May–June 1930

The ambassador's voice was newly deferential when he called her on May 25; the man Flor had come to think of as her own personal Hermes, bearer of news both good and bad, was clearly moved.

The school year is ending, and Flor, now a teenager, is living in a maelstrom of complex emotions: uncertainty, sadness, anxiety over the future, the occasional sharp surge of joy.

She won't be going back to the island for the summer holidays this year, either.

For a few weeks now, everything has been different. With that deep sensitivity that has always been her weak spot, she's noticed a thousand tiny signs: the stares, the murmured conversations among her classmates, who abruptly fall silent when she draws near; the subtly pointed remarks. Even her teachers' attitudes toward her have changed, almost imperceptibly.

For Flor de Oro is now the daughter of the president of the Dominican Republic. She found out at the end of May via a telephone call from the ambassador, quickly followed by another from her mother, who was unmistakably thrilled by the news. "Ninety-five percent of the votes—can you believe it, *mi'ja*? The support of the country's entire elite—unheard of! An incredible victory!"

What Aminta failed to mention was that, besieged by death threats, T's political opponents had chosen to throw in the towel. And that the members of the electoral committee had been forced to resign, replaced by military yes-men. That the whole presidential campaign had taken place in an atmosphere of real terror.

Flor won't learn any of this until much later.

For now, she feels very proud of her father, but she also wonders if she should start acting differently. How *should* a president's daughter act? Since there's no one around to explain it to her, she doesn't change anything. But she can certainly feel it: *everything* is different. And with the new assurance of wealth and respect, far removed from the poverty of her childhood, there is something even more potent that settles in her, a kind of self-confidence that goes along with being close to power.

Not that Flor is truly aware of any of this. She's too young to understand what has really happened. She doesn't know what "coup d'état" means, and it's certainly not at Bouffémont, where housekeeping and cooking classes are a vital part of the curriculum, that anyone is likely to gain political awareness. What Flor *does* know, on the other hand, is that she's not part of this family event. Does that mean she doesn't count? Her father has a million things to do besides worry about his daughter—consolidating his new position and neutralizing the opposition, for a start, since the conditions of his election are questionable. But where is Flor in all this?

It has been agreed that she will spend this year's summer holidays with the ambassador's family. When the ambassador tells Flor, with a small, rather embarrassed smile, she pretends to be pleased at the news, hiding her real feelings, just as she's been taught.

But O joy!—just before the school year ends, a cable arrives from Aminta, who has talked the newly elected president into authorizing—and, more importantly, funding—a visit to her daughter. Flor is relieved, the threat of a vacation with the ambassador's family receding; goodness knows, she's sick and tired of spending time with them. She's so happy and excited at the prospect of seeing her dear Mami again. She and Lucie draw up a list of everything she wants to do. It's been decided that mother and daughter will visit the Côte d'Azur and Italy, with all expenses paid by the office of the President of the Dominican Republic. Aminta agrees to everything. Pleasing Flor de Oro, whom she hasn't seen in two years, is all that counts.

* * *

It's a wonderful summer. Flor reconnects with the mother she's grown up so far away from. They luxuriate in the joys of the fresh bouillabaisse, rocky inlets, and rosé wine of Provence; the endless, rather gloomy beaches of the Lido of Venice; the rolling hills of Tuscany; the shops on the Ponte Vecchio in Florence; the *vedute* of Canaletto and the imaginative portraits of Arcimboldo; lampredotti and truffle ravioli and chianti; the Tower of Pisa. Flor, who has the eyes, heart, and stomach of a true gourmand, is enraptured by all of it. But her favorite place of all is Venice. Someday, she vows to herself, when she's found her Prince Charming, she'll come back here on her honeymoon.

One morning in early August, over croissants and cappuccino, Flor sees a photograph in the newspaper. Her father, in full dress uniform, his chest covered with ribbons and medals. It's his inauguration. Flor is overcome with pride. So is Aminta, in whom this feeling mingles with a great deal of unconcealed bitterness. She will not be First Lady. She wasn't patient enough, or clever enough; she allowed herself to be usurped by Bienvenida, that empty-headed girl who can't even give T an heir. But Flor doesn't care about court intrigues; she peppers her mother with questions about young Trujillo, the father Aminta knew before he became El Jefe.

"He was operating a telegraph when I met him," Aminta says, "earning 25 pesos a month. He was proud and arrogant even then, wild and brutal like an animal, incredibly good at imposing his will. I never really understood him," she adds with a sigh.

Inspired by this confidence, Flor tells her mother something she's never dared to mention before: occasionally, back at her island school, anonymous notes were left on her desk that said: *YOUR FATHER IS A CATTLE THIEF*. She and Aminta laugh about it together. T has come a long way from being that short, telegraph-operating cattle thief!

Flor spends that summer eating and swimming, tanning nut-brown in the sunshine, her body filling out and her spirit flourishing, and she develops a new, deep closeness with her mother. She talks to Aminta about herself, her friends, the literature she loves, the poetry she sees as almost another companion, about music, Brahms, and Paris, that magical city she never grows tired of. When Aminta asks her what she wants to do in the future, Flor says that she's too young, she doesn't know yet. But she'd love to work in the service of her country, like Papi.

That summer, Flor is happy.

The end of August arrives, and with it the close of the summer holidays. Aminta boards the steamship again, and Flor heads back to Bouffémont. It's there, just a few days later, as she's settling back into her room, that she learns of the catastrophe. The ambassador again. His voice is hollow, as if coming from beyond the grave. The words come haltingly, at first, reluctantly, and then they flow thick and dark, like mud, and Flor's blood runs cold.

On the third of September, at six o'clock in the evening, Hurricane San Zénon hit Santo Domingo, a monstrous horror with winds of 250 kilometers an hour. The capital lies in ruins, and thousands of people have been killed; the death toll will eventually rise above eight thousand. All communications have been cut off. There is no electricity, no water, no food, the threat of cholera and famine looming large, not to mention violence. The telephone receiver shakes in Flor's numb hand, and she feels as if she might faint. She imagines the worst: her mother's ship sunk in the storm-churned ocean, and her father—where is he? Anxiety grips her and doesn't let go. She can't sleep, and Rosita is no comfort.

After a few days, the ambassador is able to reassure her. Aminta has reached San Cristóbal safely, and her father is working tirelessly to bandage the wounds of the country now in his charge. He deployed the entire army within twenty-four hours of the hurricane and has managed to reestablish some means of communication, even though the newspapers are out of commission. He's appealed to the United States for aid, and the Red Cross has sent workers and supplies.

Flor can breathe again. Her father has the situation in hand, burning the candle at both ends to restore the capital. Still, this is a dark and unhappy time. There is a permanent knot of worry in her gut. She can't eat, and she has nightmares. She loses weight and begins biting her fingernails and even sucking her thumb again, like a baby.

Those summer weeks spent with her mother were so happy. But now she knows that nothing is ever, ever guaranteed.

Nothing lasts. Happiness least of all.

In the Dominican Republic they have just declared it Year 1 of the T Era. The era of her father.

* * *

June 1932

Flor has been awarded her *brevet*. She's proud; it's no small feat for a foreign student. The diploma marks the end of one phase of her life. She'd like to continue her education. T wants her to study Dominican history and literature. A veneer of French sophistication is all well and good, but what does she know about her *own* country?

Flor leaves France that summer not knowing whether she'll return to Bouffémont. Lucie goes home to Germany; she will not be back. She hopes to move to America. The friends embrace tearfully when it's time to part. When will they see each other again? "Soon," they promise. "Cross my heart."

Santo Domingo
July 1932

Flor sits at the dressing table in her first-class cabin on the Santo Domingo Line steamship, trying to tame that bane of her existence, her mane of frizzy hair. She studies her reflection in the mirror. What she sees is no longer the face of the little girl who left her home and family eight years ago to be educated in France. Has she become the polished young woman her father and mother wanted? She'd like to believe the answer is yes. She speaks French and English fluently, along with a bit of German; she's intimately familiar with the works of Ovid and Leonardo da Vinci, Brahms and Verdi. She's mastered the recipes for boeuf bourguignon and crêpes and the art of the buttonhole stitch, can tell a steak knife from a fish knife, plays golf and tennis, and, most importantly, has become an expert horseback rider. As good as her father. It's where she excels most, and she's burning to prove it to him. So, yes. The years in France have unquestionably improved her.

She's desperately impatient to be home, to be back on her beloved island with her adored mother and her father, the most important man in the country. Already she can almost hear the birdsong, smell the perfume of ripe bananas, taste the sweetness of coconut water. A broad, childlike grin lights up her face, revealing her white teeth. There seems no end to her happiness. She is going home, to the land of turquoise seas and giant mango trees, bright green parrots and tiny hummingbirds.

The truth is, she wasn't really expecting to come back. Particularly because, on each of her two previous trips home, her welcoming committee consisted of a driver at the wheel of an official car and some other faceless bureaucrat in the passenger seat, who would accompany her to her father's house.

She received a telegram from Aminta here on the ship during the crossing: PEOPLE HAVE STARTED CALLING YOUR FATHER THE BENEFACTOR OF THE FATHERLAND. HE'S PLANNING TO CELEBRATE YOUR HOMECOMING IN GRAND STYLE. MAKE SURE YOU LOOK YOUR NICEST, QUERIDA! But Flor is certain that Mami wasn't expecting her to come home, either.

No sooner have the ocean liner's mooring lines been secured to the dock in the Santo Domingo port than a brass band erupts in a joyous rendition of "Quisqueyanos Valientes,"[7] a stirring military anthem. Flor de Oro, moved, squares her shoulders and lifts her chin, holding her head high, and descends the gangplank with small, measured steps. She's followed her mother's advice, applying her makeup carefully and dressing in a finely tailored suit, with a rakish little hat perched Parisian-style on her head. She carries a crocodile handbag in the crook of her arm and wears high-heeled shoes—she's short, which is a major flaw. Her hair, trimmed so that it just reaches her earlobes, curls wildly around her head—that untamable hair, her other flaw. She's looked to photos of models in fashion magazines for inspiration in crafting her look, hoping for a sort of elegance *à la française*, but the attempt hasn't been entirely successful. Flor herself isn't especially pretty, or tall, or elegant; she's just a seventeen-year-old girl with a visibly mixed-race appearance who is still trying to find herself. But that doesn't matter; she's the president's daughter, and that alone imparts her with a tangible aura. She can feel every eye turn toward her. Her heart hammers in her chest, her breast heaving until it feels as if the mother-of-pearl buttons on her blouse will burst right off.

She blinks in the brilliant midday light, astonished at the welcoming fanfare. She truly didn't expect this. There are rows of

---

[7] "Quisqueyanos Valientes" would be made the official national anthem on May 23, 1934.

military officers, aides-de-camp in full dress uniform, and high-ranking government officials in sharp suits. And at the center of them, dressed to the nines, standing at attention, is her father. His general's uniform is impeccably crisp, the creases on the legs of his trousers razor-sharp, his black shoes polished to a mirrorlike shine and his hair neatly combed. Flor smooths her skirt self-consciously, aware that her father won't tolerate even the slightest hint of sloppiness.

T's hard, commanding expression softens as he catches sight of his daughter, a hint of a smile touching his lips beneath the neatly trimmed black mustache. Flor's father is even more imposing in the flesh than in her memory, radiating energy and purpose. She wants to run into his arms, but quashes the impulse. She knows he's expecting her to behave differently.

Flor is definitely being welcomed home in grand style. T is flanked by his second wife, Bienvenida Ricardo, now the First Lady; she is standing so stiffly that she might have swallowed a coconut palm. T steps out of the receiving line now and advances toward Flor, the faint smile still on his lips. Dazzled by what he has become, by the air of majesty emanating from him, Flor's whole body thrills with pride. He embraces her; she melts in his arms and, just as she would have done at age five, kisses him affectionately, unable to hold back her tears. T stiffens. She's going to ruin her makeup. A flashbulb pops. Then another. The press has come out in force. Flor doesn't know it, but tomorrow she'll be headline news in every national paper, and, in the years to come, they'll scrutinize her every move. She'll be called beautiful, elegant, distinguished, refined, and, truth be told, she'll find a great deal of pleasure in it. But all that is in the future.

"Come, come, the president's daughter mustn't show her emotions," T murmurs in Flor's ear, straightening up.

Taking her father's arm, she moves toward the platform where a number of prominent ladies are waiting beneath a canopy. The band starts playing again, accompanied now by a chorus that is, Flor realizes, entirely composed of soldiers. She catches sight of her mother, who waves vigorously, visibly impatient to embrace her. And then, Flor sees him.

He's dressed in a spotless white uniform, buttons gleaming golden in the sun. Back perfectly straight. Uncommonly elegant. There's a beauty mark on his left cheek. Like everyone else, he's looking straight at her. Nothing noteworthy about that, of course; she's the star of the moment, the undisputed center of attention. But there's something different about his gaze. She feels it on her like something hot, fiery, piercing her to the depths of her soul. No, it isn't the sun, or the effects of the heat. This is something else altogether, something she's never felt before. Like a delicate bird hypnotized by a beast of prey, Flor quivers with exquisite fear. Just then Aminta swoops down and gathers her in her arms, weeping openly with joy.

"Oh, Flor, *mi'ja*, you're back home with us at last! How happy I am!"

"Me, too, Mami," Flor murmurs, shaken, her cheek pressed to her mothers. Her heart thunders in her chest, her gaze still held fast, helplessly, by that of the man in uniform, his smoldering eyes fixed unswervingly on hers.

Has anyone noticed? Flor pulls herself together, answers her mother's questions, allows herself to be led toward the refreshment table, accepts a glass of champagne. She speaks distractedly to one well-wisher here, another there—*hello, yes, very happy*—and scans the crowd. Where is he? Some distance away, she spies the white uniform. He's unmistakable, impossible to confuse with anyone else, with that straight back, those broad shoulders, that princely bearing. Wildly attractive, even from behind, even if he isn't very tall. Flor is desperate to be introduced to him, instead of the graybeards and bourgeoise matrons currently vying to be photographed with her. She edges subtly from handshake to handshake, eager face to eager face, inching closer to the spot where the white uniform is standing with a few other military types. Her progress is slow and difficult, people jostling to get near her, to catch her attention. She sees him turn his head. He's even more handsome in profile.

Still she can't quite reach him. "Who is he?" she asks her mother.

"An aide-de-camp. Part of your father's personal guard, I think."

She can find out no more. Already the reception is breaking up; the dignitaries must return to their business. And Flor de Oro must be tired, after such a long journey. T signals that he's ready to depart; he has a country to run. The uniforms assemble, gathering according to color. The white ones begin to move. She watches them go. He turns. A pointed look, an almost imperceptible nod. Then he's gone.

Flor moves into the presidential residence, where she's been given a room. She hardly has time to set down her bags and change clothes before she's herded into one of a convoy of official cars; T has decided that he and his family will spend the weekend at his newly acquired country house in San José de las Matas. Flor is pleased; her childhood friend Lina Lovatón Pittaluga has been invited along to keep her company. Lina is the only daughter of a powerful attorney from an old aristocratic family, and that flatters T's ego. Flor is delighted to see Lina again. There's so much to tell her.

During this first weekend home, Flor is distracted, her thoughts elsewhere. She feels as if she's moving automatically, mindlessly, like a wind-up doll. Meals stretch on forever and are dreadfully dull, full of droning conversation that's really nothing more than a surreal kind of background noise. She answers questions absently, lets her own sentences trail off. She cares nothing for any of the guests, can hardly even pay attention to Lina. Everyone's gracious about her blankness, attributing it to fatigue from the journey home. *Ten whole days at sea, she has to get accustomed to the heat again, she's just not used to her new life as the president's daughter . . .*

Flor perks up a bit whenever she manages to get away, out into the open air of the countryside, riding hard for hours with Lina, who's always been a tomboy. It's pure bliss to rediscover the caress of the salty breeze, the damp scent of the red earth and sweet perfume of wild orchids, the colorful secluded huts, the shady mango trees and swaying palms, and the wild landscape of the lomas, which stretch away toward distant, verdant mountains.

But gallop as she might, she can't outrun her obsession. She's never felt like this before. The white uniform is there, all the time, in her every thought.

Santo Domingo
July 1932

Back to Santo Domingo.
The presidential residence will be Flor's home now, so T introduces her to his aides-de-camp. They step into his office one after another, silent and impassive, these hand-picked young men, the cream of the country's patrician youth. T has drastically overhauled his personal guard, recruiting from the best upper-class families, hoping to curry favor with the Dominican elite.

Flor's heart starts to race. She feels as if she can't breathe. Lieutenant Porfirio Rubirosa. He's even more handsome up close. He inclines his head slightly, just for a moment. She thinks she sees a brief glint of something in his eyes—triumph, perhaps. The air between them is charged. Already he's stepping back, dismissed by a flick of the presidential hand, but now the white uniform has a name, which Flor rolls around on her tongue silently, like a sweetmeat.

Porfirio Rubirosa.

Discreetly, she finds out all she can about him.

He's the son of a retired general and former ambassador. Like her, he was raised abroad. Paris, London. Flor sees this as a sign. She wanders the halls and grounds of the immense residence, hoping to run into the lieutenant.

In vain.

She's only just met him, and already Porfirio Rubirosa is dominating her every thought.

What happens next is straight out of a romantic *fotonovela*. The family has retreated to San José de las Matas for the weekend again. T likes the countryside and is fond of the grand mansion he's had built there, where he can invite close associates to congregate away from the stifling heat of the capital. Tonight, he's planned a dinner party with a ball to follow.

Flor has begged T to invite Aminta, but to no avail. The guest list is composed of government ministers, high-ranking military types, and a few wealthy industrialists, along with their prim and proper spouses. There are also several young women who take every opportunity to flutter around Flor, trying to get into her good graces because, after all, being close to El Jefe's daughter is almost like being close to him.

Flor, far from being fooled, knows exactly what's behind these calculated, self-serving attempts at friendship; she had a taste of that back at Bouffémont. But she finds it hard to tell who's being sincere and who isn't, so she doesn't allow herself to trust anyone. She feels completely disconnected from Dominican society, utterly ignorant of its social cues and codes. The only person she can rely on is Lina, who continues to be looked on approvingly by T.

She hopes Porfirio is here tonight. She looks around for him, and finds him. Alone among the rest of the officers, whether innocently or from a desire to provoke, he's left off his military uniform in favor of an elegant cream linen suit. Flor wonders what her father will think of that. Prevented by protocol from doing anything other than exchanging a timid greeting with the lieutenant, Flor languishes at the head table. All through dinner, she gazes at the table at the far end of the banquet hall, set slightly apart from the rest, where the young aides-de-camp are seated. The meal finished, the atmosphere lightens somewhat, the guests separating and scattering.

There is fine old rum, catchy music, heady cigars, boring political talk, and, among the ladies, superficial chit-chat. Heart pounding in her chest, Flor edges closer to Porfirio. A few more silent steps, and then they're sitting side by side, a bit apart from everyone else, in a pair of garden chairs on the terrace. She sees the barest curve of a satisfied smile, quickly suppressed, on his lips. Finally, they can get to know one another. They talk. The conversation flows with wonderful ease. There's not a single moment of awkward silence. They have so much in common.

"I've just come back from eight years at school in France," Flor tells him, with a hint of pride.

"I lived there, too, from when I was six until I was nineteen. My father was the ambassador. Then my family moved to London, and I stayed in Paris on my own."

Flor scrunches up her nose impishly. Her memories of the Dominican ambassador from her own time in France aren't very positive. "My dear Porfirio," she says, "*quelle coincidence!*"

"Quite so, Mademoiselle Fleur," he replies in the language of Molière, his accent impeccable.

Flor laughs. Their newfound complicity is so unexpected. It pleases them both. She talks of Bouffémont, he of the École des Roches. They speak of Paris, the Eiffel Tower, even the fables of La Fontaine. Flor tells him proudly about her *brevet*, awarded with honors; Porfirio is careful not to mention that he failed the baccalaureate exam. He took boxing lessons, she, tennis. He rhapsodizes about horses, telling Flor of the family farm where he first learned to ride, sitting in the saddle in front of his father, his back pressed against the general's middle. Flor loves horses too, and riding is a real passion for her, she says—in fact, she's known for her skill at it. "We'll soon see about that, Mademoiselle Fleur!" he teases her. They even discover a mutual love for limoncillos, the small, tart, yellow-green fruit native to the island. Another thing in common. It's incredible! They chatter in French, laughing like children. No one else can understand them, which delights them both. It's as if they've created their own private bubble, with the rest of the world firmly shut out.

Nobody pays them any attention—except for one woman.

Bienvenida watches them intently, burning with curiosity and sick with jealousy.

Flor and Porfirio talk for hours. He lights a cigarette and smokes it with careless elegance. She takes it from him and inhales like a movie star, the way she used to with Lucie at Bouffémont. He takes her hand—so small, the nails cut short like a little girl's—and presses it against his own, palm to palm, comparing sizes. He finds her charming, with her sparkling dark eyes and hair black as night, and that beaming smile, radiantly hopeful. They're like two puppies sizing each other up. They stay like that, comfortably close, until the wee hours of the morning, long after most of the guests have left the ball and retired to their bedrooms.

Something has begun between them, something electric, only waiting to be set alight.

But the next morning, reality hits like a freight train. Porfirio doesn't reappear, nor does he send word. Flor looks everywhere for him, not daring to question anyone. It's Lina who breaks the news. Flor can't believe her ears. Lieutenant Rubirosa has been placed under arrest and transferred to the garrison at San Francisco de Macorís. T doesn't bother to explain, but everyone knows the reason. His Majesty has taken offense. Flor is aghast. This is her fault. She wonders who gave them away, because her father retired to his room very early last night—she'd made sure of it before approaching Porfirio.

Bienvenida reproaches her stepdaughter for her undignified behavior. And confesses: it was she who complained to T. How dare she? Flor can't believe it. She's only just returned home, and her stepmother has already betrayed her. Moreover, she's done nothing wrong. Flirted a bit, maybe. In France . . .

In France, maybe. But not here. If only she could talk to her mother. Aminta would understand. Flor takes herself off to a remote corner of the garden and cries her heart out, bitter tears of sadness and rage.

Porfirio, meanwhile, is languishing in semi-detention. He isn't really in prison, just in a sort of holding cell, waiting for his fate to be determined. He's furious with himself. He should have been more careful; he took an enormous risk. What made him think he could sweet-talk the Generalissimo's daughter with impunity, in a country where no well-brought-up young woman is permitted to spend time with a man without a chaperone? It was practically a crime of high treason, an attack on the family honor, a blow aimed straight at El Jefe's ego. But Flor is at fault, too. She approached him, after all. They thought they were being so clever, speaking in French. And this is the result. Porfirio is at risk of being tossed out of the army, of falling into disgrace. And he'd poured so much energy into his military career, which had begun so auspiciously . . .

He spends two days stewing, long enough to have a good, hard think about the consequences of his behavior. Then he receives a note, written in French. Flor has bribed a servant to deliver it.

Dear Porfirio, I've been informed that you're gone. I'm so desperately sorry. I hope to see you again soon. I'm furious and sad at the same time. I hope we can see each other again very soon. Flor de Oro.

Porfirio scribbles a reply: *I hope so too, Mademoiselle Fleur.* He folds Flor's note carefully and tucks it into his breast pocket, close to his heart. Flor, for her part, will keep his reply in a little box made of precious hardwood.

The exchange has warmed Rubirosa's heart. She's a hot-blooded little thing, that Flor. But it doesn't change his situation. He ponders the best way to get out of it. After two seemingly endless weeks of incarceration with no prospect of any light at the end of the tunnel, he's taken to the office of the colonel in charge of the garrison. He's wanted on the telephone.

It's Flor de Oro. After being harshly reprimanded by T and forbidden to go out, she's spent the last two weeks pacing the presidential residence, dreaming up a thousand scenarios to free Porfirio and run away with him.

"I can't talk for long," she says, breathlessly. "Next week, on Saturday, there's going to be a ball at the Santiago Country Club. Look in the paper—there's an announcement. And I want you to be there. This is our chance!"

"What time is the ball?"

"Five o'clock. Come. I'm begging you."

"I'll do my best."

"Do whatever it takes. But be there."

It's an order. She sounds eerily like her father.

Porfirio gets hold of a paper and confirms it: a grand ball in Flor's honor is being given at the Santiago Country Club, a kind of christening to launch the young woman into society. He knows a doctor in Santiago, one Grullón. Porfirio isn't a prisoner, only under house arrest. And his jailers are fellow soldiers, not disposed to be too hard on him; after all, this is a matter of the heart, and men understand each other when it comes to these things. Claiming a sore throat, Porfirio requests permission to go see the doctor. Permission granted.

It's a lovely evening. The club is full to bursting, overflowing with members of high society, a full orchestra, fresh flowers, champagne.

Flor, in a sage-green evening gown, stands nervously in the midst of a group of well-born young ladies. No one dares ask her to dance; they know, now, the fate reserved for anyone who gets too close to the president's daughter. Flor's eyes rove the crowd ceaselessly. Porfirio isn't there.

The son of the provincial governor approaches and bows. She can't refuse, and they take to the dance floor, followed immediately by a wave of other couples. Flor, tense and distracted, dances badly, unable to follow her partner's lead. Suddenly she sees him, and from that moment on, nothing else matters. Porfirio makes his way toward her through the crowd. No one else exists for Flor, only him. Then he's there before her, back very straight, unmoving. She feels like she might faint. They gaze at each other, both of them sensing that there's no turning back. He reaches out and takes her hand, with delicacy and a sort of restraint. "I was so afraid you wouldn't come," Flor breathes, unutterably relieved. He takes her in his arms and holds her close. The noise of the ball recedes.

The orchestra starts playing a Parisian-style waltz. They whirl among the other dancers, alone in their own private fairy tale, feeling something deeper than happiness. Hope. Flor feels as if her heart might burst.

One dance, then another. Rubirosa knows they're breaking the rules of protocol and propriety, not to mention threatening a father's honor. And in this country, that's all it takes

By dancing in the arms of her Prince Charming, Flor is openly defying T. The other guests watch them, frowning and murmuring. For a man to dance more than three dances with a young woman he isn't engaged to! It just isn't done. It's *scandalous*. And the insolent lieutenant's going to pay dearly for it. Though the girl *was* brought up in France, it's true. And so was he, if what people say is true . . .

By the fifth bolero, Porfirio is in love. Flor, of course, had no need of dancing to know the same was true for her. She loves him. She's absolutely certain of it. She loves him the way one loves at seventeen: ferociously, determinedly, stubbornly.

All night they revel in the closeness of their bodies, the scents of their skin, murmured words. Flor's chaperone watches, vexed and powerless, when they leave the dance floor and head out into the gardens. One kiss. Just one. Flor closes her eyes, letting her body melt against his, shivering deliciously, a fiery heat burning low in her belly. Another kiss. It's torture when they have to part in the early hours. Porfirio goes back to his barracks, Flor, to the presidential residence in Santo Domingo.

She sits in the back seat of the limousine and closes her eyes, silent and stunned by what has just happened.

* * *

Flor is resting in her room. The sun's rays filter in through the Venetian blinds, caressing her skin. Porfirio's smiling face is all she can see behind her closed eyelids. She has chosen him, body and soul. Already she can see the world only through the prism of her feelings for him, the way her father can only see his country through the prism of his ambition.

There's a knock at the door. It's Bienvenida. "Your father's furious about your scandalous behavior last night," she tells Flor sharply. "Get ready for a real punishment." She turns on her heel and leaves.

A short time later, a servant appears and announces that the president has summoned Flor to his office. Well, she won't go. She shuts her bedroom door and locks it.

It's madness to defy her father, and she knows it. But her love for Porfirio overrides everything else. A tiny voice in her head murmurs that she's at risk of burning her wings, Icarus-style, but she ignores it.

Now T is there, pounding furiously on her door. He's in a black mood; his masseur is ill and was unable to keep their daily eight A.M. appointment. He orders Flor to come out. She refuses. She is undoubtedly the only person in the entire country who dares to resist him. T can't allow himself to make a scene in front of the household help. He stomps away, bent on revenge, driven far more by anger at his wounded dignity than by fatherly love. It's he who's going to keep Flor prisoner. Until she bends to his will.

He confines her to her room indefinitely. So Flor disappears. She knows very well how to do that; it's easy. She simply withdraws into herself, loses herself, and voilà, she's gone. Her already-slight body becomes light, as light as a feather. She learned to do this back at Bouffémont, when the loneliness and homesickness became more than she could bear. She becomes a mere shell lying in bed, inert and vacant, almost ethereal. The world around her loses its reality, turning silent, black and white, devoid of anything but Porfirio's voice whispering in her ear. She disappears, and there is nowhere left for her father's anger to cling.

* * *

Rubirosa is stripped of his status. His uniform and pistol are confiscated, and he is forced to return to civilian life. He's distraught. He loves the army. The uniform that so impresses the girls; the horse; the guns. His grand dreams are collapsing before his eyes. He takes refuge at his grandfather's house. There's no future for him left in this country. He's considering a return to Paris when a friend arrives in a hurry and advises him to hide. No one angers El Jefe with impunity. Porfirio has no desire to add his name to the list of suspicious disappearances and convenient accidents. So he hides himself away on a family cacao plantation in the depths of the Dominican campo.

Two weeks pass.

One day a messenger shows up from God knows where and tells him to go to the telephone booth in the village at precisely nine o'clock that night and wait.

At nine o'clock on the dot, the phone rings. Porfirio picks up the receiver. It's Flor.

"*Mon amour*, don't give up. Everything will work out. I haven't left my room. I'm refusing to see my father, but I've sent word to him. I want to marry you."

Porfirio didn't know that little Flor had locked herself in her room, that she was refusing to eat, that she'd even threatened suicide. A bit dramatic, maybe, but effective. For Flor has never wanted anything so much in her whole life. Yes, this is the first time she's ever stood up to her father, but she's doing it with everything she's got.

Shut up in her bedroom, Flor has now turned the paternal punishment into a personal choice. Lina Lovatón, her co-conspirator in romance, comes to visit her (an order, it turns out, from the president; she is the only person permitted to see Flor). She's been looking into Rubirosa, she tells Flor. He's got an awful reputation; he's a wastrel with no future; they say he led a dissolute life in Paris, that he'll flirt with anyone at the drop of a hat, that he's already gotten himself in trouble with other girls' fathers.

But none of this matters to Flor. She loves Porfirio, *all* of him: the slight dent in his chin that's almost a dimple, his dark eyes, his frank smile, his perfect manners and natural elegance, the virility that emanates from his every pore. She loves it when he calls her *Fleur*. She loves him.

Doña Ana Antonia Ariza Almànazar requests an audience with the president to plead her son's case. She doesn't want to see his military career ruined. He is, after all, the son of a general and diplomat who has spent his life serving his country. And really, an alliance between a Rubirosa and a Trujillo would be far from unsuitable; the Rubirosas have long enjoyed a solid reputation among the Dominican elite. Why shouldn't Flor and Porfirio marry? They love each other.

In the end, T gives in.

Begrudgingly, but he gives in.

When Aminta finds out, she tries to dissuade Flor from marrying so young, but in vain. What weight could her arguments possibly have against this love, against her daughter's will, against El Jefe's decision?

* * *

Porfirio returns to Santo Domingo.

In the end, El Jefe has decided that the union is a good idea, a way of guaranteeing the subservience of a prominent young member of high society through familial ties. It'll be one more card up his sleeve, to be played when the need arises. And there are always moments of such need. Yes, he concludes, he will find a way for Porfirio to serve his interests.

The lovebirds are allowed to see one another for a few hours a day, chaperoned by a duenna, to plan their wedding. The whole city feels bright and shining, the hills glowing green, the sound of the sea pure music. Occasionally the chaperone will turn away discreetly so that Porfirio can steal a kiss.

She's seventeen years old. Porfirio is twenty-three.

The notice of marriage is published.

Aminta's name is absent from the announcement, replaced by that of Bienvenida. Flor's family name, printed in bold typeface, overshadows Rubirosa's completely.

San José de las Matas
Saturday, December 3, 1932

The streets of San José de las Matas are in chaos. The hundreds of brightly colored crêpe-paper garlands festooning the village in celebration of Flor and Porfirio's wedding have been stripped from trees and buildings by the kind of downpour unique to the Caribbean during hurricane season, mixing into a kind of colorful soup that swirls ankle-deep. The guests cluster in the forecourt of the church, trying vainly to find shelter from the pouring rain that came without warning. Expensive high-heeled shoes are soaked, meticulously applied makeup ruined, carefully arranged hairstyles demolished.

In the back of a limousine at the head of the motorcade progressing slowly toward the presidential residence, Flor de Oro wipes away the bead of sweat that has trickled down her neck into the hollow of her collarbone beneath the clinging lace of her wedding gown. Her hair, painstakingly smoothed for the day, curls rebelliously beneath her mantilla, unable to resist the overwhelming humidity.

She's disappointed. This isn't how she imagined her wedding day. She'd pictured bright sun, the Cathedral of Santa María la Menor[8] full to bursting. The tomb of Christopher Columbus, the great pipe organ. Cascades of white flowers. A gown with a long train trailing all the way down the nave. An entrance on her father's arm, her mother in the first row, so proud, smiling at her. A solemn and regal ceremony. But this . . .

Porfirio is pensive next to her, gazing blankly at the fogged-up

---

[8] Cathedral of Santa María la Menor: The oldest cathedral in the Americas.

windshield. The rain has a cold, sharp, disheartening quality. The young husband gathers himself and takes Flor's hand in his own, squeezing it gently, that small, childlike hand, and smiles at her.

"Rainy marriage, happy marriage," he says.

Flor's regrets evaporate instantaneously. With Porfirio beside her, everything—absolutely everything—becomes wonderful. Even her wedding day, ruined by rain. Even the frumpy wedding dress, chosen by her father, that swamps her petite figure. She tucks a wayward curl behind her ear and beams at her husband radiantly. The motorcade continues its progress toward the wedding reception, two kilometers of rain and mud away.

* * *

"I, Flor de Oro Anacaona Dominicana Trujillo Ledesma, take you, Porfirio Enrique Rubirosa Ariza, to be my husband. I promise to remain faithful to you for better or for worse, in sickness and in health, until death parts us."

As Porfirio had just done, Flor recited her vows smoothly and clearly, without the slightest hesitation, her voice strong and confident, and perhaps a hint of defiance in her eyes when she looked at the chubby face—almost as red as his vestments—of Monsignor Nouel, Archbishop of Santo Domingo and ex-president of the Republic, who was conducting the ceremony. She pledged herself without hesitation, the words a cry of love flung in the face of Dominican high society.

For in San Jose, not to mention the rest of the country, since the banns were published in the newspapers a month ago, people had talked about nothing else. El Jefe had declared the wedding day a national holiday, and the country was in full celebration. Flor de Oro Trujillo, the daughter of Generalissimo Rafael Leonidas Trujillo, the Honorable President of the Republic and Benefactor of the Fatherland, was marrying. And the man she had chosen was one Porfirio Rubirosa, a lowly lieutenant from a respectable but down-on-its-luck bourgeois family. The gossips had taken delight in pointing out the groom's unimportance, naturally. But he was very handsome, and the couple was very young, and they were undeniably, incandescently smitten. A true love match.

The archbishop continued the service in Latin. No one understood a word of it, except maybe Flor, remembering her studies at Bouffémont.

* * *

The setting for the royal wedding was the villa of Los Pinares, T's country residence. He was the one who selected it, of course. Everything had been meticulously orchestrated, gone perfectly to plan. The civil union contract was signed at 4:30 P.M. sharp, and at 4:45 Flor and Porfirio were officially married by Francisco Rodríguez Liriano, known as Panchito, the civil registrar for San José de las Matas. At exactly 5:15, Flor entered the dignitary-crammed church on her father's arm, T puffed up with pride in full dress uniform.

She was wearing a plain, rather austere gown and fought to control its long, heavy train. The dress was straight from Paris, made of the finest Calais lace, but it was a bit old-fashioned and, truth be told, not very pretty. Flor's delicate hands and slender arms were hidden by opera-length gloves that reached almost to her shoulders, revealing only a few centimeters of bare skin below her sleeves. All of this, combined with the mantilla on her head, made Flor look more like a little girl taking first communion than a bride.

Porfirio, for his part, was dazzlingly handsome in a black tuxedo set off by a simple white pocket square. Flor glanced sideways at him when he came to stand beside her at the altar, his emotions concealed by his half-lidded eyes with their ridiculously long, almost feminine lashes. In that instant she knew she would belong to him, body and soul, forever.

And then, the storm. No photographs, no congratulations; all of that would have to wait. Everyone dashed pell-mell through the downpour to their waiting cars, and the motorcade set off for the official reception.

* * *

Now, leaving behind the pathetic sight of the soaked and tattered garlands bedecking the village, the guests gather in the vast ballroom at Los Pinares, which has been splendidly decorated with two enormous crystal chandeliers and flowers everywhere. Everyone in the place is a high-ranking member of the Church or the military or a prominent diplomat, industrialist, exporter, newspaper-owner, or foreign dignitary, all carefully cherry-picked for the guest list. Flor hardly knows anyone except her own relatives: her uncles and aunts, T's brothers and sisters. T has denied Aminta permission to attend the wedding—the ultimate revenge of the Trujillo family, and a victory for Bienvenida.

That decision has caused Flor inexpressible agony. What bride gets married without her own mother? How can T have been so cruel as to prevent her and Aminta from sharing this singular experience, the most beautiful day of her life? Flor would have loved to have her mother at her side as she became a wife, to feel the tenderness radiating from her. She would so much have loved Mami to see her in her white dress.

Flor can't begin to understand why her father would do something so deliberately hurtful. Is it out of possessiveness? Jealousy, pride? Spite? Pure sadism? She's nothing but a toy in T's hands, she realizes. A means for him to demonstrate his power. It's a bitter pill to swallow. Thankfully, she has Porfirio now, and soon she'll be far away from all of this.

The guests of honor at the wedding are the minister plenipotentiary from the United States to the Dominican Republic,

Hans Frederick Arthur Schoenfeld, and his wife. Adding insult to injury, the American served as an official witness and signed the register, along with Flor's uncle Virgilio Trujillo. Neither she nor Porfirio were consulted.

Lina Lovatón, Flor's longtime confidante, is one of the rare guests her own age. More than once Flor catches El Jefe's gaze lingering on her friend's décolletage. But Lina is perfectly at ease. Thanks to Flor's father, she knows every high-ranking politician present. She points them out to Flor, explaining who's who. "That one is the minister of agriculture and commerce; that one's labor and communications; and there's the minister of health, and the minister of public works is over there..."

This isn't a wedding reception. It's a cabinet meeting.

The commander-in-chief of the army is here, and the chief of naval operations, and a whole host of generals and colonels.

This isn't a wedding reception. It's a military gathering.

Lina discreetly points out Dr. Max Henríquez Ureña, the minister of foreign affairs.

"Salomé Ureña's son?" Flor asks, eyeing the aristocratic-looking gentleman with the piercing gaze.

Lina nods. Flor would love to talk to him, to ask him about his mother, the acclaimed Dominican poetess whose efforts on behalf of national independence and the education of young girls have lately begun to interest her. But she's too intimidated; she doesn't dare approach him. Instead, Flor de Oro does what's expected of her, exchanging a moment of polite chatter with one guest after another. With Charles de Mondesert, the French trade advisor, for example, she converses in "almost accentless French," in the complimentary words of Jean Morlet and his wife, who are introduced to her as "distinguished members of the French community." She's proud of herself; this is where she shines. If only Aminta were here to see it.

Eventually, Flor ends up standing next to her Aunt Mercedes, nicknamed Machichi, her favorite of T's sisters and the only woman in the room not putting on airs. They smile at one another conspiratorially at the sight of El Jefe surrounded by a group of simpering, fluttering women, all of them willing to act as ridiculous as necessary to spend a few hours in his bed. They laugh discreetly together at Bienvenida, the ignored wife who is well aware of her husband's appetites and stares at him openly from across the room. As for Porfirio, he has been swept up by his former comrades in the president's personal guard and is matching them glass for glass, taking full advantage of the unending flow of Médoc and Napa Valley wines, champagne, and Brugal rum.

Flor grows bored. The endless cocktail hour is dull; dinner is dull; the speeches are dull. But she comes back to life in her father's arms, when the dancing finally begins. T really does dance very well. Flor remembers the merengues of her childhood in San Cristóbal, her little feet balancing atop his army-cadet boots. It seems so long ago now . . .

And then she's in Porfirio's arms. They whirl gracefully, joyously, and it's like a fairy tale, the couple at its center drawing every eye. They radiate the invincibility of youth, that golden aura that belongs only to those who are just beginning their lives, that eagerness to meet a future that stretches ahead of them without limit.

Flor looks at the other women, at their bare shoulders and the flattering necklines of their gowns, and feels aggrieved. If only her father hadn't insisted on choosing her bridal outfit himself . . . She consoles herself by gazing admiringly at Porfirio. Her husband. His princely bearing, his beautifully manicured hands, his poise, his dark eyes, his handsome face, the warm richness of his voice. None of those women in their lovely gowns can keep their eyes off him. He is so beautiful.

And tonight, he'll be hers.

Despite her mother's absence, her stepmother's jealousy, her father's diktats, and the many lustful feminine gazes directed at her brand-new husband, this is the most wonderful day of her life.

Though perhaps, for a single blurred instant, Flor glimpses the ordeal that awaits, the misery that her life will be alongside this man who is too handsome, too magnetic, too confident, too self-assured; this man who is so pleasing to women, and who loves women too much.

* * *

The wedding night finds Flor in the bed of the man she loves, her husband of a few hours' standing. She offers herself to him unhesitatingly. This will be no gentle, romantic disrobing, though. In his haste to undress her, Porfirio wrenches the back of her dress open, ripping the white lace and sending mother-of-pearl buttons skittering across the marble tiles. Flor was hoping to keep the gown pristine so she could show it to Aminta, but it's too late now. Porfirio strips his own clothes off feverishly, as if possessed by some uncontrollable urgency. When he's standing naked before her, Flor is seized by panic. The sight of his erect member horrifies her, and she flees into the bathroom. As Porfirio calls to her helplessly from the other side of the door, she kneels next to the bathtub and crosses herself with a trembling hand. "Santa Virgen de la Altagracia, help me through this." Then she returns to the bedroom, determined to face whatever awaits.

Flor lets a palm rest on Porfirio's chest. Shyly at first, and then with fingers spread, feeling the rapid beat of his heart. She closes her eyes. This heart belongs to her. Porfirio is her husband before God, for better or worse, and she's ready.

Then her delicate body is beneath his strong one. He forces himself to go gently, tenderly. She is so young, not even a woman yet. Images flash through his mind: the faces, buttocks, breasts of the ripe-bodied women who educated him, loved him, perhaps. He sees himself at age fourteen, taken to a Paris brothel by his father. The coarse, blowsy features of the woman who took his virginity rise up in his memory with incredible clarity, superimposing themselves onto Flor's dainty, innocent ones, her little face screwed up with tension, frizzy hair spread out on the pillow, gaze riveted to his. She is his wife before God. He has vowed to be faithful to her, and already he knows it won't be easy.

His fingers dig into her skin. He plunges into her, pushes, loses control. A sudden, hard thrust. A stab of pain. A tearing. Flor can't hold back her cry of pain. Is *this* what love is, then? Porfirio isn't trying to be careful anymore; his movements are wild, almost savage, and it's all over very quickly. There is brutality in the way he takes her, and awkwardness, and the fierceness of long pent-up desire. A last groan and he rolls off her with a sigh of satisfaction. Flor snuggles up against him, a painful burning between her thighs, aching and overwhelmed, but happy. He has branded her in the most intimate of ways. She never imagined losing her virginity would be so . . . violent. Not to this extent. The blood, the pain, the absolute possession. It's one more bond between them.

The next morning, Flor spreads her wedding gown out on the bed, which she's covered with a duvet to hide the bloodstains. The dress is beyond repair. Flor's eyes fill with tears. She can't show it off to her mother now.

* * *

"Porfirio, listen to this . . . "

Flor giggles.

"I didn't know the reporters at *La Opinión* were such poets! Our wedding was the most opulent ever seen in the country, 'awash in distinction and elegance, perfumed with youth and beauty.' And you and I are 'a single heart beneath a veil of love, dreams, and promise.'"

In her clear voice, Flor reads the article out loud as they finish their breakfast.

"In a glorious tropical setting, a symphony of light, color, and scent, like in a love-ballad . . . There, where Mother Nature sings her triumphal hymn amidst dazzling tropical lushness, blah blah blah . . . with the delightful and enchanting Miss Flor de Oro Trujillo, a young lady of exquisite refinement, all delicacy and sweetness, befitting both her name, 'Flower,' and the many graces that blossom within her, beloved daughter of the country's president, General Rafael Leonidas Trujillo Molina . . . "

"Quite a flight of fancy," Porfirio observes.

"It's absolutely terrible!" Flor says, laughing. "They describe Bienvenida the same way: 'a *grande dame* in every sense of the word.'"

"And about me? What does it say?"

"'Proper and distinguished.' That's all. And that you come from an honorable Dominican family, that your father was a general and diplomat . . . "

"No flowery scents or enchanted moonbeams? I might as well not exist," Porfirio concludes, bitterly recalling Flor's name on the marriage certificate, printed in type twice as large as his.

It hurts, but he's determined not to show Flor how he feels. His pride won't let him complain. This is the price he must pay for becoming the son-in-law of the most powerful man in the country.

And this is only the beginning.

* * *

T has been generous to the newlyweds. Very generous. He's showered them with gifts: a five-bedroom house with a patio and pool in the chic Gazcue neighborhood, not far from the presidential residence; a beach cottage in La Romana; and a cream-colored 1930 Packard sedan with a 12-cylinder engine and the couple's initials in gold on its doors—not to mention an on-call chauffeur, Ignacio, a Creole most known for organizing cockfights in the capital. There's also a large Italian-made wardrobe for Porfirio and an even larger one, French, for Flor, and a mountain of jewelry from the finest jewelers in the Place Vendôme. And all of this is on top of the $50,000[9] dowry deposited in a new bank account, with the sole caveat that El Jefe must sign off in order for Flor and Porfirio to access the money.

The newlyweds prepare to leave for a luxurious honeymoon in Venice, following in the footsteps of Stendhal. A sumptuous suite at the Cipriani hotel, Florian chocolates, Gritti orange juice, scotch at the new Harry's Bar. Porfirio loves the idea of getting reacquainted with the Europe of his childhood, which he hasn't seen in ten years. And Flor is returning to Venice with the man she secretly calls her Prince Charming, exactly as she once dreamed of during her travels in Italy with Aminta.

Almost exactly, anyway.

In Venice, the young couple spends money lavishly. Porfirio truly loves his Fleur, though he does find her a bit too skinny (his taste runs to full-bodied women—a very Latin preference). But despite his sincere fondness for his wife, he can't keep from indulging in certain old habits. Some nights, after sharing a romantic candlelit dinner with Flor, he leaves her in the plush comfort of their hotel suite and heads for his favorite seedy little bar in the Cannaregio district, where he can gamble incognito until the wee hours. When he returns home just before sunrise, his eyes ringed with dark circles and his chin covered in stubble, he collapses into their bed without the slightest explanation. Flor watches him sleep with a mixture of tenderness and puzzlement, not daring to reproach him.

She doesn't know it yet, but the cage door has just closed on her, a cage whose bars will only become thicker.

---

[9] Around $1 million in today's money.

Santo Domingo
1934–1935

It hasn't even been a month since the wedding, and already T has started to press the newlyweds. They'd hardly returned from Venice when it began, and it's quickly become an obsession, putting unbearable pressure on the young couple. El Jefe stops by their home every morning to ask. Is there an heir on the way yet?

T, lord of the Dominican Republic, is determined to found a dynasty. And since he has no legitimate male offspring—that useless Bienvenida keeps having miscarriage after miscarriage—he's counting on Flor de Oro. In the absence of an officially recognized son, a grandson. A bit of masculine blood in the Trujillo henhouse.

* * *

They're too young. And clearly unequipped for married life, even in the luxurious conditions provided by T's fortune and rank.

Instead of conceiving, Flor and Porfirio live in a perpetual state of carefree pleasure, becoming the best-dressed, most elegant, and most well-educated couple in the international society pages, and certainly the most popular pair in the Dominican capital. Which, naturally, doesn't exactly please El Jefe.

Flor has two personal maids, Porfirio a valet, a masseur, and a boxing trainer, Kid Gogo. He has even transformed a room of the house into a boxing ring. His military ambitions have evaporated at the same speed with which he goes through his father-in-law's money. Having taken up a diplomatic post, a mostly ceremonial function without real responsibility, he's confident in the future. His life is full of new horizons, luxurious surroundings, trips abroad, glittering parties. Everything he loves. No more worrying about what tomorrow might hold.

The marriage is a godsend for the Rubirosa clan, as well; they've gone from shame to prosperity overnight. Not only is Porfirio generous to his loved ones, but numerous family members have been given desirable government jobs.

Flor, though, is proving to be ill-prepared for the duties of a wife, despite the practical education she received at Bouffémont. She doesn't know how to assert her authority over the servants, or make them respect her, and she has no idea how to run a household. Planning menus, receiving guests, assigning seats for a dinner party, giving instructions to the gardener, paying bills—all of it baffles her, and bores her even more. So she takes refuge in the lightheartedness that has always served her so well. She goes shopping in the city, often driving herself (Porfirio has taught her how), frequents tearooms and salons, or relaxes on a chaise longue in the garden with a stack of American fashion and movie magazines. The house is less than tidy, and dinners are unpredictable. This soon begins to annoy Porfirio.

But the thing weighing most heavily on their marriage is the close surveillance under which they've been placed. Thanks to his agents and secret police, not to mention the bribes he uses to loosen the servants' lips, T is aware of the couple's every move.

In a country that has nearly as many government informers as it does citizens, it's extremely difficult to live a low-profile life, especially in Flor and Porfirio's position. Even their most insignificant acts are duly reported. T is determined to keep a close eye on his son-in-law, in particular. He's still sizing the young man up, considering the best way to make use of this scion of an upper class still wary of his regime. Sooner or later, the right moment will come for El Jefe to put this pawn into play—for no individual is much more to him than a means of accomplishing his grand dream: developing this country that, little by little, is becoming his own private estate and reigning over it as its uncontested lord and master.

Flor and Porfirio are obliged to have lunch with T and Bienvenida at La Mansión, the president's official residence, almost every day. These are formal events, and the young couple is painfully conscious of every word, every gesture, feeling as if they're a pair of slaves at the master's table. Flor is disillusioned; she thought getting married would free her from such tight paternal control. But T continues to stick his nose into every corner of their lives, including the bedroom. His main interest is invariably whether Flor is pregnant, and his constant, blunt questions make the young woman extremely uncomfortable. Despite regular sexual activity, there is no sign of pregnancy—and, for now at least, Flor doesn't want there to be. They're too new of a couple to become a family. For the moment, all she wants is to keep her husband happy.

* * *

Living with a playboy isn't always a picnic. Flor learns this gradually, the hard way. Porfirio has resumed his gallivanting ways. He often goes out alone, not coming home until the wee hours. Worse, when they have dinner in a restaurant, he takes her home and then goes back out to drink and gamble. Exactly as he began to do in Venice. Exactly as he has never stopped doing.

Like any good Latin husband, Porfirio expects his wife to be submissive. Just like his mother was. And little by little, he discovers now that Flor is not only stubborn; she's also a spoiled child, thin-skinned and quick to anger. They often argue over insignificant trifles. He snaps at her. She provokes him. He gets angrier. The argument turns nasty. Insults fly. And then they patch things up in bed.

As the months pass, Flor becomes morose, questioning her choices. Has she gotten out from under her father's thumb only to fall beneath a husband's? She confides her feelings to Lina, her closest friend since her return from France. Lina has also struck up a friendship with El Jefe, often spending time alone with him, a rare privilege. "He's really wonderful! He's like a father to me," she tells Flor, who feels a prickle of jealousy in her gut.

"I can't be *just* an obedient wife. I don't want to live like a bird in a cage," she says.

"*Querida*, you knew what to expect when you got married. You know how it goes. Just look around."

"What if I went back to school? I could be a journalist, or a writer. Have a profession."

"A profession! You're dreaming, my dear. You're El Jefe's daughter. You're married. And to a man every woman wants for herself! If I were you, I'd watch him like a hawk."

Flor shrugs and rolls her eyes, secure in Porfirio's love.

"The best thing you could do," Lina—who is full of good advice—continues, "is to show up at official ceremonies, do charitable work, and be socially prominent. Because, heaven knows, that drip Bienvenida can't handle any of it."

Lina bites her lip—she didn't mean to say that last bit. Flor doesn't reply. It's true that Bienvenida has become a shadow of her former self, so reclusive that sometimes it's as if she doesn't even exist. The only person T's wife lashes out at is her stepdaughter, who is a kind of personification of all her resentment and jealousy. And Flor is beginning to hate her. But her stepmother, and her father's marriage, are really none of her business.

Flor complains to T about her husband's nightly outings, hoping El Jefe will support her and give his son-in-law a good talking-to.

"Porfirio keeps leaving me at home to go out with his friends, and I spend most of my evenings alone. He comes home drunk a lot . . ."

"That's what happens when you get married too young," T retorts, without batting an eyelash.

"But Papi, you're the one who wouldn't let me see Porfirio!"

"Because your way of 'seeing' each other, as you call it, went beyond what was proper. You had no respect for etiquette or decorum. You have no one to blame but yourself."

"Papi, *por Dios*, wake up! It's the twentieth century! A girl has the right to spend time with a young man without being forced to marry him on the spot!"

Flor is angry now. It's all she can do not to fling her father's notorious womanizing right back in his face. It's common knowledge, though everyone feigns ignorance.

El Jefe doesn't take the bait. "Kindly do not speak to me in that tone, Flor. And leave God out of this."

Flor stiffens. When T calls her just "Flor," it means he's irritated with her.

"And anyway, it's almost definitely your own fault," El Jefe continues. "Are you doing everything you should to keep your husband at home?"

After all, he reminds her, a wife's job is to support her husband, to continue his line. To raise his children and keep house for him. Didn't he send her to Bouffémont precisely to learn how to do all that?

And so, guilt-stricken and defeated by these pointless conversations, Flor forces herself to focus on dreams of a family.

* * *

Porfirio can't take much more. His father-in-law won't stop meddling in his business. And his wife is becoming more of a killjoy by the day.

The straw that breaks the camel's back is the dredging

operation carried out in the port of Santo Domingo. It's an enormous endeavor. T has decided to enlarge the capital's port so it can accommodate large vessels, and to do that, the mouth of the Ozama River must be dredged. How on earth Porfirio got himself mixed up in this project, co-financed by Puerto Rican businessman Felix Benítez Rexach, Flor will never know. At any rate, he somehow unearthed an old dredger for sale in New Orleans. Its purchase price, including transport? $50,000. Flor's entire dowry. T approves of the plan, and grants Porfirio access to the Rubirosas' bank account.

But, whether out of adaptability or spite, despite his previous support of his son-in-law, El Jefe abruptly changes his tune when Benítez Rexach deems the dredger unusable. Now Porfirio finds himself with a useless piece of machinery on his hands, and the couple without a penny to their names. Even worse, there are rumors that Flor's husband has been dallying with the famous French singer Môme Moineau, who also happens to be the companion of Benítez Rexach, and that the latter has ruined Flor and Porfirio deliberately for revenge. Whatever the truth, the young couple is now completely dependent on El Jefe's generosity.

Despondent, his dreams of acquiring a fortune of his own shattered, Porfirio is relieved of his government job and resigns himself to rejoining the army with the rank of captain, at a fixed salary. It's some consolation that he already knows the effect the uniform has on women.

* * *

Soon, though, Porfirio is left with only one desire: escape. To be far away from El Jefe, whose toxic maneuvering is affecting everyone around him, including his own daughter.

Europe is too far, so Porfirio's thoughts turn to America, the land of opportunity. Miami is just a stone's throw away from the island: too close. So it has to be New York.

Flor is initially skeptical, but Porfirio cajoles her, makes promises, and soon she warms to the idea. Yes, New York is a good idea. Porfirio has cousins there. And there are intellectuals, and many Dominicans in political exile, at odds with what isn't *quite* a dictatorship . . . yet.

Flor informs her father of their plans. T is adamantly opposed to it at first, but he knows how determined his daughter can be, how far she's willing to go to get what she wants. He knows just how long she can hold out, if necessary. She's proven that already. She isn't his daughter for nothing.

In the end, El Jefe gives in.

Flor and Porfirio can go, if that's what they want. But it will mean the end of T's financial support.

Flor feels as if she's sprouting wings. To start over from scratch—a new adventure! It's wildly romantic.

The first hint of clouds in the clear blue sky of their future soon makes itself known, though. A distant warning, a faint rumble of danger.

NEW YORK
1934–1935

The Rubirosas leave the island quietly, almost as if they're on the run.

Flor doesn't let go of Porfirio's hand for the entire four-hour flight, clinging to him with her eyes shut tight, soothing herself with hopeful daydreams. They're finally escaping the horrible glass-walled cage that has kept them confined, barely able to move, for so long, painfully excluded from the real life going on outside. But now it's theirs for the taking. Real life. They're together, souls as intertwined as their fingers—together against T, against the whole world, and nothing else matters.

All too quickly, however, real life shows a face very different to the one Flor has imagined, the initial bright landscape of their new existence concealing a dark and craggy horizon.

Flor and Porfirio's first residence in New York is a rundown little hotel on Broadway with a battered sign out front and a steep and dingy staircase leading to a tiny room that reeks of failure. Flor, used to a life of luxury, is miserable, and it isn't long before their dismal living conditions start to take a toll on their relationship. The delirious exhilaration of escape fades rapidly, the dreary days blurring into one another. Porfirio pounds the pavement, calling on every connection he can muster in search of a job to stave off both poverty and boredom. Flor waits up for him night after night, the neon lights of the city blinking endlessly beyond the thin curtains of their room. She has absolutely nothing to do. No friends, no money. And she's always cold, the winter chill seeping into her bones. They're a long way from the opulent suite at the

Cipriani Hotel, the luxurious home in Gazcue. It's a heavy price to pay for their freedom.

Flor is already feeling the sting of regret. Maybe, she says to Porfirio, they should alert the press to their presence in New York. Tell the story of how El Jefe has abandoned his disgraced daughter, who's been headline news throughout her entire marriage. But Rubirosa is reluctant to indulge this desire for vengeance. He really doesn't think the papers would be interested in their situation. And he's experienced his father-in-law's rages before. It would be both pointless and imprudent to provoke him again.

The couple moves from their dingy hotel room into an apartment that isn't much better. Porfirio is adjusting to New York more easily than Flor is. He spends a lot of time with his cousins, young punks mixed up in all sorts of shady business; one of them, Luis de la Fuente Rubirosa, known as Chichi, youngest child of Porfirio's father's older sister, has already done five years in prison for various types of trafficking. Flor, who finds these dubious relations vulgar and shudders to think of their potential influence on her husband, avoids them as much as she can.

Porfirio finds a job tending bar in a nightclub. He also begins frequenting dodgy gambling dens, playing poker with a circle of unsavory Cubans while Flor waits miserably for him—again, and as always—in their shabby apartment. One day he wins, and they eat; the next, he loses, and they tighten their belts. Flor never knows what tomorrow will hold. In conditions like these, it's impossible to establish any sort of proper life. Dependent on Porfirio for her measly pocket money, she does her best to pass the time, but there isn't enough for any extras, and life is far from fun. Porfirio continues his nightly outings; his bartender job relieves him of the need to justify these nocturnal absences—he's *working*, of course. Flor becomes reacquainted with the cold and loneliness of her time at Bouffémont. She misses her island. The sunshine, the smells, the colors, the smiling faces. Not to mention the easy life . . .

* * *

One morning, Flor is searching for a few dollars to go downstairs, buy a newspaper, and treat herself to a coffee in the diner next door. Porfirio is snoring like a freight train; he came home in the early hours, stinking of whiskey and cheap perfume, and is still sound asleep. She doesn't dare wake him. His beautifully tailored jacket, a rumpled remnant of the wardrobe he received from T as a wedding gift, has been tossed carelessly on the sofa. Flor strokes the Italian silk, then makes up her mind. This won't be the first time that, her jealousy and curiosity stoked white-hot, she's gone through her husband's pockets. Her questing fingertips touch cold metal. A ring. Porfirio's wedding band. He took it off. Flor's stomach lurches. She extracts a piece of paper, folded twice, from one pocket. Unfolds it and smooths it out. A phone number. Her gut tightens painfully. Bile rises in her throat. Quietly, she picks up the telephone receiver and dials the number.

"Hello?"

The voice is hoarse, sleepy. The voice of a good-time girl. Flor is paralyzed. She feels like she's trapped in a tinderbox—somewhere very hot, very uncomfortable. This isn't a surprise, merely a confirmation. She hangs up the telephone. What did she expect? Porfirio is a party boy, a pleasure-seeker. Even T warned her about him.

From that moment on, Flor begins to fade. She hardly speaks, compensating for her inner turmoil by gorging herself on cakes and sweets and then vomiting it all up, nauseated and miserable. Soon she can't keep anything down and loses weight rapidly. And when she does speak, it's always to complain. Porfirio finds her unbearably tedious. She was too thin before, and now she's positively skeletal. She's not even pretty anymore, her shoulder blades and hipbones jutting out beneath the fabric of her dresses.

Flor dreams of the magical early days of their marriage, not so very long ago, but the idea of their relationship going back to the way it was becomes more hypothetical every day. Their union is hanging by a thread, and even that is fraying, and Flor, already suffering deeply, can tell there is far worse to come.

For her, every day is the same. She waits for him. They argue. She flings accusations at him, calls him names: Cheater. Gambler. Liar. *Mujeriego*. The fights often erupt over tiny things, trivial nothings. One provocation follows another until Flor goes too far.

One day, frustrated and pushed to the extreme limit of her self-restraint, she lashes out at Porfirio more cruelly than she ever has, with names intended to wound. *Cabron, coño de su madre, pendejo, come mierda*. She waits for a reaction that doesn't come, growing more and more furious, until—

"You're nothing but a horny *goat!* And I don't want to live with a goat!"

Porfirio actually turns green. Flor's gone too far. She bites the inside of her cheek, wishing she could take the words back, but it's too late. She stares at him, still defiant, her facial expressions the only weapons she has left.

Without thinking, without even really meaning to do it, he slaps her.

* * *

The first slap.

It's hard, sharp, landing high on her cheekbone, just below her eye, leaving a bright red mark and almost knocking her over. Flor stands there, so stunned that she can't move. Her husband has just dared to raise his hand to her. She's wide-eyed, open-mouthed. Speechless. Slowly, she lifts a hand to her stinging cheek. She can hardly breathe. No one has ever struck her before. Not her mother, not even her father, despite T's reputation for violently disciplining the Haitian workers on the sugar cane plantation. Flor is tempted to leap on Porfirio, to hammer on his chest with her fists, but suddenly the idea seems overdone, false, like a temper tantrum in the movies. She feels ridiculous. She knots her fingers together behind her back to keep herself from hitting him.

Porfirio realizes what has just happened. Without a word, he turns his back on his wife and leaves the apartment. After all, she was asking for it. She's always provoking him. But he knows he shouldn't have slapped her, that it was a mistake, an open door.

The face-off ends without a winner or loser, only Flor's threat to tell T, which she won't do. Not this time. She's hurt, but the prospect of complaining to the father she left her country to escape doesn't exactly make her feel better about herself or the situation. She consoles herself with the thought that this was surely a one-off, that it won't happen again. Porfirio is already regretting it. He's apologized and vowed never to be carried away by anger again, a promise they seal between the sheets. The sex isn't gentle. Porfirio has grown bolder with his wife since the early days of their marriage, and he prefers rough sex. He doesn't hurt her, but he comes close. Flor, for her part, participates in the role-play willingly, even passionately. She doesn't know any other way of making love. And more than that, every time they engage in these games, it brings back the intoxicating feeling that she belongs to him completely, and he to her. More often than not, they come at the same time, and it's a momentary victory over their mutual disenchantment. She holds her husband tightly to her the moment the sex is over, his body lying heavily on hers, and feels a rush of pure triumph. For these fleeting instants, she knows there will never be anyone for her but him. That she is his, forever.

Porfirio feels it, too. There's something indescribable between them, an unbreakable bond. Is this because she's the first woman he's ever truly loved? Because she's his wife before

God? Because their life together has been straight out of a Hollywood movie? Or is it because the scent and taste of Flor's skin take him back to the island that is such an integral part of him? The truth is that it's a little bit of each.

* * *

But Flor is unhappy. And their life in America is putting her under immense strain.

She doesn't like New York. Or her husband's shady friends, who have made the Rubirosa apartment their headquarters. Or the snobbish Americans who look down on her, a mixed-race immigrant with a Hispanic accent. She doesn't like their threadbare apartment, or the gray clouds that fill the sky, or the cold rain they bring. The beautiful house in Gazcue—Ignacio, their chauffeur—the tropical sun—the hours spent giggling with Lina—all of it combines to form a heavy tangle of regrets that weighs on her more and more each day.

She desperately wants to call her mother and pour out all her troubles. Mami to the rescue. But she's too ashamed to do it. And anyway, what can Aminta possibly do? T is the only one with the ability to change things. Flor and Porfirio can't even return to the country without his permission.

Every day that goes by pushes husband and wife further and further apart. Porfirio loses at poker more often than he wins. The couple is in dire straits. And it's at this precise moment that El Jefe, fully cognizant of their situation thanks to his spies, emerges from the woodwork.

Flor is twenty years old, with a philandering husband and a tyrant masquerading as a father who completely controls her. She's still without a child. And without hope.

New York
April 1935

This morning, as on so many mornings, Flor's coffee has the bitter taste of loneliness and disappointment. Porfirio came home in the wee hours again, fumbling noisily with his key in the lock and then stripping off his clothes before collapsing into bed, openly drunk. His snores are audible through the thin wall, unpleasantly punctuating the news broadcast Flor is half-listening to on the kitchen radio.

The sharp sound of the doorbell makes her jump. She's not expecting anyone. She looks at the wall clock: 10:30. Vaguely unsettled, she goes to the door and stands on tiptoe—these Americans are so tall!—to look out the peephole. A uniformed telegraph boy. "Telegram for Mr. Rubirosa."

"That's my husband. I don't want to disturb him—he's sleeping."

The telegraph boy glances at his watch disapprovingly. "Well, you're gonna have to wake him up," he says. "You can't sign for him."

Flor replaces the security chain on the door and goes into the bedroom, where she shakes Porfirio awake. He rolls over, grumbling, and finally heaves himself out of bed with a loud sigh of irritation.

Flor watches his face as he opens the telegram. Shock washes over his features. It's disconcerting; it takes a great deal to surprise Porfirio. He sinks into a chair, his eyes still heavy-lidded with sleep, and rereads the telegram, incredulous. Is this some kind of prank? But the message has been personally signed by El Jefe . . .

"I've been elected," he stammers finally. "To Congress."

Flor is shocked. "But you weren't running!"

Porfirio waves her words away. "I've got go to Santo Domingo. Your father's summoning me back. He's the one who arranged the election."

There's a note of scorn in his voice. Flor is stunned by the enormity of this news, not yet able to wrap her mind around the consequences. All she knows for now is that T will never leave them alone. That much, at least, is crystal clear. And Porfirio knows full well that there has to be some ulterior motive behind his father-in-law's machinations. As always. But what?

The newly-minted diplomat catches the next plane to Santo Domingo. It's a flying visit, and Flor isn't invited. She's disappointed at first, but really, it's for the best, because she isn't sure how she'd act around T.

What passes between the young man and his father-in-law, Flor never knows. Porfirio cuts short the questions she peppers him with when he comes home three days later; all that matters, he tells her, is that their future is looking much brighter, that they've been restored to El Jefe's good graces. T has generously forgiven them for their New York escapade. It's time to return to the fold. There's just one minor formality left.

These vague explanations leave Flor unsatisfied. Her intuition tells her there's more to the story. One night soon after Porfirio's return, she comes across a black leather briefcase he's hidden in the back of a closet. He's gone out—a "business meeting," he said—and her fingers itch to open the clasps. She fiddles with them nervously, but they're locked. Caught between excitement and guilt, she fetches a kitchen knife, a thin but sturdy one, and eases the point of the blade into one of the locks. A bit of wiggling, and it gives way. Then the second lock. *Porfirio's going to be furious*, she thinks. But to hell with it—she's used to his rages, and anyway, her curiosity is stronger than her fear.

What she sees when she opens the briefcase takes her breath away. Her heart begins to pound. Bundles and bundles of banknotes. Dollars. Flor doesn't count the money, but there's a lot of it. She tries to close the case, but the forced locks refuse to catch. She leaves it on the bed, wide open.

When Porfirio gets home, he's in a good mood. Flor pounces.

"Why did you bring a bag full of money back from Santo Domingo?"

She squares her shoulders, ready for a dressing-down. But her husband really is in a *very* good mood. He just laughs.

"Couldn't help yourself, could you, my little snoop? It's an advance on my salary. So we can settle our debts. And also some cash I'm delivering to the ambassador, plus a bit more to cover my expenses—I've been assigned to investigate some anti-Trujillists in Washington Heights. What do you say we go out and celebrate over dinner?" he suggests, sounding so light-hearted that Flor agrees, smiling.

Dinner in a restaurant with her husband is such a rare pleasure that she jumps at the chance, but Flor isn't fooled. The amount of money in the briefcase was enormous, and T has never been one for gratuitous generosity.

* * *

It happens on Sunday, April 28. In an apartment on Hamilton Place. At night.

That evening, Flor and Porfirio dine at Marcello's, a trattoria in Little Italy. Porfirio is at his most attentive, and she's relishing the peaceful atmosphere that's existed since his return from Santo Domingo. In her pretty dress, the picture of a demure little wife, Flor is the perfect alibi.

She won't discover this until later, of course.

For now, she's happy. This is what every day should be like. Porfirio is sweet and tender, covering her hand with his own several times during dinner, and giving her one of those looks of his, the sort that kindles a fire within her. Flor is slightly tipsy when they emerge from the restaurant; she adores chianti.

She takes Porfirio's arm, her head barely reaching his shoulder despite the high heels she wears, which click against the pavement. They decide to prolong the evening in a jazz club that has just opened in Greenwich Village. This is a night on which to be seen. They push back the club's little round tables, and Flor dances with the musicians, Porfirio looking on, amused. They take a taxi home well after midnight, and he kisses her hungrily, sliding a hand beneath her skirt, one finger slipping beneath the lace of her stocking where the flesh is soft and sensitive, tugging at the elastic of her panties. She gasps, giggling. He carries her up the stairs to their bed, where he lets her fall. She's feather-light. Easy prey. His expression is predatory above her. She falls asleep content and satiated. A few hours later, FBI agents knock on their door. It took them less than 24 hours to find the Rubirosas.

* * *

Porfirio laid the plan carefully, using the money in the briefcase. The target designated by El Jefe was Dr. Ángel Morales, a charismatic man who had held several ministerial and ambassadorial posts in Europe and the United States, and around whom T's exiled political opponents in New York had congregated. Morales, the undisputed leader of this anti-Trujillo movement, was planning to run for president in the next election; he'd even gained the support of the powerful Dupont industrialist family, whose loans to T were never repaid. The danger he presented was undeniable.

Rubirosa chose his cousin Luis de la Fuente Rubirosa to carry out the plan. Chichi was an obvious choice—except, of course, for the fact that he lacked both discretion and good judgment and tended to dive in headfirst. The apartment door opened to reveal a man, razor in hand, his face covered in shaving lather. Chichi opened fire immediately—two bullets in the chest at close range—and killed Morales's roommate,

Sergio Bencosme, son of General Ciprián Bencosme (whose assassination was ordered by T) and former defense minister in the government of Horacio Vásquez, as well as the intended vice-president in the event of Morales's election. Two pistol-shots, and his brainless killer fled without looking back.

The Rubirosas' apartment is searched from top to bottom. Flor watches, trembling, as the federal agents rummage through their meager possessions, going through every pocket and even her lingerie drawer. They find nothing. Not in the closets, not under the mattress. No weapons, no incriminating correspondence, nothing but twenty or thirty dollars in cash in a leather briefcase. Nothing to look twice at. Beneath the disapproving gazes of the neighbors gathered in the hallway, Flor and Porfirio are taken to the police station to be interrogated. Bencosme's death is a political assassination, and T's methods are only too well known. Is his daughter complicit?

Flor isn't afraid. She loses herself in contemplation of her surroundings, absorbing every detail: the drab walls, the desks with their chipped varnish and brown rings from countless cups of coffee, the straight-backed chairs with iron legs, the station duty officer behind his window. It's all like something out of a police movie.

But Flor de Oro Trujillo de Rubirosa is blameless, as white as snow. The president's daughter doesn't know a thing, and neither does her husband. Besides, he has an alibi for last night: he was dining out with his wife. They were even seen dancing at the Village Vanguard. In any case, he's a congressman in his country, and his diplomatic immunity protects him. And he's needed urgently back home.

The FBI lets them go.

The matter is consigned to file no. NY-97-2078.

End of story.

The Rubirosas go back to the Dominican Republic.

* * *

It's not until a year later that Chichi is charged with the murder. He returns to the island the day after the killing and takes up a place in the Dominican Army at the rank of lieutenant, despite never having undergone training. El Jefe doesn't make him disappear for good until a few years later when, threatening to reveal everything, he demands a promotion to captain. It's the last attempt at blackmail this truly brainless thug will ever make.

On the plane home, Porfirio and Flor giggle like children. What an adventure! He swears to her that the whole thing was a simple misunderstanding, and Flor suppresses her guilty conscience, willing herself with all her strength to believe him. She's so relieved to be going home. She's missed her island, and the life of a penniless exile is definitely not for her. Freedom without money, it turns out, leaves a lot to be desired. The idea of being under T's thumb again is irritating, but she'll go along with it. And things are so much better with Porfirio. They're partners again, inseparable.

She'll get used to life back home, Flor tells herself. Her mother nearby, T's omnipresence, her stepmother's pettiness, financial comfort and security. And this man who attracts women like flies to honey, and whom she wouldn't trade for anything in the world. He belongs to her, this man. He's hers.

If only El Jefe would give him some real responsibility.

Flor wraps these soothing illusions around herself like a feather quilt, stifling the little voice in her head whispering that this is only a reprieve.

Quietly, dutifully, she settles back into the house in Gazcue and allows her days to be filled by society events, her old friends, her mother. Meanwhile her husband, now firmly in El Jefe's good graces, takes the reins of the San Rafael Insurance Company, attending the occasional legislative session as required by his mandate.

Santo Domingo
1935

Three years married, and still nothing.

Flor is losing hope. Despite their near-constant arguing, Porfirio hasn't abandoned the conjugal bed. Quite the contrary; it remains their sacred place, where every quarrel ends, where every problem is solved. It's what keeps them together. He might play away, he might engage in frequent affairs, but there's something primal between them, something unbreakable. Just like in the movies, Porfirio is under Flor's skin, in spite of it all.

Their time in bed aside, however, Flor often feels deeply alone. What she needs now is a family of her own. A child that will bind Porfirio to her forever. A link that can never be broken, the kind El Jefe so wanted. A child that's hers. Only hers. A baby to cuddle and cherish, like she used to do with Rosita. And when she does have a baby, she'll manage things so T can't get his hooks into it. She'll raise it like a little prince or princess. And she'll never abandon her own child to the care of strangers—never send it away to study at some elite boarding school in Europe or the States. She'll let her child choose his or her own friendships, no matter who they're with.

Flor lets herself be swept away by dreams of a little girl.

And the months pass.

And hope shrivels, like a fallen *chinola*[10] in the sun. Blackened, trodden on, rotted.

T's obsession has become Flor's. Each month she waits,

---

[10] *Chinola*: Passion fruit.

agonizing, and each month she's disappointed. Is it her? Is she the problem? Porfirio smokes like a chimney and drinks like a fish, and she's never complained. But what if it's him? Could this man who's so incredibly desirable to women have such a fundamental defect? Flor doesn't share her worries with her husband, who is too preoccupied by nightlife and shady business deals to listen anyway.

* * *

Flor has been given an address. The taxi clatters through the roughly cobbled streets of the old town and stops at the entrance to a narrow *calléjon* choked with pink and orange bougainvillea. A few *mecedoras* stand empty in front of the half-open doors of the silent houses lining the alley.

"Come and pick me up in an hour." Flor is already stepping out of the vehicle.

"Are you sure, Señora? You don't want me to wait for you?"

"Quite sure. Be back here in an hour."

Flor doesn't want the taxi driver to chat with any locals that might be around—too much risk of him discovering the reason for her visit, if he doesn't know it already. Ignacio, their chauffeur, reports her slightest movements to T, which is why she hasn't asked him to bring her here. Anyway, the limousine would have been much too conspicuous in this working-class neighborhood. And Flor is determined to keep this outing as discreet as possible. She's even put on the cheapest, plainest clothes in her wardrobe.

The heat envelops her like a wet blanket the moment she steps out of the car. One of her high heels catches between two of the uneven cobbles paving the alley, and she stumbles, narrowly avoiding a stray football. A little boy runs after the ball, laughing at Flor as she frees her foot. "Where does the *santa cubana* live?" she asks him.

He points to the far end of the alleyway.

The small hut is dilapidated, a sheet-metal roof atop a cube of boards sloppily nailed together, resting on a brick foundation. Flor pushes the door open warily. The interior is dark, forbidding. Dressed in white from her turbaned head to her canvas-slippered feet, as wrinkled as a dried tobacco leaf, the *santa* looks to be a thousand years old. Flor feels her resolve wavering, but it's too late to turn back.

The priestess has her sit down on a rough-hewn three-legged wooden stool across from her, so close that their knees touch. On a small altar made of a rickety bookcase covered with a piece of brightly colored cloth, candles burn beneath an array of images and figurines of saints, giving off a smell of rancid smoke. Flor gathers up her skirt, which is brushing the floor, and tucks it between her thighs. The old woman gazes at her for a long time without moving, her eyes black slits, and Flor feels as if she's looking straight into her soul. With one gnarled hand, the woman reaches for a cylinder of rolled tobacco leaves and lights one end of it using a candle, then inhales deeply on the makeshift cigar, its tip glowing. Her thin cheeks hollow out, highlighting the sharp points of her cheekbones. Then she exhales the smoke directly into Flor's face. Flor coughs, then apologizes, waving a hand in front of her mouth to fan away the smoke. As if possessed, the old woman invokes Damballah Wedo[11] in an incomprehensible gibberish, waving her arms like an octopus. The tiny hut seems filled with magical sounds. Flor holds her breath, her heart thumping in her chest, and submits to it all: the cabalistic symbols, the incantations, the old woman's hands on her, the droning chants. Something porcelain-white and iridescent appears between the dark fingers; in the dim light, the small conch shell gleams as if it's been polished. The *santa* presses her wrinkled lips to the shell's serrated slit, which resembles a vagina, then blows a cloud of white smoke

---

[11] Damballah Wedo is the voodoo god of fertility, benevolence, and wisdom. He is portrayed as a large serpent or boa constrictor.

that surrounds it completely. Flor holds her breath again. The old woman seizes her hand and presses the shell into her palm, then closes her fingers over it with a claw-like hand.

All of a sudden, it's as if all the energy drains out of the *santa*. She sags like a rag doll on her wobbly chair. The session is over. Flor is still clutching the seashell. The old woman gestures ambiguously. Flor slips the talisman into her handbag and takes out her wallet, handing over a generous sum, then leaves.

She's very aware of the shell's weight in her bag. It's the weight of hope.

That night before falling asleep, Flor strokes the little shell with the pad of her thumb, caressing the smooth, shining surface, silently imploring.

Three weeks later, she starts to bleed as usual.

The *santeria* has been unable to help her.

* * *

Desperate times call for desperate measures.

Flor has been hearing about a blind woman named Elupina Cordero,[12] who people say can perform miracles. They say she's a holy woman, that she can heal the sick. T himself visited her shortly after his rise to power. She made him wait for more than an hour, and he had to leave his gun outside. What did she heal, Flor wonders? His prostate trouble? His skin problems? He was clearly pleased with the result, in any case, because he paid her the lavish sum of 200 pesos. The next member of the family to visit her was Doña Julia, Flor's grandmother, T's mother, a fervent believer who sought relief from her arthritis. Eventually, T began to pay Señora Cordero a monthly pension of 30 pesos. And now it's Flor's turn to seek her help.

---

[12] Elupina Cordero (1892–1939) is currently in the process of being canonized.

The hermitess lives on the other side of the island, in Sabana de la Mar. It's a long way away, hours and hours of driving, almost a whole day's travel from the capital, even with a pre-dawn start. Flor sees no other solution but to bring Lina in on the plan. They'll go together—a girls' adventure—and Lina's chauffeur will drive them. If they are followed by T's spies, it can't be helped. This, Flor thinks, is her last chance.

The trip is tedious. Lina will *not* stop talking: "your father" this, "your father" that, his great work, his accomplishments, the world at his feet, *what* a dancer, all the women under his spell. At this last remark, Lina blushes. Flor, staring out the car window at the bleak landscape of sugarcane fields in the hot white light of a blazing sun, is hardly listening. She clings desperately to her last shreds of hope, curling her body around them so they can't escape, and eventually dozes off with her head on Lina's shoulder.

The little fishing port of Sabana, a cluster of brightly painted palmwood huts facing the calm waters of the bay, is napping through the stifling midday heat. There's not a soul to be seen; even the animals are tucked away. In a small *colmado*, the town's general store, they're given directions to the healer's home, a tiny, dilapidated shack where the blind woman spends her days praying and dispensing her unique brand of medical care. Lina waits outside.

At the back of the single dimly lit room there is a prie-dieu adorned with images of the apostles, various religious trinkets, a few candles that provide the only bit of illumination, and a metal bowl full of yellowish oil. Doña Cordero has smooth, white skin. Her hair is hidden beneath the beige wimple of a nun, though she isn't one. Her blind eyes are covered by a milky white film. She wears a crucifix around her neck, and a slight smile on her lips. She looks much younger than her forty-five years.

Flor kneels in front of her, explains the reason for her visit, and lays her head in Doña Cordero's lap like an imploring child. The woman rests her hands on Flor's head for a long time, and then on her heart, and finally on her belly, fixing her milky white gaze on Flor's abdomen. Then they pray together, Flor shivering despite the humid warmth. She emerges from the hut after some twenty minutes inside, blinking hard, giving the bright sunlight as the reason for her tear-filled eyes. She pretends to sleep the whole way home, while Lina continues to chatter.

The verdict comes a few weeks later. An indescribably devastating blow.

Even religion—even faith—are powerless to help Flor.

She shudders at the thought of T's reaction.

* * *

In despair, Flor swallows her pride and asks T for permission to travel to New York and consult an infertility specialist there. There must be a remedy. Surely she can be repaired.

Permission granted.

And so Flor finds herself back in the city into which she poured all her hopes not so very long ago, and where all those hopes were cruelly dashed. Even so, she loves the unique energy of New York. She stays at the Warwick Hotel this time, a far cry from her shabby marital apartment.

Skirts hiked up, legs open, abdomen palpated, arms stiff, fists clenched, eyes shut tight, Flor endures a week of humiliating physical exploration and mortifying specimen collection, subjected to every possible examination. In the evenings, she seeks refuge in jazz clubs. Her diamonds sparkle in the spotlights. Men ogle her décolletage, rush to light her cigarettes, offer to buy her drinks. She regards them with disdain, narrows her eyes, exhales a long ribbon of smoke with languid elegance. Exactly as she learned at Bouffémont.

The answer, when it comes, is final.

Flor will never know the joy of motherhood, the bliss of giving and receiving unconditional love. Her body, still thin and flat-chested as a teenager's, will never oblige her by becoming pregnant.

Infertile. The single word says it all.

The diagnosis is a bombshell, blasting a bottomless hole in her life and leaving her desolate, completely without hope.

Flor's return to the Dominican Republic is like stepping into a cold shower. Any hopes of finding sympathy or compassion in Porfirio are immediately dashed. Their pool is full of cheap costume jewelry, and the servants tell Flor that every whore in Santo Domingo has been swimming in it. Utterly devastated, consumed by her own pain, Flor can't even muster the strength to rebuke him.

* * *

The marriage continues to deteriorate. Porfirio has little reaction to the news that his wife is infertile. In truth, he doesn't really care. It's almost a relief, actually. After all, it's probably better this way, simpler, more comfortable. He doesn't see himself as a man with deep emotional needs. Flor, badly raised and childish as she is, is basically enough for him, especially now that he's made sure she knows her place. Or thinks he has. A little slap every now and then when she gets too bossy, and that's his Fleur set straight.

But, for the first time, Flor is having doubts about her husband. A man who doesn't care that he can never have a child—a man who can remain impassive in the face of his wife's inconsolable sorrow—does a man like that truly deserve her love?

SANTO DOMINGO
SEPTEMBER 1935

La Españolita has waited with infinite patience for her moment to come.

María Martínez is an intriguer of easy virtue, a former stenographer whom T has made his mistress and who considers herself a grand lady because of her Spanish origins and pale skin.

Bienvenida fell from grace long ago now, a slow and irrevocable downward slide from the role of spouse to that of bit player, from El Jefe's bed to separate rooms. However wellborn, Bienvenida is neither beautiful nor brilliant, neither ambitious nor fertile, and she has left T's hopes for more progeny bitterly dashed.

Flor has never liked this dull stepmother who was always so jealous of her father's shows of affection toward his daughter, infrequent as they might have been. But the truth is that Bienvenida has never posed any real danger, and everyone knows it. She's never actually counted for much. Flor almost feels sorry for her. Even Aminta pities her.

But in the case of the Spanish woman, T's seed took root. Flor has known this for years, ever since her father had the temerity to introduce to her, with puffed-up pride and not even a hint of shame, a half-brother approximately four years old. She remembers it perfectly; it was only a few days after her wedding. Ramfis, a pretty little boy raised behind the scenes, with big brown eyes and hair as long and curly as a girl's, which T had ruffled fondly. He'd brought the child along on the pretext of giving Flor a gift—a case of jewelry and Parisian lace—from Ramfis's mother. Was the visit aimed at making Flor and Porfirio want to procreate? Flor's new husband had certainly fallen under the moppet's spell; the two of them had played croquet, and Flor had been filled with emotion at the thought of giving Porfirio a son of his own.

La Españolita is in a completely different league from Bienvenida; there's no comparison between them. If Flor's right about Ramfis's age (the boy has just been made an honorary army colonel), it means the Martínez woman has been "secretly" sharing T's bed for at least nine years, despite being married the entire time to a Cuban officer serving in the Dominican Army. There have been plenty of other mistresses through the years, but she is by far the most determined—and she has the advantage.

El Jefe wanted to exile both María and her husband to Cuba when he learned of her pregnancy, particularly after she refused to get an abortion. But she came to him once the baby was born, daring to hold him to account and bringing the little boy along to entice him.

In the end, she won her case, because in 1935, T has just divorced Bienvenida on the grounds of her infertility. He has, in fact, introduced a new law to that effect: from now on, if a woman does not produce an heir within five years, her husband can divorce her. *Exeunt* Bienvenida Ricardo. "Gallant" as ever, T, who had sent his erstwhile wife to Paris so he could play around as much as he liked, informs her of the divorce via a letter delivered by his ambassador.

T marries his Spanish lover on September 28, 1935. Showing a bit of restraint for once, he decides not to mark this civil marriage with an elaborate ceremony. Both the bride and groom are divorcés, and their illegitimate child is eight years old. No point in ruffling the feathers of the Catholic Church, and better, too, not to offend the delicate sensibilities of the upper class.

Flor attends the wedding in the company of her half-brother, who wears the full dress uniform of an army colonel, but she's well aware that her days of being welcome at the presidential palace—and in her father's life—are over. She knows exactly which game La Españolita is playing; the woman will do everything in her power, not just to advance the cause of her son, whom many doubt is actually El Jefe's, but to get rid of anything that reminds T of his former lives.

Including, and especially, Flor de Oro.

Ciudad Trujillo
June 1936

Flor folds away the newspaper, sighing. The news isn't good, and she can understand why T is so angry. He's been in a viciously bad mood for days, becoming more and more unpredictable, more and more uncontrollable, more and more unbearable. She's avoiding him as much as possible.

The reason for El Jefe's fury is a film being shown in American theaters, an episode of the documentary series *The March of Time*.[13] Sandwiched between the vagaries of French politics and illegal practices in British Jockey Club races, the five minutes and forty-seven seconds entitled "An American Dictator" aren't exactly flattering.

In the film, the *Yanquis* deride what El Jefe is most proud of, including the ceremonial pageantry that has marked his presidency—which, Flor must admit, *is* a bit ostentatious. She remembers the term her friend Mathilde de Cadeville used at Bouffémont: *tacky*. That's it. Tacky. In addition to a natural penchant for glitz and flamboyance, T has developed a liking for Napoleonic pomp. He likes showiness and theatricality, imagining that it gives him more cachet, solidifies his position. He's passionately fond of parade uniforms, even designing them himself. He has an enormous collection of medals, and he's often seen wearing feather-bedecked bicorn hats. Lately, he's also

---

[13] *The March of Time* was an American newsreel series, sponsored by Time Inc., that was shown in American movie theaters from 1935 to 1951. The series won an Academy Award in 1937.
  "An American Dictator": https://search.alexanderstreet.com/preview/work/bibliographic_entity%7Cvideo_work%7C1792756.

adopted the greatcoat and heavy boots favored by Chancellor Hitler, despite their total unsuitability for the tropical climate. This newest affectation is made all the more disconcerting by his recent creation, also in imitation of the German chancellor, of the so-called Trujillist Youth Movement.

Journalists are also mocking the fact that T has renamed the Dominican capital city "Ciudad Trujillo";[14] it's the third place he has named after himself, following the province of San Cristóbal and the mountain formerly known as Pico Duarte. They ridicule his motto, "*Rectitud, Libertad, Trabajo, Moralidad*"[15]—the first letters of which just happen to coincide with his initials, Rafael Leonidas Trujillo Molina—and make fun of the plaques bearing his likeness that are becoming a fixture of the Dominican landscape, from cast iron plates on aqueducts to enameled tablets in private homes. El Jefe has even let slip his belief that, unlike Mussolini, whom he admires greatly, he's "acting on a stage too small for his talents."

None of this has gone unnoticed.

Flor is neither blind nor stupid. T's whims and fantasies are clearly making him an easy target for criticism. But many strong Latin American men are the same way. And really, since he's working tirelessly to develop his country, to raise it out of poverty and civil disorder, surely he's entitled to reward himself in whatever way he chooses—and who understands a man's tastes better than the man himself?

Flor can't help but be devastated on T's behalf. There's the person the newsreels are talking about, and then there's the father she loves. They're two different men, and yet she recognizes, in the portrait of the dictator, the pain she experienced as a child. The pain she's still experiencing now. She wanted for so

---

[14] Ciudad Trujillo was the official name of the Dominican capital from January 11, 1936, to November 21, 1961 (law no. 1067 of January 9, 1936).

[15] Rectitude, Liberty, Toil, Morality.

long to believe that her father was like Janus, a being with two faces, but in the end she's had to acknowledge the undeniable truth: there's only face, and it isn't kind, or loving, or even really worthy of love.

* * *

T couldn't care less what the Americans think. He's the Benefactor of the Nation, master of his own domain, and if the *Yanquis* don't like it, they can go to hell—or maybe the battlefront in Europe. It may be true that the Dominican Republic is still dependent on America, but that's only for now. El Jefe has vowed that, as soon as possible, he'll repay the debt forcing his country and his people into subservience to the United States. And then the *Yanquis* will have to shut their mouths.[16]

T is angry at everyone. Why wasn't he warned about the American newsreel? He fires his ambassador to Washington and, to humiliate the man, assigns him to a low-ranking desk job in the municipal government of a town on the Haitian border. Isn't he paying his informers generously enough? Idiots! He's surrounded by useless idiots! He resolves to create an intelligence service worthy of the name. He needs men who are devoted to him body and soul, unshakably loyal and able to operate abroad under the cover of diplomatic missions.

Men like . . . Rubirosa, for example! Yes—his son-in-law is the perfect example of a pawn he can put into play on the international chessboard. He's a born liar, and women love him. It's true that the young man didn't handle the New York mission very well—it was a real mess, in fact—but it proved that he's not easily frightened, at least. It's just fortunate that T had, with

---

[16] Trujillo would free the Dominican Republic from its financial dependence on the United States in 1945 by repaying the $20 million debt owed to the latter. July 17 would mark the repayment of the debt, a day on which it was henceforth mandatory for all citizens to display the national flag outside their homes or face a fine.

incredible foresight, ensured Rubirosa's election to Congress, which had saved his bacon from the law. With time, El Jefe is confident he can bring Rubirosa firmly under his thumb, turning him into a good little soldier.

* * *

Flor's marriage is on the rocks, and she's determined to take matters in hand. It would do them good to get out to sea, to get away from El Jefe's watchdogs, from turbulent politics and bad influences. There's no point trying to live in a country where she has no freedom, where her every move is monitored, her every purchase scrutinized. Where her marriage is in continuous decline.

She pleads with T. A European post for Porfirio. Please, Papi. It's her last chance to save her marriage. T looks at his daughter tenderly, sadly. He loves her, his Flower of Gold. She's his link to a distant past where his only worry was what he would make of his future, a future that was yet to be forged. She is his only daughter. He loves her, and it pains him to see her so unhappily married. But he warned her. She didn't want to hear it, and look where that got her.

T gives in.

Flor was hoping for France, but instead it's Germany, a country in turmoil and one every leader on the globe is watching like a hawk. A diplomatic post in Berlin. Rubirosa's duties will be mostly ceremonial, but he can act as an informer. T never does anything for anyone without expecting something in return.

Flor is filled with childlike hope. Europe has always been good to her, something she and Porfirio have in common. She pushes for a rapid departure. There's nothing to keep them in Ciudad Trujillo now.

Paris
June 1936

On their way to Berlin, the Rubirosas make a brief stop in Paris. Flor is in raptures. This side trip will be like a second honeymoon for them; Porfirio has promised to take her to dinner at Maxim's and introduce her to the Parisian nightlife. The scene is dominated by White Russians these days, the tango and jazz orchestras of the previous decade replaced by Slavic musicians who play a sort of Romany music, melancholy and dramatic. The couple slums it at the Monseigneur Club, the Casanova, the Sheherazade, but the madcap lightheartedness of the 1920s has vanished. In the cafés of the Boulevard Saint-Germain, they're welcomed by members of the Comité des Amis de la République Dominicaine, established after T's rise to power. But despite the cheerful atmosphere, a heavy gray cloud of foreboding hangs over the city. And Porfirio has just told Flor the real reason for their Parisian stopover.

* * *

Flor is crushed. She'd thought El Jefe wanted to help her save her failing marriage. But, in the strictest confidentiality, T has given Porfirio a delicate mission: to find him the best possible urologist to treat an embarrassing problem. The Benefactor of the Fatherland is suffering from an acute and worsening case of urethritis, a humiliating malady that he is keeping as secret as possible. No one dares speculate about how he contracted it. But it's becoming more and more difficult for him to control his bladder, and a story is quietly circulating that El Jefe recently wet his trousers during an official reception. The quick-thinking aide-de-camp who conveniently spilled his beer in the presidential lap at the opportune moment has received a promotion, of course. But such a thing *must* not happen again.

Porfirio has a discreet meeting with Doctor Georges Marion, an eminent specialist at the Hôtel-Dieu, who—under the pretext of giving a series of university lectures—immediately flies to the Dominican Republic to treat El Jefe, staying in the Rubirosas' vacant house in Gazcue.

Mission accomplished. Porfirio is securely in his father-in-law's good graces once again, and the Rubirosas board a train for Berlin.

Berlin
July 1936

"You'll be representing me in Berlin—never forget that." Those words, murmured in Flor's ear by T as she and Porfirio took their leave, echo in her head like a threat.

The women's jewels sparkle in the light from the crystal chandeliers, the silk of their modest yet elegant gowns rustling softly, and the men's brillantined hair gleaming like so many steel helmets. All the men wear black tuxedos and bow ties or full dress uniforms laden with medals. The ballroom smells of pomade, tobacco, and expensive perfumes.

Faced with such a sophisticated crowd, Flor—who thought she was accustomed to high society—thinks that this world is as far away from the Caribbean as Earth is from the moon. She feels tiny, gauche, and ashamed of her best dress, which suddenly feels old-fashioned, its cut too severe. She might have bought it from a famous Parisian couturier, but on her it's neither chic nor alluring. Despite the superficial polish she acquired at Bouffémont, despite the many official receptions given by her father, Flor is starkly, painfully aware that she will never have the natural grace and self-confidence of a woman born into wealth and prominence. After all, Flor de Oro is nothing more, deep down, than a simple girl from the Dominican campo.

She knows, too, that everything about her is unnerving to these people: her youth, her olive skin, her frizzy hair, her too-musical accent, her too-handsome husband. Him, especially. She pastes on a vacant smile, one that reveals nothing of her thoughts. It's what's expected of her, after all. And it gives her something to hide behind while she studies the other guests. No one pays her the slightest attention, and that suits her just fine. Porfirio, on the other hand, has been in his element all evening, strutting around like a peacock, flashing that perfect white smile, women clamoring for his attention. Particularly the platinum blonde who's been eyeing him hungrily for what feels like hours.

Flor sits next to her husband like some kind of decorative tropical plant. They've been seated together for dinner, which is a stroke of luck and, she'd like to believe, a deliberate kindness. But it's also true that no one's exactly competing for the place next to the little mixed-race girl who can speak maybe three words of German. With a sudden flash of clarity, she wonders what they're doing there, both she and Porfirio. She knows they've only been invited to this dinner because of Porfirio's posting to the Dominican legation, itself due solely to her father's will and not any particular merit of her husband's. El Jefe, a president protected by the United States, is a mere pawn on the international chessboard as far as the Nazi government is concerned, a bridgehead for the Reich on the other side of the Atlantic. In the German strategy of straddling the fence, any foreign political support is welcome, and Flor's father, in his island stronghold, appears to be incredibly rich; it's said that all the fixtures in his mansion are made of solid gold, from bathtub faucets to door hinges. The Dominican Republic's capital city bears his name now, and the airport, and even a mountain; there are copper plaques with his face on them fixed on aqueducts all over the country, and new statues are erected all the time. His nationalist politics are appreciated, too; he's said to be fiercely racist, obsessed with white skin—to a ridiculous extent, even, since he looks to have some black blood himself, even though he denies it. All you have to do is look at his daughter, a silly little goose without a thing to say for herself . . .

So the Rubirosas are tolerated.

The dinner seems to drag on forever. Flor half-listens to the men's endless discussions, which blur into a single dull rumble punctuated by the clink of silverware on fine china. She can't understand most of it, but she gets the gist. Recriminations, frustration, demands, occasional dry, forced laughter. These men are annoyed, and tempers are rising. This is a long way from her education at Bouffémont, from French history, the Revolution, the Declaration of the Rights of Man. Book history and real life have nothing to do with one another. Dictators and strongmen are the fashion now. Stalin, Batista, Hitler, Duvalier. And T. This is the truth of the modern world.

Flor observes the women and speculates. In Germany, unlike New York, there's absolutely no question of a wife going out to work. Dutiful German women confine themselves to the domestic sphere and keep out of men's discussions, focusing instead on managing their households ("I had to fire the maid; she turned out to be Jewish."); bearing children ("Franz, my eldest, just joined the Hitler Youth; his younger brother will do the same soon."); and dressing up for receptions like this one ("The other evening at the Austrian ambassador's . . . "). Flor, who has no real household of her own and almost nothing in common with these women, is astonished that such a powerful, modern country is so regressive when it comes to feminism. But these are reflections best kept to herself, so she simply smiles her wide, dazzling smile. And she drinks.

These good German wives are perfectly content to leave Mrs. Rubirosa alone with her boredom, emptying glass after glass. *Mr.* Rubirosa is a different story, however. He may be of almost no political interest to the men, but the women . . .

Porfirio exudes an aura of sensuality that drives them wild. Everything about him is exotic, from his Italian silk suits, to his Latin charm, to his athletic physique. They can't help but be aware of the virile eroticism that emanates from the new Dominican attaché. He's so different from the strait-laced German men with their stiff manners and guttural voices.

Porfirio's accent when he speaks English is charming, his voice warm, his manners impeccable, his movements graceful, his ease and confidence manifestly clear. And when his dark eyes crinkle at the corners, he's quite simply irresistible. And every woman at the table is thinking it.

Porfirio has no difficulty interpreting their kittenish behavior toward him, so he unleashes his most devastating smiles, aiming his come-hither looks like darts. Flor loses herself in contemplation of her gold-rimmed Saxe porcelain dinner plate. The conversations buzz around her. She hardly hears them. Another swallow of wine.

The blonde countess seated across from them, Martha von something-or-other, is laughing at every remark Porfirio makes as if he were the wittiest man on earth. She's also staring unapologetically at Flor, musing that this little mongrel is lucky indeed to have bedded a man like that, her thoughts so obvious that she might as well have stated them out loud. Fluttering her eyelashes as she gazes at him with big blue eyes, she's like a doe caught in his trap, fully ready to surrender.

Suddenly, Flor is ashamed. Of him, and of herself. Is she the only one that can see the game-playing going on? Something twists in her gut and rises slowly up into her throat. She tries to keep from fidgeting, but her fingers play nervously with her napkin, and she reduces a piece of bread to crumbs. Her leg starts jiggling beneath the table—and then a sudden pain. Without looking at her, Porfirio has just stamped heavily on her foot, remaining as calm and elegant as always in sophisticated company. Flor tries to suppress the disgust mounting in her, the nausea. Excusing herself, she leaves the table hurriedly.

In the ladies' restroom, Flor, still gripped by painful spasms, tries to wash away the acrid taste in her mouth with large gulps of water. She wipes cold sweat from her forehead and smooths her hair, grimacing at the sight of herself in the mirror. She isn't very pretty. She's too young. She's awkward and self-conscious.

How can she compete with these women? How will she keep Porfirio? Her eyes fill with tears. Forcing them back, her heart in her mouth, she rejoins the other guests.

At home, Porfirio reproaches her for not talking enough, not mingling enough. For not shining, and not making him shine. It's a good thing he was sociable enough for both of them, he huffs. And on top of all that, she's slightly drunk. He makes love to her distractedly, thinking of the blonde Valkyrie who smoldered at him all through dinner.

After this, things happen very quickly. Porfirio embarks on an affair with the woman, the wife of a high-ranking Reich official, while Flor sinks deeper and deeper into depression, watching helplessly as her marriage flounders. A vague sort of ache, composed of sorrow, grief, and the remnants of her shattered ego, becomes her constant companion.

She finally admits to herself what she's known deep down for a long time: no one woman can ever be enough for Porfirio. Not even her.

Berlin
Summer 1936

The Rubirosas have taken up residence at 23 Dessauerstrasse, in a residential area where the Dominican ambassador, Burgos Bonetti, has provided them with a large, elegant house complete with housekeeper and chauffeur. Porfirio hardly ever sets foot in the embassy, which doesn't worry anyone; after all, it isn't really what's expected of him. As third secretary to the legation, he's of no real use, and everyone knows it. But they accommodate El Jefe's son-in-law, and some of them are even afraid of him, because the truth is that no one really knows what he's been sent to Berlin to do. Espionage? Surveillance of the delegation? Informing? Anything seems possible.

Porfirio himself prefers to spend his time playing polo, fencing, and going every day to the Olympic games, which have just begun. He obligingly gave the Nazi salute during the opening ceremonies, like all the guests in the official box. Flor stiffened at his side, her hand feeling as if it weighed a ton, hanging uselessly at her side. Porfirio elbowed her in the ribs, and she saluted weakly. "Heil!" She dropped her arm, sickened, disgusted at herself for having gone along with the others. That evening Porfirio treated her to a long lecture about her duty as a diplomat's wife.

The Rubirosas' lives are utterly dominated by social obligations, their days full of receptions, dinners, and horseback rides. This frivolous existence makes Flor feel like a dead weight that her husband is forced to drag around, as if she's the price he has to pay to dwell among the rich and powerful.

They attend one parade after another, always sitting on the

VIP platform. Flor is bored, Porfirio impressed by the Nazis' military might and the modernity of German armaments, which he reports on in detail to El Jefe. He's even struck up a friendship with Hermann Goering, the medal- and uniform-obsessed Luftwaffe chief whose bizarre mannerisms Flor has noticed, and whose high, nasal voice reminds her disagreeably of her father's. Porfirio has arranged to obtain some Dominican Army medals for Goering's collection, a surefire way into the German's good graces. This means that the Rubirosas are spending quite a bit of time among the highest-ranking members of the regime, and Flor finds it difficult to hide her uneasiness about the Nazis. For one thing, because she's not stupid, and despite her lack of political savvy, she's well aware of the government's disturbing proclivities. And on a more personal level, there's the condescension, the palpable disdain toward her, which she feels on her skin like a burn. Simply put, Flor—short, dark, and mixed-race in an openly racist country—doesn't feel good in Germany. She never thought she'd find herself on the other side of the racial divide, and yet the frequent looks of distaste aimed at her are unmistakable. She retreats into herself, as if she's shrinking. More and more often she shuts herself into the bathroom after a meal. Porfirio, engrossed in his affair, doesn't even notice as Flor slowly withers away.

On the rare occasion that they have a peaceful evening at home, Porfirio sometimes imitates the men with their goosestepping and their stiff-armed salutes. And he imitates their leader with the ridiculous mustache that might be hiding a harelip, cutting a cigar in half and wedging it beneath his nose. This makes Flor laugh. It's a victory, one evening's victory. Tomorrow will be another day of debauchery.

Porfirio isn't even trying to hide his infidelity anymore.

* * *

Flor stretches after a night of unsettled, broken sleep and

glances at the bedside clock. Ten A.M. Leaving the warm comfort of bed, she slips on a silk robe and pads barefoot into the living room, where the sofa still bears the imprint of a body. Having told her he'd be out late at a gathering of foreign diplomats, Porfirio woke her in the wee hours, fumbling with his key in the lock. Most likely very drunk, at least he hadn't had the gall to climb into bed beside her. And now he's gone again. To the embassy? A polo field? A bar?

A sudden smell of charred onions makes Flor's stomach lurch. Herta, the cook, is starting to prepare lunch. Flor drags herself into the kitchen and asks for a strong coffee, then goes back to bed, where she flips through a stack of magazines.

The doorbell rings, the sound dampened by the apartment's wool carpet and heavy wall hangings. Flor hears the door open, two voices speaking, the door closing again.

"Herta, who was that?" she calls.

"A bouquet's just been delivered, Frau Rubirosa."

Another invitation. That's all life is these days. Flor gets out of bed again, listlessly, prodded by a dim spark of curiosity. A bunch of magnificent red roses is lying on the table in the foyer. She counts them: twenty-one. An interesting choice for an invitation.

There's a small white envelope addressed to Mr. Porfirio Rubirosa pinned to the tissue paper wrapping the bouquet. Flor plucks it off, pricking her index finger in the process. She tears open the envelope, leaving a pinkish smear on the thick paper.

For the 21 days we've loved each other.

There's no signature. There doesn't need to be. Martha. Or someone else. It doesn't matter. Porfirio's mistresses are becoming brazen enough to infiltrate Flor's actual home. She can put up with his infidelities, but this is a step too far. She dissolves into tears. Yesterday she could have borne this. But not today. How can Porfirio be so cruel? He's acting like she doesn't even exist.

When he gets home that evening, she's still in her robe and

nightgown. She hands him the note silently, then knots her hands tightly behind her back to keep from hitting him, from leaping at him and hammering on his chest. She knows that wouldn't accomplish anything, anyway. He'd only see it as a joke or, worse, a slap on the wrist. So, without losing her calm, she makes him eat the twenty-one roses, one by one. Porfirio does it without a word. When he's finished, his lips are as red as a prostitute's. There's a trickle of pink saliva on his chin. He's a sorry sight, this husband who is constantly being stolen from her by other women. With queenly hauteur, she turns her back on him, goes into the bedroom, and shuts the door.

BERLIN
NOVEMBER 1936

"*Mein Gott*, Flor! Flor de Oro, is that you? I can't believe it!"

Flor, aimlessly roaming the aisles of the Karstadt department store, has just run into Lucie Mayer, her old friend from Bouffémont. The other woman is utterly astonished.

"Lucie?" Flor says. "I thought you were in America."

"I didn't go. What are *you* doing in Berlin?"

It's a long story, and Flor would rather tell it in a café.

"Come on, let's go for a *moka* at the Café Schön—my treat—and you can tell me everything," Lucie says, taking Flor's arm.

They walk along Unter den Linden to the Schön, a large, modern café, vast enough to ensure a bit of privacy. Flor is so happy to see a familiar face that the encounter feels like more than chance; it feels like a sign. Once they've been seated at a small table, the two women look at one another, both deeply curious. Lucie hails a waiter and orders two *mokas*, then takes out a lacquered cigarette case.

"You still smoke?" Flor asks, laughing.

"Yes, but I've changed my brand. These are American ones. The Nazis disapprove; they want a healthy population. What about you?"

"Like a chimney! No—like a Hollywood star, actually. Remember? But I've gotten better at it!"

They both giggle. It's so good to be together again.

Lucie listens open-mouthed to Flor's story. Marriage, Venice, New York, the Dominican legation, polo. How lucky Flor's been to travel so much! Of course, she *is* the daughter of a sitting president . . .

Lucie's own life is nowhere near as glamorous these days. She might belong to Berlin's high society, and she might have married Walter Kahn, a wealthy businessman, but she's Jewish, and so is her husband. She sizes Flor up and decides to be truthful.

"Life is becoming more and more difficult for us here. Since the Nuremberg Laws were passed last year, we've become second-class citizens. I'm going out less every week, and I always make sure to dress inconspicuously. My blonde hair protects me a bit, but only the other day someone called me a Jewish bitch."

Flor is wide-eyed, appalled. And she can empathize.

"I understand! They look at me like I'm dirt, too. I'm mixed-race, you know, and here . . . "

"But it's worse for us, because we're German! The government has decided that Jews are responsible for all Germany's problems, and they don't want us here, yet they're keeping us from leaving. Walter and I both want to go to America. I could continue my studies. I've got an uncle there. But you have to have a visa, and all kinds of documents. And you have to give up your whole life here . . . "

Lucie has a nervous tic; she blinks more often than normal, and frequently bites her lip, ruining her makeup. She looks around defiantly at the café's other patrons. "It's hard to live normally when everyone you meet might be an enemy, and give you away."

Flor is genuinely moved. She knows well what it's like to live under constant surveillance.

"Lucie, if there's anything I can do . . . "

Lucie jumps at this chance. "Could you help me get visas? Your husband's a diplomat; surely he could . . . "

Flor puts a hand on Lucie's. "Of course. I'll ask him."

She says it without hesitation, without equivocation. No one ever asks her to do anything useful. No one ever asks her to do *anything* except be a decorative accessory. Flor, who has never asked for a single favor, never exploited her position or family connections to benefit herself, has finally been given an opportunity to be of service to someone else, to right an injustice. And moreover, Lucie isn't a stranger; she's a link to a happy time in Flor's life.

Flor promises.

Now Flor has a friend, and a kind of secret garden. Lucie shows her a whole new side of Berlin. They take long walks together, passing the Kroll Opera House (the seat of the Reichstag since the 1933 fire, Lucie tells her) and the Apollo Theater, going to see *The Testament of Dr. Mabuse* at the Universum movie theater, lunching at the Horcher restaurant.

Flor regains some of her sparkle, and Porfirio starts to find her desirable again. Despite his lifelong weakness for voluptuous women, he's used to her thinness, even enjoys the feeling of her jutting hipbones colliding with his own. Why does Flor's skinny body arouse him so much? It's their own private mystery.

When she asks him for the visas, Porfirio just shrugs. He has other, far more pressing concerns. Like playing polo? Flor wonders. She keeps pushing him. "Two visas in the names of Walter and Lucie Kahn. It's important. I've never asked you for anything." Porfirio reads the steely resolve in his wife's eyes. She can be so stubborn sometimes. If he doesn't act, she might go directly to the ambassador. He gazes at his wife—so small, so delicate, so determined. He knows what she's capable of. She's never been afraid of anything. In the end, he capitulates. Not out of human kindness, or personal conviction, or love. He simply has no choice.

When Flor tells Lucie the news, her friend's gratitude warms her heart. This is proof to Flor that she does exist, that she's alive and of use. How she wishes she had some real responsibility. If

El Jefe ever gave her the opportunity, she'd leap at it without hesitation.

But this will be Flor's sole heroic act during her time in Germany. This, and her enthusiastic applause for Jesse Owens and his four gold medals, even while seated just behind Hitler and his inner circle.

Months later, Flor will receive a letter of thanks from Lucie, who has settled with her husband in Ciudad Trujillo. They're planning to invest in the tobacco industry.

But what Flor can't know is that El Jefe, himself the owner of multiple tobacco plantations and factories, will resent Walter Kahn's commercial success. He will ruin the man deliberately, leaving him no choice but to move to America with his wife. Flor will never see Lucie again.

* * *

Berlin is becoming more unbearable by the day.

Porfirio's affair with Martha has been discovered.

The scandal quickly makes the Rubirosas personae non gratae, as the cuckolded German count proves to be both jealous and vindictive. The volatile situation finally explodes in a swanky nightclub, with the husband confronting Porfirio in full view of the other guests.

The matter is quickly hushed up; Rubirosa is a foreign diplomat, after all. But the couple is ordered to pack their bags.

Flor feels as if everything has aligned to make her miserable: her infertility, Porfirio's unfaithfulness, the missions assigned by T, the lack of a real home. The feeling of time, and life, passing her by.

* * *

> Berlin, February 8, 1937[17]
>
> Dear Papa,
> It's been seven months since we moved to Berlin to please you, because you wanted it that way.
> My basic German has improved, and we've toured a large part of the country, and I admire the great work Hitler is doing. But I'm not happy.
> Diplomatic secretaries count for absolutely nothing in Germany. We're only ever invited to public balls, and I never have the chance to meet anyone.
> If it isn't asking too much, I would like it if you transferred us to Paris. The Exposition Internationale is happening soon. It's going to be a huge event, and I'd like to be there from the beginning.
> I'll be able to go to a lot of lectures in Paris, and gain a deeper understanding of the French literature I love so much.
> Let me know if I can plan on moving by April 1, the start of spring.
> With my love to María and Ramfis,
> Your loving daughter,
> Flor

It pains Flor to lie about the Nazi regime; she has no admiration for it whatsoever. But her request is granted. El Jefe hardly has to lift a finger to make it happen.

That March, Flor de Oro closes the lid on trunks loaded with an added weight of disillusionment and bitterness. The Rubirosas leave the Reich by the back door as the thud of Nazi boots echoes louder and louder on the Berlin pavement.

---

[17] The original letter is shown on p. 368 in the Image Section.

PARIS
SPRING–SUMMER 1937

Flor leaves Berlin with absolutely no regret.
Will the City of Light work its magic on her crumbling marriage?
She hopes so. With all her heart, with the mad, unbridled hope of a child. She's determined to fight to keep her man. For, beneath her fragile exterior, little Flor de Oro is a tigress. There's something inside her that holds on to what she loves and won't let go. And she's still clinging to illusion, too, to the belief that revisiting the years they both spent in France as adolescents will spin a thread of nostalgia strong enough to knit them together again.

She's in Paris again, and, as always, it's a joy. She feels at home in this city that is infinitely more sophisticated than Ciudad Trujillo.

The Parisian spring has a certain quality sure to enchant the child of an island without seasons. The cool clarity of the light, the tender new leaves on the trees, the café terraces and banks of the Seine, the music of the language, the chic and self-assured women, the splendor of the Haussmanian buildings, the brightly illuminated store windows, and especially the museums, galleries, and theaters—it's like a fairyland. Flor is filled with hope, and *want*. It's been so long since she really wanted anything. She'll get rid of anything that reminds her of Germany, she decides: she'll buy a new wardrobe, splash out on designs by Patou and Heim. She'll buy out the Guerlain perfume store and stroll the city streets with her head held high—no more fear of encountering those horrible Nazis and their looks of distaste. All her troubles with food will get better here, too, she's certain of it. She's hungry already.

The Rubirosas spend a few days at the ambassador's residence, whose gaudy furnishings have aged very badly indeed. Flor remembers fondly how enormous the place used to seem, back in her Bouffémont days. She finds an apartment as quickly as possible, and she and Porfirio settle in Neuilly.

Paris may not be Berlin, but soon enough Flor's life there settles into the same rhythm: waiting and solitude. Porfirio, too, picks up where he left off: women, parties, clubs, bars, casinos. He rapidly renews old friendships and goes out every night, coming home shortly before dawn reeking of sweat and perfume, the smooth lies soon giving way to an almost disdainful silence. His sexual reputation precedes him everywhere he goes, even becoming the subject of mockery in some circles. In the end, Flor is forced to admit to herself that nothing, not latitude or longitude or time zones, will ever change her husband. He'll never be faithful to her, no matter where they are. He doesn't belong to her. She has just two options: to resign herself to the state of things, or to leave him.

In early May, the Dominican newspaper *Listín Diario* trumpets the news that the Rubirosas will be representing their country at the coronation of King George VI in London. Flor makes a good showing among the crowned heads in her pink lamé Molyneux gown, T having given her $3,500 and told her to buy anything she wanted for the occasion. Porfirio, for his part, is relaxed and charming as ever, even in such august company, befriending several maharajahs.

The International Exposition opens in Paris at the end of the month, and Porfirio has conveniently been made a judge. Visitors flock from all over the world to experience the

"Exposition international des arts et des techniques appliqués à la vie modern," held at the Palais de Chaillot.

One of Flor's cousins on her father's side, Livia Ruiz Trujillo de Beres, invites herself to stay with the Rubirosas for the occasion. A single woman older than Flor, an old maid even if she refuses to admit it, Livia puts Flor in mind of one of the Salem witches, her grayish skin turned wrinkled and leathery from too much sun. She's also a busybody who likes nothing better than to stick her nose into other people's business—and the Rubirosas provide endless grist for the mill. Flor tolerates her, while Porfirio can't stand her. She sticks to them like glue, inserting herself into every part of their married life: every meal, every outing, every dispute.

Almost immediately, Livia becomes their self-appointed referee. A human Apple of Discord straight out of Greek mythology, she keeps their mutual resentment simmering in a way that almost seems deliberate. Loyal to her cousin, whose side she invariably takes, she gives Porfirio no quarter, pointing out his every falsehood and failure, causing Flor immense pain. "Porfirio Rubirosa," she shrieks—she only ever addresses him by his full name—"they're preparing a bed of hot coals for you in Hell!" She never stops trying to stir Flor up, to rouse her anger. What is she playing at, this cousin whom they never even invited to stay? Flor breathes a sigh of relief when Livia finally leaves.

She's learned to put up with a great deal in her marriage. The affairs, the lies, even the occasional slap from her husband. But it's getting harder and harder, and sometimes she can't control herself. Like the day when, delirious with rage, she breaks a vase and chases Porfirio around the apartment, barefoot and brandishing a kitchen knife, then threatens to kill herself. It's too dramatic a scene to be taken seriously, and she knows it. Porfirio only mocks her, pretending to be terrified and then dissolving into laughter. She slips, thudding into a wall and then crumpling to the floor, skewering the point d'Hongrie parquet. Porfirio helps her up. He's stopped laughing. There's incomprehension on his face, and a kind of pity. But at least it isn't disgust. Flor breaks down in tears, the knife dangling uselessly from one hand. She retreats to their bedroom, defeated. Her scarlet-painted toenails poke through holes in the feet of her stockings like drops of blood. She's pathetic. All she's managed to do is inflict a deep scratch on the oak floorboards.

Porfirio, with his characteristic coolness, takes refuge behind a wall of indifference that his wife's reproaches can't penetrate. And Flor endures it. Until the day she discovers that her husband, her Prince Charming, is taking advantage of his embassy post to make money from official stamps, selling Dominican visas to Jews anxious to leave Europe and its looming dangers. The memory of Lucie whispers in Flor's ear; this is beyond disgraceful. Porfirio tries to defend himself, but for Flor this is the last straw; he's crossed an invisible line. The time for endurance is past. She's had enough of his self-absorption, his arrogance, his bullying, his opportunism. Enough of his volatility and unreliability, too. She can't look the other way anymore. Her father was right, and she has to face facts: she's been deluded about Rubirosa from the very beginning. She has to break the connection between them before it destroys her.

Flor returns to the Dominican Republic in 1937, when El Jefe summons her to Ciudad Trujillo for an important family matter. Some time and distance are what's needed to restore the foundations of their marriage. But for Flor, both the thought of staying with Porfirio and the idea of a future without him are deeply painful.

* * *

She tells T about all the humiliations she's suffered at her cheating husband's hands, hoping he'll show some understanding and send her back to Paris with a mission, a way to do something with her life at last. But no. T is furious. To dishonor Flor de Oro is to dishonor him, and that is unforgivable. He tries to soothe his daughter the only way he knows how—with money. "Choose any one you like," he says, handing her an automobile catalogue. Flor picks out a deluxe Buick and asks for it to be sent to Neuilly.

T refuses. "I'll never let you go back to that man!"

The next day Flor receives a visit from her father's personal attorney, Jacinto Peynado.

She submits docilely as the legal proceedings begin, convinced that she must make a clean sweep of the past, that it's absolutely necessary. That she can do it, that she owes it to herself. And then she'll remarry, and this time she'll choose a suitable husband, with her father's approval.

She writes to Porfirio, swearing that the "family matter" that brought her to the island was no lie. She loves him, she says, and she forgives him. But she's not coming back.

* * *

> *My beloved Fleur,*
>
> *A day without you is a day wasted. Paris is desperately sad, and your absence weighs more heavily on me every day. Our big apartment has become a dark and dreary place.*
>
> *I can't bring myself to do any work. I'm not even going to the legation.*
>
> *I'm not myself without you. I miss you terribly. I miss your body, your smile, your energy and zest for life, your hand in mine. Your shadow is everywhere—in the Place Furstenberg, the Parc Bagatelle, the Luxembourg Gardens.*
>
> *I'm so deeply sorry for hurting you with my behavior.*
>
> *Come back to me, my love. I love you, and I'll do everything in my power to make you happy, the way you deserve. I promise.*
>
> *Your husband, Porfirio*

Fleur,
How could you leave and abandon me on a false pretext? It's an act of betrayal.
You're my wife before God. You have no right to put asunder what God has joined together.
Your place is with your husband.
If you don't come back, I'm joining the Foreign Legion.
I'll do it, I swear. And you'll never see me again.
If you love me the way you say you do in your letter, come back.
I love you. I'm begging you, come back. I'll do anything to keep you.
Porfirio, your husband before God

As each new letter from Flor's husband arrives, their tone shifts. Tender at first, they quickly degenerate into blackmail and threats. Panicking, Porfirio uses every argument he can think of, not least those based on religion. Having neither the intention nor the ability to change his ways, he's acutely aware of everything he'll lose if his marriage to Flor ends. Thanks to her, his life is one of wealth and ease—well, except for their time in New York, but that was a youthful error, all but forgotten.

What would he gain from a divorce? His freedom, certainly, but the price—disgrace, poverty, El Jefe's hatred—would be far too high. Not to mention the consequences for his family back home. His father-in-law has never been one to hold back when it comes to revenge.

And there's something else. Porfirio loves his Fleur. In his own way, he truly does love her. They have a great deal in common, and they've had some unforgettable experiences together. He hasn't lost his hopes of turning her into a submissive wife who will turn the other cheek to his infidelities.

The weeks pass. The letters peter out.

There's a new feeling growing between them. The harsh, gut-wrenching acknowledgment of the inevitable.

Ciudad Trujillo
November 1937

They've agreed to meet for a walk along the Malécon, the capital city's seafront promenade. They have so much to tell one another.

Lina hugs Flor tightly. Flor can't believe her eyes. The tearaway tomboy of Lina's youth is nowhere to be seen. Flor knew Lina had been elected queen of the *Carnaval Dominicano* back in February, but she didn't expect *this*. It's like being face-to-face with a fashion plate. Lina's elegantly pale skin is set off by a luxuriant mass of dark hair held off her face by two tortoiseshell combs. Her eyes and lips are perfectly made up, her fingernails painted a deep crimson. Her chic dress emphasizes her small waist and flatters her slim, angular silhouette. Flor is speechless.

Lina leans in close to her friend, who's a full head shorter than she is, and murmurs confidentially, "It was your father who got me elected Carnaval queen!"

It was so much fun, she bubbles. The long robe, the crown and scepter, riding in the parade in a flower-bedecked float, the photographers and receptions, the headlines in national newspapers.

Lina can hardly contain her excitement, hopping up and down and clapping her hands. A flashing sparkle catches Flor's eye, and it's only then that she notices the solitaire on Lina's ring finger. A diamond as big as a passion fruit seed.

"Oh, Lina! Are you engaged?" she asks, smiling fondly.

"Oh, that . . . "

Lina flutters her fingers. The diamond glitters. Her expression shifts, suddenly uneasy. "Not engaged, exactly, no. It was a gift . . . a gift from your father. After my coronation."

Flor swallows hard. She's afraid to hear what comes next. The two friends walk for a moment in silence. A few meters behind them, a black Volkswagen with tinted windows that has been parked nearby starts up again and follows them slowly, its driver not even making a pretense of discretion. Flor shivers. Bodyguards? Spies? T never lets her out of his sight for a minute. Unless it's Lina who's under surveillance. Waves crash noisily on the shore, leaving ribbons of mossy seafoam along the rocky barrier supporting the promenade. The scent of salt reaches her nostrils. A seagull soars above the water in search of food, crying out raucously.

Flor waits.

At last, Lina makes up her mind. Her secret won't keep for much longer anyway.

"I'm in love with your father!" she bursts out.

Flor turns white. Lina is a year younger than her.

"He's much too old for you, Lina. He's old enough to be *your* father!" she says weakly, knowing there's no point in objecting.

"I know, but these things happen. He's a lovely man. I adore him, and he adores me."

A lovely man! Surely Lina can't be serious!

"So you're his mistress, is that it?"

Lina gives a small nod. Her eyes shine. "It's still a secret. Promise you won't say anything! Do you promise, Flor? My family wouldn't approve."

Flor nods, defeated. "He's only been married to La Españolita for two years," she can't help saying. "They have a son."

"Oh, *her*." Lina's voice drips with scorn for María Martínez, T's third wife. "She forced him to marry her," she says, smugly knowledgeable. "She made him think Ramfis was his. That's what people are saying, anyway. But he's going to marry *me* for love."

"Marry you?" Flor gasps. "You're crazy, Lina."

Lina flushes, stung. "You don't understand," she retorts hotly. "Your father's *madly* in love with me. I'm not exaggerating. We see each other in secret every day, or almost. He's so passionate, and he's been spoiling me tremendously. He's going to get a divorce, and then we'll be married."

Her father. Passionate.

About Lina.

Flor does a swift calculation in her head. There's a twenty-five year age difference.

She studies her friend. Lina conforms perfectly to the prototype for El Jefe's mistresses: pale-skinned, beautiful, elegant, and young enough to be his daughter.

"This won't ruin our friendship, will it, Flor?" Lina asks anxiously. "We'll still be close, won't we? You can be my confidante, like I was yours when you fell in love with Rubirosa."

Flor knows she has no choice but to accept Lina's relationship with T. Lina is her only friend, the only person who knows her intimately, the only one she's ever been able to confide in. And she needs a friend now more than ever.

But from now on, there can be no question of opening up to Lina, of telling her anything secret. Flor will have to remain on her guard, because Lina's in T's camp now; she's fallen for him wholly and recklessly, friendship or no friendship, and Flor can never trust her again. She's not naïve enough to believe that T won't take advantage of his influence over Lina to keep an even closer eye on his daughter.

Flor resigns herself to this latest abandonment. Another one. She feels as if something precious has been lost forever.

"Of course we'll still be friends, Lina. But I can't possibly be your confidante. I don't want to know *anything* about your passionate relationship with my father. It . . . bothers me. I'm sure you understand."

CIUDAD TRUJILLO
JANUARY 31, 1938

Their marriage before God, their pledge to remain together until separated by death, lasted just five years. Almost to the day.

There are better ways to start a new year than with a divorce. Flor de Oro and Porfirio's, managed by El Jefe, is finalized on January 31, 1938.

The whole thing takes only a few minutes in T's office, overseen by Jacinto Peynado, his personal attorney. The grounds are the same cited by T as his reason for divorcing Bienvenida: failure to produce offspring within five years of the wedding.

They sign the papers quickly in the presence of a registrar. Flor goes first, her anger and grief concealed by a thin veneer of indifference, her heart thudding heavily in her chest. Then, drawn and silent, she sits back and waits for the axe to fall. Porfirio's face is expressionless. Flor looks at his hand resting on the paper. His beautiful hand. He's taken off his wedding ring, leaving a pale groove in his finger. Flor's heart sinks. Her anger vanishes, and she struggles to hold back her tears. The ringless hand trembles very slightly as Porfirio signs the document giving him his freedom.

They rise in leaden silence. Flor can hardly breathe. Porfirio has lost some of his haughtiness. He looks at the woman who is no longer his wife, hesitating. Should he kiss her cheek? Shake her hand? Flor is frozen. In the end, he simply gives her a brief nod. A salute. A farewell. A thank-you-for-everything.

Before turning away from her for the last time, Porfirio gives Flor a final look, in which she could read, if she chose, a sort of wistful tenderness, resignation, and also relief. "Goodbye, Fleur," he says at last. "I wish you the best."

Flor flinches. It's almost cruel of him to use the pet name, the one no has ever called her but him.

Then he's gone. She still hasn't moved. She watches him walk away down the corridor, shoulders slightly less square than usual, as if the weight of failure is pressing down on him. Sadness washes over Flor. Her eyes fill with tears, a lump forming in her throat. She looks at El Jefe, across the table from her. He's her father again now, his face loving and sympathetic, an expression she yearns for and hardly ever sees. She thanks him, her voice made low and husky by the years of smoking. "Thank you, Papi." Then she straightens up and leaves his office, walking stiffly, her handbag tucked beneath one arm.

T lets out a breath, repressing a smile, quietly triumphant. He's just gotten his daughter back.

Tomorrow, the punishment will begin. El Jefe never forgives an offense, and Rubirosa will pay dearly. The diplomatic post in Paris will be terminated. All Rubirosa family property will be confiscated by the government so he can't inherit any of it. And T will declare him persona non grata in the Dominican Republic.

As for Flor, he'll only tighten his grip.

Ciudad Trujillo
1938

No longer Mrs. Rubirosa, she's now Flor de Oro Trujillo again. The name alone, so unwieldy, so heavy to bear, is enough to let her know that she's firmly back under El Jefe's thumb.

Now come the long, empty, weary days of doing nothing, of watching time slip away. Flor feels utterly hollow. After Germany and France, this is a new world, one of regret and remorse, loneliness and devastation. Night and sleep bring solace, but the pain reawakens with her in the morning, growing sharper and deeper like a wound doused in salt.

And it's not only that.

Flor can tell that something is very wrong in T's administration. Only last October, he had thousands of Haitians massacred near the Dajabon River, which marks the border between the two countries. People are saying that more than 25,000 people were killed by the Dominican soldiers, bludgeoned and shot and hacked to death with machetes, victims of El Jefe's xenophobia. The rumors have reached the Ministry of External Relations, and both the American government and its public have decried the mass slaughter, their criticism picked up and repeated by the international press. T's image as the Father of the Nation has been badly tarnished.

Flor isn't so young that she can't grasp the political implications of things, and she can clearly see El Jefe's characteristic authoritarianism and lack of restraint in every aspect of the country's governance. His tight control over the national economy, even in minor matters. The people in bondage. The newspapers and radio stations brought to heel, competing with one another to see who can lavish the most praise on the president. The briefcases stuffed with cash that T distributes like alms to the poor whenever he makes a public appearance. The cult of personality he encourages so shamelessly. The giant portraits of him popping up ad nauseam all over the country. The *droit du seigneur* he takes full advantage of exercising over any woman who catches his eye? Flor could bear it all as long as she was far away, but here . . .

She knows that if she allows herself to admit fully what her father is, what he's doing to the country and his people, she'll sink into total despair. She knows it for a fact. So, to survive, she pushes away the thoughts and images, distancing herself from them, refusing to give them any power over her.

Hiding herself away in the big, empty house in Gazcue, Flor is confronted with memories of Porfirio in every room. Her sense of his absence is overwhelming, his image seeming to fill the empty space, and she seethes with fury at his affairs, his gambling debts, his wheeling and dealing.

She studies her reflection in the full-length cheval mirror in her bedroom—one of the possessions she's had sent over from the apartment in Neuilly. She was always slender, but now she's bone-thin. The dress that used to flatter her figure hangs loosely on her now. She tries putting a jacket over it, but then she's too hot. She takes the jacket off and decides to make over her entire wardrobe. It'll be something to occupy her time.

The solitude and the agonizing slowness with which the days creep by leave her prostrate in her bedroom, curtains drawn. She doesn't want to see the sunlit street outside. She's not hungry or thirsty. She doesn't even feel the need to smoke, or go to the bathroom. Her anger burns red-hot beneath her closed eyelids, her rage at having failed, her disappointment. She'll force herself to hate Porfirio. She's almost there already. But then another wave of sadness comes, and leaves her gasping for breath, curled up in the fetal position. The pain starts in her chest and spreads throughout her body, until her whole being is a knot of pain.

She tries with all her strength to convince herself that it's over, that she's free, that she loathes him. But it's so difficult. She loved him the way a seventeen-year-old loves, with a heart bursting with hope, with the feeling that the whole world was theirs for the taking.

At twenty-three, she's being forced to confront the fleeting nature of happiness, the deceptive reality of love. It's a bitter pill to swallow. All she can do now is try to banish her sorrow to the depths of her memory, to turn the page, as she knows she must.

* * *

Aminta is the only other person to regret the failure of Flor's marriage. She blames herself; she didn't prepare her daughter for married life, nor did she show her a good example of how a couple should behave. But how could she have, with a husband like T? To soothe her conscience, Aminta moves in with Flor to take care of her for a while.

Fussing over Flor de Oro and trying to salve her wounded soul is her duty as a mother, and Aminta applies herself to the task with determination, despite not being sure how to act with this prickly, grieving daughter who was taken from her so young, and whom she doesn't really know as an adult. Maternal love quickly overcomes any awkwardness.

Flor has relapsed. She's stopped eating properly once again and is plagued by intense headaches. "This is the start of a new life; you just have to get through this rough patch," Aminta repeats endlessly. "We'll get you better, you'll see, *mi'jita*. Everything's going to be fine."

Flor nods. She believes it. But where will she get the strength to move forward? Though she's unable to give it a name, Aminta senses the nature of her daughter's malady. She encourages her to go out, to see friends or travel, but to no avail. At last Lina comes to the rescue, and in the end it's she who manages to pull Flor back from the brink.

* * *

A few months later, the pendulum of Flor's mood has swung the other way, and she picks up her life again with a sort of frenetic energy. For anyone with money, and Flor certainly doesn't lack for that, the Dominican capital offers plenty of diversions—not to mention the possibility of jaunts to Havana, Miami, and New York, which she now considers with new eyes. Money makes everything possible. Flor stays in palatial hotels, attends the premieres of top musicals, frequents jazz clubs. She drowns her sorrows in tobacco, alcohol, shopping, parties. Anxious to help his daughter rediscover her joie de vivre, T has opened a virtually unlimited line of credit for her. Anything, so long as he can keep an eye on her.

Little by little, Fleur fades away, and Flor de Oro returns. She rediscovers some of her zest for life, her expressions and movements regaining confidence and grace. Every day offers new possibilities, just as Aminta predicted. Rubi—Flor has decided to call him that in her mind—has been relegated to a memory. A scar, nothing more. He was a disease, and she has healed from it. And besides, he's left the island. He's far away now. He may have recovered some of his standing, occupying a low-ranking position in some European embassy, but the important thing is that she doesn't need to worry about running into him here in Ciudad Trujillo. The sum total of all this is that Flor has convinced herself that the disaster of her marriage is behind her. She's ready to start over from scratch, and this time T will approve of her choices. She's sure of it.

At a reception some months later, Flor meets Ramón Brea Messina, the son of a well-to-do family, educated in France like her, and a pediatrician by trade—a real profession. He's an ordinary, rather serious man devoted to his work. The complete opposite of Porfirio. He's far less charismatic, of course, even a bit awkward, but with a solid, reassuring physical presence. Certainly not the kind of man who has women falling at his feet.

Ramón knows perfectly well who Flor is, but, charmed, he takes the risk of seeing her again. There's something about her that touches him deeply. And T quickly makes it clear to his daughter that he finds the physician acceptable. A green light. Though it's not as if he could actually do anything to stop Flor; she's an adult. And hopefully old enough now to know a good-for-nothing man when she sees one.

A new man—what better way to draw a permanent line under Rubirosa, who is still showing up in Flor's mind on far too many sleepless nights?

Ramón puts only one condition on their union: he will never work for El Jefe. Ever.

Flor marries Ramón.

It's been less than a year since her divorce.

* * *

The actual civil ceremony for this second marriage is far less ostentatious than the first. But El Jefe doesn't know how to do things discreetly. A planeload of pink and white peonies arrives from Miami, and T throws an opulent reception at the presidential residence. He also offers his daughter the generous sum of $10,000 for her trousseau and a new apartment in Gazcue—she's eager to be rid of everything that reminds her of Porfirio.

The press is in attendance, naturally, and the young bride displays her newfound happiness proudly, knowing that the information will make its way quickly round the embassy circuit. Porfirio will learn of the wedding soon enough, wherever he might be. Flor de Oro, his Fleur, has found comfort in the arms of another. *You see, Rubi, you're far from irreplaceable. You see, Rubi, I hardly had to lift a finger. You see, Rubi, your Fleur can blossom without you.*

Swept up in the excitement of the moment, Flor isn't clear-eyed enough to recognize that her desire for revenge has driven her to act without thinking. And she has no idea how heavily the game is rigged against her.

* * *

It doesn't take T even three weeks to start meddling in the couple's affairs, and Ramón is not pleased. He's made director of the new Ramfis Hospital, an appointment he has no choice but to accept; no one dares oppose one of El Jefe's decisions. He's forced to close his private practice, which breaks his heart.

Determined to make the best of a bad situation, Ramón, who takes his work extremely seriously, decides to introduce new French medical techniques into his hospital. A fateful initiative. Because El Jefe has another job in mind for his son-in-law.

Ciudad Trujillo
1939

Scandal. Lina is pregnant. The Lovatón Pittaluga family's disgrace is smoothed over with large infusions of cash and honorary government posts.

"Your father's going to divorce that Spanish woman soon and marry me," Lina insists to Flor again and again, caressing her swollen belly with its cargo of all her hopes for the future.

The young woman is surrounded by the capital city's finest doctors. On some perverse whim, El Jefe orders his son-in-law to assist in the delivery. Ramón protests that he's a pediatrician, not an obstetrician, but to no avail, and he has no choice but to agree. "Your little doctor," T says to Flor—this is how he's begun referring to her husband—"is an easy man to control." The remark, offhand and yet pointed, cuts her to the quick.

Yolanda Lovatón is born in the greatest secrecy, though it's an open secret that doesn't keep for long. Flor's new half-sister is twenty-four years her junior.

A few weeks after that comes the birth of Odette, the daughter of Bienvenida, whose bed T continues to visit despite their divorce. It's a slap in the face for Lina. This is followed in June, in France, at Neuilly, by the arrival of Angelita, daughter of La Españolita, whom El Jefe has entrusted to the care of Rubirosa, now firmly back in the president's good books. Flor receives a letter from María Martínez, who has been utterly charmed by Porfirio. "How could you divorce such a handsome and charming man?" she asks Flor, whose fury is tinged with jealousy. Three half-sisters in less than a year. More than enough.

* * *

Her young marriage also leaves much to be desired. The Brea Messinas' already-full cup runs over when Ramón is accused of abusing his authority at the hospital. His administrative performance and the new medical techniques he's introduced are called into question, and he finds himself under fire. "Your little doctor only married you so he'd be made a hospital director," T says to Flor scornfully, forgetting that he appointed Ramón to the position himself, against the pediatrician's own wishes. El Jefe isn't above distorting the truth, as long as it keeps his eldest daughter under his control.

Ramón is summarily dismissed from his duties. No more hospital, and no more private practice. "Your marriage is a disaster," El Jefe says to Flor smugly, his mouth twisted in a disdainful little smile. Flor is devastated. T has only been toying with them. Quite simply, he wants to destroy Ramón. And her, for good measure. Demeaning people, humiliating them, making them feel small, demolishing their self-esteem and their relationships—El Jefe is a master at these sadistic, life-ruining games.

Very quickly, Flor's fear and despair give way to a feeling that takes root deep inside her, terrifying her. She doesn't want to admit it, but it's there. Hatred. Twisting itself around her heart, penetrating it. She hates T, she fears him, and yet the little girl inside her loves him, admires him, desires his approval more than anything. The result of all this is a fierce internal struggle.

Why is everything so difficult?

Why can't she and T simply love one another?

Why—*why*—can't her father just let her live in peace?

Why does he always have to get involved in her life, define its contours and boundaries? Is he jealous of her affection for her new husband? Aren't his mistresses, his bastard children, and his one-night conquests enough to satisfy his appetite for domination?

Under these incredibly stressful conditions, Flor's rebound marriage falters. She and Ramón decide to leave the country and settle in New York, to escape El Jefe's clutches.

There's a strong sense of déjà vu about it all.

New York
1940–1941

Ramón comes home exhausted one evening, after a fruitless day spent pounding the New York pavement in search of work. Not being an American national, he's unable to practice medicine, and it's devastating for him. He spends his time roaming the streets, hoping against hope to be hired on at a clinic.

Flor hurries to pour him a drink. Crystal tumbler, bourbon, ice cubes. They clink their glasses, looking into one another's eyes. It's a ritual they always make sure to follow, a mutual pretense that their lives are normal.

The phone rings. Flor seizes the receiver.

"*Holà,* Flor!"

She doesn't recognize the voice.

"Flor, it's me! Lina!"

"Lina! My God, where are you?"

"Here, in New York! I live here now!"

Lina's voice is cheerful—no, more than that, almost hysterically excited. Flor doesn't have time to express her surprise before her friend hurries on:

"Wait, don't go anywhere! There's someone here who wants to talk to you!"

A moment of silence, then: "Flor de Oro?"

There's only one person who ever calls her by her full name, at least when he's in a good mood. Otherwise it's simply Flor.

"Yes . . ." Her voice shrivels inside her, the word barely making it past her lips. A drop of cold sweat trickles down her spine.

"Come over, I want to see you!"

It's an order, and T's orders aren't up for discussion. El Jefe gives her the address. "I'll be waiting." He hangs up.

Ramón declines to go with her. He's had enough of El Jefe's humiliations. He calls a taxi for his wife.

* * *

Flor is driven to a grand building on East Riverside Drive, where the elevator takes her to the top floor, its doors opening directly into a gigantic penthouse suite with a view of the Hudson River.

Lina welcomes Flor with open arms. She's put on some weight, but she's still very beautiful. She takes her friend into the living room, where Flor nearly trips over a relaxed, smiling man she struggles to recognize. T, on his hands and knees on the carpet, is playing with a baby. "This is Landy," he coos.

The Ogre of the Caribbean, transformed into a doting papa. Flor can't believe her eyes. The sight cuts straight to heart. Has she ever inspired her father to act this way, even once?

Flor looks curiously at the baby, who crawls toward her. She searches the tiny face for any resemblance to T, but there is none. Yolanda is pure Lovatón. Flor can't help but be relieved. She—with her frizzy curls, olive skin, and dark eyes—*she's* the one who looks like El Jefe.

"I've never been so happy," T says dreamily, sinking into an armchair. "I want you to be part of this life."

Flor has never heard her father sound like this. He has installed Lina comfortably here in New York—more comfortably than Flor herself is living—to protect her from María's vengefulness and her own parents' criticism; the affair is common knowledge now. Two birds with one stone.

"I'll be coming to New York once a month from now on, to visit Lina and Yolanda. Bring your husband next time, Flor de Oro, and we'll all go out together," T says. It's a command, not a request.

T's contentment is no less conspicuous when the next time comes. "I want you to be as happy with Flor de Oro as I am with Lina," he says to Ramón.

No longer is Flor's husband simply her "little doctor" to El Jefe. Pretending to act on impulse, T takes $1,000 out of his wallet and presses the money into his son-in-law's hand. The truth is that he's well aware of Flor and Ramón's precarious financial situation, and he's brought the cash for the express purpose of giving it to them.

This marks the start of a peaceful period in Flor's stormy relationship with her father. He's not El Jefe during that winter in New York, exchanging the uniforms for civilian suits the moment he arrives in the States. The two couples dine in the best restaurants and become regulars at the Rainbow Club, where they dance boisterous congas, cha-chas, and merengues, the Dominican dance popularized by El Jefe. He's still such a good dancer! Flor whirls in her father's arms. Their fingers intertwine and they sway together. Sometimes he presses a kiss to her hair, and it's happiness unlike any she's ever known.

There are often press photographers around, of course. T poses between his mistress, his daughter, and his son-in-law. Flor is thrilled. When Porfirio sees how much fun she's having with T and her new husband, he'll be sorry. He'll miss her then, her and the opulent life they shared.

At Christmas, T decorates Lina's tree himself and heaps expensive gifts beneath it. Flor is happy, but can't keep from being melancholy at the same time; this is the only Christmas she can remember celebrating with her father. T gives Lina a magnificent white mink coat, which she immediately puts on over her evening gown. She looks stunning. Moved, T takes her in his arms, gently tucking a stray wisp of hair behind her ear. Flor shivers, memory slicing through her like a blade. T did the same for her once, in San Cristóbal, when she was a little girl dancing on his feet.

Pulling herself together, she unties the ribbon on her own gift with her long, nervous fingers. It's a large box made of thick, high-quality cardboard. Inside, on a bed of silk, lies a white mink coat. Exactly the same as Lina's. It's beautiful. Lina is delighted, but Flor can't help but feel unsettled. The exact same coat for both of them? Really? And the same gestures . . .

But, in the face of Lina's genuine joy, Flor tells herself that she's just being difficult, that it doesn't mean anything, that she's making too much out of small things. So she puts on a smile. And T makes his entrance at the Rainbow Club that night with his daughter on one arm and his mistress on the other, both of them swathed in dazzling white fur.

No one else seems to think twice about the matching gifts, and everyone seems happy, so Flor decides to be happy, too. The good times never last; she knows that all too well. Best to enjoy them while she can.

This is when Rubirosa chooses to come out of the woodwork.

New York
April–May 1941

Flor recognizes the elegant handwriting immediately. Her mouth goes dry. She feels as if she can't breathe. Palms moist, fingers trembling, she rips open the envelope clumsily, as if it contains something dangerous.

Neuilly, April 14, 1941

How I miss you, my Fleur! More than I ever could have imagined.

Your father has had me posted to the Paris legation again, in the city we both love so much, and despite my heavy workload and all my social obligations, you're always in my thoughts. I think about you constantly, and I still believe your place is by my side.

I know you've remarried, but I don't care. I'm sure you were trying to get your revenge on me, and you succeeded, because it's broken my heart. But you can't be happy without me, any more than I can be happy without you. After all we've been through together, our destinies are linked forever. For better and for worse, remember? I love you. And I know you love me. And love is stronger than anything.

I've been invited to Bali by a friend I met at King George's coronation. The Maharajah of Kaipur, you remember him? I'm begging you, Flor, join me in Paris, and we'll travel to Bali together. It's a wild and exotic island, and they say the beaches are magnificent. We'll be treated like royalty there. It'll be like a fairy tale, like when we first fell in love. A new start for us, without all the youthful mistakes we made.

Write back quickly, my love. I'm waiting for you.
Your husband, forever,
Porfirio

The letter, delivered to Flor through the Dominican embassy, was sent via diplomatic courier. Her hands are still shaking as she refolds the single sheet of paper. She closes her eyes, trying to calm the thunderous pounding of her heart. Porfirio. Resistance is impossible; she's already in his arms, smelling his woodsy scent, running a fingertip lightly over the dimple in his chin, pressing her lips to his.

That's her initial reaction. One of the heart, and the body, too. She realizes with a start that she's never stopped thinking about Porfirio. That void, that nothingness, that longing—that was him. There's no point in denying it.

But then comes the counterblow, like an aftershock after an earthquake. A short-circuiting. The voice of reason. He has some nerve, writing to her like this when she's married to someone else, after everything he put her through. He thinks he's irresistible, all-powerful. He thinks he can toy with her as he pleases.

And then the cycle starts all over again. Flor tries to control her imagination, but she can't. She's swimming in Porfirio's wake in the turquoise waters of Bali. They're walking on the beach, fingers interlaced, gazing at the horizon, their feet leaving twin prints in the white sand. They're meditating in a temple with a thousand stupas. They're sipping cocktails and watching a glorious sunset. It's what she's always wanted. To be with him. That, and only that.

She falls asleep in a daze next to Ramón that night. The seed of destruction has been sown in their already shaky marriage.

A second letter arrives. A forceful declaration of love. That chapter of her life is not over. Porfirio continues to send her dramatic missives full of regret. Before long, Flor is utterly overwhelmed by a single, all-consuming desire. To rejoin Porfirio in France and set off on a second honeymoon.

And of course, fate intervenes to muddy the waters.

* * *

El Jefe has been negotiating for months to end American control over Dominican customs enforcement, and he's finally winning the battle. His trips to the United States become fewer and farther between.

He's taken ill at the end of May, painful abscesses sprouting on his neck, and seeks treatment in New York. While the Spanish woman is busy summoning the gods of the voodoo pantheon in Ciudad Trujillo, Flor keeps vigil at El Jefe's bedside with Lina. She takes advantage of the opportunity to confide in her father.

"I've decided to go back to Porfirio as soon as you're better. My place is with him."

El Jefe reacts with fury.

"Out of the question! I forbid it! Remember how he treated you. He didn't just cheat on you—he beat you! How many times did you come cry on my shoulder?"

Ramón discovers Porfirio's letters. Flor hasn't hidden them very well. Perhaps by design? Even she isn't sure. For the honest and respectable physician, it's the last straw. First his career is ruined, and now his impetuous wife is reconnecting with Rubirosa. And really, what did he expect?

Ramón doesn't make a fuss. He simply resigns himself to the situation, as he has done so many other times since their marriage. If Flor wants to leave him, let her leave. The couple drifts further and further apart, Flor's yearning for Rubi growing stronger every day.

But the Nazis invaded France a year ago. Paris is occupied, and Flor can't join Porfirio there. And his letters have stopped, anyway, Flor's own to him going unanswered. In the pressure of the European political climate, he has forgotten her. Or maybe he's simply begun a new affair. Flor's puzzlement is mingled with anguish and humiliation. She sinks into depression. Her hopes have been dashed, and her whole life is crumbling. Again.

The bubble of happiness in which Flor has been living with her father and Lina finally bursts. With no more business to conduct in Washington, T resumes married life in Ciudad Trujillo. Disappointed, Lina relocates to Miami with her baby, taking up residence in a luxurious apartment at the expense of the Dominican taxpayers, a convenient two-hour flight away from El Jefe.

Flor quietly divorces the kind and decent Ramón Brea Messina, who could have made any woman in the world happy but her. Ramón himself leaves the marriage with his head held high, soon embarking on a diplomatic career of his own: T appoints him to the post of chargé d'affaires in Mexico, in return for which Ramón gives Flor back her freedom without asking for anything else.

A brief, impulsive interlude, a meteorite flashing through Flor's world; in that end, that was her second marriage. A parenthesis in a life that seems to be getting away from her. She can't help but feel cheated. If T hadn't stuck his nose into their lives . . . if Rubi hadn't written to her . . .

Her pain is deeper than regret, sharper than loneliness. She's haunted by a ghost, one whose presence she can't exorcise, whose image she can't banish from her thoughts, whose stamp on her body she can't erase.

Her unhappiness grows and grows until it swells into a flood of despair.

That's the way you drown.

New York
Autumn 1941

Twenty-six years old and divorced twice. A dismal track record.

T has stopped paying any attention to her, completely absorbed in his new family, not to mention his ongoing affair with Lina. The only ones he cares about now are Angelita, his baby daughter with the doll-like prettiness, and Ramfis, who has now been appointed "Protector of Poor and Unfortunate Children" in a lavish ceremony. Though she's fully aware of how ridiculous it is to give such a title to an eleven-year-old boy, Flor can't help but feel a stab of jealousy, too. El Jefe has never given her any formal role. She would truly love to give of her time, to be of service to her country, to take part in charitable works or cultural events.

Her country has become a gilded cage, its door locked tight, its bars forged of domination, authority, possessiveness, demands, and limitations. Flor is watched by T's spies day and night. Once again she chooses to flee, and she runs toward what she knows: New York, again, where she loses herself in a Bohemian lifestyle not wholly unlike the one she criticized Porfirio for, minus the shady wheeling and dealing. She also becomes reacquainted with her old demons, alcohol and eating disorders. Old demons, already, at age twenty-six.

She is determined, despite everything, to be an ordinary young woman. But Flor de Oro is anything but an ordinary young woman.

Her exile is threefold.

Firstly, she's in exile from her home island. She deeply misses the beautiful place of her birth, with its abundant food for every one of the five senses. She misses the landscape of her childhood, her language and her loved ones, and it's as if holes have been carved in her heart. She misses it all: the colors and scents, the music, the kindness of the Dominican people.

She's also in exile from T, the father who has controlled every aspect of her life since birth, the source of every punishment and every reward according to his mood, the father whose hold over her is so strong that she can't shake free of it no matter how hard she tries. The powerful, charismatic father she does nothing but disappoint.

And finally, there's Rubirosa. Yes, she feels as if she's in exile from Porfirio. Without him, she isn't whole. She had so much hope, only a few months ago.

Without the two men in her life, her father and her great love, Flor is nothing. A painful reality that is truly dawning on her for the very first time. She's incapable of living by herself.

She embarks on the single life in New York in near-total isolation. Her name, far from opening doors, proves a heavy weight to bear. She'd like to get a job, but has to admit the obvious: she doesn't know how to do anything except sparkle at high-society cocktail parties. No one trusts her, her fellow Dominican expatriates least of all. For opponents of the regime, she's just El Jefe's daughter. Forging a new identity for herself is impossible.

She hides away in her Fifth Avenue apartment, spending her days on the sofa, leafing through magazines and putting away glass after glass of whiskey. On certain days, when the loneliness is at its worst, she drinks until she passes out, until she sinks into darkness and disappears.

When she feels strong enough, she goes shopping. She's well known to the credit department at Saks Fifth Avenue, which sends stacks of bills to El Jefe. But no amount of shopping dulls the pain. It's just not enough anymore.

Two days ago, she was wandering the city aimlessly when she was attacked by a swarm of black flies, which buzzed thickly around her head until she fainted on the pavement. When she came to and saw the anxious faces bent over her, she closed her eyes again, overcome with self-loathing. Her first thought? *I'm an embarrassment to El Jefe.* Helped back to her apartment by a Good Samaritan who advised her to consult a doctor, she locked herself inside and hasn't gone out since.

Having closed the door on a world that doesn't interest her, she wants nothing more than to take herself out of it forever—but she lacks the courage. So she decides to simply fade away. The idea quickly becomes an obsession. She all but stops eating again, and makes herself vomit up any food she does consume.

Fade away, Flor.

Lina calls. She's living in Miami with her daughter now, far from the threats made against her by La Españolita, who people say is fervent believer in the bewitchments of Santeria. Lina is still being maintained in lavish style by El Jefe despite the fact that his passion has flagged over the years, and he only visits her every so often. As soon as Lina hears Flor's faint, slurring voice, she can tell that something is very wrong with her friend, and decides to alert El Jefe.

"You've got to pull yourself together, *querida*. If you're tired, go and see a doctor. Promise me you'll do that, Flor."

Flor agrees, the same way she does everything these days, listlessly.

Flor still keeps her promises, and now she puts on her mink coat, which swamps her thin body, and steps into the elevator. She's made an appointment at a doctor's office nearby. She's eaten no solid food since the previous evening. In the lobby of her building, her head fills with a sort of loud buzzing, and she feels a wave of nausea. She tries to lean against the wall for support but falls, semiconscious, to the marble floor. A rustle of silk and fur, a whispering sigh of breath—it's as if she's already ceased to exist.

Horrified, the concierge hastily phones a doctor who lives in the building. Flor is feather-light, almost weightless in the man's arms as he carries her up to Dr. Berck's apartment. When the physician removes her fur coat, he's shocked by her emaciated condition. He examines her quickly, then pushes up the sleeve of her dress, exposing her twiglike upper arm, and administers a vitamin shot. Flor gamely allows him to do it, like a ghost with no will of her own.

Anorexia, alcoholism, exhaustion. A textbook case. These conditions aren't Maurice Marshall Berck's specialty; he's a surgeon at Mount Sinai Hospital. But he insists on seeing Flor again, then again, then a third time. He's genuinely alarmed by the condition of this young woman who seems so intent on destroying herself. It's painful for him to see the way she's mistreating her own body, and he can see that hers is a deeply troubled soul. All he knows of her is her ravaged body and her grim clinical presentation. But he's pleasantly surprised by the vitality of this patient of his who, after just a few visits, is more or less back on her feet.

New York
Late 1941–1942

Dr. Berck finds himself intrigued by Flor Ledesma—for this is the name she gave when they met. He can sense that she isn't telling him everything. He's also eager to learn the reasons for her neuroticism. Very quickly, he gains a good deal of insight into her character. She's intelligent, lively, and has a strong personality. Possessive, too, even jealous, and certainly extravagant, but none of that is important. Beneath it all, there's a wounded young woman. Why does he insist on continuing to treat her, rather than referring her to a psychiatrist? He finds himself moved by her, and, even though he doesn't want to admit it, she touches his heart. This is more than simple kindness toward someone who's suffering. It's crazy, foolish. But Maurice is falling in love.

For Flor's part, the doctor doesn't make much of an impression on her, except maybe as a skilled and trustworthy professional. But even though she doesn't realize it, with each consultation, a bond is forming between them. He's her only link to real life. She looks forward to their appointments with an impatience that gradually turns into feverish excitement. She's made promises to him. To drink less alcohol. To smoke less. To eat fruits and vegetables. To keep to a normal schedule of sleep and wakefulness. To call him if she slips up at all. And this is exactly what she needs. A promise is like a crutch, something solid in her hand, something to make sure she doesn't stumble.

For the first time in her life, Flor finds herself trusting a man.

***

The day Dr. Berck invites her to dinner, Flor accepts. It's as if he's opened the cage door a crack, slipped a hand in to stroke the feathers of a frightened bird with a fingertip, without being attacked in return. How has he managed it?

The confession comes between the appetizer and the entrée.

"Trujillo. My real name is Flor de Oro Trujillo."

Maurice doesn't understand right away. He frowns. Flor toys with her pearl necklace nervously. Looking deep into the doctor's gray eyes with her dark ones, she drives the point home.

"I'm the daughter of the Ogre of the Caribbean."

The words are said the way a child might confide a secret, but it's a painful reality. This is how Flor refers to her father. It's almost a deliberate provocation. Is it a defense mechanism? A way of keeping Maurice at arm's length?

He's frustrated with himself for not realizing it sooner. The Fifth Avenue apartment, the expensive clothes—too large, but expensive—and jewelry.

The Ogre of the Caribbean. People call him the Little Caesar of the Caribbean, too, and the Generalissimo, and the Benefactor of the Fatherland. Every self-respecting Democrat detests the tyrant reigning over half the island some 600 miles from Florida. And Maurice Marshall Berck votes Democrat.

She's a patient. She's the Ogre's daughter. Two strikes.

But in this unexpected love, Maurice is already too far gone.

***

The physician has absolutely no connection to T. And so Flor opens her heart to him. She tells him everything. The two failed marriages, the pressure, the dependance, the jealousy, El Jefe's omnipotence and control, the conflicting desires that have turned her life into a constant internal struggle, her three half-sisters born a few weeks apart, her flight from the Dominican Republic, Ramfis being made an army colonel at age four, the heavy burden of her love for her father, the dictator, the Ogre, from which she can't free herself.

She tells Maurice about T's spies. "Even here, in New York?"

"Yes, even here."

Maurice understands now.

Her nervous glances over her shoulder when she walks through the revolving door of a restaurant.

The pause before she enters a nightclub.

The way she recoiled when a man offered her a light at a coffee shop counter.

Her wariness of other patrons at the beauty salon.

The way she freezes when a stranger speaks to her in the street.

Her panic, even terror, when the telephone rings.

There's a name for all of it.

Paranoia.

"No one can understand what it's like to be T's daughter."

Yes. Doctor Berck understands. And he sympathizes. His eyes on hers are like a spotlight illuminating the darkest corners of her soul.

Flor is going to have to admit some truths.

That she isn't an adult.

That she's dependent on an unhealthy relationship.

That a single desire is governing her entire life: to please her father.

That when she displeases T, she flees to escape punishment.

That the punishment always catches up with her.

That she must free herself from this unhealthy cycle.

It's time for Flor to grow up, to stop being a marionette whose father is pulling the strings. Until she's a real adult, she can't be anyone's wife.

Every day, the physician gives way a little bit more to the man.

***

Flor was drowning, and she's found a lifeline. She must grasp it and pull herself toward the light. Little by little, she blossoms under Maurice's wing. She rediscovers her enjoyment of food and puts on weight. The color comes back into her cheeks. They go out to the movies, the theater, art exhibitions. Flor clings to Maurice's arm, and it's far more than a life preserver.

They laugh about the way they met: there are better ways to meet a man than nearly drinking yourself to death.

He finds her beautiful, and tells her so. Better, he proves it to her in the intimacy of the bedroom. He doesn't turn his back to her after they make love, like Rubi. Instead he rests a hand gently on one small breast to calm the pounding of her heart, caressing her slight body all over, tracing designs on her belly, pressing kisses to her neck, playing with her curls, which he adores. Flor closes her eyes, calm and peaceful, and falls asleep in his arms. In the mornings, Maurice wakes her up with a steaming cup of coffee on a tray, accompanied by a rose— pulled from the bouquet in the living room—in a glass of water. Then he leaves for the hospital, but not until she promises to go out and get some fresh air. When the door closes behind him, Flor stretches luxuriously in bed and buries her head in the pillow, breathing in his scent. Then she drinks her coffee, thinking that today will be a good day.

Their idyll lasts for a few blissful weeks.

But real life catches up to them. Flor has warned Maurice; she can never escape T's spies, who have been ordered to watch her every move.

The Dominican consul telephones. El Jefe "knows what she's up to."

He asks the inevitable question. When is she getting married?

Flor panics and tells Maurice. She warned him, she says.

Spending time with T's daughter is putting him in danger, threatening his freedom.

Calmly, Maurice assesses the situation, weighs the pros and cons of the relationship.

But Flor is devastated. She's never been able to have a normal courtship. Never enjoyed a romantic escapade without T's shadow darkening it.

* * *

In early December, Flor learns—via official public announcement—that her half-brother Radhames was born on the first of the month. T certainly draws a lot of inspiration from Verdi.[18] Flor would find it funny if she weren't so consumed with jealousy. She will never have children of her own, while El Jefe's family continues to grow. And there can be no doubt that this new baby is his—unlike Ramfis, whom people say is the son of Doña María's Cuban ex-husband. It's crystal-clear that, for the Trujillos, Flor no longer exists. So why won't T loosen her shackles?

* * *

The news that breaks on December 8, 1941, changes everything.

The United States enters the war.

And the Dominican Republic follows suit.

Despite his admiration for Mussolini and Hitler, El Jefe listens to the voice of reason and aligns himself with the detested *Yanquis*. He's taken steps in this direction already, at the Evian Conference of 1938, offering a hundred thousand visas to Jews fleeing the Reich; even before that, in 1936, he'd set up a small number of European immigrants in an enclave in the northern

---

[18] Ramphis and Radamès are both characters in Giuseppe Verdi's opera *Aida*.

part of the Dominican Republic. Flor, who hated the Nazis so much during her time in Berlin, had been pleasantly surprised by this maneuver, which, despite the dubiousness of the motives behind it, had put T on the right side of history. She tells Maurice how proud she was at the time. And she feels the same way now.

Maurice feels as if a hurdle has been cleared. The Ogre has taken America's side. It's a small consolation, but it's enough for him.

For Flor, it's now or never. The chance to be with a man who truly loves her and is good for her, an opportunity to break with the past, with her country, and to settle for good beyond the reach of her father's tyranny.

Maurice is no playboy, and he's not beholden to T.

Maurice loves her.

She agrees to marry him.

NEW YORK
SPRING 1942

The wedding takes place in Manhattan on March 6, 1942, in near-total secrecy. Between international politicking, running his country, his family, his mistresses, and his bastards, El Jefe is too preoccupied to make much of it. But he provides the couple with a duplex at 784 Park Avenue, along with a monthly wire transfer of $2,000, as a wedding gift for Flor de Oro's third marriage. In exchange, they're tasked with a few social obligations, such as the party the Bercks throw for T's birthday on October 24. The next day Maurice sees his own face splashed all over the *Times*'s society pages, directly opposite an advertisement for Van Cleef & Arpels. He isn't sure he likes it.

Flor and Maurice's life as newlyweds is content and comfortable. He loves books, classical music, and small dinner parties with friends. It's Flor's first taste of peaceful domesticity, and she dons the model-wife role he creates for her with delight. The simple pleasure of being a normal woman is enough to make her happy. Her monthly allowance enables her to enjoy herself, and she takes advantage of all New York has to offer without hesitation, as she's never been able to do before.

From time to time, as she strolls the busy Manhattan streets, almost without meaning to she finds herself outside a restaurant she used to frequent with Porfirio, or the bar where he used to hold court. Once, her curiosity even takes her to the hotel where they first stayed after their escape from the island. Everything looks unchanged, and she's tempted to go inside and ask for the key to their old room. It's an unhealthy pilgrimage, and she realizes it. She promised Maurice she would stop harming herself, both body and soul. So she forces herself to return to Park Avenue. She takes long walks in Central Park, past children playing tag, and allows herself to dream of giving Maurice a child. If only. A lump rises in her throat at the memory of the shell given to her by the old priestess in Sabana de la Mar, still buried somewhere among her things. She's never been able to part with it.

She stops on the way home to buy a few fashion magazines from a newsstand. The concierge greets her respectfully and calls the elevator for her. She enters the immense apartment that has become her sanctuary and sinks into the sofa, magazines in her lap, casting a reproachful glance at the glaringly empty liquor cabinet.

Flor keeps her vow. Total abstinence from alcohol, moderate smoking, eight hours' sleep a night, plenty of fruits and vegetables. Peaceful days, weeks, months. Not particularly exciting, but mundanely happy.

Sometimes Flor and Maurice seek a few days' escape from the tumult of the city. Maurice enjoys mountain hikes, and the nearest place for that is in the Catskills. Flor, in sturdy boots, learns to love walking. She has a surprising level of stamina, which delights her husband. With Maurice, it's easy for her. Everything seems easy with him. There is an occasional stab of memory: winter weekends in Jarabacoa with Porfirio, surrounded by T's court, women in fur stoles gathered around the hearth . . . but that's all behind her now.

For the first time, Flor admires and respects the man with whom she's sharing her life. She loves Maurice's devotion to her, his work ethic, his selflessness, his honesty and calm. He's her friend, her protector, her mate. She loves him.

The love between Flor and Maurice is a complex tapestry, its pattern unique. There's the skill and influence of the physician, and the patient's trust in the man of science. There's the compassion of a human who has rescued a trapped and wounded animal, and that animal's boundless gratitude toward its savior. Then there is Flor's sensuality and exotic magnetism, and Maurice's flesh-and-blood attraction to her. The Dominican president's tyranny, which is so distasteful to the American's political convictions. And the fear, even terror, that El Jefe rouses in his daughter, and her continually thwarted desire to be free.

And there is, too, what Flor has carefully buried in the deepest recesses of her soul: the dulled but ever-present yearning for Rubi.

NEW YORK
SEPTEMBER 1942

"*Pendejo! Hijo de la gran puta!*"

The words slip out before she can stop them.

When it comes to swearing, Flor learned from the best. When she's shocked, her control slipping, she invariably lets loose a stream of curses, like the princess in the old fairy tale spitting snakes and toads. And the expletives that come to her most naturally happen to be the ones El Jefe prefers, too, the ones he bellows at anyone guilty of the slightest lapse in conduct, particularly if he feels he hasn't been treated with enough respect, or his dignity has been compromised—his Achilles heel.

"*Pendejo! Hijo de la gran puta!*" Flor repeats. A chill runs down her spine.

There it is, printed in black and white on the *New York Times* society page. The news hits Flor like the lash of a whip, like a bucket of ice water thrown in her face.

Porfirio has remarried.

Her Rubi.

Remarried.

In Vichy, where her father transferred him after his restoration to El Jefe's good graces.

To an actress.

The most beautiful woman in the world.

Flor's heart races, thudding painfully against her ribcage. A dark red flush creeps up her neck.

She studies the photograph. It's a bit blurry, but not so blurry that she can't make it out.

"*Fea! Narizua!*"

Ugly, big-nosed. Pallid.
Danielle Darrieux.
Rubi looks happy. He's smiling beatifically, even a little foolishly. Did he think of her, Flor, when he slipped the ring on that French woman's finger? He can't have forgotten Flor's hand trembling in his, her gaze lifted shyly to meet his own, her eyes full of hope, overflowing with love, tears glistening on her lashes. That other ring, symbolic of their future, that he slid slowly, carefully, onto her slender finger, fine as a matchstick. The ring he made a mockery of so many times.

Crushed, Flor rises and goes to the liquor cabinet.
Swaying slightly, like a boxer who's just taken an uppercut to the jaw.
She braces herself with both hands on its marble top.
Breathes deeply.
Picks up a decanter. Puts it down again.
Pulls out the stopper. Wrinkles her nose at the scent.
Whiskey. It will do the job.
Fills a tumbler to overflowing.
Takes a large swallow.
Immediately, a wave of guilt washes over her.
Maurice has warned her.
Resolutely, she pads to the kitchen and pours the rest of the whiskey down the sink. She'll be good. She promised him.
Flor de Oro is Fleur no longer.

But *por Dios*, Porfirio had no right to remarry! As long as she was married but he wasn't, she had the upper hand; she could feel like she'd won. But in marrying that French woman, he's one-upped her. The proof is right there on the society page.
His ability to hurt her, even now, leaves her breathless.

The sound of a key in the front door. Maurice.
Flor crumples up the newspaper and throws it in the garbage,

hurries to the kitchen, rinses her mouth under the faucet. She can still feel the whiskey scorching her throat.

She greets her husband with a smile.

She's so unhappy she could die.

Somewhere across the ocean, the man she's never stopped loving has just taken a new bride.

WASHINGTON, D.C.
NOVEMBER–DECEMBER 1942

Since the United States entered the war, Maurice, who holds the rank of captain, has been assigned to the Walter Reed military hospital in Bethesda, treating a constant stream of soldiers wounded on the front.

Flor has rented an apartment in Washington to be closer to her husband. Very quickly, life accelerates to a hellish pace. Maurice is always on call and works day and night. He persuades Flor to return to New York, where things are calmer. She can visit him whenever he gets a few days' leave.

Thanksgiving Day finds them in a cozy inn on the banks of the Potomac. Maurice is so exhausted that he doesn't even want to go walking. They spend two days lazing in bed, then Flor goes back to New York and Maurice to the operating room.

* * *

She hasn't seen Maurice in three weeks, and she misses him terribly. More than she expected to, in fact. The big duplex is empty without him. She listens to his favorite string quartets, leaves his old science journals lying around and his cigarettes on the coffee table, just to create the illusion that he's there.

In the evenings, she puts on a pretty dress, makeup, and elegant shoes, then examines herself in the mirror, the click of her high heels echoing mournfully off the marble floor. Then she undresses again. The coquetry is wasted without her husband there. She thinks of him constantly. Is he thinking of her? Does he even have time for that? Yet he telephones her every evening. Flor is determinedly cheerful during these calls; there's no point letting on how lonely she is. Maurice has enough to worry about as it is.

She has little desire to go out in the evenings, and turns down most invitations. Being alone among their married friends would make her miss Maurice even more. She sits in an armchair, contemplating the thick rectangle of cardstock with its ostentatious gilded lettering. An invitation to the Dominican embassy in Washington to celebrate the New Year, the thirteenth of the Trujillo Era.[19] She's declined, citing her husband's absence as the reason, hoping it won't be held against her. She has no desire to spend an evening being put under the microscope by El Jefe's cronies. It's an immense relief to have distanced herself from him.

* * *

Maurice phoned the day before yesterday with good news. "Darling, I've been granted three days' leave starting January 2. Come to Washington, and we'll go and stay in the country somewhere. I have a surprise for you. Dress warmly!"

Excited by the prospect of a getaway with her husband, Flor goes shopping on Fifth Avenue. All the shops are beautifully decorated for Christmas, and she browses happily. Warm clothes, he said? She buys Maurice a cashmere scarf, fur-lined gloves, a woolen undershirt, and a gold cigarette lighter, which she has engraved with his initials, for the physician doesn't practice what he preaches, and continues to smoke like a chimney. She has the gifts beautifully wrapped and selects a Christmas card decorated with a tree covered in sparkling sequins, in which she writes: "For the best husband in the world, with all my love, Flor."

January 2 can't come soon enough.

---

[19] "The Trujillo Era" was the name given to Rafael Trujillo's years in office, 1930–1961.

New York
December 31, 1942

1 "54 East 54th Street, please. El Morocco."

Flor arranges her evening gown around her in the back seat of the taxi and pulls her mink stole more closely around her neck. The driver closes the door and eases into the flow of traffic.

It's New Year's Eve, and Flor, her reclusiveness easing slightly, has agreed to celebrate with a few couples she and Maurice are friendly with. The former speakeasy of the Prohibition years has changed; El Morocco is now *the* place to see and be seen for New York's smart set.

One thing is worrying her: pictures taken by Jerome Zerbe, El Morocco's official photographer, often make the gossip columns. There's no doubt that she'll be snapped tonight, or that Porfirio will see the photo, because he gets all the American papers at the legation in Vichy, she's certain.

With this in mind, she's chosen her outfit carefully and spent extra time on her hair and makeup, parading back and forth in front of the full-length mirror, her evening gowns strewn across the bed. No patterns—they'd clash with the blue zebra-print banquettes the club is known for. She was torn between the green dress and the black one. In the end, she went with the black.

Flashbulbs pop as Flor steps from the taxi onto the red carpet in front of El Morocco. She smiles, the little girl in her delighted by the attention. She feels like a star, like María Montez, one of her favorite actresses. It occurs to her that she should have brought someone else along. It probably looks pathetic, coming to a New Year's celebration alone.

No matter. Tonight, she's decided to be happy. She banishes Porfirio from her thoughts. Tomorrow, she'll fly to Washington to join her husband. A divine way to start the year. She wonders what her gift will be; Maurice always chooses them with care. She can already see him untying the ribbons on his own presents, a fond smile on his lips. *You're crazy, darling! You're spoiling me too much!* he'll say, hugging her. And she'll answer, *Nothing is too much for you, my love.* And it's true; nothing is too good for Maurice. She just hopes he likes his gifts.

* * *

They have a wonderful time at El Morocco. Everyone smokes, laughs, dances, drinks. Flor is the only abstemious one: just a drop to drink, and cigarettes in moderation. The others find her a spoilsport, but a promise is a promise, and Flor always keeps hers. She chatters with her friends, whirls about the dance floor, and permits herself a glass of champagne at midnight.

As everyone embraces, Flor mentally sends a kiss to Maurice. *Happy New Year, my darling.* She hopes the war will be over soon; they have so many plans for their life together. She allows herself to dream. A child. Yes, why not? Nothing is impossible . . .

After that, the party seems to drag on forever. Flor listens to the drone of conversation around her, growing bored, drawing spirals with her index finger in the condensation on her champagne glass. She'll ask the club's maître d' to call her a taxi soon; she still needs to finish packing and get some rest before her flight, to be in good form for her arrival in Washington.

Someone taps her on the shoulder. She turns. A pit opens in her stomach. Her brilliant smile fades. It's Marieke, her coat buttoned crookedly, a scarf wound haphazardly around her neck. She shouldn't be here. Flor can't look away from those crooked coat buttons. She already knows that whatever her

German housemaid is about to say isn't going to be good. She shrinks into her chair, bracing for the blow. She stops breathing, almost feels as if her heart has stopped beating. Marieke's lips are trembling. She waits.

"Ma'am, you have to come home right away, please. The taxi is waiting outside."

Flor stares at the zebra-print fabric of the seating. The stripes seem to be moving, slowly, sinuously. She grips the edge of the table. Her father? Her mother? Not Maurice, surely ... no, not Maurice ...

A wave of dizziness washes over her. She retrieves her mink stole from the coat check and makes her way to the taxi, clinging to Marieke's arm. As soon as the driver closes the back door, Marieke bursts into tears, managing to gasp out a few phrases between sobs.

"They called . . . the police . . . your husband . . . fell asleep ... a fire ... sleeping pills ... cigarette ... dead ... "

Flor hears only one word. Just one.

Dead.

It's a two-line news item at most.

So mundane that it wouldn't even make the front page.

Maurice took a sleeping pill and fell asleep with a lit cigarette in his hand. His room caught fire and he died in the blaze.

End of story.

But he was T's son-in-law. So the police are on the case, already waiting at the Berck apartment. The FBI, too. Was it murder? It wouldn't be El Jefe's first attempt. Flor is questioned. She's suffering badly from shock. Swaying over to the liquor cabinet, she stretches a trembling hand toward the whiskey decanter, then hesitates. Maurice has forbidden it. But Maurice is dead. He isn't here to tell her not to do things anymore, to keep her away from the abyss. Flor pours herself a glass, which she downs in one long swallow. Then she collapses into an armchair beneath the detectives' baleful gazes.

The matter doesn't warrant an in-depth investigation, and the case is soon closed. During the first hours of questioning and ice-cold shock, Flor feels as if she's floating outside her own body. There is no one to support her. So she lets her mind wander, far from the unbearable reality.

There's nothing lurking beneath the surface of the placid life Flor and Maurice have been leading. No conspiracies, no espionage, no fraud. Nothing. The final verdict? Death by misadventure.

Aided by the military authorities, Flor has Maurice's body brought back to New York, where he is buried.

The days pass, and gradually Flor pulls herself together. Despite herself, she can't help feeling a hint of doubt. Suspicion. That Maurice's death wasn't natural. That he was murdered. The thought takes root deep in her brain, casting a dark shadow day and night. El Jefe was behind this death. He's managed to take away the husband who never asked him for anything, never owed him anything, and in this way evaded his grasp, and even succeeded in stealing his daughter. Maurice became her protector, her bulwark against adversity. He enabled her to be free from El Jefe's dictates. He made her completely happy. And El Jefe could never tolerate that.

In taking Maurice away from her, T has regained the upper hand. Flor feels more trapped than ever in the net El Jefe has woven around her.

But she doesn't want to believe it. She forces herself to listen to the voice of reason inside her. It's vital, for her own mental health. Overwork and exhaustion, those were the causes of Maurice's death. A simple accident, nothing more. She has to make herself believe that, or it'll be impossible to go on living.

Flor's third marriage has ended with her husband's death.

They were married for ten months.

She's twenty-eight years old.

It's a photo of her dressed in black, dark shadows beneath her eyes and lips twisted with bitter grief, that will make international headlines, not one of the snapshots taken at El Morocco in her pretty gown.

Rio de Janeiro and Ciudad Trujillo
1943

Flor doesn't have the heart or the strength to play the emancipated young woman anymore. Defeated, she takes refuge in Ciudad Trujillo. T moves her into a large house in Gazcue, far from the intrigues of his court, and summons Aminta to care for her. The days pass interminably, their emptiness reducing Flor to a near-catatonic state.

Maurice's passing has left her utterly drained. Beyond the violent shock of the news and the tragic circumstances of his death, she simply misses him. The way he protected her, his tenderness and solicitude, his determination to get her back on her feet, sober and clear-headed—all of that appeased her demons. With him, she wasn't afraid anymore. She'd even begun to believe in herself. But now the nightmares have returned, and with them the terror, deep and ever-present.

To calm herself, she allows herself a small drink in the evenings. No more than one. Maurice wouldn't approve, and it's just to help her sleep. Sleep—and forget, for a while, that she doesn't have a man to watch over her. It's a question of survival, Flor knows. And so alcohol is back on the table.

* * *

But somewhere deep inside Flor is a core of strength. She never gives up. She never stops hoping.

And so, when the invitation arrives, she doesn't hesitate.

Arturo Despradel, the uncle of her childhood friend Idalina, invites her to rest and recover in sunny Brazil, where he's currently serving as the Dominican ambassador.

To leave Ciudad Trujillo, to forget Washington and the ghost of Maurice, to discover a new country . . .

T, who has largely left her in peace since she was widowed, raises no objection.

* * *

The Despradel residence is huge and very comfortable. The ambassador's wife can't do enough for Flor, who gradually reacquaints herself with the high-society life. Cocktails, art exhibitions, dinners. Life is pleasant in Rio, which has a large European expatriate community. Here, the war is almost an abstraction, even though Brazil is preparing to send its first troops to fight alongside the Americans on the European front.

The Despradels are eager to show off their famous guest. Flor de Oro isn't just anyone. She feels like a marionette with someone else pulling the strings, but she doesn't care. Any feelings of discomfort are soothed by caipirinha cocktails and the rhythms of the samba.

* * *

Late one morning, Flor is still in bed. She stretches, gazing idly at the stripes cast on her body by the rays of the sun, already high in the sky, filtering through wooden shutters and silk hangings. Her head throbs dully. She mixed alcohols last night—champagne, wine, aged rum, bourbon. Maurice would not approve. But Maurice isn't here to hold her hand anymore, or to keep her from overindulging. The official dinner put on by the Dominican chargé d'affaires, to which Brazil's top industrialists were invited, was an unmitigated bore, made bearable for Flor only by copious amounts of alcohol.

There's a knock at the door, and it's as if someone's hammering a nail into her skull. Señora Despradel comes in, followed by a maid in a white apron who's staggering beneath the weight of an enormous bunch of roses. The girl, who looks to be mixed-race, makes it over the threshold only with difficulty. She sets her burden down on the rosewood dresser, bobs a curtsey, and withdraws.

Beneath the inquisitive gaze of her hostess, who now hands her an envelope, Flor sits up in bed, slides a lacquered fingernail beneath the seal of the envelope, and unfolds the little note that came with the extravagant floral offering. She can't keep her lips from curling in a slightly scornful smile as she reads the message: "A few flowers for the loveliest of flowers." The play on her first name is so banal, so overdone. Señora Despradel is shifting from one foot to the other, and it's clear that only good manners are preventing her from pressing Flor for more information.

"Who is Antenor Mayrink Veiga?" Flor enquires, taking pity on her hostess's curiosity.

The ambassador's wife is astonished. What a silly goose Flor de Oro is!

"Why, he's the gentleman who was sitting next to you at dinner, my dear! He spent the whole evening staring at you!"

Lord, how stupid does Señora Despradel think she is? The man ogled her décolletage with those bulging eyes of his all night. How could she *not* have noticed?

"I know that much, of course," Flor retorts, picturing the man's shiny bald head and baby face. "That's not what I was asking."

The remark comes out more dryly than she meant it to. The ambassador's wife blinks, but recovers quickly and begins to reel off the list of Mayrink Veiga's impressive qualities. It's a long one. Excellent family, industrialists, machine tools, armaments, munitions. Multimillionaire. Married three times (*like me*, Flor muses). A real charmer, political ambitions, a possible Senate seat. He owns a whole media empire—newspapers and radio stations (*like T*, thinks Flor, now decidedly amused by the mounting coincidences). In short, this new admirer of hers isn't exactly a nobody in this land of rubber trees and samba music.

"How old is he?" Flor asks.

"Around forty-five, I'd say."

Seventeen years older than her. Bald and round-faced.

At dinner that night, the Despradels don't hold back in singing Antenor's praises. The ambassador is even quite insistent: Mayrink Veiga is a close friend of Eurico Gaspar Dutra, a military leader with his eye on the presidency, and a very good chance of winning it.

That night, despite her fatigue and the softness of her silk sheets, Flor can't sleep. She tosses and turns, her mind whirling, one face after another seeming to float in front of her: T, Maurice, Porfirio, Antenor. *Antenor*, what a strange name! She goes over the events of yesterday evening: the smooth, gleaming pate, the plump-cheeked face, the tightly-knotted bow tie, the fleshy roll beneath the chin, the slightly coarse laugh, the vest buttons straining across the round belly. He won't win any beauty contests, that's certain. Still, Flor must admit, she's flattered.

It doesn't matter anyway, because she's packing her bags tomorrow. It's time to return to the island.

WASHINGTON, D.C.
1943

Flor's brief interlude as the demure wife of a North American physician over, T moves to take control of her life again.

When she returns from Brazil, there's a major surprise in store. Flor has been appointed first secretary to the Dominican embassy in Washington, a post that comes with a stipend of $60,000 for the purchase of a home worthy of her rank.

Flor can't help but be delighted. A whole diplomatic career is opening up for her. She knows El Jefe has given government jobs to almost everyone in his family, and her own personal merits have nothing to do with this posting. But it's her first official role in service of her country, and she's thrilled. She vows to herself that she'll do everything she can to be worthy of the opportunity she's been given. A real job, finally—and a salary! Is this a consolation prize, an attempt to ward off the bad luck that has dogged her marriages? Isn't it proof that T cares about her? That he wants to help her recover from the tragedy she's just suffered? Flor convinces herself that these things are true, and they only strengthen her determination to succeed.

Settling in the US capital, Flor quickly becomes part of Washington's smart set. When she's promoted to ministerial advisor for cultural relations between the US and the Dominican Republic, she feels as if she has sprouted wings. Helping her country be better understood by the rest of the world—promoting its culture—what a mission! It's more than she could have dreamed of. Bursting with energy and full of ideas, she gives a series of lectures on Dominican culture. She sponsors a university research project on the merengue, that irresistible music born of African and Spanish tradition and made widely popular by T. She works with the producer Spyros Kouras on a documentary about the country. She meets with everyone who matters, even having tea at the White House with Eleanor Roosevelt. Her name frequently appears in the society columns and—even better—the cultural sections of American newspapers.

For the first time in her life, Flor feels useful.

* * *

Coincidentally, or perhaps not, Flor crosses paths with Mayrink Veiga again, an event orchestrated by Herbert May, an industrialist and lobbyist who often does favors for El Jefe on the sly. Antenor wastes no time in picking up where he left off in Rio. Flowers, expensive gifts, elegant garments. He lavishes Flor with gowns, jewels, and roses, always roses. She's never been courted this way, with such dedication and extravagance. Making her entrance on the Brazilian billionaire's arm dressed in an evening gown by Mainbocher or Valentina, Flor is shown off like a trophy: *Look, everyone, it's the daughter of T, the Generalissimo, the Little Caesar of the Caribbean.* They frequent the most fashionable restaurants and the hottest nightclubs, swanning from reception to reception without pausing for breath.

The fling is anything but discreet.

LOS ANGELES
SEPTEMBER 1943

P*RINCESS OF A THOUSAND SEQUINS DAZZLES!* In her suite at the Biltmore, Flor sets down the newspaper still open to the society page, stubs out her cigarette in a crystal ashtray, and pours herself another cup of coffee, thinking how proud El Jefe will be of her. And Porfirio, in whatever far-flung embassy he's posted to these days, will undoubtedly come across the article. He'll see her, too.

The Queen of Technicolor in the center of the photo draws the attention first, of course, but despite her small stature, Flor doesn't come off too badly herself. She's shown in three-quarter profile; you can make out her pretty face, her pert little nose. Her face is guileless, her every emotion clearly visible on it. Pride, joy, and a kind of submission, an anticipation. Looking at the picture now, Flor wishes she weren't gazing at the actress quite so reverently; she should have looked straight at the photographer. She also regrets her choice of hat, which looks like a sparkling tulle hairpiece, and her ridiculous manicure. The false fingernails are so long that they'd bothered her when she tried to pin the decorations to María's lapel. *My God, they're all you can see!* They aren't in the best taste; Flor can see that now. They make her look silly, rather than sophisticated. She'll make another appointment with the manicurist pronto and have them taken off.

The previous evening in Los Angeles, on behalf of the Dominican government and in accordance with decree no. 1370 of September 1, 1943, Flor de Oro Trujillo awarded the Juan Pablo Duarte Order of Merit in the Grade of Officer—her homeland's highest honor—and the Order of Trujillo to the actress María Montez, the first Dominican woman to be so decorated (except for La Españolita, who was given the Grand Gold Cross of the Order of Juan Pablo Duarte during the presidency of T's straw man, Jacinto Peynado, but El Jefe's wife doesn't count). The actress, currently filming *Gypsy Wildcat*, was unable to travel to the island, so it had fallen to Flor, as first secretary of the Dominican embassy in Washington, to do the honors.

María is only three years older than Flor—hardly more than thirty—and she's already reached the peak of success. The United States has been at war for more than two years, and Hollywood's directors, working to boost the morale of American troops with lighthearted films, have been showcasing the charms of the woman the press has nicknamed the Latin Bombshell. In her latest film, *Arabian Nights*, María Montez plays Scheherazade. Universal Studios movie sets, premieres, rubbing elbows with the handsomest actors, the cream of Hollywood—Flor has often envied the Dominican star. Not anymore, though. Not now that she has a real role to play, too. The ambassador, Manuel de Moya Alonso, is entrusting her with all sorts of missions. She's representing her country and relishing every moment of it.

Sometimes, in a flash of clarity, Flor wonders if she's making these "missions" more important than they really are. Where do her personal strengths come into play? But she banishes these thoughts as quickly as they occur to her, choosing instead to focus on her duties and think of as many ways as possible to shine even brighter.

She's all too aware of her insatiable need for her father's recognition and love. All too aware of how vital it is that he acknowledge her, pay attention to her, approve of her, be proud of her. If she doesn't exist in his eyes, she doesn't exist at all. It's as simple as that. Nothing has changed since the days of agonizing over her grades at Bouffémont.

Ciudad Trujillo
1944

When Flor returns to Ciudad Trujillo in February to celebrate the centenary of Dominican independence, she's accompanied by Mayrink Veiga, on the flimsiest of pretexts: her devoted admirer is the bearer of a gift from Brazil's President Vargas for El Jefe, an ornamental Brazilian Army sword with a scabbard of solid gold. Antenor is impressed by the Benefactor of the Fatherland. "Your father's an extraordinary man. I've never met anyone like him!" he gushes to Flor, who swells with pride.

T is fully aware of their affair, and of the Brazilian's pedigree and situation. Mayrink Veiga has no need of his fortune, nor of a post in his government, and he isn't looking to marry any member of El Jefe's family for their millions. Antenor is so rich, so powerful, so far removed from Hispaniola and T's meddling and spies, that when he asks Flor to marry him, she persuades herself to say yes. It feels like a triumph over misfortune. He *must* be truly in love with her. Even after everything she's been through, Flor hasn't lost her innocence.

El Jefe has taken careful stock of this new suitor. "A woman is nothing without a husband. You have to marry him," he tells her.

Why does she agree to the marriage? Deep down, a small voice is already murmuring that she doesn't love Antenor.

Then why?

Because he spoils her beyond reason?

To assert her independence?

To escape her father's control?

Or because, who knows, this new hand of cards might just turn out to be four aces?

* * *

T insists that the wedding ceremony take place in Ciudad Trujillo. The newlyweds exchange vows on May 1, 1944, in what virtually amounts to a state occasion. The wedding is headline news on the society page of the Brazilian newspaper *O Globo* and in every Dominican paper. In the photographs, Antenor is stiff and awkward, his expression almost irritated. Flor's smile is mechanical.

She's twenty-nine years old.

He's forty-two, and looks much older.

* * *

Flor had only one condition when she agreed to marry Mayrink Veiga: that she would continue her cultural work. Antenor agreed unhesitatingly to divide their time between Washington and Brazil.

But a few days after the wedding, the axe falls, as sharply and irrevocably as any guillotine blade. T revokes his daughter's diplomatic posting. Antenor denies it, but Flor knows that he and T, cut from the same cloth, have conspired behind her back to put an end to her career and reduce her to nothing more than a housewife again. If only she could break each link of the chains confining her, one by one, reducing them to useless bits of iron . . . maybe then, she would finally be free. But her life is not her own; it's men's business. She knows that. And it's utterly devastating.

Depressed and sick at heart, Flor moves to Rio. She was so proud of her work. Why did they take it away from her? Because a woman's place is with her husband. Because the sun rises and sets at El Jefe's command. Because Antenor is nothing but a macho swine, and he intends to take complete control of her life. Because Flor herself is nothing.

* * *

Flor, a foreigner whose scandalous reputation precedes her, and the heir's *fourth* wife, isn't exactly made welcome by the Mayrink Veiga family. She's quickly left to her own devices in Antenor's too-big penthouse with its vast terrace, in an overstaffed, extravagant household she has no idea how to run—a situation made exponentially worse by her lack of Portuguese. Antenor shows her virtually no affection besides the distracted kiss he gives her when he leaves in the morning. He does, however, control her every action, opening her letters and scrutinizing her every expenditure. Evenings consist of the inevitable public display, the eternal circus. And at night . . .

Flor starts to yearn for her nightly acrobatic sessions with Porfirio. At least he made her *body* feel good.

Her days drag on endlessly, the hours ticking slowly by, time seeming to expand. This is far from the life Flor has dreamed of. She begins to focus on a single thought, which rapidly becomes an obsession: failure. She loses her appetite, picking listlessly at her food, pushing it around and around on the plate with her fork. Later, when everyone else is asleep, she sneaks into the kitchen and gorges herself. Then she locks herself away in her bathroom. The nameless something she has dreaded so much is back again, draining away her vitality, her health. She grows thinner and thinner until there's almost nothing left of her.

* * *

One day, Flor insists on visiting a Veiga family finca. She needs this, if only to pretend to herself for a few hours that she exists. When she goes to the stables, something comes back to life in her. She can already feel the wind in her hair, her hands gripping the reins, her calves tight against the horse's flanks.

She wants to gallop until she's breathless, until her body is exhausted.

She convinces Antenor to ride with her. Then, spurring her own mount, she takes off at a gallop and is immediately awash in forgotten sensation. The warm wind caresses her face, her legs pressing against the pureblood's flanks, her body melding with the saddle. A slight squeeze with her heels, a slight tightening of the reins, and the horse speeds up. *Faster!* She can hear Porfirio's horse behind her; she doesn't want him to catch up with her. *Faster, faster!* Breath short, heart pounding, Flor slows and stops, turning to look behind her. The blissful illusion shatters. It's only Antenor. He's a mediocre rider, even a poor one, trotting in her wake, his bald head sheltered by a Panama hat. Flor feels sorry for him. And for herself, too. Nostalgia, which rears its head at the slightest opportunity, shoots through her like a lightning bolt at the memory of the thrilling rides she used to take with Rubi. How they would gallop madly up the slopes, challenging one another with a glance. How beautiful the landscape was, the view of the rolling hills from the summit of the lomas. How Rubi would grasp her by the waist to help her down from the saddle, then hold her tightly in his arms and kiss her passionately. How her body would burn at his touch. How young they were.

Flor gasps for breath, realizing with shock just how deep a chasm the memory has gouged out inside her.

* * *

Flor has learned her lessons well. She knows exactly what to expect. Antenor is T, more or less, just a few years younger, and he controls an industrial empire instead of a country. He also rapidly reveals himself to be an unparalleled domestic tyrant. Latin down to his fingertips, sole captain of the ship, domineering, possessive, and jealous, he views Flor as a submissive little thing obliged to put up with his frequent infidelities—which he conducts in broad daylight without a hint of shame, even confiding in Flor about Helen, his American mistress, how unhappy she is, how she has just given him a bastard.

Flor lacks even the strength to put on a happy face in public. Nothing—not the Veiga family's private island, not the sumptuous wardrobe, not the priceless jewelry, not the lavish parties at which Antenor has the orchestra play the merengue for her—is enough to soothe her despair.

Washington, D.C.
September 1945

There is no choice. It's a question of survival, Flor knows. She absolutely must free herself from Mayrink Veiga's clutches. On the pretext of selling her apartment in Washington, she departs for the United States, duly chaperoned by her mother-in-law and one of Antenor's nieces—it's as if they think a single escort isn't enough to keep a wild, brazen thing like Flor in line. It would be absolutely unacceptable for the fourth Mrs. Mayrink Veiga to be seen out alone in the evening. Because she's Flor de Oro, El Jefe's daughter, and men are drawn to her like flies to honey.

The war is over, and the country is euphoric. Flor has kept in touch with her friends in the US capital, and all she has to do is make her presence known for the invitations to start streaming in. At one cocktail party, she makes the acquaintance of a charming American captain and talks with him long into the evening. He isn't a war hero, but he isn't far from being one, to judge by the rows of medals, including the Croix de Guerre, shining on his chest. Charles Edward Stehlin, his aura burnished by soldierly glamour, is a pilot who fought in France alongside the Free French Forces. He emanates an air of masculine adventurousness, refreshing to a young woman who spends all her time with rearguard politicians, diplomats, and intriguers.

France. Ah, la France. All she has to do is hear the country mentioned, and Flor is strolling the paths of the Luxembourg Gardens, sitting in a box at the Opéra, idling on the Champs-Elysées. She can't help but flirt. She needs to understand her own ability to charm, to prove to herself that she's just as attractive and bewitching as her husband's mistresses. She unleashes her smile, that wide, brilliant smile that lights up the room. Captain Stehlin feels the bite of the harpoon, but it's too late: he can't tear his eyes from that laughing, full-lipped mouth, those ocean-deep dark eyes. Flor's conversation is light and beguiling, switching from English to French with startling ease. She talks about the arts, Brazil, Mexico—anything but politics, a subject she carefully avoids. And Charles, a down-to-earth young officer trying to put the horrors of war out of his mind, finds himself utterly entranced. Someone murmurs to him that Flor is the wife of a Brazilian billionaire and the daughter of a dictator, but that only makes the game more exciting. Besides, this tropical flower gives every appearance of being free to do as she chooses.

Flor and Charles see each other again, and then again, enjoying each other's company. Charles, the son of an aristocratic Spanish mother and an American father, is seven years older than Flor, combining old-world sophistication with American modernity, a man of the world and an outdoorsman, an intellectual and an adventurer. It's a heady mixture, one that effortlessly outclasses Antenor and his millions.

Flor reluctantly leaves Washington and returns to Rio, her two chaperones clinging to her like shadows.

Where there's no love, there's nothing to hope for.
And there's no doubt about it now. Flor doesn't love Antenor any more than he loves her. Indeed, there's never been any question of love between them.
Flor has nothing left to lose.
Nothing to regret.
Especially not the failure of this fourth marriage.
She asks for a divorce. Antenor agrees without rancor. He even gives her a $30,000 diamond ring as a sort of reparation. The price of Flor de Oro. It's rather humiliating, actually. It

shows just how much Antenor regarded their marriage as a simple transaction—not to mention his desire to continue cordial relations with El Jefe, who, for his part, reimburses his former son-in-law for the premature divorce with cold hard cash. A favor for a favor. They really are two of a kind, T and Mayrink Veiga.

Flor has had enough of tyrants.

She'll be stronger than either of them. She'll take her revenge.

And, in her own inimitable way, she already knows how.

In November 1945, freed from her shackles, she leaves Rio behind and returns to the United States, the taste of whiskey already sweet on her lips.

NEW YORK – MEXICO
LATE 1945–1946

Flor checks into the Carlyle Hotel in Manhattan.
The telephone rings.
"It's Charles."
"Charles?"
"Charles Stehlin!"
"Here in New York? What a surprise!"
Before they hang up, Charles tells Flor jokingly that he supposes he'll have to sleep in the park, since he hasn't been able to find a hotel room. Flor bites her lip. Hesitates. Decides to be bold.
"Oh, Charles, really? I can't let you sleep outside in the cold! Come here; there's an empty bedroom in my suite."
"I accept, but with only honorable intentions!"

It's easy to earn a few dollars by selling an indiscretion to the press. There are always journalists on the prowl near the city's top hotels, ears pricked for scandal. Dolores, a young Hispanic maid, can't resist the temptation. Her boyfriend works as an errand boy for a newspaper owned by William Randolph Hearst, and they pay well, cash in hand, for any juicy tidbit. So Dolores spills the beans. After all, those rich people treat poor ones like her as if they were dirt, and since the occasion has presented itself, why not take advantage?
The papers quickly seize on the opportunity to mock Antenor, the Brazilian magnate cuckolded by the valiant American aviator. They praise the bravery of Flor de Oro, the only Dominican woman courageous enough to defy El Jefe and follow her heart. The whole business is painted with a golden sheen of romance,

a welcome touch in the complex social climate of postwar America. The newspapers cloak Flor in glamour, turning her into the fabulous Flor de Oro, mixed-race daughter of the Ogre of the Caribbean, whose drop of slave blood reminds her father of his plebeian roots.

Emilio García Godoy, Dominican consul and presidential spy, makes a full report to the Generalissimo. It's a slap in the face. Worse, an embarrassment. El Jefe goes mad with rage. Nothing makes him angrier than being savaged in the American press. He's convinced that Flor has criticized him openly. His own daughter, dishonoring him! She is, quite simply, a walking scandal. A few days later, the dutiful Godoy informs Flor that she's been disinherited. El Jefe has just caused a law to be passed in the Dominican Congress authorizing a father to disinherit his daughter if she brings shame on him.

Flor is stunned. She can't imagine how she could possibly have compromised the respectability of a man who publicly sports with girls younger than his daughter, who claims *droit de seigneur* over his whole country, a man whose mistresses and bastards are too numerous to be counted. How many high-society families has *he* dishonored by shamelessly pursuing their daughters?

It's a gut-punch, yet another humiliation, but Flor keeps her calm, refusing to be cowed. She knows how deeply she harms herself by letting anger and resentment swallow her up—the torrent of bile that engulfs her heart, destroying her fragile equilibrium—and so she resists. She contains the devastating fire raging inside her, tamps it down, extinguishes it. She will be stronger than El Jefe. She's not afraid of his wrath anymore. She has her own plans for the future.

* * *

Flor joins Charles Stehlin in Mexico and, on January 16,

1946, privately, euphorically, marries him. The newlyweds are in a mutual state of bliss. They're well aware of how different they are from one another. That they aren't, perhaps, a natural match. Yet they set about planning a life together with feverish excitement.

They will sell Flor's Washington apartment, they decide. With the proceeds—a fortune, probably—they'll buy a ranch in Mexico. A vast one in Oaxaca, or maybe Chiapas. Flor finds the Yucatán, with its Caribbean tang, especially appealing. She can imagine herself there already. An outdoor life! Cattle and horses, vaqueros, long rides across the deserted pampas, falling asleep under the stars to the nostalgic strains of a *ranchera*, campfires. And a dog. A big black one she'll name Coffee. With this adventurous new husband at her side, life seems full of glorious possibility again.

Everything is intoxicating. For every suggestion Charles makes, Flor makes an even more extravagant one, clapping her hands like a little girl on Christmas morning. There's a Technicolor film playing in her imagination, and the leading lady with a sombrero on her head and the wind in her hair isn't María Montez anymore, but Flor herself. And Charles is John Wayne or, even better, Gregory Peck . . .

In her exhilaration, it's as if Flor's a child again, or a character in an epic novel. She loses herself in daydreams and illusion, while her dream slowly sinks in the marshy swamp of reality.

That reality catches up to her when a buyer who insists on remaining anonymous shows interest in the Washington apartment through a proxy. Flor knows, beyond the shadow of a doubt, that the anonymous buyer is T. He purchases the apartment for peanuts—a cheap way of recovering the gift given to his daughter in 1943. A few weeks later, as if to taunt her, the Dominican military attaché moves into the place. When the business is over, Flor and Charles's dream hacienda has shrunk by several hectares.

El Jefe will never loosen his grip on the halter around Flor's neck.

He will never, ever leave her in peace.

* * *

On January 31, 1946, Eurico Gaspar Dutra is elected president of Brazil. It's all the radio and newspapers can talk about. That, and Dutra's friendship with T.

In October 1946, Flor learns from a newspaper article that a corvette sailing from Rio, purchased in Canada and christened the *Cristóbal Colón*, has arrived in the port of Ciudad Trujillo, loaded to the gills with mortars, rifles, and munitions produced by factories owned by the Veiga family. A profitable affair for the Brazilians and a crucial means for El Jefe, deprived of weaponry by the Americans, to show his independence. Further strengthening his country's ties to Brazil, T has even decided to replace French, the language all Dominicans study in their final year of school, with Portuguese. What better way for two friendly nations to understand one another?

Flor thinks back to the sword with the golden scabbard sent by General Dutra, then Minister of War in the government of President Getúlio Vargas, and delivered by Antenor, a pathetic echo of the Dominican medals given by T to Hermann Goering and delivered by Porfirio. It was a prelude to the pact between them. It occurs to Flor how they all used her: El Jefe, Ambassador Despradel, Mayrink Veiga, Dutra. An entente, an arms trade, and her a pawn in the middle of it all, her marriage a seal on their alliances.

It was all there, right before her eyes, and despite the blatancy of the maneuvering, she saw nothing. Once again she was nothing but a piece on El Jefe's chessboard, quickly played, quickly sacrificed, quickly forgotten.

Flor is angry at herself for being so childishly naïve—for *still* being so, despite everything. Always forgetting the lessons life has taught her. But she and El Jefe can never be evenly matched.

Gritting her teeth, she forces down the murderous thoughts.

She summons up the courage to tell Charles everything. He feels sorry for her, while at the same time the vastness of the gulf separating them is driven home. His wife's world is utterly foreign to him.

* * *

Flor and Charles don't find the Mexican hacienda they've been dreaming of.

Charles, a man genuinely and deeply committed to the cause of freedom, is no weekend warrior for the cause. He spent several years of his life fighting to rid the world of a dictator. The thought of owing his new life to money shelled out by the man the press calls the Ogre of the Caribbean weighs heavily on him. Morally, it's unacceptable. To agree to such a momentous compromise, he would have to be madly in love. He wonders if he really is. He wonders that more and more often, in fact, as Flor, with her diamonds and mink stoles, continues to behave like a spoiled child. Will she really be able to adapt to the rough-and-tumble life he wants? Will she be happy without her society parties and posh restaurants? And, most importantly, does she truly love him? The heady passion of their first few months together gives way to doubt, and their relationship fizzles out in a series of disappointments. Very quickly, Charles concludes that he's just one more whim in the capricious life of T's daughter.

The Dominican ambassador to Mexico cuts in. Flor knows him well; it's Ramón Brea Messina, her second husband. El Jefe doesn't approve of her plans at all, Ramón tells her. The threat is clear, and Charles realizes that they will never be free. It's the last straw. Nothing solid can be built on such a shaky foundation.

The dreams of a hacienda evaporate.

Quick marriage, intense emotional turmoil, quick divorce.

Charles goes off to forge a life in Argentina, taking his dreams of an outdoor life with him. Flor departs for Paris, the city she loves most, and where she feels most at home.

Does she have even an ounce of regret over this fifth husband? They had a lot of fun together, while it lasted. She's left with a faint bitter taste in her mouth, the sense of an extraordinary adventure cut short before it could begin.

Flor will pick up her life again, post-banishment by El Jefe, in France.

A whole ocean between them. It's exactly what she needs.

Paris
May 1947

It was here that Flor's marriage to Porfirio underwent its death throes. She remembers how she walked out on him, on the convenient pretext of seeing to some family business on the island. How, despite his pleas, she never came back. How many years has it been? Almost ten. An eternity.

She can sense Rubi everywhere. She's heard about his divorce from that actress, the French woman with the big nose, and there are rumors that he's about to marry again, to the richest woman in the United States, the heiress of a tobacco magnate. There are also rumors that Doris Duke bought him from the French woman like a prize stallion, with a check for the tidy sum of $1 million.

A million dollars. The price of Rubi, relegated to the category of an expensive whim. It's all people can talk about.

This isn't a healthy place for Flor. That reality is drummed home for her with every step she takes. Paris was a bad idea. Worse, a mistake. She can't stop thinking about him here. About the man he's become. Has he aged well? Is he still as handsome as he looks in the magazine photos? Would she still find him attractive? She looks at her reflection in the shop windows as she passes: her angular silhouette; her hair, tamed through copious use of pomade; her smile, as brilliant as ever. In spite of the years and the disappointments and the slings and arrows life has thrown at her, she doesn't think she looks too bad. Thirty-two years old. She's no longer a self-conscious high-school girl, or a young Dominican woman humiliated by a cheating husband. She's Flor de Oro Trujillo, a woman of the world whose father is rich and powerful, a woman who's experienced a great deal, whom the vagaries of fate have buffeted and battered, but who is unafraid of the future. Thirty-two years old, her whole life still ahead of her. She glances at her reflection in the window again, defiant. She'll go for a drink at the Ritz tonight. Who knows what might be waiting for her there . . .

But first, she decides to visit Benito Pardo, one of her old Parisian friends, vaguely assigned to the Dominican embassy as a sort of fixer, most probably a lobbyist on El Jefe's behalf.

Benito welcomes Flor with undisguised pleasure, lavishing her with compliments. To her it's the same pussyfooting as always, a kind of schizophrenic dual reality that engulfs her in every situation like this: is Benito sincerely glad to see his friend Flor de Oro, or is it T's daughter he's flattering? It's impossible to separate the two, so Flor makes the best of it. This is made slightly easier by the fact that she's able to glean a few tidbits about Porfirio.

"He's been minister plenipotentiary to Rome since last year. He speaks of you often," Benito confides. "Last time I saw him—it was only a few weeks ago—he talked nostalgically about your years together."

Flor is lapping up Benito's words, but she shrugs with feigned indifference. "Ah, well, you never forget your first love," she says coolly. "We were so young. I think about him from time to time myself. But it would be hard to forget all his shady business, you know, his affairs. He's getting married again, I hear?"

"Oh, that! It's quite a story. I'm not sure Porfirio's completely in control of his own life."

Flor laughs nervously. "His own impulses, you mean!"

"Only the rich get richer, as they say," Benito smiles.

So Rubi's in Italy. Flor can breathe easier knowing there's no chance of bumping into him on the Champs-Elysées. Still, she leaves Benito's place feeling reinvigorated. All it took was a few words. The scar has reopened, just a bit.

* * *

"May I buy you a drink?"

Perched on a stool, elbows on the bar, Flor looks up, smiling automatically. The invitation, issued in English, is a frank one, leaving no doubt as to the gentleman's intentions. He's nice-looking, if you like the Irish type; Flor has noticed the reddish hairs on the backs of his hands. He looks her straight in the eye with the self-assurance of a man unafraid of being rebuffed. He leans toward her slightly, a vague inclination of his upper body, like a prelude.

The soft lighting of the Ritz bar, which has become known as a favorite haunt of American expatriates, whether soldiers, diplomats, or spies, creates an intimate, mellow atmosphere, just right for tete-a-tetes of all kinds.

Flor reaches into her purse and extracts a pack of cigarettes and a gold lighter engraved with her initials—a gift from Porfirio she's never been able to part with. She's used to men looking at her. There have been so many of them. She picks up her glass nonchalantly and takes a long swallow. Without the least timidity, without false shyness, with a hint of brazenness, even a sort of childlike naughtiness, she takes in the man's appearance: red hair cut short, steel-blue eyes with laugh lines at the corners, square jaw. It's a symmetrical, well-balanced face, strong-willed and determined. His shoulders are broad, his torso solid and powerful. He's the kind of man women find attractive.

Get out of my way, she's tempted to say, but she's learned to think before she speaks, and after all, the whole point of coming here was not to be alone. She gazes down into her glass again, swirling the liquor with a sinuous movement of her wrist, taking a long drag on her cigarette at the same time. Then she exhales a long ribbon of smoke and looks back up at him through her lashes, seductive and acquiescent. Finally she gives him her most irresistible smile, her breath already heavy with alcohol fumes.

"Thanks. I'll have a whiskey."
"On the rocks?"
"On the rocks."
"Spanish?" he asks.
"Cuban." Concealing her identity is like putting on a suit of armor. She's sick of all these men desiring her for what she never chose to be, so she's become an expert in being someone else. Their conversation is desultory; he's there to negotiate for the repatriation of American soldiers. "And you?" A widow, traveling for pleasure, Flor replies distractedly. A simple question is already preoccupying her: will it be her hotel room, or the American's?

* * *

He's an attentive lover, gentle and skilled. Flor refuses to be angry with herself for sleeping with him; the pleasure he's given her is a balm to her wounded self-esteem. She wakes up rested and relaxed the next morning, in a room on the third floor of a modest hotel in the first arrondissement, next to his big, comforting body.

They arrange to meet that same night for dinner, a stroll along the Seine, a jazz concert. The perfect plan for a romantic interlude. Both of them know their time together will be brief. He's made no secret of the fact that he's happily married back in the States. So, after they make love, in the privacy of pillow-talk, they both let their masks fall. He works for the CIA. Flor knew it; the Ritz is crawling with spies. Neither is he surprised to find out that she's T daughter. He's seen her photo in the papers. They both laugh about it.

As Flor toys lazily with the tawny curls on her lover's chest, he murmurs casually, "Rubirosa's in Rome. A colleague of mine at the American embassy there says he doesn't want to marry Duke anymore. He's not exactly proud of the way she bought him from Darrieux. It has nothing to do with love; it's all about money. A sordid thing, really. Rubirosa's shouting from the rooftops that he's only ever loved one woman. Can you guess who that is?"

Flor flinches. She feels an overwhelming rush of adrenaline. An electric shock runs down her spine, and her breath catches, despite herself. The American's keen eyes bore into hers.

"That might be what attracted me to you, actually. And I sure as hell don't regret it," he adds gently, stroking her hip. "Rubirosa's telling everyone he should never have divorced you, that he should remarry you, that kind of thing."

Flor's finger freezes where it's been trailing through his chest hair. She suppresses a grimace of pain. It feels like a fire's been kindled in her belly, the blood pounding at the pulse point in her neck. She closes her eyes at this sudden reappearance of her old sickness. She tries to control her emotions, to keep her face impassive. The American's lips twitch in the hint of a smile.

"I met my wife in middle school, you know. I play around a bit—I'm not made of stone—but I always go back to her. That's how strong a first love is. You should never give up on the dreams of youth. I think, my dear, that all you'd have to do is beckon and . . . "

He knows he's pouring poison into Flor's ear and, observing the tension in her face, curses himself for it. He isn't without a heart, or a conscience, after all, and both of them are screaming that this is a dirty business, what he's just done. *Never get emotionally involved.* He's been sent here on a job: to keep Rubirosa from marrying the American Tobacco Company heiress—and thus to keep T from acquiring a stake in his country's economy. That's his mission. A twisted one, to be sure, but he's learned not to question orders. Flor de Oro's ending up in his bed was an unexpected bonus, one he's allowed himself to indulge in because he was told to influence her any way he chose. Pained and slightly guilty, the agent kisses the top of Flor's head.

She has to see Rubi again.

She has to know if what the American is saying is true.

What does she have to lose?

She tries to examine her memories of their romance with a clear head, but she knows she's on the brink of succumbing again. Even with all his faults, the lying and the cheating, Porfirio seems infinitely preferable to the spineless men she keeps meeting. She's angry at herself for her own weakness, her cowardice, but she's always known it: he's her destiny.

There's something decadently romantic about falling back in love.

In her heart, Flor is already in Rome.

The American pulls her slim body to him again.

Mission accomplished.

Rome
May 1947

Dear Porfirio,
I arrived in Rome a few days ago. I'm staying at the Majestic. Someone told me you were posted here. Shall we meet up at some hole-in-the-wall bar in Trastevere and reminisce about the good old days over a bottle of chianti?
Fleur

Flor is no match for this fresh temptation. She's run straight toward what she yearns for, without any further reflection, without guilt, without hesitation. The irresistible force pushing her toward Rubi is like a strong wind reviving the smoldering embers of her love, making her feel throbbingly alive. The door she'd closed on that missing part of herself has been blown open, the part that has refused to die, the part she can no longer ignore.

When Rubirosa receives Flor's note, eager to believe that their paths have crossed again by some happy chance, he thanks the fates for this wonderful accident. Of course he'd love to see his Fleur again. He often thinks of her with tenderness, even a certain nostalgia. She must be so different now. The memories come flooding back, melting his heart. Flor is home. She's the island of his birth, the musical accent of Santo Domingo, the silky-sweet taste of mangoes, the rhythm of the merengue, the mutual remembrance of their French education. Flor is his first love, the link to his vanished youth.

They have so much history together. He remembers the first time their eyes met, over El Jefe's shoulder, at the port of Santo

Domingo, in a look already heavy with uncontrollable desire. The way they flirted shamelessly right beneath the noses of all those graybeards and dowagers. Their standoff with T. How she blew him away with her prowess on horseback, and her triumphant laugh. Their rainy wedding day, their escape to New York, their travels. The good days and the bad. He's curious to see the woman she's become. He's heard about all her marriages and divorces, even kept track of them, not without a hint of jealousy-tinged spite.

Without hesitation, Porfirio has an enormous bouquet of red roses delivered to the Majestic. Flor can hear the smile in his voice when he telephones her. She tries to control the fluttering of her heart, but in vain. Her own voice cracks slightly when she speaks to him, but she quickly collects herself. Feverish impatience sweeps through her. Rubi is the freshness of youth, the exhilaration of adventure, the sweetness of forbidden fruit—and the certainty of scandal. She finds herself literally breathless with emotion at the idea of seeing him again. Desire flares in her belly. The old wound is fully open. There's no pulling back from the brink now, she knows. She's going to let herself fall. There's no use fighting it. Suddenly, only one thing matters. Rubi must be hers again.

* * *

There's a feeling of vertigo in their first meeting, a giddy excitement mingled with a sense of irrevocable destiny. In the hotel lobby, Porfirio clasps Flor's arms at the elbows, smiling the old roguish smile. She starts to tremble. He doesn't speak, just bends toward her slightly and looks deeply into her eyes, into her soul. Then he kisses her on the cheek, very near the corner of her mouth. The kiss is tender, almost furtive—and carefully planned, its placement calculated down to the millimeter. A kiss that opens a door. He does it deliberately, and they both know what it means. Flor sways beneath the impact of a flood of emotion that crystallizes instantly into pure desire, and she struggles to keep her composure. Porfirio steps aside to let her walk through the door first. But not quite far enough aside. Deliberately. Their arms brush slightly. Their hips touch. An electric jolt sizzles through Flor. She looks down, repressing a smile. It's intoxicating, like dancing on a clifftop overlooking a choppy sea.

Flor slips her arm through Porfirio's, her hand resting lightly on his forearm. She can feel the hard muscle beneath the silk of his sports coat, even through her leather gloves. His shoulders are still broad and sturdy, his back straight, his bearing regal. He still has the beauty mark on his left cheek, the same full lips, the same dimple in his chin. She sees, too, with a painful jolt of emotion, the first threads of silver in his dark hair, the laugh lines around his eyes and mouth—this is the face of a man who's led a mostly easy life. His charm is wholly intact, touched—as it always has been—with a whisper of sex. It's what has always driven women mad for him, Flor included. She can't keep from inwardly cursing the strength of her attraction to him, her helplessness in the face of it. She's acutely aware of every point where their bodies are touching. Their steps immediately fall into the same, unforgotten rhythm. A moment or more two more, and Flor abandons any wish to be freed of her attraction to Porfirio. All that remains is the bone-deep need to belong to him again. She feels alive in a way she hasn't in a very long time.

Porfirio observes her as they head silently for the banks of the Tiber. Flor is one of those women who grows more attractive with age. Her bearing and movements have become more elegant. She's truly beautiful, an exotic beauty tinged with melancholy, muted by sadness. Her body is still slim and lithe. Her clavicles stand out sharply beneath the neckline of her blouse, a sight that touches him unexpectedly. And she still has that smile, that wide smile so irresistible to men, the one that turns her into a siren, entrancing them. It's almost indecent, in fact, that smile of hers. Porfirio has to admit the obvious: his Fleur is entrancing. Graceful neck, straight spine, the curving small of her back still ravishing. Her face has lost the roundness of youth; her features are more chiseled now. She's smoothed her unruly curls, setting off her domed forehead, high cheekbones, delicate nose, finely-cut lips. There's something untamed in her, something wild and fierce, so different from the sophisticated, artificial women he's around every day. She's like a coral gemstone from their home island. Golden, warm, enticing. The ghosts of all his fleeting love affairs vanish like smoke. Next to this tropical flower of his, that boozing Duke woman, with her pointed nose and protruding chin, pales into insignificance.

"Fleur," he says. "You look incredible. Beautiful."

Flor smiles, delighted. Porfirio meant the compliment sincerely. She can see it in his eyes.

Porfirio, always so silver-tongued around women, asks her a series of silly questions. His voice, an echo of those long-ago days of passion, suggests untold possibility, chipping away at Flor's resolution. She makes a few idle remarks of her own, but is unable to keep her voice from shaking. The pretense of small talk is ridiculous, and they both know it: a thin shell just waiting to be cracked. There is something undeniable between them, an intimate knowledge of one another, and always that desire, never quenched, always on a low simmer. After a few more moments of chit-chat, the masks fall. There's a glint in her eye when she looks at him. He smiles knowingly. Neither of them are mistaken.

They know.

A silence settles between them, one laden with desire.

* * *

It's in a narrow bed in an anonymous little hotel in Trastevere that Flor and Porfirio seal their reunion, both of them ravenous for each other, their hunger fueled by memories of long-ago passion. After a momentary hesitation, quickly banished, Flor loses any hint of shyness; in Porfirio's arms there's no room for coherent thought. Their skin feels aflame where their bodies touch, and Flor wants to believe Porfirio only experiences that heat when he's with her. She feels once again, at last, unique.

Gasping for breath, she presses her body to his with all her strength, like a person touching the riverbank after a treacherous crossing, with the relief of knowing they're home again at last. In his haste to undress her, Porfirio rips a button from her blouse, and it rolls under the bed. With a rush of emotion, he rediscovers the protruding bones where her clavicles meet her shoulders. Flor briefly remembers her torn wedding dress, but the thought quickly evaporates in the heat of passion.

The erotic charge between them is as unquenchable as it ever was, keeping them awake through the night. Flor allows herself to sink into the intimacy between them, the beautiful familiarity between their bodies.

She knows him inside and out. She knows his deepest sexual secrets. His insatiable lusts, his attentiveness, the way he moves, the way he alternates between gentleness and roughness. She's forgotten nothing: his broad torso, the scar on his shoulder, the smell of his skin, the force of his thrusts, his tight embrace, the weight of his body on hers.

She loses herself in him, tracing the old scar with her finger and finding another, thinks of how much time has passed, and yet has shrunk to nothing in just a few hours.

Porfirio has become even more of a master in the art of pleasuring women. He can't keep his thoughts from drifting to his other lovers, the women he's had, the ones he's still to conquer. But Fleur is a different story. He knows all her tender places, all her weak spots. The body has a long memory, and his has retained the imprint of Flor, unshakeable, indelible.

It's all very simple.
For a brief moment, the two of them are one.

* * *

Porfirio has rented a speedboat and reserved a large room in a hotel on the southern tip of Capri. The champagne flows endlessly, and the bed is immense. Their bougainvillea-draped terrace has a view of the Faraglioni rising from the blue depths of the sea. They walk hand-in-hand through narrow cobbled streets, browse shop windows, lunch on grilled fish washed down with cold glasses of Vermentino in a little trattoria. It's the life with Porfirio Flor used to dream of. Life is a trickster, she thinks, springing surprises on you when you least expect it. She wears a wide-brimmed hat to ward off the hot sun, and it seems like Porfirio never stops smiling at her, with a smile that takes her back to the days when he was just an ambitious young lieutenant in T's personal guard. Gazing at him, she's flooded with a tenderness unlike anything she's ever felt for him. He really is a beautiful man. She's never met anyone handsomer. And she knows she'll never stop loving him.

Porfirio is watching Flor, too, through half-lidded eyes. She's beaming. She's changed, his Fleur, and for the better. The flush of renewed love and his irresistible attraction to her leave him disarmed. No other woman can ever be what Flor is to him. His country, his beloved tropics, his first love, his wife before God. No one else has ever been able to make him forget her. They defied El Jefe together. They flouted convention. They moved mountains.

Together, they're invincible.

Even the smallest remarks and gestures bring renewed intimacy, and hope flares in both of them. Flor dreams of starting over from scratch, of forgetting everything that separated them: the nightclubbing, the gambling, the women. Especially the women. Bursting with optimism, she convinces herself that it's really possible this time, because they both want it.

They reminisce, giggling like children over how careless, how irreverent they'd been back then. Without bitterness, Porfirio tells Flor that she shouldn't have abandoned him in Paris like that, shouldn't have ignored his pleas. "You didn't understand," she retorts. But there was nothing to understand, really. She was just a girl, naïve and capricious. And he was an incorrigible Don Juan.

Their feelings are far too powerful for either of them to resist.
They're lying in bed, Flor's body curled around his, when he says the word.
Remarriage.
The word is like infinite, dazzling sunlight.
It was always going to be this way.

* * *

Word of the affair gets out, of course. That was the whole reason for ensnaring Flor in the first place. An American photographer follows them all over Capri, rapidly joined by an Italian colleague. It's a delicious morsel, then a whole feast for the scandal-sheets, with a postwar public hungry for light-hearted salaciousness. Snapshots telling the tale make their way to T via the Dominican embassy. And the American tobacco heiress learns of her fiancé's infidelity by reading about it in a New York paper.

Flor and Porfirio, bent on remarrying, don't care in the least.

Rome
May 1947

"Flor de Oro?"

Flor recognizes the nasal voice immediately, despite the crackle of static on the telephone line. It's hard, flat, threatening. It cuts. Decrees. Orders. Suddenly, despite the spring sunshine flooding her suite, Flor feels as if the blood has drained from her body. Pain. She can't move. Sweat beads on her forehead, her hands start to shake, and her heart thumps so hard she can feel it in her fingertips.

"Haven't you learned anything from past mistakes? You keep embarrassing yourself—and dishonoring me at the same time."

It's a rhetorical question, no response needed. Swamped by a wave of all-too-familiar emotion—shame, tinged with both hatred and the instinctive urge to yield—Flor can't speak. Silent, paralyzed by fear, she's already preparing for defeat. The last of her hopes for a new life are brutally dashed by T's next words.

"I forbid it. Do you hear me, Flor de Oro? I forbid you to reunite with Rubirosa. You will stop this circus immediately and return to Ciudad Trujillo. You will leave Rubirosa to live his own life. Listen to your own sense of propriety—if you even have one!"

Flor takes a deep breath, trying to calm the pounding of her heart. "We . . . we've found our way back to each other, and we . . . we're going to get married again . . . " she says, summoning all her courage. Her voice is weak, quavering, as she tries to hold back the tears. Suddenly the whole plan seems utterly ridiculous.

Then, more firmly: "Porfirio is the love of my life. I'm sure of that now. And—"

"Nonsense! This is just another of Rubirosa's dalliances! Remarriage is out of the question. I formally refuse my consent. You will not make the same mistake twice. This 'rekindling' is just another illusion conjured up by your sick mind."

El Jefe goes on and on, ridiculing the couple's renewed love, reducing it to a vulgar sexual escapade in a few hard words hurled blindly, spitting on Flor's hopes for a new life with Rubi. And in the end, perhaps he's right.

"Don't let your feelings overwhelm your rationality, or you're going to get badly hurt again, Flor de Oro. And if personal reasons aren't enough for you, there are others, greater ones than you. Political reasons."

Politics. A word perfectly calculated to burst the bubble of Flor's romantic dreams. How could she have been so stupid? El Jefe doesn't need to elaborate on the strategic importance of inserting a pawn into the heart of the American tobacco lobby. Or on the potential financial advantages of his own plantations exporting tons of the precious brown leaves to the Duke family factories. There are millions of dollars on the line. There can be no question of some sappy little fling, even one with his own silly daughter, interfering with his plans. Rubirosa will marry Miss Duke and her cigarette factories. The fiancée's assets are simply too abundant to pass up.

A heavy silence stretches over the telephone line. Flor's throat is too tight to speak. Her whole body is trembling, but of course El Jefe can't see that.

"Have I made myself understood, Flor de Oro?"

Silence.

"Flor de Oro? I repeat, a remarriage—even a simple affair—between you and Rubirosa is out of the question. I'll send someone to retrieve you if I have to."

The last thing El Jefe needs right now is for the Duke woman, humiliated, to break off her engagement. Used to giving orders that are then immediately carried out, T has remained perfectly calm.

And what about Flor de Oro in all of this? T's conscience doesn't bother him even a little. Flor doesn't matter. She bounces from man to man. She's already done it—what, four? No—*five* times. (He's forgotten, conveniently, that it was he who forced her hand every time.) Flor de Oro, like every other Dominican and every other member of his family, has no choice but to submit to his will.

He hangs up.

Slowly, Flor removes her earrings, wipes off her lipstick with the back of her hand, takes off her high-heeled shoes. The mirror shows her the grotesque image of a sad clown.

Broken by El Jefe. Again.

* * *

There's no appealing T's ultimatum. Flor is resigned. Shattered. She knows she can only give in. It's as if she doesn't even have the right to feel cheated, really, because that's how her and Porfirio's relationship has always been. Doomed to failure.

Porfirio has received the same warning at the Dominican legation, along with a series of thinly veiled threats. He must cease all contact with Flor de Oro immediately. Having been one of T's henchmen himself, he's better placed than most to know the cost of disobeying one of El Jefe's orders. And so Rubirosa throws in the towel without even a pretense of resistance. Strength of will has never been foremost among his personality traits. He remembers their disastrous time in New York. He's not ready to go through that hell again. Living without money? He and Flor are both too old for that. And after all, he reasons with himself, Doris may not be a beautiful woman, but she's pleasant enough, she knows everyone who counts, and she's extremely rich. Almost as rich as T. And, perhaps most compellingly, Miss Duke has decided to give Rubirosa to herself as a gift. It might be a fantasy, but the simple fact is that the heiress has the money to indulge herself this way. So, if it also happens to suit El Jefe . . .

Pragmatically, Porfirio gives in. A shame for Flor. He scribbles a vague little note of regret.

> *My dear Fleur,*
> *I've had to leave unexpectedly for Brussels. El Jefe has a plan, and we can't go against it; you know as well as I do how dearly that could cost us. We owe ourselves the truth: that our love is in the past, and there it must stay. We've got to move on.*
> *Capri will forever be a magical interlude that I'll remember fondly. I'll always cherish the memory of these few days together. They'll be our beautiful secret.*
> *I wish you the best.*
> *You'll always be my beloved, my only, Fleur.*
> *All my love, Porfirio*

What a coward! With a sense that things were always going to turn out this way, Flor tears up the note. A single tear splashes on the paper, ink and heartbreak running together in black smears. What a waste. Any disappointment she feels is aimed at herself alone. What did she expect? As if *she* could inspire unconditional, unyielding love! It was just a fleeting instant of glorious madness. How could she have been stupid enough to believe it was real? She acted like a teenage girl drunk on romantic dreams. But really, deep down, didn't she *know* this was how it would end?

Love stories like that only happen in Hollywood. But this? This was all a foregone conclusion. In real life, there are puppets—weak, cowardly, submissive men and women—and there are those who pull the strings. Rubi is a puppet. Soft and spineless, with no dignity and no courage. And so is she.

Flor has never really mattered, and she knows it. Compared to Porfirio's fear of El Jefe or the Duke woman's millions, even though she was the first woman Porfirio ever truly loved, despite everything they have in common, all the memories, the island blood that flows in their veins, she doesn't matter. And so she steps aside.

She let herself be swept away by a fantasy that went up in smoke. All very predictable. Just another disillusionment to add to her collection.
And, well . . . they did have a lot of fun. Capri will always be a delicious slap in the face from Flor to all those women who throw themselves so shamelessly at Rubi.

Flor learns the rest of the story by reading the newspapers.
Doris Duke hasn't given up on her precious conquest, and quickly gets over the sting of Rubirosa's infidelity. She wants him, at any price. Porfirio rejoins his fiancée in Paris and marries her at the Dominican embassy on September 1, 1947. Doris Duke gives him a house in Paris's sixteenth arrondissement as a wedding gift, and El Jefe rewards his former son-in-law's obedience by making him ambassador to Argentina. And the Dominican Republic prepares to sign a series of lucrative contracts to export tobacco to the United States.

For Flor, this latest chapter of her life has the bitter taste of déjà vu. She remembers the armaments contracts signed by El Jefe and her Brazilian ex-husband.
It would be funny if it weren't so pathetic.
It would be funny if it weren't her real life.
The time has come to draw a line under her relationship with Rubi, Flor decides. Her memories of the interlude in Capri will eventually fade, like the last wisps of a bad dream. She can't know, yet, that her first husband will forever remain an unhealed wound.
Defeated and humiliated, full of regret, Flor de Oro leaves Rome for Paris. She could deal with T's fatherly anger; it will

pass. But his indifference, his lack of love—that casts a shadow over her whole life, permeating her soul, crushing, destroying.

In an office at Langley Air Force Base in Virginia, an Irish-American man is given a severe dressing-down. Does he feel the slightest bit guilty?

A woman's breakup is no business of his.

Paris
1949–1952

Paris in the early 1950s is a merry place, the war relegated to the status of a bad memory. After a period of despair and isolation, Flor renews some old friendships from the era of Porfirio's embassy job and their life in Neuilly, though she avoids diplomatic circles like the plague. Instead, she begins to frequent the city's more Bohemian spaces, where artists and intellectuals of all nationalities mingle freely. At thirty-five, Flor is determined to shake off her father's lingering influence. She's managed to put an ocean between them, and, after five failed marriages, she's bent on taking full advantage of her liberty, on grabbing life by the horns. *Here I am*, she wants to shout. *I'm Flor de Oro! I am who I am! I drink whiskey like a man and daiquiris like a woman of the world! I like seedy clubs and posh hotel bars! I dance like a daughter of the pueblo and waltz like a Viennese countess!*

She quickly becomes popular, a drink in one hand, a cigarette in the other, and a wide smile on her lips, always ready to break into laughter. The men don't fail to take notice of her, and Flor, after all, isn't made of stone . . .

* * *

Paul Louis Frédéric Guérin is a handsome young man a few years younger than Flor, with an easygoing temperament that might even be called wishy-washy. Flor's dalliance with him turns out to have more staying power than the others. Paul really is very good-looking, and, though a bit dim, he's harmless, nice, and uncomplicated.

The Guérins are a model middle-class French family, Catholic and conservative, residents of a well-heeled neighborhood on the east side of Paris. Their money was made in perfume, an industry emblematic of the country. Three sons, one daughter, and a demure mother completely in the shadow of her autocratic and domineering husband.

Paul works for the family business during the day and spends his evenings and nights with Flor, who flourishes in this easy relationship where no one has to compromise—all the more so because she is quickly adopted by the Guérins. They know exactly who she is, of course, but whatever their feelings about it, they don't say anything, and the lovebirds are left alone.

That is, until the day the Dominican ambassador informs Flor that El Jefe would like to know the wedding date. Flor is stunned. No matter how far away she is, even all the way in Europe, even in Paris, she's within reach of her father's tyranny. He hasn't relaxed his hold on her at all. He still has every intention of controlling her life.

Flor confides in Paul. His reaction is lukewarm. Their current situation suits him perfectly. He hasn't been considering marriage any more than she has.

Monsieur Guérin, however, is thrilled. His son, engaged to a woman with a pedigree as long as her arm! The daughter of one of the richest men on the planet, the legendary El Jefe, and the ex-wife of the no-less-storied Rubirosa! Maybe he sees the whole thing as a promising business opportunity. At any rate, he's one hundred percent in favor of the marriage, and evidently happy for his religious convictions to take a back seat. The businessman's eternal philosophy: when money is involved, don't ask too many questions.

So at the age of thirty-five, Flor takes her sixth husband. T gifts her the usual furnished apartment in Paris and a check for $25,000, more or less the going rate. Flor is happy, with the happiness of the schoolgirl she was at Bouffémont, to belong to a bourgeois French family, where everything is tasteful and nothing is tacky.

The newlyweds honeymoon in Cannes, and it's in their suite at the Hôtel Martínez that Paul confesses. Monsieur Guérin is a real dictator, he says (Flor opts not to point out the irony of this remark), who has been controlling Paul by confining him to a low-ranking position in the family business and paying him a pathetically low salary. He doesn't know how he will support his new wife. It's a good thing El Jefe is generous, he says. Flor is alarmed. The $25,000 dowry isn't going to last them long.

Monsieur Guérin quickly proves to be just as mercenary as Paul has said. His son has married an heiress (whom he doesn't know has been disinherited), and like any businessman worth his salt, he expects to benefit from the alliance. Figures in hand, he proposes a trade with T: "perfume for tobacco," a win-win arrangement. El Jefe, who doesn't even like being given advice, much less being told what to do, especially by some foreign small businessman, takes umbrage. His reply is brief and to the point: "I'm the one who proposes things. And I have no desire to do business with the Guérins, or with France."

Informed of the exchange by her husband, Flor has to swallow the pill, however bitter it might be. She knows that T's flat refusal is his way of punishing her for a marriage he doesn't approve of, even though it was he who forced her into it. T still has a thousand ways of harming her, no matter where she is. He can keep her from being happy. Tighten the leash around her neck. He's done it so many times. And now he's just won for the umpteenth time.

Monsieur Guérin, who was already picturing himself among the world's top international businessmen, is fiercely disappointed. He takes his anger out on his son, by demoting him to an even lower-ranking position and reducing his salary accordingly. Paul, no rebel, goes along with it all uncomplainingly.

Flor is appalled by her husband's weakness, but at the end of the day, he's simply a reflection of her: a plaything, a doormat, a punching bag. Forever under the thumb of a tyrant who never tires of toying with people.

Their divorce is inevitable.

1952. *Exeunt* Husband Number Six.

* * *

Returning to the Dominican Republic is out of the question. El Jefe will only stick her in a cage again, as he's so skilled at doing. The ties that bind them, woven of love, jealousy, frustration, guilt, and hatred, soaked in seawater, toughened by salt, dried hard in the sun, can't be untied. The only solution is to cut them completely, so that nothing remains.

Flor is too old to be told what to do. Almost forty. It feels like a yawning chasm is opening up before her. She's digging in hard, sinking her nails into the wall of the ravine and doing her best not to fall, but she knows she can't keep from sliding down that slippery slope into the dark forever. So she decides to make the best of what remains of her life.

Alone, without work or money, Flor remains in Paris—a Paris that no longer bears any resemblance to the one of her youth. In the eyes of society columnists she becomes the vivacious, the tempestuous, the fabulous Flor de Oro, veteran of multiple marriages, rebellious daughter of the Ogre of the Caribbean.

In reality, however, she's beginning a descent into hell. A rootless life, a headlong rush to nowhere. Mired in alcohol abuse, the nightlife, and an endless series of parties, Flor begins to frequent less-than-respectable places and the sort of men that go with them: petty criminals, drug dealers, weekend gangsters. She throws herself headlong into any new adventure that happens to cross her bumpy path. She drinks more and more, chain-smokes, racks up a series of flirtations, stormy relationships, and passing flings with men only interested in her last name. Her reputation, already tarnished, blackens inexorably until, all too soon, nothing remains of it. *Flor de Horror*, she nicknames her reflection in the mirror.

From one fleeting liaison to the next, from drinking binges to the debilitating hangovers that follow, Flor is simply drifting. Parisian life stopped being enchanting some time ago. She's drowning in debt. Complaints pile up. Like the one from the French viscount from whom she borrowed several thousand dollars and repaid with a bad check, who sends El Jefe a vaguely threatening letter demanding his money. Flor has, at last, wholeheartedly embraced the role of disobedient daughter, the one wasting her life, the one forever disappointing her father, trailing distress in her wake like a desperate cry for help.

Informed of the situation, T dispatches a trusted henchman to Paris: General Paulino Álvarez, a half-black giant feared by all Dominicans, nicknamed "Magic Eye"[20] because of a childhood accident that caused one of his eyes to be replaced by a glass one. Flor knows who he is, and she knows how deep his devotion to El Jefe runs. People even say he sleeps with his single eye open, in full military uniform including his boots, just in case T has need of him.

Magic Eye doesn't beat around the bush. The circus is over. It's time for Flor to return to the Dominican Republic. But she'll have to enter through the back door, since she won't exactly be a welcome guest.

It's thinly disguised as advice, but it's an order. Flor is under no illusions about that.

---

[20] General Anselmo Paulino Álvarez, "Magic Eye," one of Trujillo's right-hand men during the second half of his regime, developed an extensive network of informers throughout the Dominican Republic. Falling into disgrace, he was imprisoned and finally permitted to leave the country at the end of Trujillo's presidency.

Ciudad Trujillo
1952

Thirty-seven years old. Six marriages.

Six against three. Flor has beaten Porfirio in the matrimonial marathon. It's certainly the only area in which she's winning.

Her life is a fiasco, her future an oncoming disaster.

More than that, Flor is ill. She's spent too many years plagued by depression, neurasthenia, and eating disorders. She needs serious medical care, and she knows it.

El Jefe is right. It's time to go home. After all the years of wandering, all Flor wants now is to rest. And she wants to do it in her own country, at least for now. Exhausted and out of resources, she tries to convince herself that going home is her decision. What other choice is there? Adding insult to injury, once the decision is made, she's reduced to begging a plane ticket at the Dominican embassy, where they look at her with a mixture of compassion and scorn that cuts her to the quick.

* * *

When she lands in Ciudad Trujillo, it's a relief that no one is there to greet her. She'll keep out of the way of El Jefe, who doesn't even want to hear her name spoken, and take refuge with her mother, whom she hopes will ease her loneliness while she recovers. Aminta has already found a physician who's agreed to treat her daughter. Flor imagines an endless stream of antidepressants and vitamin cures, along with complete abstinence from alcohol, a balanced diet, and above all, rest. Lots and lots of rest.

But despite her mother's attentive and devoted presence, the reality is far harder to endure than Flor expected. It's like she's suspended in a void, in mourning for herself, waiting for a hypothetical return to T's good graces that doesn't come. Manuel de Moya, El Jefe's chief diplomat and lobbyist in the United States, has told her American friends that they aren't allowed to visit her. Flor shuttles back and forth between her mother's home in San Cristóbal and a modest rental house in Gazcue. The days of a personal chauffeur are in the past; Flor now travels via *guagua*[21] for a handful of *cheles*,[22] just another anonymous face among the chattering passengers. No one recognizes her, and if she's somewhat disappointed by this, it's also a relief. She's not anyone anymore. She has disappeared, been erased, disowned by the father who patiently, methodically destroyed her. She wasn't strong or brave enough to defy him, just like the millions of other Dominicans whose fates he holds in his clenched fist. Draped in an ever-present pall of fear, Ciudad Trujillo has become a cowering, lethargic place. No one dares to go out anymore, and they lack the heart to dance or make merry in this grim city, a city of dulled colors, muzzled words, forgotten laughter.

---

[21] *Guagua*: A public bus.
[22] *Chele*: A coin worth one hundredth of a Dominican peso, no longer in circulation today.

CIUDAD TRUJILLO
MARCH 1953

"H*ola, Señora.*"
Flor starts. She hadn't heard him approach. He's come up from behind to surprise her. Unsettled by the softness of his lips against her ear, intoxicated by the familiar scent of his eau de cologne—the same as always, Guerlain's Impériale, she turns her head slightly. And there he is, close enough to touch her shoulder, wearing a benign smile. As if nothing has happened. As if they just saw each other yesterday. Flor feels a surge of panic, her pulse speeding up. The sounds of the room around them fade away, the other guests' silhouettes blurring, as if the two of them are enveloped in a kind of enchanted bubble. "Papi," she murmurs in a little girl's voice that she can't keep from quivering. That one word is all she can manage as he brushes her cheek with his lips. She sways, as lightheaded as if she were drunk.

Is she back in T's good graces?
Can it really be as simple as that?

* * *

That morning, Doña Amelia Vicini herself—the Vicinis, one of the most powerful families in the country, are on a first-name basis with El Jefe—had come to personally deliver a message inviting Flor to a Trujillo family party at San Isidro Air Force Base, Ramfis's territory. Doña Amelia hadn't elaborated on the invitation, but had given Flor a knowing look.

Perplexed, Flor turned the card with its presidential insignia over and over in her hands. This was the first time in three years that she'd been invited to any kind of family event. In all that time, she hadn't been invited to any of her father's birthday parties, or New Year's Eve galas, or official ceremonies. Could this be the long-awaited thaw in her relationship with T? Flor couldn't help but be wary. *It could be a trap*, she thought. But she would go, because she couldn't decline even if she wanted to. An invitation from T was as good as an order. So, obediently, she put on her most elegant dress, applied her makeup with care, and went to San Isidro.

* * *

This afternoon, Flor feels as if she's floating on a cloud of happiness. Brothers, sister, uncles, aunts, cousins—she's gotten reacquainted with all of them, and it's a deliverance. El Jefe asks how she's been and listens placidly to her answer. They drink, eat, joke around like a real family, a world away from all those glitzy official receptions. When the party is over, T sends her home in a presidential limousine.

Infinitely relieved, almost euphoric, Flor can't hold back any longer, and proceeds to get drunk with a determination matched only by her joy. Waking up the next morning is difficult. She can't believe what happened yesterday.

But there's no time to reflect. A chauffeur comes to fetch her and drives her to the Palacio Nacional, a pretentious building erected by El Jefe in 1947 and modeled after the American White House. T is waiting for her in his office. The whole way there, Flor, mouth dry and head aching, wonders what on earth this is all about.

Hardly has the presidential office door closed behind her when Flor finds herself with her back to the wall. El Jefe doesn't beat around the bush. He wants her to persuade her mother to agree to annul their marriage, which Aminta is refusing to do, believing that, despite T's two other civil marriages, he still remains her husband before God.

There it is. It *is* as simple as that. Flor must convince Aminta to accept the annulment of her marriage. T makes the request without the least hint of delicacy, the slightest visible prickle of conscience. He only just deigns to explain that María Martínez is demanding a Church-sanctioned wedding.

The hypocrisy of it! A civil ceremony wasn't enough for her, and now La Españolita, more obsessed than ever with the idea of "respectability," is insisting on a religious one.[23] What an evil woman she is. Petty and egotistical. She and T are a perfect match.

El Jefe did try to sway the Church initially, but the Vatican, which doesn't recognize divorce, refused to annul his first marriage. So now T is trying to convince Aminta, and their daughter is his emissary of choice. Flor senses that this piece of maneuvering is T's final attempt before he resorts to force. She's furious with herself. How can she have been so stupid as to believe that yesterday's invitation was sincere? Nothing is free when it comes to El Jefe. Everything is calculated, including his relationship with his own daughter. Will she never learn, never rid herself of the deep, childlike desire for her father's love?

Despite her anger and disgust, despite everything, Flor goes to Aminta's house to relay El Jefe's demand. But Aminta remains intractable. It's less her Catholic faith than it is the remnants of her pride that are keeping her from giving in. And anyway, she has nothing left to lose. Except her life, perhaps. That thought fills Flor with terror.

Two days later, Flor opens the door of the house in San Cristóbal to a singular delegation. Magic Eye has come accompanied by two priests in cassocks, including a Spanish Jesuit. Flor watches incredulously, the colonel fingering his pistol in a thinly veiled threat, as the priests subject poor Aminta to

---

[23] On August 9, 1955, Trujillo married María Martínez in a religious ceremony in the chapel of the Nunciature, according to his wife's wishes.

a barrage of sordid questions, the worst of them concerning the nature of her intimate relationship with Virgilio, T's older brother, whom she hardly knows. How convenient it would be for these men if Aminta confessed to having a lover, and since the dutiful Virgilio is willing to swear to anything . . .

Flor is sickened by this merciless interrogation, by the groundless accusations being hurled at her mother. Aminta, terrified, finally signs her name with a shaking hand in the spot pointed at by the Jesuit priest, not even bothering to read the rest of the document consigning her to total obscurity once again.

* * *

The marriage of Flor's parents is officially dissolved by the Church on May 19, 1953.

For Aminta it's the ultimate humiliation. True heartbreak. She's no one now.

For Flor, the wound goes deep. Worse, it's an annihilation. T has already disinherited her once, and now, in annulling the marriage that bound him to her mother, T is renouncing his daughter, too, erasing her once again, with the simple stroke of a pen. It's as if none of it ever existed: the palm-roofed house in San Cristóbal, the horseback rides, the dances standing on her father's boots, Snowball.

Flor makes a vow. It's a trivial thing, she knows, but she will never again walk through the Parque Piedras Vivas, which El Jefe has constructed (razing several blocks of houses in the process) in the heart of San Cristóbal, an equestrian statue of him lording over its center.

* * *

Following the annulment of his first marriage, T lavishes the Church with gifts, investing a million dollars in various institutions, presenting foreign priests with luxury cars and magnificent houses, decreeing that soldiers must attend mass every Sunday, and becoming godfather to hundreds of children in mass baptisms. He even signs a concordat with the Vatican.

Flor, for her part, has lost more than her identity; she's also lost all faith in the integrity of the Church.

Is she still El Jefe's legitimate daughter, or just one more bastard? The question gnaws at her so painfully that she retreats for several days into one of the luxury retreats T has gifted to the Church. There, she cries her heart out, confiding in a priest about her suffering during her own divorces, and how deeply hurt she was by the Church's complicity in the annulment of her parents' marriage. The priest's reply is hardly comforting:

"Sometimes it's best just to accept these things in life. Perhaps, Flor de Oro, you were born to suffer. Why not accept it, and give your soul to God?"

"Can I take Communion even after my civil marriages—because I'm still married to Porfirio Rubirosa in the eyes of the Church?"

Permission granted, which doesn't make Flor feel much better. She still hasn't found an answer to the questions plaguing her: who is El Jefe really? Does he love her, or hate her? How should she behave toward him?

T begins to haunt her nights again, reproaching her for a thousand things, loosening his grip on the leash and tightening it again, mocking her. Flor's mysterious fevers and fainting spells return.

Ciudad Trujillo
1953

Flor has no choice. She has to try to enjoy this life because it's the only one she's been given. Her existence these days is aimless, meaningless. She's no more than a leaf blowing in the wind. It takes courage to keep living while going nowhere. To keep living just for living's sake.

She breaks this stultifying routine however she can, taking comfort in simple pleasures and trivial projects. She's gradually transformed her little house in Gazcue into a Bohemian artists' retreat full of mementos from her time in France: books, knick-knacks, a few pieces of furniture. The few friends daring enough to visit here there—poets, writers, musicians, painters—are, like her, pariahs, much too modern to fit into a Dominican society that has modeled itself on El Jefe's tastes: pretentious, flashy, kitschy. None of these artistic types have a *palmita*[24] in their wallets—a crime, incidentally, that would result in immediate imprisonment at La Cuarenta if they were found out.[25] You never know when—or if—you'll emerge from a dungeon run by the Benefactor of the Fatherland. If, that is, you're lucky enough not to get thrown to the sharks off La Caleta.

Flor is taking a risk by entertaining these friends in her home, and it would be delusional to think El Jefe isn't being kept informed of her every move. But these friendships are the oxygen she needs to survive in the prison the island has

---

[24] *Palmita* was the popular nickname for a Dominican Party membership card. The Dominican Party was the country's sole political party, created by Trujillo on August 16, 1931, and had a palm tree as its emblem.

[25] La Cuarenta was a prison and torture center during the Trujillo dictatorship, located not far from the Christopher Columbus Cemetery.

become. Even abroad, there are rumblings of discomfort at her treatment; people are saying that Flor de Oro is a prisoner in her own country.

Truly, there's no limit to the Ogre's cruelty. His own daughter . . .

* * *

From time to time, Flor's half-brother Ramfis comes to pick her up, and they escape to his beach house at Boca Chica. A strange, sweet bond has formed between them, despite the major difference in their ages. On these occasions, El Pato[26] exchanges his uniform for a white linen *guayabera*—the open-necked, short-sleeved shirt ubiquitous in Latin America—and a pair of canvas trousers, removes his ever-present Ray-Bans to reveal his large, mournful eyes, and lets his mask drop. They're no longer El Jefe's children, but a simple brother and sister.

They listen to nostalgic tango music at the beach house and drink more than they should, lulled by the sound of the waves on the strand. They make fun of the literary pretentions of Doña María, who fancies herself a poetess and moralist, mocking her current theatrical success, *False Friendship*, and her book *Moral Meditations* (ghostwritten by the Spanish refugee José Almoina), which is required reading in every Dominican school. And they commiserate about their impossible father. Beneath his womanizing, bossy façade, Ramfis is just as heartsick over his parentage as Flor is. Like her, he's perpetually unable to live up to T's expectations. He has no desire for responsibility of any kind and suffers from depression and abulia, the inability to make decisions. He veers between ennui and hysteria and, like Flor, seeks refuge in alcohol and drugs. She,

---

[26] Ramfis was nicknamed *El Pato*, "the Duck," because he was in charge of the land, sea, and air branches of the military and therefore marched, swam, and flew.

the eldest daughter, and he, the heir and favorite son, are forced to live as parasites, all while endlessly disappointing El Jefe. Ramfis, though, isn't in disgrace.

It's through her brother that Flor gets the latest family news. And because Ramfis is also close friends with Porfirio, who introduced him to Hollywood and infected him with a taste for polo and women, Flor uses him as a source of information on Rubi's latest conquests as often as possible—not without a prickle of jealousy, of course. Today, she can't repress a small surge of triumph at the news that Rubi's fourth marriage, to Barbara Hutton, is already on the rocks, not even two months after the wedding.

Summoning up her courage, she asks: "How's Chapitas?"

She didn't even use El Jefe's other less-than-affectionate secret nickname, El Chivo.[27] Still, Ramfis flushes. He doesn't like it when people make fun of his father. T's sexual appetite is bad enough, but his obsession with medals makes him ridiculous.

"You should be more careful, Flor. You know he's keeping an eye on you."

"I honestly don't understand why. Is it to be sure I'm not a Communist? Or worse, an anti-Trujillist?" She tries to sound scornful, even though she doesn't even feel rebellious toward T anymore, just sad, and resigned.

"Couldn't it be that he just cares about you?"

"If he had any interest in me whatsoever, he'd show it, don't you think? And not by having me spied on. I'm the bad child, and he's punished me by sending me to my room, like a disobedient little girl—and at my age!" Flor sighs fatalistically. "He's even made me believe that being caged like this is for my own good."

Ramfis gazes with unusual tenderness at this sister who's almost old enough to be his mother.

---

[27] *Chapitas*, "Bottlecaps," and *El Chivo*, "the [horny] Goat," were secret nicknames given to Trujillo by his opponents.

"If you could leave the country," he asks, "where would you go?"

Flor looks at Ramfis, surprised. A tiny spark of hope kindles inside her. She smiles dreamily. The cigarette between her fingertips emits a thin ribbon of smoke as she waves her hand, sketching a hypothetical horizon.

"Oh, not all that far, really. I'd go to Havana. It's so much jollier than this place."

Ramfis eyes her through the smoke and doesn't say any more on the subject.

Havana
1954

In Havana, the atmosphere is more boisterously festive than ever. Rum, sex, money, music—the Cuban capital is nothing but an enormous pleasure machine. The city lives in time to the rhythm of the rumba and the mambo. People dance frenetically, drink day and night, and gamble away mountains of dollars on green baize tables. They dance the bolero and the guajira to the strains of the *charangas*, accompanied by the voices of the *soneros*. Prostitutes linger beneath the garish neon signs of casinos where high rollers throw down their cash without bothering to count it. The streets are packed with revelers until dawn, when the cabarets with their tantalizing posters finally shut their doors on the last dancers. Tough guys and kingpins, including Lucky Luciano and his cronies, are a common sight around the city, indulging themselves and raking in the money.

A new passport, and a generous new allowance. Flor's life has taken an unexpected turn for the better. Ramfis pleaded his sister's case with El Jefe, and several days ago she took up residence at the Hotel Nacional, settling into a vast suite on the seventh floor with a balcony overlooking the long esplanade of the Malécon and the turquoise ocean beyond.

The Cuban capital is far more entertaining than Ciudad Trujillo, which is like an open-air tomb in comparison. In Havana, the daughter of President Fulgencio Batista's friend is persona grata, with every door open to her, red carpets, piano bars, casinos, cabarets. People gawk and elbow one another when she walks into a restaurant. *It's her!* Still, her checkered reputation has preceded her. She's the woman who flits from man to man, collecting husbands only to drop them immediately. A libertine, an alcoholic, maybe a drug addict, too—and even, some say, a nymphomaniac. Flor doesn't give a straw for the whispers. She feels as if she's come back to life. The looks, the murmurs and judgments are like the raindrops that roll off her tanned skin: a fleeting sensation of cold, quickly drowned in a daiquiri and gone without a trace.

Turning her back on the teetotaling lifestyle prescribed by the good doctor in San Cristóbal, Flor celebrates coming back to life with endless cocktails and sleepless nights. She chain-smokes, dances until dawn, loses fortunes at the poker and blackjack and baccarat tables, naps in the shade of poolside parasols. There's no better place to live like this than Havana. And yet... she's already growing bored.

* * *

Rubi's scandalous exploits are headline news; it's impossible to ignore them. He's begun a stormy relationship with a former Miss Hungary. She's a beautiful woman, Flor has to admit: tall and slim as a reed, with a gorgeous figure set off to advantage by her clinging dress and a perfect, doll-like face with high cheekbones, a small, straight nose, and almond-shaped eyes slightly upturned at the corners. She's also much younger than Rubi, judging by appearances. They're appearing together publicly without a hint of shame, which has caused a major scandal, since both of them are married. Zsa Zsa sometimes hides her face behind an enormous pair of sunglasses—and she's even made Hollywood tongues wag by wearing an eyepatch over a black eye. So Rubi beats her, too. But the starlet proudly displays her bruises, which she calls "marks of love." Flor knows her ex-husband well enough to know exactly what their relationship is like behind closed doors, full of conflict and lust. But she doesn't care. It has nothing to do with her anymore. She's got her own life, far away from him, and it's for the best. She throws the newspaper in the garbage.

* * *

Flor stands naked in front of the full-length mirror in her suite, examining her figure. Flawless. Even now. Short, but flawless. Not deformed by pregnancies like those of most women her age—the silver lining in the cloud, she supposes. Stress and self-starvation have made her lean; there isn't an ounce of excess fat on her body. Her waist is narrow, her breasts high and small like a young girl's. Her face, though, is looking a bit worn. Weary. Life hasn't seen fit to give her much happiness. With an effort, she smiles. That still-magnificent, wide smile, showing every perfect white tooth, that her mother loves so much. The smile that defies the whole world.

She's received an invitation for the evening. Lope Balaguer, the famous singer nicknamed "The Tenor of the Youth," a cousin of the bandleader Johnny Pacheco and the favorite nephew of Joaquín Balaguer, one of T's most loyal associates, is appearing at the Sans Souci later tonight, at the hour when people take to the dance floor.

The Sans Souci is the hottest nightclub of the moment, with the possible exception of the Tropicana. Its patrons represent everything that matters in Havana, a motley assortment of criminals, artists, broke bootleggers, corrupt diplomats, femmes fatales, mafiosi and the heads of powerful Italian families, high-class call girls, sultry cabaret dancers, famous musicians, double agents. There are always a few goggling tourists, too, drifting in and out so they can say they set foot in the famous Sans Souci. Flor's gaze wanders disinterestedly over the crowd.

* * *

In the ten years his career has spanned so far, from his beginnings on a Cibao radio station to his first performance in Ciudad Trujillo, at the Café Ariete in January 1945, to his first album, recorded in Puerto Rico in 1946 with the Antonio Morel Orchestra, Lope Balaguer has navigated his fame with aplomb. He's become a true international star across Latin America, from Panama to Colombia to Chile.

Flor has dressed to kill that evening. High heels, smoky eyeshadow, scarlet lips and fingernails. Her green silk taffeta evening gown sets off her tanned skin beautifully, displaying a tantalizing amount of cleavage. Seated at a table with a few other VIPs, a wide smile plastered on her face, Flor alternates daiquiris and Cuba libres with puffs on her cigarette.

El Cantantazo—another of Lope Balaguer's nicknames—takes the stage to cheers and applause, accompanied by a barrage of drumbeats on the *tambora*. His trim-fitting satin-backed vest gleams in the spotlight. He's very young, not even thirty. His figure is small and neat, his face boyish and pleasing, his eyes soft. He sports a pencil-thin mustache like the famous Mexican singer Jorge Negrete, and his hair is worthy of an advertisement for pomade. He certainly doesn't have Rubi's sex appeal. In fact, he doesn't have any sex appeal at all. Flor is fascinated by the dark fuzz on his upper lip. She imagines that mustache tickling her neck and suppresses a smile. Stubbing out her cigarette in a crystal ashtray, she fixes her gaze on the singer, acutely aware of her kohled eyes, her red lips, her bosom rising and falling like a bottle bobbing in the ocean. *Speak to me of home . . .*

The orchestra has launched into a saccharine bolero, piano weeping and brass instruments whining. Lope has a lovely voice, warm and well-modulated, and he sings the insipid lyrics with conviction.

The American chargé d'affaires, who has been ogling Flor all night, asks her to dance. "Yes, of course." They cut a swath through the sea of people on the dance floor. The concept of decorum has clearly been left at the front door; the men sway and grope at the women, who give way beneath the assault, melting into their partners' bodies. Flor is aiming for a single spot on the floor: the one right in front of the singer. She directs her gaze over her partner's shoulder, looking fixedly at Lope until his eyes meet hers. And then she unleashes her most enchanting smile, banishing the niggling image of Rubi and Zsa Zsa from her mind.

After his performance, Lope Balaguer invites himself to sit down at the table—overflowing with champagne, whiskey, rum, and gin bottles—over which Flor is reigning like a diva. She leans forward, the neckline of her dress dipping to reveal the curves of her pert breasts. She knows exactly what she's doing. The young singer goggles at this woman who has shamelessly stolen the spotlight from him. Flor de Oro Trujillo?

He bows.

Low.

Signed, sealed, delivered.

In reality, it isn't quite that easy.

Ciudad Trujillo
1954

The flirtation between Flor and Maney—Lope Balaguer's first name is José Manuel—only lasts for as long as it takes the orchestra to play a few more boleros. The singer is leaving Cuba almost immediately for a scheduled performance in Puerto Rico, and Flor is going back to Ciudad Trujillo. Swept up in the voluptuous atmosphere of the Sans Souci, they promise to meet again in the Dominican capital.

Lope is thrilled to have met El Jefe's daughter. He finds her warm, funny, and far more unpretentious than he would have expected. But Flor, once the excitement of their tipsy evening wears off, finds herself back on earth. It was a few hours' flirtation, nothing more. She doesn't even think Lope is particularly attractive. Despite the golden glow of success surrounding him, he's singularly lacking in charm. If she compared him to Rubi . . . but best not to do that.

Her life resumes its gray routine beneath the relentless tropical sun. Several weeks later, her friend Felipe, an interior decorator, invites her to spend the day in Boca Chica. Lope is back on the island, which is good timing; she invites him to come along. At the beach, she wears a low-cut orange bathing suit that flatters her slender figure and tanned skin. They swim, they sing, they frolic in the turquoise water and roll in the white sand. How nice it is to plunge into the sea, to wash away poisoned memories, to lift the ever-present weight on her chest and escape, if only for a moment, T's omnipresent shadow.

The sun sets—but why go home? The road back isn't well-lit, and a fisherman has offered to grill lobsters for them. The little group decides to spend the night in Boca Chica. There's a modest hotel nearby, perfectly serviceable. But the surprise awaiting Flor there couldn't be greater. The hotel manager is none other than Ramón, her second husband. Like every Dominican, his life has been a series of highs and lows, all dictated by the mercurial cycle of El Jefe's favor and disfavor. At the moment, the pediatrician-turned ambassador-turned seaside hotel manager is clearly at a low point.

They might be thirty years old, or they might be ten. For this evening they become children again. Forgotten is the fear that hangs like a dark cloud over Ciudad Trujillo, forgotten the *calies*[28] of the SIM.[29] The lobsters, enlivened with a squeeze of lemon and washed down with ice-cold Presidente[30] beer, are delicious. They sit on the sand and roast marshmallows over an open fire. They drink Brugal rum, not forgetting to follow the dictates of tradition and pour out the first drops from the bottle on the ground, for the dead.

Lope picks up his guitar and begins to sing a romantic bolero in his warm, sensual voice. Felipe holds a hand out to Flor. He pulls her to her feet, and they dance barefoot in the sand. Elena laughingly makes up a game: they'll share the marshmallows, taking bites directly from the stick. Soon Flor knows what it feels like to have Lope's mustache against her lips, and it ends with a kiss. Then a swim beneath the stars, the full moon transforming the sea into a sheet of silver. What didn't quite get started between Flor and Lope in Havana becomes fully realized in Boca Chica.

In the morning, Flor wakes up next to the singer. Lighting a cigarette, she gazes with soft wonder at him, still asleep

---

[28] *Calies*: Secret police in the employ of the SIM (Military Intelligence Service), assigned to keep the Dominican public under surveillance.

[29] The SIM: The dictatorship's intelligence service. Colonel Johnny Abbes Garcia, a childhood friend of Rubirosa, was its last director.

[30] Presidente: The national beer.

beside her, his rounded face, plump cheeks, body still with its cushion of puppy fat. It's been so long since she last shared a man's bed.

* * *

Sometimes, the morning after turns out to be a disappointment.

The atmosphere in the hotel is thick with tension. Four men are pacing back and forth on the pavement outside, not even attempting to be discreet, their official *cepillo*[31] parked in full view nearby. There's no need to wonder about them; everyone knows exactly who they are. Flor learns that Magic Eye is here, speaking to Ramón. Who snitched on them? The general emerges from Ramón's office without even glancing at Flor, whom he knows well, or her friends. The secret police follow him out and pile into their sinister black Volkswagen. El Jefe's emissaries have just left the crime scene.

Flor's stomach is in knots the whole way back to the capital, the pain growing worse the closer they get to Ciudad Trujillo. A leaden silence fills Felipe's old Chevrolet, everyone battling their own feelings of dread. Lope has gone off separately.

Back home, Flor closes her front door with a sigh. She's safe. She's just about to pour herself a rum and Coke when the telephone jangles, paralyzing her with terror. She eyes the phone for a long moment as if it were a deadly viper preparing to strike, then picks up the receiver. It's Lope's mother, her voice thick with fear.

"They came and arrested Maney. They were waiting for him; they seized him the moment he arrived and took him to La Cuarenta. They'll kill him if you don't step in. Please, Señorita Trujillo—do something!"

---

[31] *Cepillos* ("brushes"): The black Volkswagen Beetles used by *calies*.

Flor immediately calls Felipe to warn him, to tell him to be on his guard, but it's too late. He's been arrested, too.

Swallowing her pride, she tries to call General Álvarez at the presidential palace. Conveniently, he's busy and can't speak to her. She tries a few more times, then gives up. Finally, Magic Eye calls her back.

"Brea Messina's with your father as we speak, giving him all the details of your outrageous behavior."

Ramón, you bastard, thinks Flor. To think she was once married to him. What a piece of garbage. And what about Álvarez? What did he see with his glass eye? How dare he judge her?

"Stay home until you're told differently, or he'll make you pay for it," Magic Eye orders, and hangs up.

* * *

What's the punishment for having slept with Flor de Oro Trujillo? Will Lope be introduced to the Throne, an electric chair mounted on a Jeep seat that's become disturbingly well-known? Or will he be sent to the torture center at Isla Beata, or fed to the sharks at La Caleta?

The singer's mother tries to convince her brother-in-law, Joaquín Balaguer, to intervene. He's Minister of Education, an important enough position that his opinion is likely to carry some weight. But, servile and cautious, he refuses to say a word to aid his nephew.

Finally, several days later, Lope is released. He was "only" severely beaten as a warning, a relatively minor punishment. Both he and Felipe have gotten off lightly, but the message is clear: he must not see Flor de Oro again.

In the meantime, Flor, who hasn't set foot outside her house, is summoned to SIM headquarters. She tries to contact El Jefe to find out why, but it's a wasted effort. Her heart in her throat, she drives herself shakily to the intelligence offices. A glance in the rearview mirror confirms her fears: a black Volkswagen is tailing her. Then a cry of rage jerks her back to herself and she brakes hard. She's narrowly avoided running down a cyclist.

SIM headquarters is located on the corner of Avenida Mexico and 30 de Marzo. She's never been here before. The building is hunkered down behind barbed wire and piles of sandbags, guarded by an army of uniformed police with machine guns, swarms of Beetles parked nearby, ready to fly off on their next sinister mission. Flor, recognized as T's daughter, is allowed to enter. Inside, she can't repress a shiver of disgust. The air is thick and close, the lighting dim. And the *smell*. Sweat, stale tobacco, brutality, and fear. Her insides contract. An armed sentry leads her to Johnny Abbes's office, looking her up and down disdainfully all the while. The people summoned here are the dregs of Dominican society, after all.

The colonel's office is a gray, forbidding space that perfectly matches its cold-blooded occupant. The room's sole decoration is a portrait of the Generalissimo in full dress uniform, complete with an ostrich-feathered tricorn hat and a chestful of medals. *Hi, Chapitas*, Flor thinks, in a vain attempt at self-soothing. After all, he might have disowned her, but she's still his daughter. They can't do anything to her.

Through a cloud of yellowish cigarette smoke, Johnny Abbes jerks his chin at a chair across from his desk, indicating that Flor should sit down. Obeying, she looks at him; this is the first time she's ever seen him up close. Short and pudgy, he wears a military uniform, the buttons on his jacket straining across his belly, unattractive sweat stains beneath both armpits. He has sharp little eyes that burn with impersonal hatred, a double chin with an incongruous dimple in it, and a ridiculous little inverted 'v' of a mustache atop a thin-lipped mouth permanently set in a scornful sneer. He's every bit as sinister-looking as his picture in the newspapers.

Abbes's fingers toy restlessly with a red handkerchief. They say he's never without the square of red cloth, that it was his Mexican wife, a witch proficient in spells and curses, who gave it to him. He takes a pull on his cigarette, its tip glowing red. The silence in the room thickens. Since her placement under unofficial house arrest, Flor has perfected her "resigned" body language: lips pressed together, shoulders slumped, eyes downcast. But she can feel her insides turning liquid beneath Abbes's gaze. It's unbearable. She feels as if she's been stripped naked. She tries to gather herself, but still can't meet his eyes. He's a torturer and an executioner, and she's afraid of him, as is everyone who sets foot in this lair of his, her blouse sticking to her back with cold sweat. At last she takes a deep breath and breaks the silence.

"Why am I here?" she asks. "What am I being accused of?"

She can't keep her voice from trembling, and even breaking on the word "accused." There's more fear in the question than there was in all the previous years of fear put together. It's so very terrifying to find herself facing this man with his blood-drenched hands. Abbes's lips twitch in an ironic little smirk.

"Your behavior is causing a serious disturbance of public order, and, as you know, I'm responsible for peace and security in this country. You're corrupting respectable citizens, dragging them into debauchery. It's unacceptable."

Abbes speaks flatly, without emotion. Flor knows there's no point in pleading her innocence, trying to justify herself. In a surge of pride, she fights hard to hold back her tears. The colonel drums his fingers restlessly on a typewritten sheet of paper on the desk in front of him.

"The Balaguer family has filed a complaint against you," he says.

Flor's stomach drops. They did this? Would Lope betray her this way? Or is it a lie, a ruse to intimidate her? She tries to think of a retort, but the predatory look in the colonel's eyes stops her from speaking. He smiles mirthlessly.

"Of course, we can ask them to withdraw it. But, in view of the problems you've been causing, it's complicated."

Flor grits her teeth. How unfair this is. She squares her shoulders and stares back at Abbes defiantly, her cheeks red with shame and anger. Especially anger. They're as red as that stupid handkerchief he's mopping his forehead with. There's nothing complicated here. She's El Jefe's daughter. He can issue orders as he sees fit.

Which the colonel confirms. "El Jefe will not tolerate having his reputation besmirched by members of his own family," Abbes says calmly. "If he orders me to, I'll arrest you. For now, I'm telling you to go home and stay there. Oh, and give me your car keys. That way you won't be tempted to go swimming nude at Boca Chica again."

Abbes is completely unbothered by any of this. He knows full well that El Jefe is toying with his daughter, but he's not there to judge. He's perfectly happy just to carry out orders.

Flor throws her keys angrily down on his desk, her awareness of just how powerless she is filling her with deep hatred for these men controlling her life. With one last furious, disdainful glance at the chief of the secret police, she turns on her heel and leaves his office.

A black Beetle full of *calies* follows her taxi home.

Cooped up at home with no car and her conversations most likely being monitored, Flor succumbs to a bad case of "Dominican neurosis"—the tendency to believe anything as long as it comes from El Jefe. Nasty rumors about her are flying thick and fast: that she was swimming in the nude, that she got drunk on the beach, that she insulted the residents of Boca Chica. That there's talk of exiling her abroad, far from the father on whom she's brought dishonor. She no longer communicates with anyone except a few close friends, and even then it's in code, for she knows the SIM has developed a sophisticated system of wiretaps. She tries to get a message to Lope, but their go-between, a gardener, mysteriously disappears. For long weeks, Flor is literally a prisoner in her own home.

One evening at sunset, her faithful friend Idalina Despradel braves the interdict and comes to pick her up for a clandestine meeting. Flor sneaks out of the house, hiding beneath a blanket on the back seat of a battered old car. On the Malecón, the police stop Ida. Flor's heart pounds. She lies perfectly still beneath the stifling wool blanket. The fear that's never far from her mind floods every cell of her body. This is around the time El Jefe takes his daily walk, surrounded by advisors and bodyguards, always making a stop at the home of Doña Julia, his adored mother and Flor's grandmother. Idalina rolls down her window and smiles at the police officers. Her papers are in order; the check is a brief one, purely routine. Flor starts breathing again.

Lope has arranged to meet her at the home of a Cuban friend in the Miramar neighborhood. Flor hardly recognizes him. His blithe self-assurance has vanished, and he's pale and thin. Lope tells her the story of what he was put through, the fate of any man with the gall to appear in public with her or, even worse, to share her bed. His exclusive contract with the radio program *La Voz del Yuna* has been terminated, and he's been fired without reason or notice from the TV show he was hosting on La Voz Dominicana, the new TV channel run by T's brother Petàn. A scathing letter has been published in the dreaded "Foro Público," a column in the daily newspaper *El Caribe* dedicated to anonymous denunciation and defamation, a pernicious tool to control the public, most of whose "tips" come directly from the presidential palace. In the letter, Lope is described as a mediocre performer notorious for his scandalous relationships with women, though the author doesn't dare go so far as to mention Flor.

She describes her own ordeal of the past few weeks. Lope hangs his head, defeated. He's on the verge of tears. Flor feels a rush of scorn. Not exactly brave, is he? Just like all his fellow countrymen—one threat, and he folds like a cheap suit, beaten, broken. But after a moment she softens. She can't truly know what he endured in prison. Music and his career are his reason for living. She can't begrudge his weakness. She lays a hand on his arm, stroking it softly, smiling to boost his spirits. Lope takes a deep breath and plunges ahead.

"Marriage is the only solution," he says. "If we get married, El Jefe's honor will be safe, and they won't be able to touch us anymore."

Get married? For the seventh time? To a one-night stand? It hadn't even occurred to Flor.

"You're forgetting that I'm in disgrace," she reminds him. "He's disowned me. I've been cut off without a penny to live on."

"Think, Flor. We're being watched, harassed. We can't go on like this. I had concerts scheduled abroad. Recording sessions. My career is ruined. Our whole lives have been shut down overnight."

Maybe your life has, thinks Flor. *Mine never even started. I've always been on El Jefe's leash.*

They aren't in love, that's for sure. But it's equally certain that they can't keep living this hell. Flor knows how much stock T puts in his image. She knows he won't tolerate any kind of affair or casual relationship on her part. There's only one way to get him to loosen his grip: appeasement. Lope is right.

Flor sends a message to María Martínez, asking her to test the waters and intercede on their behalf. That moral zealot of a Spanish woman is in agreement, of course; only marriage can redeem them in T's eyes. She consents on El Jefe's behalf.

* * *

Flor marries José Manuel López Balaguer a few weeks later, in a shotgun wedding that feels more like a funeral. It's Lope's first marriage—and Flor's seventh. It's a farce, and a sparsely attended one at that. Not a single member of Flor's family is present at the ceremony other than, for once, her mother. Ramfis, who'd agreed to stand witness for his sister, begs off on some flimsy pretext at the last minute. The bride is emaciated, almost haggard, the groom's triumph restrained.

Still, the couple makes national headlines—and gives rise to a great deal of gossip. No matter. The important thing is that El Jefe's honor has been restored.

Flor's spirits are momentarily boosted by the thought of Porfirio finding out about the wedding. He has his actress; she has her singer. Maybe he'll be jealous. Maybe. It's little consolation.

As a symbol of her return to T's good graces, a check for $20,000 is deposited into Flor's account. A wedding gift from El Jefe. The usual rate, more or less. Lope's passport is returned to him, allowing him to travel and to honor his commitments.

Bogotá – Ciudad Trujillo
1954

The newlyweds honeymoon in Colombia, where Lope's uncle Joaquín Balaguer is now the ambassador. In Bogotá, they stay at the ambassadorial residence in the chic El Dorado neighborhood.

Balaguer, no lover of the society life, sends Flor and Lope to represent the country at the official party for the Colombian national holiday. And there, deliberately or not, they cause quite a scandal. Puffed up with renewed confidence—after all, now he's the Generalissimo's son-in-law—Lope feels as if he owns the room. Not only does the couple instantly draw every eye, but Lope seizes a microphone and, without being asked, decides to serenade his fellow partygoers with a few of his hits: "Arenas del desierto," "Nunca te lo he dicho." Launching into "Ni pie ni pisa," he accompanies the lyrics with a fiery merengue, and there's something obscene about the sight, his plump backside wiggling with deep conviction. The quintessence of the merengue is desire, seduction, the imminence of pleasure, and Flor and Lope set the rhythm, leading the dancing into the wee hours of the morning.

The bureaucrats and officials gathered to celebrate their national holiday are shocked at the way the event has been stolen from them. The ladies tut in dismay; the reporters snap photos and scribble in their notebooks. In the official car provided by the Colombian government to drive them back to the ambassador's residence, Lope, passions inflamed, launches himself at his wife, who doesn't resist his advances. Their driver, eyes glued to the rearview mirror, doesn't miss a detail of the lascivious scene, and gives a full account of the couple's shocking backseat romp to the press the next morning.

Back in Ciudad Trujillo, T chokes with rage when he reads the Colombian newspaper articles lambasting the "shameless spectacle provided by the singer and the passive attitude of the Dominican lady diplomat." Flor never misses an opportunity to blacken his reputation. And she'll pay for it. When the couple returns to the island, they're met by armed policemen. Summoned to the presidential palace, Flor and Lope are given a furious dressing-down by El Jefe, and Ambassador Balaguer is raked over the coals, as well.

Disgrace. Again.

* * *

Life with a professional singer is incredibly boring. It's nothing like what Flor had imagined. Recording sessions, interviews, tours. Not to mention his female fan club. Deep down, the truth is that Flor finds Lope's music embarrassing, syrupy and overly sentimental. His looks are dowdy, old-fashioned. And, despite appearances, he's a real wet blanket—including in the bedroom, where his performance doesn't live up to its early promise. A creature of habit with no sense of fantasy or whimsy, he's the complete opposite of his stage persona. Flor wishes he would shave the mustache that makes him look like a mariachi. He dreams of having children, and that, Flor can't do.

Now that he has access to money and free reign to use it, Lope hatches a plan.

He wants to buy a nightclub with Flor's dowry. He'll use it as a home base for his own performances and host other singers, too. It's an appealing idea—a bit of gaiety in the gloomy Dominican capital. Lope's found the perfect place, on the Malécon, not far from Parque Ramfis. Flor takes to the idea with enthusiasm. A few renovations, some frescoes painted by Flor's artist friends, and the Do-Ré-Mi is born. Lope is the club's artistic director, while Flor looks after the books.

They go bankrupt in less than five months.

The Dominicans aren't much for nightlife, and tourists are few and far between. And, most damagingly, Lope treats the club's coffers like his own wallet. A new personality emerges, that of El Jefe's son-in-law. And for that personality, anything goes. What's Flor's is his, right? After all, they're husband and wife! At one point, she reports a theft when two gold bracelets go missing—only to be located by the police at the pawn shop where Lope took them, in desperate need of ready cash. The house of cards that is their marriage collapses when Lope forges his wife's signature on a check for $700 that ends up bouncing. Self-important and sure of his own untouchability, Maney has played with fire and lost. The whole affair is a disaster. Passionate love exists only in his songs.

Flor asks herself why. Why did she give way? Why did she marry Lope, why didn't she stand up to El Jefe, why did she let him dictate her behavior yet again? In the hopes of reconciliation? Yet she knows the rules of his sadistic game, running hot and cold without warning according to the whims of his own ego, breaking ties, humiliating, controlling by fear, by force, destroying self-esteem, breaking spirits . . .

Flor leaves Lope.
Her seventh marriage hasn't quite lasted a year.
Back to an empty existence, a deep void in her soul, and El Jefe's close surveillance. Back to never knowing whether he's angry with her or not, whether the axe is about to fall, where the next blow will come from. Back to the same life as always. Isolated, penniless, and totally disillusioned, Flor de Oro is easy prey for her demons once again. She surrenders to them body and soul.

***

The years that follow are nothing but a series of ascents and crashes, brief upturns, then backsliding. Flor ekes out an existence marked by uncertainty and punctuated by fleeting friendships, frequently seeking refuge with her mother.

She's vexed to learn that El Jefe has renovated and redecorated her old house in Gazcue, the one she used to share with Porfirio, for his mistress Lina Lovatón and their children to stay in when they visit the island. Lina, the childhood friend of Flor's whom El Jefe never married, has, like Flor, had plenty of time to become bitter. Long gone are the days of their friendship; Flor hasn't spoken to Lina since New York and her divorce from Brea Messina. She's intuitively, acutely aware of everything cynical and equivocating in her father's decision to house his mistress where his daughter used to live. It's a way to humiliate both of them, a way to cause Flor de Oro extra pain. The memory of their matching white mink coats comes back to haunt her.

When someone tells Flor that Lina has had the nerve to complain about the décor, including what remains of Flor's Parisian furniture, she resolves never to see her old friend again.

CIUDAD TRUJILLO
DECEMBER 1955

Dios mio! How *grotesque* it is, the picture on the front page! If mockery could kill, this newspaper would be the end of the Trujillo clan. Every foreign leader in the world must be laughing at them.

Flor crumples the paper into a ball and throws it in the direction of the wastebasket.

She misses.

Getting up, she picks up the paper and slams it angrily into the basket. Then she goes to the bar and reaches for a cut-glass decanter. She needs a nice large cognac to wash away the bad taste in her mouth. And a cigarillo, too! *If Maurice could see me now, wherever he is*, she thinks, fondly, fleetingly.

Outrage and dejection war within her. That dim-witted little Angelita with her scepter and jeweled crown, sitting on a throne next to Flor's thug brother in full dress uniform. It makes Flor nauseous. They look like bad actors in a cheap sword-and-sandal epic. Except that this is real life. Their real life, anyway. How can El Jefe have allowed himself to look so ridiculous in the eyes of the world? Has he lost any remaining shred of good judgment?

Flor has never liked Angelita.

María de los Ángeles del Sagrado Corazón, to be precise. Simple.

Raised by a French "lady" in Paris, this half-sister Flor barely knows, twenty-four years her junior, has been T's precious little princess since her birth. He even named his latest toy after her, a four-masted yacht 110 meters long with 3,000 square meters of sails. Everything Flor knows about her suggests that she's a fussy girl, never satisfied, who's only ever known a life of privilege and luxury. And El Jefe indulges her every whim.

Flor can't keep from feeling slightly jealous of La Españolita's daughter. At sixteen years old, on T's orders, Flor was a student at Bouffémont, far away from everyone she loved. Angelita, at the same age, has just been crowned "Queen Angelita I.".
Not that Flor would want to be sitting on that throne as queen of some ridiculous fair. It's all truly grotesque, and in terrible taste both aesthetically and politically. No, what Flor envies is her half-sister's place in their father's heart. Still, she would *never* have taken part in this kind of buffoonery. Her childhood dreams were of Hollywood, its film studios and exotic settings. Of having a life like the actress María Montez, with a Prince Charming like Porfirio. Those may have just been childish fantasies, but Flor has always loved to lose herself in daydreams, and she sinks into a soothing one now.

She sits there for a long time, thinking of the past, of what never was, what could have been, and will never be. Pointless, all of it. She drains her glass of cognac and takes a long drag on her cigarillo, savoring the burn in her chest that reminds her she's alive, that she's doing the best she can. That she has her own life, away from *them*.

She gets up, retrieves the newspaper from the wastebasket, smooths it out, and reads the article about her half-sister's coronation.

> ... *Her Gracious Majesty Angelita I ... white gown created in Rome by the Sorelle Fontana fashion house ... trimmed with 600 ermine pelts ... golden scepter ... retinue of ladies-in-waiting ... parade of magnificent flag-bedecked carriages on the Malécon ... presiding over it all was Héctor Trujillo ... the Generalissimo's long speech ... economic progress ... modern*

hospitals . . . new roads . . . literacy rate increased from 30% to 96% . . .

It was Flor's uncle Héctor who officially opened this "Fair of Peace and Fraternity of the Free World." An international festival that began on December 20 to mark the twenty-fifth anniversary of T's reign and celebrate the spectacular advances made by the country since his rise to power. They've unveiled a monumental bronze statue of the Benefactor of the Fatherland, university degrees in hand.

Flor can't repress a bark of laughter. What a joke! T left school before he was even a teenager. He always has had a remarkable knack for lavishing himself with honors, not to mention rewriting history.

Forty-two national delegations, showgirls from the Lido de Paris, figure skaters from the Ice Capades. All of it staggeringly expensive, especially at a time when many of the country's people are starving and T gives Aminta just 100 pesos a month to live on. He really has lost all sense of perspective.

Flor isn't stupid. The whole fair is a rather crude illusion, a display of smoke and mirrors to distract the world's superpowers, especially America, from the atrocities committed every day in her country. Kidnappings, torture, political assassinations.

Flor sighs. For the first time, she feels sorry for Angelita.

She remembers when, two years ago, El Jefe proposed that Angelita represent the Dominican Republic in London at the coronation of Queen Elizabeth II, claiming that the girl was eighteen. Imagine Angelita, aged fourteen, parading around amid the crowned heads of Europe! Buckingham Palace had flatly refused the suggestion. The story was hushed up, but it cost British ambassador Stanley Gudgeon his job, with El Jefe sending him back to England amid accusations of misconduct. It's very likely that the idea of the scepter and diadem, imitating those worn by the new English queen, are a reaction to Britain's snubbing of Angelita. The royal pomp, the crown, the long white tulle-and-lace dress designed in Rome, the three-meter-long train and forty-five meters of Russian ermine, the pageboys and maids of honor holding bouquets of roses, the entrance of Her Gracious Majesty by ship, saluted by the marina's sirens and the bells of every church in Ciudad Trujillo—all of it straight out of a fairy tale. But Queen Angelita I and her pathetic little coronation can't hold a candle to British royalty.

Angelita will crash and burn, sooner or later.

What chance does the girl have of ever becoming a normal woman, after something like this?

None.

Flor knows a bit about such things.

And every day, she pays the price.

She pours herself another cognac and drinks a toast to her own bad mood.

CIUDAD TRUJILLO
MARCH 1956–1957

The disappearance in New York of Jesús de Galíndez makes headline news.

The Spanish Republican had sought asylum in the Dominican Republic, where he represented the Basque government in exile. He'd even served as legal advisor to the Dominican Minister of Labor before moving to the United States and becoming an American citizen, Columbia University professor, and, it's rumored, FBI and CIA informant. Galíndez disappeared after defending his PhD thesis, later to become a book called *La Era de Trujillo*,[32] which analyzed the machinations of a "megalomaniacal and stupid tyrant." But what's made El Jefe angrier than anything else is Galíndez's allegation that Ramfis isn't his son, but rather the child of Rafael Dominici, La Españolita's first husband.

The Basque nationalist was seen for the last time at about ten P.M. on March 12, coming out of a subway station on Broadway. Since then, nothing. Every eye has turned toward El Jefe, suspicion rapidly transforming into certainty. The Benefactor ordered the kidnapping, transport by plane via Miami and Puerto Plata, imprisonment, torture, and execution of an inconvenient eyewitness who'd exposed the inner workings of his dictatorship and made him look ridiculous, then disposing of the body in the shark-infested waters of the Caribbean. Every single person involved in the operation, from the main players down to the most minor witness, from Galíndez's kidnappers to his

---

[32] Jesús de Galíndez, *The Era of Trujillo: Dominican Dictator*, ed. Russell H. Fitzgibbon (Tucson: University of Arizona Press, 1973).

jailers to the pilot of the plane that brought him to the island, has been carefully eliminated, one by one. And Rubirosa, it seems, played some role in the dirty business. It becomes a matter of state. There's widespread outcry in the US, despite the rumor that the American intelligence services knew about the kidnapping plan and allowed it to happen.

"Big brother America" is growing tired of El Jefe. Flor can see it. Cracks are appearing in the regime's façade.

* * *

That isn't the only bad news 1956 brings.

In October, Rubi's fifth marriage makes international headlines. This time, his fiancée, a French actress, is barely even a woman. She's nineteen, thirty years younger than Porfirio and two years older than Flor was when she became his first bride. It was so long ago. An eternity.

Scrutinizing the newspaper photos of the couple, Flor can't hold back a fond sigh. Rubi is as handsome as ever. Handsomer, even. He never throws in the towel, never hangs up the gloves. A sudden realization startles her. This is the first time she's been able to look at a picture of Porfirio with another woman without being jealous. The thought makes her blood run cold. *Age makes us* feel *less*. She realizes just how far boredom and apathy have sapped her vital energy. She is distancing herself, at last, from this love that has dogged her all her adult life.

* * *

Can El Jefe really be intending to play referee in the complex tangle of Latin American politics? By the middle of 1957, rumors are swirling. In May, three pseudo-agents of T's are arrested in San José, Costa Rica: Jesús Gonzàlez Cartas, alias El Extraño; Herminio Díaz García; and Ernesto Puigvert Thron, alias El Francesito, a former French Army officer, are charged with conspiring to assassinate President Figueres. In July, Carlos Castillo Armas, the Guatemalan president, is killed by one of his own bodyguards. The affair is a murky one, but many believe the SIM chief Johnny Abbes was behind the Armas assassination, with El Jefe's approval.

Flor tries not to listen to the gossip, concentrating instead on her own limited life. She opens an art gallery and interior décor showroom that she names Studio Ledesma after her mother, catering to young newlywed couples. From time to time, she joins Idalina Despradel and her brother in the town of La Vega, where Ida works at the city hall. With them, Flor can speak freely about politics and analyze the rumors buzzing throughout the country without having to worry about being overheard by the wrong people.

Flor's interior décor business isn't making much of a profit, so when a San Cristóbal architect asks her to redecorate the Casa de Caoba,[33] she leaps at the opportunity. T has gotten her a job; is this a glimmer of light at the end of the tunnel? Has he finally forgiven her? Or is this just a way for him to keep an even closer eye on her? You never know how to interpret a gesture made by El Jefe. It could be a genuine gift, a momentary whim, a trap. In her permanent state of uncertainty, never knowing when she'll take a wrong step, always on her guard and under endless stress, Flor's everyday life is much like that of every other Dominican. But she throws herself enthusiastically into the decorating project, spending a fortune on Oriental carpets, purple velvet drapes, crystal chandeliers, and luxury furniture, and rediscovering a spark of her zest for living at the same time. The endeavor fills her with hope.

But in the end, there's no reconciliation on the horizon. El Jefe doesn't thank her when the work is completed, doesn't

---

[33] Casa de Caoba: The Trujillo residence in San Cristóbal.

congratulate her. He just pays Flor for her labor, as if she were any common contractor.

One more humiliation.

Nothing changes.

This is Flor's life: cheap, confined, constantly watched. A life without laughter, without love, without joy.

What does she have left? An aging body and a withering soul.

That, and the comfort to be found at the bottom of a glass.

Flor lights a cigarette and pours herself a whiskey. She smokes slowly. No, she isn't dead, she decides. Not quite. Not yet.

Ciudad Trujillo
1958

The letter was posted a month ago. It's been opened and resealed. Clumsily. Just in case Flor had any doubts that the secret police were still reading her mail.

> *Havana, April 15, 1958*
> *Mi querida Fleur,*
> *It's been such a long time since I've had any news of you. I know you're living in Ciudad Trujillo now, but I don't have your address, so I'm sending this letter care of the presidential palace.*
>
> *You probably know this already, but I've just been named ambassador to Havana. I'm absolutely thrilled about this new posting. After so many years in Paris, it's like coming home, or almost. I think, despite all the traveling and exile, I am and always will be a child of the tropics, and above all a Dominican. This is something I don't tend to share with anyone but you, that no one else could understand, because it's impossible to explain; it's just something in the blood. It's the essence of us, what makes us who we are, and it will never change.*
>
> *I'm living in a beautiful house in the Vedado neighborhood, with a swimming pool and extensive gardens.*
>
> *I'd really love it if you visited me. After all these years, any hard feelings between us should be a thing of the past, don't you think?*
>
> *We share so many memories. All the happiest and most innocent moments of my life were with you. Venice, New York, Berlin, Paris . . . how young we were. And Rome . . . I*

remember Capri with such fondness. I think we were the closest we've ever been, during those few days.

Fleur, no one has ever taken your place in my heart. It's a place all its own, a secret place, untouchable by time.

You will always be my Fleur.

Will you come? I'm waiting, and hoping.

Forever yours,

Porfirio

* * *

Flor's throat tightens. Porfirio's words strike her to the heart, and a bitter tear slides down her cheek. She really believed she was over him. Nothing could be further from the truth.

A sense of urgency, mingled with what she knows is unhealthy curiosity, comes over her.

She imagines it.

Satisfying herself that time hasn't eroded the bond between them.

Seeing the old tenderness in his eyes.

Hearing him call her *Fleur*.

No one else has ever called her that. Only him.

But then, a cruel realization.

The ravages of time have not been kind.

Flor has caught sight of her reflection in the mirror. What she sees is an emaciated, sharp-featured woman. Her honey-colored tan is a distant memory now. Her skin is gray in the light, almost green, like a dead person's, and her hollow cheeks are crisscrossed with deep lines. Gone is the perfect oval of her face. Her features have hardened, begun to sag, and the skin under her jaw has slackened. Her eyes are dull, dark-circled. And her hair, streaked now with gray, is an undisciplined mass she doesn't even try to tame anymore.

There's a single wrinkle, just one, on her still-smooth

forehead. She forces herself to smile, and the expression is one of pure sadness.

To see Rubi again . . .
Ni modo. No, thank you.
Fleur no longer exists. Flor is ashamed of the woman she has become, aging and faded, struggling vainly against ill health.

The thought of facing Rubi's new wife is more than she can bear. There's no competing with youth.

Besides, she no longer has a passport, and any foreign travel is subject to police authorization.

And that's the end of that.

Flor buries her memories deep in her heart and covers them with the ashes of her life.

She makes a vow to herself. She will never let Porfirio see her looking like this.

Never.

* * *

In December, a ray of sunshine arrives to brighten up the rainy season. Margaret, a recently divorced American friend, comes to visit Flor for the holidays.

The two women go slumming at the Bombillo Rojo, a popular cabaret whose owner puts on merengue contests. Too bad if anyone's following them. "El Pichoncito," "El Chucu Chucu," "San Rafael" . . . the orchestra is on fire, the party in full swing.

On New Year's Eve, they go dancing at the Jaragua, one of the city's chicest hotels, where they spend the evening twirling breathlessly in the arms of one flirtatious partner after another. The next morning, Flor's doorbell rings. A loud, insistent ringing like a threat. Then there's a police officer in the doorway and a military Jeep idling in front of the house—a *lovely* start to the new year. Maggie is summarily arrested. El Jefe has been waiting to pounce. The slightest faux pas, the most minor of indiscretions—such as having the nerve to dance in public—is wholly intolerable, and Flor has no right to have friends. Under threat of torture and imprisonment, Margaret is forced to sign a document acknowledging her membership in the Communist Party and given forty-eight hours to leave the country.

El Jefe is furious. Flor continues both to make a public spectacle of herself and to have disreputable friends. Americans have fallen from grace in the Ogre's country; any one of them is a potential threat. In his fury, El Jefe talks about exiling Flor again—perhaps to Paris, since she loves it so much. But Aminta and Ramfis, worried for Flor's health, talk him out of it. In the end, she isn't sent away. But now, suspected of pro-Communist and anti-Trujillist activities, she's under house arrest, under constant surveillance, for several months. There's nothing really new about that, though. Flor's used to it.

Still, it worries her. El Jefe's mental stability is obviously in decline. His mania and paranoia are only getting worse.

CIUDAD TRUJILLO
JANUARY 1959

Havana has fallen.
The city is a mere stone's throw from Ciudad Trujillo. Immediately after the coup, loaded down with around $40 million, Cuba's President Batista requested permission to land at the military base in San Isidro. El Jefe agreed to lodge the Cubans for a week at the Hotel Paz—at the rate of $1 million per day in exchange for his hospitality, all of which went directly into his pocket. Batista, his former friend and ally, had no choice but to agree. The Cubans have now departed again, first for Miami and then for Spain. In addition to the money, El Jefe has taken possession of six planes from the Cuban presidential fleet.

Flor folds away the newspaper, sighing. There's no limit to the Benefactor of the Nation's avarice. Friendship, fidelity, loyalty, moral rectitude—none of them mean a thing to him anymore, all swept away by opportunism and greed. El Jefe has always been an expert at gaining the maximum benefit from every situation. His methods are unethical, perhaps, but effective. The Cuban coup has made him look like an opponent of Communism at the very least, and, at best, an ally of the *Yanquis* in their fight against the Eastern bloc.

In washing his hands of his old friend Fulgencio Batista, El Jefe has turned his back on a man who could almost have been his brother. Both of them are olive-skinned, both of humble origins, both laborers risen to the presidency, pulling themselves up from nothing through sheer force of will and ambition to lead first their armies and then their countries, both ruling for three decades, sometimes through figurehead presidents. Batista's path has been identical to T's. The parallels are so obvious it's unsettling.

Flor wonders how similar their destinies might prove to be in the future, as well. If the outcome will be the same. If, like the Cubans, the Dominican people will eventually rise up. If the *Yanquis* will abandon T completely in the same way they did Batista. If T, too, will be forced into ignominious flight.

One of El Jefe's nicknames is "the Little Caesar of the Caribbean," and Flor has retained the irritating tendency to believe in signs. She remembers her studies at Bouffémont. Caesar, dictator for life, was assassinated by members of a conspiracy that included Brutus, whom he regarded as a son. A civil war followed the killing. There have been two attempts on El Jefe's life already. Would Ramfis be capable of eliminating his father? No—not Ramfis. Not El Pato!

Flor wonders, briefly, about Rubi. Where will he end up next? A mental shrug. His future has nothing to do with her. It's T she's worried about.

A pigeon flies overhead, black as the forebodings that send a shiver down her spine.

Ciudad Trujillo
Spring 1960

The year has begun amid a tense political atmosphere, with mass round-ups across the country following a failed invasion by anti-Trujillist forces at Estero Hondo and Constanza several months previously.[34] The dictators of neighboring countries have been falling one by one since the end of the war, like dominoes. El Jefe's position grows more tenuous every day. If the Americans are still supporting him, it's only because he's the last bastion against Communism. For months, though, rumors have been circulating among Dominican political exiles, and have now made their way to the island: the middle class has turned against Trujillo, the Catholic Church has abandoned him, and longstanding allies are planning his demise. The CIA is working to incite a coup.

* * *

It's this precise moment that Joseph Farland,[35] the US ambassador (and only American diplomat not to have forged his career by licking T's boots), chooses to make contact with Flor. He shows up at her house after dark, having driven his wife's car instead of an embassy one with its diplomatic plates.

When Flor opens the door a crack, the ambassador shoulders it the rest of the way open and slips into the house. Flor

---

[34] June 14, 1959.

[35] Former FBI agent Joseph Farland was the US ambassador to the Dominican Republic from May 1957 to May 1960. He was forced to leave his posting when the OAS imposed sanctions on the country in August 1960, cutting diplomatic ties with numerous countries.

greets him warily, fearing some new threat against El Jefe. Farland sinks into a chair without waiting for an invitation. His face, normally impassive, is stamped with a mixture of irritation, fear, and urgency.

He gets right to the point. "I've come to warn you."

Flor swallows hard. This is exactly what she was afraid of. Farland leans close and continues, his tone grave, as if he's confiding a secret.

"There's a highly active underground movement against the Generalissimo. He should be keeping a very close eye on it. You're his daughter—you must convince him to abdicate and leave the country. We can offer him a farm in Virginia, for instance, where he could live surrounded by livestock and the horses he loves so much. Tell him it would be the greatest patriotic act of his life, that his reign has run its course, and the time for democracy has come."

Flor is stunned. She'd expected anything but this. Why has Farland chosen her, and not one of her five uncles, or Ramfis, to warn El Jefe that a conspiracy is being hatched against him? For a brief moment, she pictures herself living in Virginia with her father, newly calm and relaxed, enjoying lighthearted horseback rides together . . . but cold, hard reality rears its head almost immediately. The American ambassador is here in her home, asking her to warn El Jefe—no, more than that—to convince him to relinquish power! It's surreal.

"Do you have any solid proof of what you're claiming, or is this just speculation?" she asks.

"Do you really think I'd have taken the trouble to come here based on speculation?" Farland's gaze is direct, almost aggressive. He's talking to her as if she were a child. Flor shakes her head.

"I'm far from the best person to relay your warnings. You know my father has cut off all communication with me. This would carry a lot more weight coming from Ramfis, or one of my uncles."

"They're all too power-hungry; they'd never listen to me," Farland retorts. "And it would put my life in danger. Only a daughter who loves him and speaks honestly to him, with no agenda other than saving his life, can talk to the Generalissimo about this."

"My father believes he's the greatest anti-Communist democrat in the Western hemisphere, and there are plenty of Americans who agree with him. Cardinal Francis Spellman, in New York, even congratulated him for his twenty-fifth anniversary in"—Flor hesitates—"office. And the former Secretary of State, Cordell Hull, called him an exceptional president, greater than any other in Latin America."

"Don't be taken in. That's all just posturing. It has nothing to do with what's brewing in secret. If you want to avoid a bloodbath, the Generalissimo must be warned. I'm urging you to trust me."

Farland is already getting to his feet. There's nothing more to say. He leaves the same way he arrived, by stealth, satisfied at having done his job. Flor is left alone, struggling to bear the weight of what she's just learned.

* * *

It's not that she doubts Farland's claims. El Jefe has already been the target of two assassination attempts, in 1956 and 1958, and the danger is clear. There's only one place where she might encounter her father. He visits his mother Julia Molina de Trujillo, the "First Mother of the Republic," every day between 6:30 and 7:30 P.M. without fail, just before his evening stroll. And so Flor goes to her grandmother's house. No one can prevent her from going inside. She steps through the front door of the house, terrified at the thought of facing El Jefe. It's been so long since she last saw him. At the very last moment, her courage fails. She's forbidden to approach T unless he's explicitly authorized her to do so. Her Uncle Héctor, a kind but spineless man and El Jefe's puppet-president, is there, and Flor delivers Farland's message to him instead. Hector listens to her, not knowing what to make of the information, not even sure whether to believe her. He's heard so much about his niece, so many things that put her mental stability in doubt. Flor hurries to leave her grandmother's house before T arrives, reassuring herself that she's done what she could.

A few days later, she telephones Héctor. Has he given T the American's warning? How did he react? All El Jefe did, her uncle tells her, was ask when the message was delivered, and by whom. Flor quakes with fear, but Héctor reassures her that he didn't mention her name, only Farland's. And then he relays her father's haughty response: "I'm riding a tiger, and if I fall it will devour me." Flor despairs at El Jefe's stubbornness. Does he think he's immortal? Is he relying on destiny? Doesn't he see the writing on the wall? T has become a caricature, mired in his own tyrannical, unbearable arrogance, blind and deaf to everything but his unshakeable faith in himself.

* * *

In the weeks following her encounter with Farland, Flor remains on high alert, anxious for any news, following political events as closely as she can on the radio and in the papers, as no one bothers to keep her informed.

On May 5, José Almoina, T's former private secretary, tutor to Ramfis, and ghostwriter for María Martínez, pays for the publication of his book *Una satrapía en el Caribe*,[36] in which he's deeply critical of El Jefe, with his life. Run down on a city street in Mexico, he's killed by three slugs from a handgun. His murder goes almost unnoticed. But no one is fooled. Everyone knows who ordered the hit.

---

[36] José Almoina, *Una satrapía en el Caribe* (Santo Domingo: Letra Gráfica, 2007). Text originally published under the pseudonym Gregorio R. Bustamante.

T's ostracization by the Western world continues, inexorably, as his abuses multiply.

In June, there's a failed assassination attempt against Venezuelan President Rómulo Betancourt in Caracas, incited by T in retaliation for Betancourt's support of Dominican pro-democracy forces. He isn't killed by the bomb, fortunately. But the attack is seen as deplorable, a grave political mistake—and the Dominican Republic is expelled from the OAS as a result.[37] This puts an end to all diplomatic and commercial relations between El Jefe's country and the OAS's member states, as well as an embargo imperiling its export agreements, including sugar quotas, which brings the economy to a grinding halt.

Ambassador Farland packs his bags.

The country enters a truly dark period.

In spite of everything, El Jefe clings to power.

---

[37] OAS: Organization of American States.

CIUDAD TRUJILLO
JULY 1960

Since the encounter with Farland, and the realization that his warning has gone completely unheeded by the Trujillo clan, Flor has been on tenterhooks. She wakes up dry-mouthed with trepidation each morning, and goes to sleep every night with a sense of having snatched one more day from the jaws of encroaching misfortune.

Her health isn't good. She's lost her battle, however feebly fought, against alcoholism. Her body is frail, thin, weak. Depression has left marks of its own. She feels as if she's losing control of her own soul, her own consciousness. She's frequently incapacitated by terrible migraines, mysterious fevers, and fainting fits. The slightest exposure to sunlight causes her skin to erupt in itchy red welts, so she hardly ever ventures outside. A dermatologist diagnoses a nervous condition and recommends a more temperate climate.

Summoning all her courage, because it's either that or succumb to madness, Flor requests a meeting with Manuel de Moya Alonzo,[38] whom she calls Manolo, as does everyone close to him. She's known him since he was the Dominican ambassador to Washington, and she a cultural attaché. He's now Secretary of State, a post without portfolio, and personal advisor to his close friend T. If anyone can help her, it's Manolo.

The son of a well-to-do family, Manuel de Moya's startling good looks as a young man earned him his first ticket to the United States, where he worked as a model, actor,

---

[38] https://www.youtube.com/watch?v=VPTHAmU6CxA and https://www.youtube.com/watch?v=g725gf-Elhw.

singer, and dancer. Legend has it that T sought out an introduction after noticing him in an ad for Colgate toothpaste and learning that he was Dominican. Manuel's intelligence, education, kindness, and selflessness—not to mention that beaming smile—did the rest. El Jefe took the youth under his wing, and Manuel became his protégé. Since 1939, de Moya has been T's near-constant shadow, occupying multiple government posts, accompanying him on his travels abroad, and serving as his interpreter in the United States. It's to Manuel that T owes his impeccable elegance; the young man selects El Jefe's wardrobe carefully, having his Italian shirts custom-tailored with a special collar made to conceal the scars from the carbuncles on his neck, and advising him on which shoes and ties to wear.

But Manuel is no fawning courtier. He's a loyal, hardworking, morally upright man who doesn't seek the spotlight for himself. Neither corrupt nor mercenary, still a handsome and charismatic man, he is the amiable face of the dictatorship. He's the diplomat Rubirosa could only dream of being, and undoubtedly the son T would have loved to have. The first time she met him, Flor remembers, she thought fleetingly that she should have fallen in love with him instead of Porfirio.

They haven't seen one another in some six years. Flor, all too aware of her physical deterioration, is dreading the encounter. When she enters Manuel's office, she sees that, unlike her, he's still handsome despite the passage of years. He rises and comes toward her with outstretched arms.

"Flor de Oro! I'm so happy to see you," he says, embracing her alarmingly thin body, and she knows he means it.

"Me, too, Manolo. Thank you for seeing me, even though I'm not on the best terms with El Jefe . . . "

Manuel waves away the remark and gazes at her, an expression of concern on his face. "How are you?"

Flor grimaces. "I've been better, as you can see."

"I'm truly sorry to hear that. Now, how can I help?"

* * *

Manolo pleads Flor's case well. She's issued a passport and authorized to travel to Quebec for medical treatment, equipped with $25,000 for expenses. She's startled by how easily the matter is settled, but rather than seeing it as a sign of new warmth in her relationship with T, she figures that he's eager to be rid of her. It's impossible to imagine any decision of T's being without ulterior motives, these days. And in the end, instead of making her happy, her father's approval of her request for a passport cuts her to the quick.

* * *

Flor settles in Montreal. Temperate climate, solitude. She rents an apartment and furnishes it with odds and ends, then begins treatment with a psychologist and a physician specializing in nervous disorders. But she's far away from the Benefactor, without news of the man to whom she owes her life, and who has orchestrated virtually every minute of it since birth. His psychological grip on her is so strong that she feels like she doesn't exist without him. But she vows that she'll find the strength to get through this difficult period, and she certainly has all the tools to do it: the freedom, the will, and the money.

MONTREAL
NOVEMBER 1960

The news reports are unthinkable. Flor is appalled as a woman, stunned and sickened as a Dominican, and horrified as a daughter.

El Jefe has gone too far. It was during his employment at the sugar cane plantation that he first overindulged in violence, in the smell of blood, the feeling of omnipotence combined with the certainty of impunity.

But now his regime is coming apart at the seams. It can't go on like this. The tide, already unfavorable, is about to turn against him. Flor wonders what will become of T, a strongman turned bogeyman, and one with feet of clay.

Things are going from bad to worse. Since the disappearance of Galíndez, El Jefe has abandoned even the pretense of judgment or discretion. Having survived two assassination attempts, he's convinced of his own invincibility.

But now he's crossed a red line. In having Galíndez kidnapped, he acted on American soil, something the *Yanquis* don't tolerate. He should have learned a lesson from that, but no. For T, there are no limits. He keeps pushing, further and further. There was the failed attempt to kill Betancourt last June—and now this.

A triple femicide. Four killings, including the driver. This time, it's El Jefe's own people who turn against him. The fate of the three Mirabal sisters is too unspeakable for the country to ignore. Who could believe the grotesque official cover story, that they all died in a car accident on the way home from a visit to the Puerto Plata prison, where their husbands were being held? The precipice where their bodies were found is indeed a dangerous one, along a steep road in the northern mountains near the village of La Cumbre, but no one is fooled. Patria, Minerva, and María Teresa were executed on El Jefe's orders. In making them martyrs to the regime, he has irrevocably doomed himself. It's he who killed them, even if he has no actual blood on his hands, those immaculately manicured hands that he never gets dirty. He's the one behind every kidnapping, every instance of torture, every political assassination.

In killing the Mirabal sisters, El Jefe has, at last, passed the point of no return. Flor senses it in every fiber of her being. This, she knows, will be the end of the story. Tomorrow, or the day after, or maybe the day after that—but soon, very soon, an era will reach its end.

She folds the newspaper and pours herself a glass of whiskey with a shaking hand. Against doctor's orders, of course, but she's always going against doctor's orders. Maurice, the only doctor she ever obeyed, isn't here to protect her. Glass in hand, she sinks back into the saggy armchair where she always takes refuge when things are going badly, its leather armrests marked where she's dug her fingernails into them in fury.

She tilts her head back. Looks up. The crack in the ceiling has gotten worse. She'll have to have it repainted.

In the depths of her solitude, Flor prays to the protective mother of the Dominican Republic and to the gods of Santeria: *Señora de la Altagracia, Ochún, Yemayá, Elegba, make this stop. Make it all end. Protect El Jefe. Protect my father.*

It's cold in Quebec. Ice cold. Like the cold flooding her heart.

Tears begin to trickle down her cheeks.

MONTREAL
SPRING 1961

Nixon has lost the election, narrowly defeated by John F. Kennedy. Catholic, inexperienced, Kennedy will be the thirty-fifth president of the United States, and the youngest in the country's history. Some people claim he owes his victory to the support—and the money—of the mafia. His position in support of civil rights delights Flor. She's particularly fond of a phrase from his inauguration speech, one that has personal resonance for her: "Ask not what your country can do for you. Ask what you can do for your country." Farland's advice, his warning of a year ago, seems to have made no impact on T; despite everything, the regime continues to limp along.

Since taking office in January, Kennedy has been bent on ridding himself of El Jefe. He's resolved to support the hemisphere's reactionary dictatorships to counter the red menace of Communism, but their former strongman in the Caribbean has shrugged off any semblance of American control and gone rogue. There is real potential for the Cuban problem to spread. If El Jefe is overthrown, if leftist forces—or even worse, Communists—seize power in Santo Domingo, total disaster could follow. A leader unquestionably loyal to the United States must be installed before it's too late.

It would be naïve to view Kennedy as a pacifist, Flor knows. The Bay of Pigs invasion is proof of that, despite its embarrassing failure.

For now, the American president is biding his time. In late April, he sends a diplomat named Murphy to Ciudad Trujillo, tasked with persuading El Jefe to abdicate peacefully—the fourth American government emissary to make the attempt. Once again, T rejects the idea of following Batista or Perón into comfortable but ignominious exile. His reply to Murphy isn't without panache: "*A mí solo me sacan en camilla!*"[39]

Reading the quote in an American newspaper, Flor is aghast.

---

[39] "The only way I'm leaving here is on a stretcher!"

MONTREAL
MAY 31, 1961

It's a beautiful Canadian spring morning. Tender young leaves are sprouting on the trees, and the sun is shining in a sky swept clean of winter's gray clouds. They aren't the warm, bright colors of the tropics, but after a bleak northern winter, they're nice to see.

This will be one of the worst days of Flor's life, but she doesn't know it yet.

A scarf worn turban-style around her head and a pair of sunglasses perched on her nose, Flor steps on the gas pedal of her coupe and indulges herself with a burst of speed. An intense feeling of freedom runs through her veins like a drug. The doctors have finally gotten her depression under control over the past few months, and she's significantly reduced her alcohol consumption. When she told Ramfis about it, he gifted her this Chevrolet Corvair as a reward for good behavior. It's a beautiful car. Flor appreciated the gesture, but she would have preferred it to come from El Jefe.

Keeping one hand on the wheel, Flor turns the radio dial with the other, looking for a station that plays Latin music.

A word catches her attention.

Her hand stills.

A name.

Hers.

She must have misheard. She turns up the volume. The reporter has already moved on to the next news item. Feverishly, she spins the dial. Another station. Another. The speaker's words are indistinct, hard to hear through the crackle of static, but eventually they manage to penetrate her brain. *Middle of the night . . . assassinated . . .*

A horn blares angrily. Flor's car has swerved. She brakes. *The San Cristóbal coastal road ... Got out ... defended himself with his revolver ... Bullet-riddled Chevrolet Bel Air ... more than fifty bullet holes of various calibers ... shot twenty-seven times, including nine at close range ... fell across the hood ... No chance ... Well-planned crime ... quick and efficient ...*

Another car horn. Flor jerks the wheel, pulling onto the shoulder. The Corvair screeches to a halt and stalls with a gasp. She hasn't put on her blinker. The truck that was behind her speeds ahead, honking furiously, the driver shaking his head and glaring.

Everything goes hazy and muffled. Flor is dizzy, her mouth dry. Suddenly she's very cold, as if the blood has drained from her body, her heart pounding so hard it feels like it's about to explode. Her vision blurs. Her temples throb. The world starts to spin. She rests her forehead on the steering wheel and takes a deep gulp of air that burns her throat. Her mind is a confused tangle, and she's unsure of the difference between dream and reality.

And then comes the grief, like a tidal wave, swallowing her up. She sobs, hiccupping and choking. The pain is unbearable. How many times has she wished for the disappearance of El Jefe? Not her father, but the dictator. Not his death, but his resignation, or deposition.

Beneath the sorrow, there is a terrifying, insidious sense of relief.

So this is how it ends. You even said it yourself: "I'm riding a tiger, and if I fall, it will devour me." Well, you fell, and it devoured you. "The only way I'm leaving here is on a stretcher!" And so it was.

It was only a matter of time. I knew that. Everyone knew it. But a daughter is never prepared for her father's death, much less his assassination. Even though I knew it couldn't turn out any other way.

Minutes pass. Thoughts whirl madly in her head. So many

*if*s. If he'd only stepped down while there was still time. If he'd relinquished power to someone else. If he'd managed to control his own bloodlust. If he hadn't been so obsessed with personal gain. If he'd listened to the people around him. If he'd spared even one thought for those who still loved him despite everything. If he'd loved her, even a little.

Then her thoughts take a new direction, with a strength that surprises her. The whole thing might be untrue. False information. *Disinformation*, as they call it. It wouldn't be the first time. She turns the key in the ignition. She has to get home, find a telephone, make a call, because it'll never occur to anyone to contact her, exiled so far away from the island. If there's one thing she can be sure of, it's that she's the least of anyone's worries.

She pulls back onto the road, feeling as if she's not fully in her own body, a ghost, a puppet moving mechanically, automatically. She passes a police station, decides to stop, and turns around. The cops look curiously at her when she enters, an obviously foreign woman in a state of extreme agitation. They listen to her.

"I'm . . . my name is Flor de Oro . . . Trujillo."

Her voice trembles when she gives her surname. It's always been such a heavy load to bear. They stare at her. *Okay, and . . . ?* They have no idea who she is.

"I'm—I heard on the radio that . . . my father's just been assassinated. Can you check . . . phone the Dominican embassy . . . "

The officers are dumbfounded. Slightly wary and more than a bit skeptical, one of them agrees to call the local newspaper.

"I've got a woman here claiming that . . . "

It's at this moment that the dam breaks. Flor sinks to her knees, weeping. The police, caught off guard, hasten to assist her. *Sit down, ma'am. Calm down.* Meanwhile, the officer on the phone has received confirmation. The leader of the Dominican Republic has just been assassinated. And his daughter . . .

His daughter has already vanished out the front door.

* * *

Flor has to see her father one last time. There's not a minute to lose. She has to get home. But there are no direct flights from Canada to the Dominican Republic; they all have layovers in New York or Miami. She books a Pan Am ticket, but she needs permission to set foot on American soil, without which she won't be allowed to board. And she, El Jefe's daughter, the Ogre's daughter, her very existence an irredeemable sin, is persona non grata in the United States. She knows the Americans won't lift a finger to help her get home.[40] Is this out of a desire for vengeance? Total indifference? Sadism? What right does anyone have to prevent a daughter from attending her father's funeral? Who could be cold-blooded enough to inflict a punishment that cruel, and for what reason? Putting her grief aside, Flor spends two whole days battling for permission to transit through the United States. Delays, foot-dragging, bureaucratic slowness. And after all that, despite her pleading, she's unable to make the American authorities budge. Eventually—why didn't she think of it sooner?—she calls Igor Cassini, a gossip and society columnist for the *New York Journal American* whom she knows well, and who has acted as a lobbyist for El Jefe in the past.

"Please, Igor, alert the press. Tell the whole world they're preventing me from going home for my father's funeral."

Cassini pulls every string in his power, and at last the required permission is granted. Disembarking at Idlewild Airport,[41] Flor is mobbed by reporters and television cameras. Cassini begs her not to make a scene; things don't need to be any more complicated than they already are. So she is silent, tight-lipped, and the photos of her published in the newspapers show a hardly

---

[40] The American State Department issued a list of individuals who would not be allowed to return to the Dominican Republic in the event of Trujillo's death.

[41] Idlewild Airport: The former name of JFK Airport.

recognizable woman in a black cloak, pale and exhausted, with dark circles beneath her eyes and a bitterly downturned mouth.

On the plane back to her island, Flor reflects on the last time she saw El Jefe alive. It was October 24, 1959, his birthday. A stiflingly hot and humid day, as is common at that time of year. She'd gone to the parade ground in Ciudad Trujillo, blending into the crowd, anonymous among all the other anonymous faces, and stood there along with several thousand other women dressed in white to keep as cool as possible in the heat. They'd waited for three hours in the blazing sun to pay homage to the Benefactor, who had finally deigned to appear at 5:30 in the evening, dressed in a gray suit and black tie, far away and impassive, a wax figure in the distance. Just like all the others, Flor had extended her right arm robotically and sworn loyalty to her father.

And he—when had he seen her for the last time?

Ramfis and Radhames, who'd been on a pleasure spree with Rubi in Paris, are stuck on French soil—but Ramfis has enough money to charter an Air France flight. It's Porfirio, who's been promoted and is now inspector general of Dominican embassies, who negotiates the $27,000 transaction. The trio flies back to the island, landing at the military base in San Isidro and disembarking with machine guns slung across their chests, poised for battle.

Ciudad Trujillo
1961

The Benefactor of the Fatherland, the Father of the New Homeland, the Restorer of the Republic's Financial Independence, the Supreme Protector of the Dominican Working Class, the Mastermind of Peace, the Generalissimo, El Jefe, is no more.

A nine-day national mourning period has been declared. Flags are torn and lowered to half-mast. Flor arrives on June 3, the day after the funeral. She's devastated to have missed it, and in all the trouble she encountered getting home, she can feel the depth of hatred that had built up against El Jefe. She wouldn't have actually been able to see him, anyway. His bullet-ridden body and battered face had necessitated a closed casket.

The Benefactor of the Fatherland was buried with all the honors due to the absolute ruler that he was. Flor didn't get to see the weeping crowds, the human tide that had tried to reach the casket as it lay in state at the Palacio Nacional, the hysterical women clawing at their faces and pulling out their hair, the thousands of men in tears who had made the pilgrimage from Ciudad Trujillo to San Cristóbal, where the casket was interred beneath the high altar of the church, exactly as El Jefe had wanted. She didn't see Ramfis, pale and strained, in full dress uniform, Ray-Bans firmly in place as always, acting as one of his father's pallbearers. She didn't see La Españolita, the widow who knows she's ruined, utterly consumed with rage, screaming curses at the entire population of the capital, wishing them all massacred. She didn't hear Balaguer, in tears in front of the coffin, promising: "We swear on his blessed remains to defend his memory and remain loyal to his directives."

Flor goes directly from the airport to the Estancia Radhames, the family seat, in a state of indescribable agitation. Around the corner from the property, the American embassy, now closed like all OAS member-state embassies in accordance with sanctions and replaced by a "mission," is guarded by a detachment of armed soldiers. Inside the house, Flor, totally disoriented, is confronted by empty rooms and distraught servants. She gazes with infinite sadness at the tinkling crystal chandeliers, heavy mahogany furniture, thick Oriental carpets and gold doorknobs—all that inordinate, pointless luxury. Ramfis sends a car to take her to another house, this one in Hainamosa, not far from the air force base in San Isidro, where the Trujillos have gathered. In the emotion of the moment, María, who has never shown her the slightest affection, hugs Flor tightly.

"Thank God I have a son," she sighs, forgetting about Radhames completely. "Ramfis will handle everything and establish order again."

"He said, '*Párate a pelear,*'"[42] Ramfis says, embracing his sister and weeping. "He didn't want to run. He died a soldier's death, fighting like a lion with his .38 revolver in his hand."

Ramfis is only repeating the words of Zacarías de la Cruz, El Jefe's driver, who was shot eight times during the assault and is in critical condition at Marion Military Hospital. The discovery of El Jefe's pistol with its chamber nearly emptied of bullets confirms this account. The idea that T died a courageous, soldierly death is clearly of great consolation for Ramfis. Flor, though, feels as if her father was put down like a rabid dog, and without being absolved of his sins.

Ray-Bans still perched on his nose, in full dress general's uniform, Ramfis fulminates, his mood veering from one extreme to another.

"They're going to pay for this. All of them. Not a single one will get away from me. Starting with Román."

---

[42] "Stop and fight."

He proceeds to share with Flor the obscene detail that their father's corpse had begun to bleed again in the presence of General Pupo Román, head of the army, who had come to pay his condolences to the family—thus marking him out as the killer. Flor doesn't put much stock in folk beliefs like this, but she listens without comment.

"I'm your father now," Ramfis adds, with a touch of boastfulness at this gain of influence over his elder sister. "And I'll be an understanding one."

Despite her grief, Flor is overwhelmed with gratitude, and she falls weeping into the arms of her half-brother, El Jefe's heir. Surrounded by bodyguards, dressed in deepest mourning, her face hidden behind a veil, she's driven in a limousine to San Cristóbal to visit T's burial place. The whole way there—ironically, it's the exact same journey that cost El Jefe his life—she thinks constantly of her father. *Will I be able to think of you with compassion now, Papi? Will I finally be able to forgive you for everything you put me through?*

Getting into the church is no easy matter. The military guards have to clear a path so she can enter. He's there, beneath the altar. *They say the dead are at rest. Are you at rest, Papi? Can you be, with so much blood on your hands?* Flor doesn't know how to say goodbye to her father. At that moment, grief overwhelms everything else in her. She should cry, to drain herself of so much bursting emotion, but it's as if she's locked up tight. She drops to her knees, struggling to breathe in the heat, beneath the smothering weight of her sorrow. *Do you see where it all got you, Papi? Was it worth it? Forgive me, Papi. It was so difficult to love you.*

How will she remember him? She wants to hold him in her heart merely as her father. Alone with her during their rare horseback rides in the hills of San José de las Matas. When he escorted her solemnly to the altar to give her in marriage to Rubirosa in the little village church. When she'd sit in his lap and he'd carefully examine her school report card before lecturing her on how to be a good student. Dancing with him, her little feet perched atop his own. The fragments of their relationship are sharp and jagged in her memory.

Then, amid the grief, the pain, a revelation. A sudden surge of euphoria at the thought of being rid of him. Free, at last. An incredibly intense feeling, followed almost immediately by guilt at having felt it, even for a moment. Such thoughts are a betrayal.

Does she have the right to mourn him? Even more than his daughter, she was his subject. The woman has been freed from her guardian, the Dominican from her dictator, the daughter from her father. How can she reconcile all that? She doesn't know which feeling is the right one, can't tell which is strongest. It's impossible to unwind the complex tangle of her emotions.

She doesn't grieve for T. She grieves for her Papi. When the tears do come, they're sincere, the tears of a daughter who hated her father for what he was, the tears of a daughter who loved her father despite what he was, the tears of a daughter who could never tell her father she loved him, the tears of a daughter whose father never told her he loved her. Such simple words. Words she waited in vain to hear all her life, words never said, words whose absence marked her cruelly with the brand of indifference, words whose absence crippled her life.

I love you, Flor de Oro.

CIUDAD TRUJILLO
JUNE 1961

"I want all my husband's children to come to me," María Martínez has declared. "All of them that he's officially recognized. No time to waste."

She's a determined woman, La Españolita. A flurry of telegrams is dispatched to the United States. Flor wonders about her stepmother's motives. Is this an attempt at reconciliation? To soothe bitter feelings? Or to avoid legal wrangling?

Within two days, they're all there: Odette, whose mother is T's second wife, Bienvenida. Yolanda and Rafael, Lina's children. And Elsa Julia and Bernadette, El Jefe's mysterious youngest daughters.

There are nine of them in total. Other than Flor and the children of María Martínez, they're all strangers to one another, meeting for the very first time. Now, summoned by La Españolita, who has made their lives hell for years, going so far as to forbid them from living in the Dominican Republic, they're not at all sure why they're here. Naively, in their common grief, they're hoping for reconciliation. They look at one another curiously, a motley battalion of the Benefactor's descendants. Odette, Yolanda, and Angelita are exactly the same age, and so are Rafael and Radhames, facts that make everyone uncomfortable. And of course, there's the inheritance. It's why they're all here. Sitting in the vast living room of the San Isidro house, on imposing lion-footed mahogany chairs, they wait.

Ramfis asks for silence and then yields the floor to "our eldest sister." Flor is moved by the sight of all the siblings together. Her voice trembles. She hasn't prepared anything to say.

"I want to welcome you all, in spite of these dreadful

circumstances. I'm happy and very touched that we're all together under one roof for the first time. We've all lost our father. Let's have a moment of silence."

Obediently, they all bow their heads, looking up when she asks them to approve Ramfis's taking over as head of the family. The atmosphere in the room becomes noticeably more relaxed when Ramfis announces that cars will be made available to them so they can pay their respects at the tomb in San Cristóbal. And then, another silence. They wait. Ramfis draws the pause out almost cruelly. Finally, he adds, there's the question of the inheritance, in which they'll all have a share. He invites them to dinner at his beach house in Boca Chica. Far from eavesdroppers and indiscreet ears.

* * *

They eye one another across the monumental dining table. The sea glitters silver in the distance beneath the pale gleam of the stars. But there's nothing poetic about the tension filling this room. The half-brothers and -sisters are finding it hard to talk to one another. They're all of different nationalities, backgrounds, and educations, and they have no history, no childhood memories in common. María asks polite questions in her mellifluous voice. The replies are brief and matter-of-fact. Yes, no. *Don't stick your neck out, don't reveal too much . . .*

Flor is the eldest. The rest of them could almost be her children.

She looks at Ramfis, the designated successor, with his evasive nature, his poorly contained anger, his stridency, his weakness, occasionally glimpsed but always present. Has her Don Juan of a brother definitively recovered from the periodic attacks of madness that have sent him to a psychiatric clinic more than once? She remembers the first time she saw him, a tiny five-year-old boy dressed like a miniature adult, with brillantined hair carefully combed and sharply parted on the side, his girlishly long eyelashes, his soft brown eyes. The immediate surge of affection she felt for this illegitimate little thing dressed in his Sunday best. The way Rubi took him under his wing—they're still close, in fact.

Ramfis frightens her a little. She hopes with all her heart that he'll be able to govern the country with the same determination as El Jefe, but without their father's excesses. Yet she dreads what is to come; there's already violence and disaster in the air, she can feel it. As if in agreement with her dark thoughts, the harsh cry of a seagull—a bad omen—pierces the silence hanging over the disparate group of siblings.

She scrutinizes Angelita's pretty face. María de los Ángeles del Sagrado Corazón de Jesús. El Jefe's favorite daughter. The one he made a queen and covered with diamonds. She seems to be the child most affected by his death. Flor used to be so jealous of her, though she never wanted to admit it to herself. How painful it must be for Angelita to be finding out about these sisters who are her exact same age. She'd thought she was the only one, but she isn't. And she's not the prettiest one, either. Elsa Julia is a real beauty. How will she manage now, this poor carnival queen whose husband, Pechito,[43] is one of the worst thugs of the regime? Flor pities her.

Next Flor's attention turns to Radhames, the third wheel of the Martínez chariot, whom she's never liked. He's weak-featured, pale-eyed, mediocre. She can sense the imbalances in him, the inadequacies, the instability. The excesses and abuses to come. He never had a real father, either. Poor Radhames, saddled with the name of a character in an opera.

Flor's gaze drifts to the lovely Yolanda, who looks so much

---

[43] Luis José León Estévez, nicknamed "Pechito," first husband of Angelita Trujillo, was one of the worst torturers and perpetrators of anti-Trujillist repression. He committed suicide in 2010, in his eighties.

like Lina when she was young, with that same wild, free-spirited air. Yolanda, who's getting married in Miami in a few days, and won't be walked down the aisle by her father. She remembers her as a chubby baby crawling on the wall-to-wall carpeting of a Park Avenue penthouse, while El Jefe, his guard lowered for once, built a pyramid of blocks for her. Does she remember him at all?

Flor is meeting young Rafael Leonidas Trujillo for the first time. He has the exact same name as El Jefe. Lina must have really loved T, to baptize her son with those names. He has his mother's dark curly hair. Flor searches his face for any resemblance to their father. His small, piercing gray eyes, maybe? Or the nasal voice struggling to crack that veers, sometimes, into sharpness? Or maybe it's his obvious indifference to his siblings, even disdain. Lina's children were born of passionate love, Flor knows, and that sets them apart from the others.

Then there's Odette Altagracia, born long after T's divorce from Bienvenida. And the two other girls, Elsa Julia—so beautiful—and Bernadette, whom Flor is meeting for the first time. Girls whom she's never even heard mentioned. Girls that must have rivalled her in their father's heart, because they're here today. He acknowledged them, which means they counted to him. As much as her? As little as her? How was it for them, growing up without a father? Did they receive checks as signs of his "affection"? How much was El Jefe's affection worth? $25,000? $20,000? A mere $10,000?

And, finally, there's Flor herself. Flor de Oro Anacaona, the black sheep, the eldest daughter, the product of T's first marriage, the child of Aminta *la campuna*.[44] The daughter who's

---

[44] *Campuna*: Country-dweller, a Dominican term often used pejoratively, as in "country bumpkin."

been married seven times, the one who burned her bridges, the rebel, temperamental and capricious. The one who's often ill, the one imprisoned for years on the island, the one who lives far away now, the one who doesn't count.

Looking at the rest of El Jefe's children, it dawns on Flor that she was for him a permanent reminder of his humble origins, and particularly of his drop of black blood. The drop of blood that coursed through his veins and bloomed on his skin, giving him away, forcing him to powder his cheeks like a woman. She was a reminder of the time before his rise to greatness, the time when he was a mere guard on a sugar cane plantation in San Cristóbal.

Hot tears sting her eyes.

She thinks of Julia Genoveva, her sister who died at barely a year old, whose life hung heavy as an anvil over her own childhood. How she missed this sister whom she never knew. How she misses her still.

Did you love your children, Jefe? Which one of us did you love most? Which of us wasn't a disappointment to you? You were the Benefactor of the Fatherland, but where was your bounty, your benefaction, for us? These questions teem agonizingly in Flor's mind as she gazes at the miserable throng that is her family, fighting to keep the tears from falling.

Then there is the stepmother. La Españolita. Her falseness is plain to see, written on her smug, bloated face. Her hypocrisy, her opportunism, her avarice, her greed, her covetousness, her egotism. She who made El Jefe believe that Ramfis was his son, who demanded the annulment of Aminta's marriage despite the immense pain it caused, who claimed authorship of books and plays produced by ghostwriters, who saw herself as a poetess, a playwright, and—the ultimate joke—a moralist. Flor doesn't believe the woman trusts even her own children. She can almost prophesy María's downfall, her end.

Flor closes her eyes. They form a sorry tableau, the heirs

of Trujillo. Ramfis continues to pursue T's killers with single-mindedtenacity. General Román, who didn't try to flee, is arrested and tortured to death over the span of several days. Attention now turns to the other conspirators, the country's entire police force working past the point of exhaustion.

Flor returns to Montreal to wind up her affairs there, then moves to Miami so she can be closer to home. There's no doubt; Balaguer may have taken the country's reins in the immediate aftermath of El Jefe's death, but it's Ramfis who will succeed his father as head of state, ruling with the same firm hand but without the various excesses. For now, as El Pato personally leads the hunt for the assassins, Flor dreams fondly of being given an official role, a government post, something to do with culture, like she had in Washington.

Balaguer, for his part, wastes no time. On July 11, he founds the National Civic Union, intended to ensure an interim power structure that excludes both the military and any civilians who supported El Jefe. Little by little, he's squeezing out Ramfis and his clan. La Españolita is furious.

* * *

In August 1961, three months after the assassination, Ramfis convenes another meeting of the siblings. Solemn-faced, dressed in black, they gather in a meeting room at the military base in San Isidro, all hoping to emerge from the gathering as millionaires. The international press is claiming that El Jefe was the fifth-richest man in the world, with an estate thought to be worth some $800 million, and his heirs know it.

Ramfis mechanically reads out an inventory of El Jefe's possessions. The simple handwritten document confirms that there is no will, that the millions are a myth, and that, contrary to rumor, there are no foreign holdings, no bank accounts in

Switzerland or France or Lebanon. All of T's residences on the island and abroad are in María's name, and Radhames is the owner of the Hacienda Fundación, the largest livestock ranch in the country.

What this all boils down to is that there is a mere $2,723,349 to be divided up. The figure is unsettling in its exactness. Disappointment is clear on every face. Flor knows that the great fair of 1955—more than $50 million worth of new structures and events and Queen Angelita's magnificent coronation outfit—and the armed struggle against the 1960 invasion must have put immense strain on the country's finances—which were often indistinguishable from El Jefe's personal ones. She has witnessed it herself over the past few years: things have gotten tougher and tougher since America began to distance itself from the regime. But—*so* little money? Not even $3 million? Even though El Jefe was the Dominican Republic's leading businessman? When his companies held the monopoly on meat, milk, rice, oil, salt, beer, shoes, cigarettes, lumber, matches? When he took a commission of 10% on all public works contracts? And the yacht, the sugar plantations and refineries, the livestock and mines and land? Flor finds it a bit hard to believe.

Her own inheritance consists of a few small parcels of land scattered throughout the country and a house in Gazcue. Ramfis surveys the dismayed faces of his siblings. Their discontent is clear. With a flourish, he announces that he's forfeiting his share of El Jefe's estate.

What he doesn't say, and Flor discovers only much later, is that for two months now, the courts have been working—on the orders of Ramfis and his mother—to modify a plethora of title deeds and transfer everything they can out of the country.

In the end, like the others, and only slightly better off than them, Flor takes what she's been offered. Yolanda and her brother Rafael are the only ones who balk, and they go back to

Miami without signing the probate agreement. Their mother, Lina, is also demanding a personal bequest of $2 million.

The pretense of succession is kept up. Flor doesn't know how to feel. Ramfis, her self-proclaimed substitute father, privately agrees to pay her an allowance of $2,500 per month. Armed with his promise, Flor returns to Miami, confident in the future.

Ciudad Trujillo
Autumn 1961

Flor arrives on the island on October 26, more anxious than ever. Ramfis sends a car to pick her up at the airport. Nose pressed to the car window, she breathes in the smell of blood and fear permeating the city. The day before yesterday, October 24, would have been T's birthday.

The country has changed. Flor can feel it. It's perceptible in a thousand small things. People are walking with more assurance in the streets, shoulders back, heads high, smiling. The exiles have come home; the political prisoners have been freed. Tongues are loosening, people belatedly expressing moral outrage at El Jefe's abuses. A few daring newspapers are even starting to air the dictatorship's dirty laundry. The removal of T's friends and family from their government positions, relegated to the ranks of the unclean no matter their previous relationship to power, has begun.

* * *

Arriving at her half-brother's beach house, Flor is shocked to encounter Ramfis's mistress of the moment, a German dancer from the Lido cabaret in Paris, who introduces herself as Hildegarde Mertinat and extends a small, dry hand. Flor is disgusted. Ramfis has a Dominican ex-wife who presented him with a gaggle of children, not to mention a new young wife, Lita Milan, an American actress of breathtaking beauty who gave up her career for him and is currently awaiting him in Paris, pregnant. True to form, even at the worst times he remains monstrously self-absorbed.

Ramfis is in a foul mood. Balaguer is gaining ground every day, making his position ever more unstable. Accused of betrayal, cowardice, and apathy, and subjected to fierce reproach by the Trujillo clan, all of whom are counting on him to regain power, El Pato has taken to seeking refuge in his house at Boca Chica to drown his sorrows in vodka and banish the specter of civil war hanging over the country. Not to mention the whole matter of the inheritance, which is growing thornier all the time.

"Lovatón's children have started legal proceedings to get their hands on their share, the little bastards. And their bitch of a mother is still claiming she's owed $2 million! Even after living in the lap of luxury for all these years with our father footing the bill! Can you believe it?"

Flor doesn't comment. She's the eldest daughter with the most unassailable claim to legitimacy of them all, born of a marriage consecrated by the Church, but even so, she's unsure of her place, or what she has a right to herself.

"Don't worry, Flor," Ramfis reassures her. "I'll support you until this whole mess is sorted out, I promise."

* * *

The massive house belonging to Radhames is a beehive of activity, every room filled with men and crates, packing up anything that can be transported. People are saying that hundreds of heavy trunks have been loaded onto the *Angelita*; they're saying that the Martínez clan is preparing to board the yacht and leave the country permanently. People are saying so many things.

Flor has asked to select a few photographs as keepsakes. Permission granted. There are many portraits of El Jefe in full regalia, his famous bicorn hat on his head, his chest dripping with medals. Flor doesn't want those. She chooses a snapshot of T on horseback, looking like a bourgeois gentleman in his impeccable lightweight linen suit. He looks happy. The picture reminds her of the times they went riding together, just the two of them, those all-too-rare moments she cherishes in the deepest, most secret part of her heart.

She also selects a photo in which she and Ramfis are sitting next to their father, who is dressed in a business suit. And another, this one familiar: she's on her father's arm, wearing an evening gown. With his bow tie and pocket square, he looks almost shy. He's proud of her; she's smiling. They're beautiful together. She remembers that night. It was during that happy time in New York when she thought she finally had him back, and he'd been photographed posing between her and Lina. Did he cut Lina out of the picture so La Españolita wouldn't destroy it?

She also finds a cardboard folder full of newspaper clippings. Filed in order, they're of her marriages, the high-society functions she attended, her months as a Washington diplomat. She recognizes her reports from Bouffémont, too, the paper yellowed, and a letter in her own little girl's handwriting. This isn't a police or intelligence file. She's sure of it. These are keepsakes collected by a loving father.

She should ask her stepmother if she can have the folder . . . shouldn't she? María certainly has plenty of other fish to fry, planning for her own future. And this is such a small thing. Yes. Flor slips the file and the snapshots into her bag. She'll treasure them. And they're all she'll take—these, and Ramfis's promise of an advance of $25,000 on the inheritance to come.

* * *

La Españolita leaves the island with Angelita and Radhames, traveling to Paris and settling at the Hotel George V. From there, supported by her younger son, she continues to rail against Ramfis and his weakness, his cowardice, his shaming of El Jefe's memory.

Flor goes to the port of Andrès, where the *Angelita* is anchored. The engines of that floating fortress are being kept running 24 hours a day, in accordance with the instructions the captain has received. In the yacht's bar, Ramfis and a few friends are downing shot after shot of vodka in an atmosphere of intrigue, intermittently taking mysterious long-distance calls. A cabinet gapes open to reveal a veritable arsenal. The men talk about the American machine guns used in the assassination. They talk about exterminating Balaguer. Rubirosa's ghost reappears. Still lurking in the back rooms of power, he's returning to the island with a new plan for Ramfis. Rubi, a political strategist? Flor doesn't believe it for a second. Feeling out of the loop, she disembarks, leaving the plotters to their fantasies.

* * *

This latest trip accomplished nothing. No progress has been made, and the political situation is still extremely chaotic. As soon as she's back in Miami, Flor receives alarming news. It's all going from bad to worse. After thirty-one years of absolute dependence, the country is in a state of shock. What remains of the Trujillo clan is in a delicate position, with Ramfis the ongoing target of a great deal of anger and resentment. The radio station El Caraibe, which he owns, has been burnt down. The people have begun methodically toppling El Jefe's statues across the country—1,872 of them, according to well-informed press reports. Plaques engraved with his name are being wrenched down in every public space. The name "Trujillo" is also vanishing from the many places that previously bore it: streets, parks, schools. Enameled signs reading "Only Trujillo Heals" are being removed from hospital rooms, as are the ones in churches that read "God in Heaven, Trujillo on Earth." Balaguer has issued an order to restore the original name given to the capital city by Spanish conquistadores, Santo Domingo de Guzmán. Ramfis doesn't object. He doesn't have the means to fight back.

With T dead, freedom of speech has been restored. People tell stories of unspeakable atrocities committed by El Jefe, far worse even than the ones whispered about during his lifetime. He's called a satrap, a rapist, a sexual obsessive, a murderer. Balaguer, the puppet president who praised T at his funeral, hasn't wasted any time in changing sides, playing the game with disconcerting skill and determination. Who would have believed this insignificant little man capable of such keen judgment, such authority? Balaguer has established himself as the architect of the Dominican Republic's democratic transition.

So as not to alienate the Trujillo clan, Balaguer initially persuaded Ramfis to agree to a two-headed government, with Ramfis taking charge of the military and Balaguer of politics, both guaranteeing to the United States that there will no infiltration by the Communists or other opposition parties—even though Balaguer's new party, the Unión Cívica Nacional, is openly against the Trujillos. As a gesture of good faith to the *Yanquis*, in order to avoid their occupation and takeover of the country, Balaguer has even managed to convince the heir to exile his uncles, El Jefe's brothers. An OAS mission is demanding that Balaguer's powers be expanded and free elections held. Buffeted by uncertainty, the Dominican people are emptying grocery shelves, storing away reserves of rice, beans, oil, and sugar.

Accounts of Ramfis's cruelty are piling up, international voices rising against him. El Pato is proving to be even worse than El Jefe: crazier, more violent, more bloodthirsty. T's assassins have been caught, Ramfis having hunted them down like animals, and were brutally tortured for weeks in the dictatorship's jails. Then, not content with that, he's had hundreds of political opponents, Communists and anti-Trujillists, arrested, tortured, and executed.

Cut off from the political decision-making process, Ramfis will have a hard time holding on to power. Flor wonders about Rubi: is he still out there intriguing with Ramfis somewhere? It's been a year since El Jefe named him inspector general of Dominican embassies. Does he still have a role to play in this hellish chess game? She can't help but be curious about his fate.

Flor has never had an affinity for politics, and she doesn't understand the whole picture. But she's under no illusions about the fall of the regime, or the defeat of the ever more vilified Trujillo clan.

In Miami, she meets with an old friend, Willmoore Kendall, a former Yale professor and editor of the conservative editorial magazine *National Review*. At Ramfis's request, Kendall has crisscrossed the Dominican Republic to assess the political situation and made suggestions for saving the regime and the Trujillo family's assets. He believes it necessary for the country to rid itself of the US State Department's control, send away the OAS mission, and launch an intensive effort to attract tourists to the island. Ramfis hasn't listened to a word of it. He didn't even cover Kendall's travel costs.

* * *

Flor reads in the newspaper that the *Angelita* set sail in secret on November 18, loaded down with trunks and cases stuffed to overflowing with dollars and bearer bonds—and El Jefe's remains, hastily exhumed from his tomb in San Cristóbal. Ramfis, abandoned by everyone, has fled the island with his tail between his legs but his moneybags crammed full. Before leaving, he robbed the central bank of all its cash and killed the six imprisoned surviving members of the assassination plot, a macabre gesture aimed at convincing himself that he was worthy of his father. The *Angelita* sails to the island of Guadeloupe, where she is left in custodianship, meant to be sailed on to Cannes. Meanwhile, Ramfis flies to France to be reunited with his family. When he learns that the Dominican navy has seized the yacht, complete with trunks and coffin, and taken it back to the port of Santo Domingo, he collapses. He's hospitalized in Belgium for a sleep cure. El Pato's short stint in power—and his life on the island—is over.

Not even Aminta is spared. Her modest house is vandalized and ransacked. She manages to join Flor in Miami with nothing but a few dozen pesos and some old photographs in her handbag.

Rubirosa holds a press conference in Paris. His hopes disappointed, he lashes out at Ramfis, "the most cowardly man in the world." Rubi had been relying on Ramfis to help him return to prominence, or at least retain his current position, but he bet on the wrong horse. The break between them is total. They've both lost everything.

Balaguer, eager to rid himself of everything reminiscent of El Jefe and to occupy the seat of power alone, has T's coffin flown to Paris aboard a Pan Am Douglas airliner. Two weeks later, the Martínez clan buries the Benefactor of the Dominican Fatherland in Père Lachaise Cemetery, to rest in peace at last. If he can.

Ramfis's promises were short-lived. Flor de Oro finds herself alone in Florida with her mother, completely abandoned and without resources. Even from beyond the grave, El Jefe has made her an undesirable in her own country. Will she ever be able to set foot in Santo Domingo again? Will she hear the waves crashing against the rocks of the Malécon, feel the burn of the Caribbean sun on her skin, smell the scent of salt and ripe fruit so unique to her island, the island forever branded on her heart?

MIAMI
JUNE 1962

In the end, with no word from the Martínezes, Flor joins the ranks of El Jefe's despoiled heirs. In concert with her other five brothers and sisters, she files suit against La Españolita's three children, all now living in Madrid, to claim her fair share of the inheritance. Leland Rosenberg, former secretary to Barbara Hutton and a Trujillo stalwart recruited in the wake of Rubirosa's fourth marriage, has revealed that T wanted his assets to be divided equally among his inheritors in the event of his death. These wishes have not been respected.

It's a declaration of war between the children in Miami and those in Madrid, and it will be a fierce one.

Flor knows that Ramfis has conned them all. T's properties and bank accounts have been put into receivership, both in the Dominican Republic and abroad. His Swiss accounts remain in the hands of the bankers. María Martínez, descending into senility, won't—or can't—give the codes even to her own children, fearing that they'll wash their hands of her once they've gotten them on the prize.

It's simple: without a miracle, no one will benefit from T's fortune—except Ramfis, Angelita, and Radhames, who had the foresight to siphon off what they could, some $30–40 million, and to transfer some assets abroad the day after the assassination.

Flor's only inheritance will be the name she's always found so heavy to bear.

So El Jefe did nothing to ensure his children's comfort.
You really didn't care much about any of us, Papi. Including

me, thinks Flor, looking at her photos, paltry relics saved from disaster.

The way forward is beginning to make itself clear.

It's time to burn her bridges. For good.

She wants nothing more to do with anyone in this family.

No one but her mother, the gentle Aminta.

She will never return to the island, with its stifling atmosphere of repression. She isn't allowed to travel there, anyway.

From now on she'll live alone. Make her own way the best she can.

A woman without a family, without a homeland. A survivor subsisting from day to day.

That's all.

If she and her siblings win the legal battle, so much the better. If not, to hell with it.

A sense of peace and relief washes over her. She buries the photos in the back of a drawer.

New York
1963

Florida turns out to be nothing more than a dreary interlude. Flor scrapes together what funds she's managed to save from bankruptcy and buys a modest apartment in New York. That's where she wants to live now, but she feels as alone as if she were in a desert, a vast desert filled with people. Aminta went back to the familiarity of San Cristóbal some time ago.

With T gone, Flor is no longer either a bargaining chip or a risk for the Americans. As Balaguer's control of the country stabilizes, the vice-grip of her identity relaxes. She loses herself among New York's teeming millions, avoiding Latino areas. The fear has changed sides, and America's Dominican exiles are of another type altogether now; they were followers of T, and are probably under surveillance by both Balaguer's spies and the CIA. Still, in spite of her name, Flor gradually becomes seen as acceptable company again. She renews old friendships, and one evening, at the Royal Box Supper Club in the Americana Hotel, she runs into Rafael Solano. They embrace warmly. He's the club's pianist now. They talk about the good old days at the Do-Ré-Mi.

"You were so angry when you left us! That was in . . . " Flor pauses to think. The years have gone by so quickly.

"October 1955. I remember it like it was yesterday. Lope had 'forgotten' to pay my wages," Rafael says, his fingers making quotation marks in the air.

"Lope's a good singer, but he can't be relied on for anything else!" Flor says, with a slightly forced chuckle.

"Do you know what he's up to these days?"

"Only what I read in the papers. He's remarried, has children now. And he's still singing."

"With mixed success," says Rafael, his tone condescending. "He's a bit old-fashioned now. Never updated his style."

Her old friend is still extremely bitter, Flor realizes. She changes the subject; flattery always does the trick. "You're still a fantastic musician, though, Rafael!"

Solano smiles, preening at the compliment. "I've carved out a niche for myself here. Things are pretty good. What about you, Flor? How are you getting on?"

Flor gives a small shake of her head. "It's been difficult since the . . . the assassination. I'm sure you know the Martínezes have fled to Spain. They've misappropriated everything they could for their own profit. Ramfis has stopped sending me money, and since I don't know how to do anything . . ."

"Still no inheritance, then?"

"I just came back from a meeting with my half-brothers and -sisters in Miami. We've agreed to be represented by an attorney in Geneva, Paul Brechbuhl. He's going to file a claim with the Swiss banks, so . . . stay tuned."[45]

"I hope it'll all work out for you. Truly."

A man in a tuxedo calls to Rafael from the stage.

"Excuse me, Flor; I'd better get back."

Flor and Rafael part with a promise to see one another again soon.

An empty promise. Like so many others.

* * *

Flor surveys herself in the full-length mirror. The coat is perfect, a delicate pale pink that flatters her olive skin. The saleswoman gently adjusts the fur collar around her neck.

---

[45] The City Bank of Miami, represented in Europe by the law firm of Nixon, Stern, Baldwin, and Todd, filed this claim in Switzerland on July 22, 1963.

"It's like it was made for you! It looks absolutely gorgeous."

Flor knows the coat suits her; she doesn't need the saleswoman to tell her that. She's already looked at the price tag, and the amount took her breath away. She always has to try on the most beautiful things, the most expensive things. She takes off the coat regretfully.

"I'll think about it."

She hates herself. Why not admit that the coat's too expensive for her? She thinks back to a time when nothing was out of her reach financially, absolutely nothing. The blithe and easy time when she could simply have any bill sent to the Dominican president's office. The time when her name was worth its weight in gold. Until the assassination, in the happy times when she was in T's good graces, Flor never even thought about money. She had an unlimited credit line at Saks Fifth Avenue. T paid all her debts. But that's over now. Without her inheritance, there are hard times ahead.

Humiliated, she leaves the boutique without saying goodbye.

New York
1963–1965

Balaguer's exile. The return from exile of Bosch, T's longtime opponent. Bosch's election to the presidency.

Flor has little interest in the ups and downs of Dominican politics, though she is pleased about the new constitution, which guarantees unprecedented freedoms such as the legality of labor unions, equality of the sexes, the legalization of divorce, and equality between biological and legitimate children.

The reality, though, is that none of it has anything to do with Flor anymore. She's practically an American now. Her island, first the cradle of her childhood and then an oppressive prison, is nothing but a mass of memories at this point. Only her mother still lives there.

After a period of calm, it starts again. In fact, it gets worse.

Bosch, too chummy with the Communists for the Americans' taste, is deposed by a military coup and flees into exile in Puerto Rico. A new dictatorship replaces him, described as "Trujillism without Trujillo." *That's the last thing I needed*, Flor thinks bitterly when she reads this catchphrase in the paper.

A sort of urban guerilla warfare is declared between the Republic's left-wing "Constitutionalists" and the "Loyalists" in power. The country is as much of a mess as ever.

* * *

When Flor learns that American troops have landed on the island,[46] she's aghast. It's the start of a real war.

---

[46] On April 28, 1965, Operation Power Pack, consisting of 23,000 American troops, landed in the Dominican Republic. The United States Army would remain in Dominican territory until September 1966.

She's worried about her mother, but a phone call reassures her. The campo remains peaceful; it's in the cities that bitter street fighting has erupted.

Flor can't help but think that El Jefe would have been able to avert the war now threatening to rip the country apart.

NEW YORK
APRIL 1965

Flor is in dire straits. It's clear that she's going to have to pawn her last remaining jewels, the ones she hasn't already sold. She's been living hand-to-mouth for four years now, relying on the occasional generosity of various friends. T's vast fortune has evaporated into thin air without her ever seeing a penny of it. She's tried more than once to remind Ramfis of the promises he made to support her after the assassination, but it's wasted effort. The lawsuit filed against the Martínez clan puts them at odds now and is nowhere near reaching a conclusion. The Trujillos aren't even responding to their legal summons.

And really, what's the point in fighting on? The fates have always been against her. The good fairies didn't bother to visit her cradle when she was born, and they've never made up for the omission.

In Spain, María Martínez, back in the land of her ancestors, is living the good life. Ramfis is still plotting to regain power, the scenarios he conjures up becoming ever more hypothetical. Radhames has assumed the role of playboy, a pale imitation of Rubi with infinitely less panache and success, the crisp suit too large for him by a mile. And Angelita has decided, ridiculously, that she wants to be a famous writer.

For Flor, after enduring a decade in disgrace, a period of numbed emotions akin to sleepwalking that she can barely remember, relieved only by the brief happy time with Lope, these last few years have been little more than an endless series of doctor visits and medical treatments, every recovery followed by an almost immediate relapse.

She's never been able to trust or confide in anyone. Never had any true defenses against the curse of her identity or the stares of people around her, their prejudices and assumptions, their scorn and hatred. All she's ever had is a desperate desire for freedom, and an unfortunate tendency to plunge headlong into every new experience.

Is it too late to rebel against crippling fate? To fight the suffering and unhappiness that have a constant grip on her heart? Too late to hope for a transformation? No longer ensnared in her father's net, she yearns to believe that a new beginning is possible.

Flor looks in the mirror, and her worst enemy looks back: the poor opinion she has of herself, the sense of her own worthlessness. Who has ever believed in her? Her mother, sweet Aminta, certainly. Porfirio, briefly. Maurice, tenderly and futilely. As for T...

She spent her childhood trying in vain to earn her father's love. For him, she wanted to be an extraordinary child, but she was only ever an ordinary, love-starved little girl, the one who didn't choose the right dog, who didn't bring home the best grades, who tripped when she tried to dance the merengue.

Her love for T has been an endless torment, her love for Porfirio a curse.

In a flash of clarity, Flor sees that her whole life has been a tragic circus. Or maybe a vulgar burlesque, or a comedic farce in which she's always been the powerless butt of the joke. No matter how desperately she's tried, despite everything, to hope for something better, the same cruel scenes have played out again and again. Her life has never been her own. Some diabolical playwright has forever been scripting its twists and turns.

* * *

Flor sits down at her dining room table—she's had to sell her pretty inlaid wood writing desk, regrettably—and uncaps her old Bakelite pen, a gift from Maurice she still treasures. She dabs the pen on a sheet of fine vellum stationery with the letterhead of the Palacio Nacional—a keepsake from the luxurious days of old that she's preserved like a superstitious child—and a large drop of ink blots the paper, staining her first and middle fingers. She crumples the ruined sheet into a ball and trades the Waterman for a cheap ballpoint lying on the table, a common clear plastic Bic. Well, it's better suited for the tell-all she's about to write.

She's thought about the title for a long time. Nothing very literary has ever come to mind.

My tormented life as T's daughter.

To hell with it. Only the truth matters.

She plunges into the project the same way she used to hold her nose and jump into the rushing waters of the *salto*[47] in San Cristóbal. Her hand trembles. The words pour out.

My tormented life . . .

Only the truth matters.

She's going to tell hers.

* * *

In the end, her tormented life doesn't fill very many pages. There are so many things Flor can't say, wouldn't know how to say, doesn't even know whether she has the *right* to say. She remembers the political killings: Bencosme, Galíndez, the Mirabal sisters. In her country, women who dare to express themselves are murdered. It sends a chill down her spine. Dominican political repression is alive and well; Balaguer, now returned from

---

[47] *Salto*: Waterfall.

exile and soon to be re-elected president, has deliberately taken up her father's torch. His "affable professor" appearance conceals a shrewd strategist and fearsome tyrant. No, Flor can't tell everything, but she's written the essence of it.

She straightens the meager stack of pages on the table. Looking at them, she knows that no reputable publishing house will be interested in her memoir. If she wants to make her voice heard, her only choice is to go to the press. She's already been approached more than once, and she knows that any number of magazines will pay handsomely for her recollections.

Her first choice is *Life*, but in the end it's *Look*[48] that wins the prize by outbidding the competition, offering Flor a tidy sum that she accepts without blinking. Her memoirs will be published in the form of an interview conducted by Laura Bergquist. It will be Flor de Oro Trujillo's swan song.

* * *

Flor has asked Don Manuel Ontañón, a Dominican industrialist, to lend her his residence for conducting the interviews. Her own is far too modest to show the *Look* journalist and photographer. She puts on a simple black dress that flatters her slender figure. Her ever-problematic hair has been tamed by a stylist, and she's done her makeup with care. Laura Bergquist is right on time. Flor is comfortably ensconced in a deep armchair in the living room, a whiskey on the rocks within easy reach, ready to begin the interview.

"I am the daughter of a very simple man and woman. They loved each other, they loved their land, the sun, the moon, and

---

[48] *Look* was a bimonthly illustrated American magazine with very high circulation, published in the United States from 1937 to 1971, the content of which centered more on photographs than articles. The interview with Flor de Oro Trujillo appeared in two parts: "My Tormented Life as Trujillo's Daughter," *Look* 29, no. 12 (June 15, 1965), and "My Life as Trujillo's Prisoner," *Look* 29, no. 13 (June 29, 1965).

me, Flor de Oro. But one day, my mother and I realized we'd lost a husband and father."

"My father's career took shape in the shadow of the military, and very quickly it became extremely rare for me to see him."

"A secret police force under his command? It's quite possible, but I never got involved with political matters. In my situation, I couldn't."

"I love my father, but I was opposed to Trujillo, the president. If I hadn't been his daughter, I would never have been a Trujillist. I never agreed with my father's political principles, but I didn't dare tell him that. No one could disagree with him. I think he made a lot of mistakes, but I agree with Stalin's daughter: I blame them on the party."

Flor knows it's not an exact parallel, but she doesn't care.

As she answers the journalist's questions, it occurs to Flor that this is like a kind of unpacking. Is it really a good idea to air the Trujillos' dirty laundry in public like this?

She's realizing, too, how much she's forgotten. Her memory is full of gaps, playing tricks on her, refusing to knit together the scattered fragments of reminiscence. The second honeymoon-that-never-was with Rubi—was it in Bali or the Bahamas? But strangely, other memories come back with startling clarity. Her visit to Elupina Cordero, Capri, the Nazis' Olympic Games . . .

"I was the only one of Trujillo's many children to be a constant target of his anger. My father and I were like two magnets that attracted and repulsed each other at the same time. I always fled from him, but I always came back because he made everything all right."

"You're right, none of my marriages lasted very long. Only two years each, on average . . . "

She describes every one of her marriages as a frustrating, tragic, and painful experience.

"On what do I blame these failures? It was my father, and he alone, who decided whether my husband was a real man or not. Most of my spouses ended up being owned by him, like a piece of property. I wasn't the only one it happened to—everyone in the whole country got used to having El Jefe think for them. For example, if someone wanted to marry off his daughter but didn't have the money for a dowry, all he had to do was make my father aware of it, and he'd take care of it. It was never-ending theater."

Flor's words reveal no bitterness. She speaks in a light, even tone, as if she were an actress in that theater herself.

"You want to know about Rubirosa, my first husband?"

Flor has been waiting for this question; she's only surprised that it took this long to be asked. She's prepared her answer carefully. She settles herself more comfortably in the armchair, crushes out her cigarette in the crystal ashtray, takes a long swallow of whiskey, and presses the glass to her knee to keep her hand from trembling. She won't say too much; she wants to remain the insignificant first wife she's always been. No one must know. She carefully adopts a tone of derision.

"I must confess, I very rarely benefited from his renowned... gifts. In fact, I'm sure I was never fully aware of them. What made him so famous? He had that charm—he still has it—so often seen in men who don't really *do* anything. Although really, being a playboy isn't a hobby for him; it's his profession." Then she adds, dreamily, "It was so romantic. Our wedding was the most splendid one ever seen in Santo Domingo."

"I remember once, in Paris, we went to see an Arab fortune teller. He had a pile of sand on a low table, and we drew lines in it with a little wand. The fortune teller didn't say very much to Rubi, but he said a lot to me. He predicted that I would marry nine times. My God, how we laughed at that! Now I've been married seven times, and I'm wondering if I'll be able to fulfill the prophecy."

"It affected me deeply when Trujillo was assassinated. He may have been a dictator, but he was also my father. I had to leave my country in great haste. There were many complications. Now I'm beginning to adapt and live for myself."

"Really? People have said Ramfis stored enough money in Swiss and French banks to support the Dominican population for a year? You know, they claim my father was worth $800 million, but I don't believe it. The country was in very poor shape financially."

"I've filed a lawsuit against Ramfis. My attorney is asking for around $40 million."

"My current situation?" Flor laughs, rattling the ice cubes in her whiskey glass and filling her lungs with air. "Whiskey on the rocks, please!" she sings out.

"My preferred arrangement," she continues, "would be to remarry. It would be my eighth time!"

"My hopes for the future? To have a stable, quiet home. I'm tired of running in these sophisticated circles, where you have to do all sorts of crazy things to get ahead. I want a calm life. My father is gone, and now I can live the way I choose."

* * *

The interview takes place over several sessions, and by the end of them Flor is completely wrung out. It's like a kind of psychoanalysis. If only it could permanently wash away the regrets bedeviling her life, the guilt that clings to her like a second skin.

New York
June 1965

Flor dresses in loose, unflattering trousers, wraps a scarf turban-like around her hair, and dons a pair of oversized sunglasses, then glances in the mirror with satisfaction. It would take a truly keen eye to recognize her like this.

She goes down to the newsstand on the corner, and there it is: her own face on full display, on top of a stack of *Look* magazines. The title of the article, "My Tormented Life as Trujillo's Daughter," leaves no room for doubt as to the interview's content.

Biting her lip nervously, Flor opens the magazine. Everyone's going to know, everyone's going to gossip, everyone's going to judge her. She's all too conscious of having exploited the only thing she had left, her name. Did she have the right? Well, it's too late now; there's no going back. She had no choice, she reassures herself. All Ramfis had to do to keep her from talking was not turn his back on her. And she'd felt such an urgent need to tell the truth. For the sake of her own health and sanity, honestly. To tell *her* truth, and to make peace with herself. Or at least try. She'd owed it to herself.

She covers her mess of a life with a copy of the *New York Times*, pays for her purchases, and walks slowly home.

New York
July 1965

It's a punch to the gut. A shot to the heart. Nausea wells up inside her.

It's as if a piece of herself has been torn away. The grief is all the more surprising for being unexpected. She'd thought for a long time that she was safe, immune. In a comfortable place where Rubi couldn't reach her.

But Rubi, it turns out, is an incurable disease.

He is her disease, gnawing away insidiously at her for decades.

Despite the passage of years, despite the pain and jealousy, the husbands and lovers, Flor knows that no one will ever be able to replace the man who has just died. He was her youth, her innocence. Her ruin and her destruction. The great love of her life.

She doesn't want to read the article, but finds herself devouring it down to the last line. Rubi has died in a car accident. His Ferrari hit a tree head-on in the Bois de Boulogne, in the wee hours of a Paris morning. True to form, Porfirio was returning from a party. For all intents and purposes, he'd seemed to be happily married and settled, his fiery passions tamed by his very young wife. But a leopard doesn't change its spots. Flor knows that all too well.

The need to *know* once again overpowering sadness and horror, she runs breathlessly to the corner newsstand and buys up every paper containing details of the accident. Rubi had won the polo Coupe de France and had been celebrating the victory with his team—of which he'd been captain—at Jimmy's nightclub in Paris. He died at nine o'clock in the morning on the way to the hospital. *Avenue de l'Hippodrome.* This detail brings a small, sad smile to Flor's lips. How callous life is, for a man who loved horses so much to die on a street named Hippodrome. Rubi's Ferrari had swerved inexplicably, clipping another car before slamming headlong into a tree.

Inevitably, doubt creeps into Flor's mind. She's still El Jefe's daughter, better placed than almost anyone to know that supposed accidents sometimes conceal ugly truths. Rubi was an incredibly skilled driver; he'd even competed in the 24 Hours of Le Mans auto race. It's hard for Flor to imagine him losing control of his car, even when exhausted, even when drunk. Could this have been murder? Did something in his past catch up with him? Was it a jealous husband's revenge? A settling of scores by the mafia? The CIA? Rubi was involved in so many things. Could he have killed himself? No. *That's* unimaginable. Flor rejects the idea out of hand, preferring to believe in the accident theory, possibly aided by fatigue, alcohol, and insomnia. It's less cruel—Rubi's life ending just as he hovered on the edge of becoming an aging playboy in decline, the thought of which must have horrified him. Flor can't help but think it was an appropriately dashing way for him to go. *This is how legends are created.*

They say your whole life flashes before your eyes as you're dying. Did Porfirio see her? His Fleur? Disembarking from the ocean liner, at the Santiago country club ball, in her wedding dress, in Venice, in Capri? Did he have an instant's regret? Flor chooses to believe that he did, and no one can ever tell her otherwise.

Flor finds herself searching through her record collection. Guided by a phantom hand, she places the vinyl disc on the record player, lifts the arm, and delicately places the needle in the groove. The first nostalgic notes sound on the guitar, and she feels a surprising prickle of tears. Wrapping her arms around herself, Flor begins to sway gently. A part of herself has just been lost. She feels completely empty. In her alcohol- and tobacco-roughened voice, she sings, softly:

Ya no estás más a mi lado, corazón,
En el alma solo tengo soledad...
Por qué Dios me hizo quererte
Para hacerme sufrir más... [49]

* * *

Within a few days, Flor finds her picture splashed all over newspapers and magazines throughout the world. The small round image shows her in her frumpy, old-fashioned wedding gown, with that ridiculous flop of white lace on her head. It's the only photo of her and Rubi together that the press could find. How they got their hands on it, she'll never know. But there she is, the first wife of Porfirio Rubirosa. And she really does come across as his insignificant, timid, youthful love, compared to the impressive record of his later life as an international playboy. All those stunning women, the most beautiful in the world, the richest in the world, the sexiest in Hollywood...

She, Flor de Oro Trujillo, is nothing, and no one cares about her grief, which suits her just fine. She chose to remain in the background a long time ago.

And yet, just for a moment, she regrets it.

At the sight of those magazines, she regrets it.

She regrets not having done anything with her life.

She regrets having let El Jefe control her existence.

She regrets not having joined the political opposition while there was still time.

She regrets not having written a book. Her memoirs. Her travails. Like Angelita, the queen of the fair, who, like her

---

[49] "Historia de un amor," 1955: "You're by my side no more, my love, nothing but loneliness in my soul... why did God make me love you, to make me suffer so..."

mother before her, is hiring ghostwriters to produce poetry and essays and then parading herself around as a woman of letters.

She regrets not having devoted herself to charitable work.

She regrets not having accepted Rubi's invitations to Bali and Havana.

She regrets never having found a replacement for Rubi. Not a worthy one, anyway.

In the many feet of newsprint eulogizing Rubi, she is nothing more than "the eldest daughter of the Little Caesar of the Caribbean." She'll never be anything but her father's daughter. And the forgotten first wife of the most famous playboy in the world.

It will never end.

She'll never be herself, Flor de Oro.

Because she's no one.

Rereading one article, Flor is struck by the words of Rubi's second wife, the French actress. "He died as he lived, with speed and passion."

That was how Flor had loved him from the first.

Speedily, and passionately.

And forever.

New York
October 1965

Her father is gone.
Rubi is dead. He's buried not far from Paris, in the cemetery of Marnes-la-Coquette.
T's resting place is in Père Lachaise Cemetery, 16 rue du Repos, division 85, cross-street 2, in a black marble mausoleum far more eye-catching than the neighboring tomb of Marcel Proust. Flor visited it last year, scraping together the money for a plane ticket to Paris. She'd wanted to have a quiet moment at her father's grave. Her memories of the trip are bitter ones.

It was a cold day, the sky gray and lowering. She'd lingered in one of the flower shops near the cemetery entrance, delaying the moment when she would actually be there, at his grave. Finally she'd emerged, clutching a wicker basket holding an arrangement of white flowers. She'd wandered the lanes of the vast cemetery for a long time before finally daring to ask a gravedigger for the exact location of the tomb. It was a massive edifice, austere and ugly. There were no flowers, no plants, nothing but the cold stone. Flor had placed her basket in front of the metal gate, locked tight with a chain that protected the crypt beyond. The loveliness of the white flowers clashed horribly with the starkness of the mausoleum. She'd bent to rip out the clumps of weeds that had invaded the twin planters cut into the marble on each side of the tomb. Straightening, she'd snagged her stocking on a gnarled shrub jutting from one of the planters. It was then that she'd wept.

Behind that gate, under the ground, lay her father. She'd stayed there for a long time, thinking of nothing, tears streaming down her cheeks. Then, gathering herself and turning around, she'd seen him. Alerted to her visit somehow, a paparazzo was watching her. She'd shouted and lifted an arm to hide her face, but too late. He'd fled. The stolen photograph shows her alone, dressed all in black in front of the mausoleum, her stocking ripped at the knee. It shows her in all her desolation, her distress, her weariness. And of course, that horrible photo had appeared in the papers the next day.

* * *

The two shadows that hovered over her whole existence, coloring and influencing even her most insignificant choices, are nothing but ghosts now.

Flor persuades herself that the deaths are a liberation. Her life will take a different direction now; she's certain of it. After all, she's still only fifty.

For a while, she thinks of going back to Europe to bid a final farewell to Rubi, the man she loved so much, whom she was never able to replace.

She plans the trip. It's a terrible financial stretch; she really doesn't have the money. She remembers the sumptuous travels of her younger years with nostalgia. How easy life used to be. It all feels like a dream now, as if it never really happened at all.

But in the end, she doesn't go.

She has met someone new.

New York
November 1965

As a treat to herself on the publication of her confessions by *Look*, Flor decides to spend some of the $10,000 they paid her on a new suit. A tailored one, made to order. Just like in the old days. And she knows just who she wants to do the job: a Cuban designer whose first Parisian fashion show she attended last year, when she went to France to visit T's tomb.

Flor enters the showroom with shoulders back and head held high, trying to recapture the confident allure of her best years. Miguel Ferreras is sketching in his studio, perched on a high stool at his drawing board, a measuring tape draped around his neck. He likes to act as if he's Oscar de la Renta, but, despite his solid reputation, he doesn't hold a candle to the Dominican couturier. A budget Oscar de la Renta—that's all Flor can afford.

Ferreras looks up at his client. Flor de Oro Trujillo. He's been expecting her. He smiles at her. He knows exactly who she is, and what people say about her. Penniless and not the best judge of character in her relationships. A drinker. There are also the rumors about the immense fortune left by her father, the assassinated Little Caesar of the Caribbean. Hundreds of millions of dollars stuck in Swiss bank accounts. He knows the competition for that jackpot is in full swing, and that the heirs are embroiled in a court battle.

* * *

Ferreras is wildly charming, with his mass of dark hair, a

thick lock flopping continually over one eye, the half-smile lifting the corner of his mouth, his frank, firm handshake, his rich, warm voice and soft accent. He and Flor discuss styles, cuts, and fabrics and come to an agreement. When he calls for an assistant to take her measurements, Flor's mouth turns down in a little pout, and she demands to be looked after by the couturier himself. That's why she came here, after all. It's out of the question for him to turn her over to one of his seamstresses.

She undresses. She's carefully chosen her undergarments and slip, white silk and lace, contrasting prettily with her olive skin. Miguel Ferreras circles her, leaning, straightening, crouching, kneeling. His light eyes meet her dark ones and hold them. Flor surveys him. This is the first time a man's ever gotten down on his hands and knees in front of her. She smiles at the thought, with that wide, guileless, dazzling smile that lights up her whole face. That's the one thing that can never be taken away from her: that tropicality, that island air, that Latin quality. Ferreras might be practically American, but he's Cuban in his blood. That similarity links them, and Flor can feel it in the deepest part of her. She sways slightly on her feet.

Euphoric, she orders a cocktail dress, too. Strapless.

Miguel and Flor breathe each other in, brushing, grazing one another's bodies, fingers on skin. He has the gray-tinged complexion of a Latino man who hasn't spent enough time in the sun, whose skin will take on the color of honey after even an hour or two outside. Flor eyes his muscular shoulders, the glimpse of smooth chest. Her nostrils quiver as she catches the faint, fresh scent of his cologne: Guerlain's Impériale. The same one T always wore. Her gaze falls on the beauty mark at the base of his neck, the curve of his ear with its slightly elongated lobe. The finely-cut groove between his nose and upper lip, the line of his jaw, the dimpled chin, the thick dark hair. She reaches out to run her fingers through the dark mass, but stops herself just in time. That forelock falling over one eye. She can see that his gaze is riveted to the line of her knee, the fingers of one hand just barely brushing her skin. She studies those long, fine fingers with their impeccably manicured nails. The tracery of veins just visible on the backs of his hands. His wedding ring.

His gaze moves from her tiny feet, the toenails painted crimson, past her dainty ankles, up the slender line of her calf. Pinning up the hem of the dress, he uncovers her knees with their perfectly delineated kneecaps, the delicate hollow at the back of her knee. Shorter. Exposing the soft skin of her thigh. His eyes run the rest of the way up her slim torso, leaving a trail of fire in their wake. The roundness of her cheekbone, the bridge of her impish little nose, the still virtually unlined dome of her forehead. The dress has a ruffle running around the bustline and he brushes a piece of lint away from it with the back of his hand, feeling the small, youthful breasts, the firm nipples. His fingers slide around to her back, pulling the fabric straight between her shoulder blades, which stand out like the wings of a bird. She closes her eyes, feeling slightly dizzy. He pins the dress along the line of her spine, fitting it to the small of her back, ensuring that the fabric hugs the curve of her bottom perfectly. Flor feels a familiar sensation, a wonderful one: the hot tingle of desire. She tries in vain to quash the feeling. She's a middle-aged woman. Her days of swooning over men are long gone. They have to be.

They meet several more times for fittings and alterations. More than they need to. Flor rapturously awaits each visit to Ferreras's studio, and at every session, the dance begins again. An extraordinary sensuality emanates from this man. Beneath the American polish, Flor can detect the perfume of the islands. By the time the suit and dress are finally ready, Miguel Ferreras knows Flor's body like the back of his hand, and what he hasn't seen, he's imagined. This is a new occurrence for him, and it unsettles him. He's never felt this way about a client before. Women's bodies hold no mystery for a couturier. But Flor's body affects him.

More than anything, it speaks to him. Of unrelenting sun, turquoise seas, sugared flavors. Of the joyous music that belongs only to those who come from that part of the world.

There is a bond, a fellowship, an indescribable *something* between the fashion designer and the dictator's daughter that no one can understand if they weren't born on a Caribbean island, beneath the tropical sun. It's sweet and sensual and violent all at once. It can't be put into words, only felt. And both Flor and Miguel are powerless to resist it.

Miguel Ferreras insists on delivering the finished clothing to Flor's home himself. She's reluctant to give him her address. Her apartment is far from luxurious, not what one would expect from T's daughter.

But she also knows the die has been cast. And so she gives in.

Miguel unzips the garment bags.

Flor smiles at him.

"One last fitting?"

He bows.

Signed, sealed, delivered.

Flor, who has only recently rediscovered that life can be worth living, is certain that this is her ticket to new happiness.

December 1965. Snowy marriage, happy marriage?

If you could only see me now, Papi! And you, Rubi!

Flor has finally become the wife she's always dreamed of being. Lovely, bursting with health and vigor. Married to an artist, rubbing elbows with creative types, photographers, journalists, publicists. Fulfilled emotionally, sexually, and socially. Miguel is handsome, easily comparable to Rubi, and artistic and intelligent into the bargain. They share so much: their love of socializing (sometimes to excess), their Hispanic heritage. How wonderful it is to follow the heart's urges again, after so long.

That's the story Flor tells herself, anyway.

Because there's always a B side to the romance. There are always the mundane underpinnings.

* * *

It starts with Ferreras's separation and divorce from his second wife Oonagh, heiress to the Guinness family fortune. The reasons for this are never made clear. Miguel owes the creation of his New York design house and its Parisian office to the Guinness wealth, and his client roster to Oonagh's mile-long address book. Not only that, but they've just adopted two babies, Mexican twins named María and Alejandro, who arrived at Orly Airport in September 1964 to great fanfare and public attention at around the same time as Miguel's fashion show.

There are the two daughters from Miguel's first marriage, whose births enabled him to obtain American citizenship.

There's his taste for luxury, his extraordinary appetite for money, his unquenchable thirst for publicity, his need to shine in the media, his preference for women older than him, preferably with famous names.

And Flor's name glitters like gold.

Flor is aware of all of this. She just chooses to ignore it.

"Remember, Flor, a woman is nothing without a husband."

El Jefe's words echo in her mind.

Are they the reason for this eighth marriage?

This will be the first marriage her father won't be able to meddle in. It's her own decision. No matter how poorly thought out.

* * *

In bed, the early promise gives way to dull routine, and Flor thinks nostalgically of the passion she shared with Rubi. What a curse, to have had her first sexual experiences with a man no one can equal.

And then there's everything she finds out during the five shaky years of her marriage to Ferreras.

He gets some credit for being attracted to a woman of fifty, some twelve years his senior, a little island bird with a smooth forehead and the figure of a teenager, who is far from looking her age. That's a "weakness" Flor can live with.

His one-night dalliances, often with young nymphets encountered at his design house or one of the city's many nightclubs, are regrettable. But they can be overlooked.

The fact that he's considered provincial and talentless by the New York elite is unfortunate—but not the end of the world.

One might even look beyond his meetings, before the marriage, with President Nixon, whose office is keeping a file on T's dispossessed children to assess the chances of gaining access to the Swiss accounts, a completely legitimate interest.

He can even be forgiven for his vexation when the dream of getting his hands on T's millions evaporates. Understandable disappointment.

But it gets worse.

Miguel Ferreras is not Miguel Ferreras.

New York
December 1969

He lingered in agony for ten days, and no one even bothered to inform her. Flor learns the bad news, as she has so many times before, via the press, and it catches her completely off-guard.

Ramfis, El Pato, the successor, has just died following a car accident in Madrid.

Flor is shocked, yes. But unmoved. As if the death has absolutely nothing to do with her. As if "Ramfis" were just any six letters printed in a newspaper. As if he weren't her half-brother, the man who'd once sworn to be another father to her.

She feels so far away from them now. A complete stranger to that family inconvenienced by her very existence, that family that has simply erased her from their lives. She knows nothing about them anymore. It's been years since she had any contact with them at all.

Then . . . the aftershock. Flor recalls the little boy with the big, sad eyes and sharply parted hair, that dark hair so carefully styled with pomade. The medal-heavy uniform swamping his tiny body. His shy smile. A sob rises painfully in her throat.

Other images follow, though. The angry teenager overindulged by T. The general in full regalia complete with dark Ray-Bans. The alcoholic blackout drunk on vodka. The debauched party-lover with his tawdry exploits. The sadistic torturer and executioner. *He's finally paid for everything he did, and everything he didn't do, for all his promises unkept.* No. Ramfis wasn't a good man. But he was still her brother.

His Ferrari had slammed into a car driven by the Duchess

of Albuquerque, who had been killed on impact. He'd fought for his life for ten days, during which speculation about the crash had run amok. Many suspect an execution by agents of Balaguer's government—unless, of course, it was a settling of scores by the mafia.

The irony of the story isn't lost on Flor. Ramfis has always followed in Porfirio's wake, now imitating him even in the way he died. A car accident. Always the understudy. Poor Ramfis. Flor wipes away the single tear that trickles down her cheek. It will be the only one. Her heart has run dry of grief.

Ramfis doesn't deserve it.

And since no one in the family bothered to notify her, she won't gratify them by reaching out.

Exeunt Ramfis.

Flor takes a deep breath, empties her mind, and decides to go for a walk in the fresh air.

New York
1970

"I'd advise you to read this with a clear head, preferably somewhere calm and quiet."

Michael Shields delivers the warning with an expression that speaks volumes. Flor pays his bill without batting an eyelash, even though it's for $380. Shields pushes a large brown envelope across his desk to her, the result of six weeks of investigation and research. It isn't very thick, but the number of sheets inside doesn't reflect the magnitude of the revelations they contain. Flor stuffs her checkbook and the envelope into her bag, trying not to reveal her distress. Murmuring a vague thank you and goodbye, she leaves Michael Shields's office on unsteady feet. Outside in the hallway, she sways, leaning against the wall for a moment to collect herself. Then she leaves the building, walking slowly and carefully, as if her handbag contains a bomb.

* * *

Flor finds an anonymous coffee shop and slides into a booth at the back. She orders a café au lait and opens the envelope with trembling hands. It takes her two fumbling tries to extract the sheets of paper inside. She fills her lungs with air and breathes out slowly, once, twice, like Maurice taught her to do whenever she's under stress. And then she starts to read.

M.S. Investigations
450 7th Avenue #805, New York
Tel: 212-748-6893

March 9, 1970

Dear Mrs. Trujillo de Ferreras,
Please find enclosed the results of the investigation I've conducted at your request concerning Mr. Miguel Ferreras, as well as my bill and expense sheet.
Sincerely yours,
Michael Shields

INVESTIGATION REPORT

The real name of the individual known as Miguel Ferreras is José Maria Ozores Laredo.

My God! A false identity? Everything has been a lie from the very beginning. Flor feels as if the blood is draining from her body. The disappointment is crushing. She keeps reading. Every new revelation is like a splash of acid to the heart.

José Maria Ozores Laredo was born in 1922 in Ribadeo, in the province of Lugo, Galicia, Spain.

He wasn't born in Havana? 1922 . . . that makes him forty-eight years old. He's been passing himself off as five years younger. That explains the contradictory remarks he's made about his age. And this explains, too, the traces of an odd accent, the strange hissing consonants. A memory rises to the surface like a flash of light; it had surprised her at the time, but, in the flush of new love, she'd brushed it off. Miguel's bewildered expression when she'd told him to when to meet her—*a la hora que mataron a Lola*—with a conspiratorial wink, proud of being able to show him how well she knew Cuba. No one knows who Lola is, or why she was killed, but every Cuban knows that the phrase refers to three P.M. Every Cuban but Miguel. These jarring little notes should have sounded louder in her mind. She feels a surge of anger at herself for not paying more attention to them.

> Born to a single mother who couldn't afford to have him educated, he was raised in an orphanage in the city before being taken in by an uncle.
> Too young to fight in the Spanish Civil War, he moved to Madrid as a teenager, where he became a petty criminal known for his bisexuality.

Well, his bisexuality is no surprise. Flor's used to that. Her years with Rubi were a complete education in the twisted sexuality of men. And as for his being a petty criminal, T, her own father, started out the same way. A youthful indiscretion. Forgivable.

> Following Franco's victory in 1939, Ozores was arrested for theft in 1941. He narrowly avoided a prison sentence and got away with a warning from the police.
> In July 1941, Ozores joined the Blue Division[50], the 250th infantry division of the Wehrmacht, and was sent to the Eastern front to fight the Communists alongside the Nazis.

It was that same hatred of the Communists that obsessed T during the last years of his life! But it's a long way from there to fighting alongside the Germans.

---

[50] The 250th infantry division of the Wehrmacht, officially called the División Española de Voluntarios, better known as the División Azul, or Blue Division, was a corps of 17,692 Spanish volunteers created by General Franco during the last week of June 1941, immediately after the German attack on the Soviet Union, and put at the disposal of the Nazi Wehrmacht to fight on the Eastern front. Recalled to Spain on October 5, 1943, it was dissolved on November 17 of that year.

> *He deserted after four months, not far from Leningrad. He was arrested by the German military police and imprisoned for a month, then sent back to Spain. He was permitted to reenlist in 1943.*
>
> *Upon the dissolution of the Blue Division in November 1943, he again returned to Spain.*
>
> *Arrested for theft by the Madrid police on two separate occasions in 1944, he returned to Nazi Germany to escape punishment.*

Flor puts the report down on the table and closes her eyes for a few seconds. She's breathing hard, her head spinning. After a moment, she keeps reading.

> *Ozores made contact with the pro-Hitler fascists of the Spanish Falange, which smuggled volunteers across the border. Several weeks later a record appears of him having joined the Waffen-SS. He became an officer, serving in Romania and Yugoslavia.*

Flor chokes. The Waffen-SS! This is only getting worse and worse. She recalls the ordeal of her months in Berlin, the quiet loathing she felt for the Nazis; her upraised arm during the opening ceremonies of the Olympics; her friend Lucie's flight. And all the horrors that have been revealed since the war. A wave of disgust for the monster described in these pages sweeps over her. Some things might be forgivable, but not this. She forces herself to keep reading.

> *Ozores was captured in Italy by the Allies and repatriated to Spain in December 1945. Once again, he fled the country to escape the law.*
>
> *Joaquin Ferreras, a Cuban who served with Ozores, had a brother named Miguel, who was being treated for*

tuberculosis in a Spanish sanatorium. Joaquin let Ozores use his brother's birth certificate to obtain a Cuban passport, Miguel having been born in Havana on January 28, 1927. The two men traveled to Havana together, where they went into petty trade.

So, in fact there's nothing Cuban about him. He hardly even knows Havana, or any of the places Flor used to love. He doesn't know the particular cadences of the language, or *la hora de Lola*, and he certainly doesn't dance like a Cuban. That might have been the first thing that made her suspicious, actually. That telltale rigidity in his hips.

The real Miguel Ferreras died in 1949, while Ozores, now using his name, was studying fashion design in New York, paying for it with the money earned in Havana. In the meantime, he married, thanks to which he obtained American citizenship. He and his wife had two daughters and quickly divorced.

Ozores did his apprenticeship in the 1950s with the couturier Charles James, but was dismissed due to conflict with his employer. His attestation of employment mentions mechanical knowledge but "no real talent, except for self-promotion."

Ozores opened his first studio in New York. He lost money but managed to be mentioned in Life *magazine with a phony story about a gown made for Elizabeth Taylor.*

Oh, Liz Taylor, is that all? What unbelievable nerve! But Flor has no trouble believing it. It smacks of Miguel's obsession with being talked about, no matter what the cost.

He married Oonagh Guinness at the Drake Hotel in New York in 1957. Joaquin Ferreras stood witness at the ceremony.

It's so simple. Marry a rich woman and use her as a springboard. Flor fell into right into the trap. And not just with Ferreras. It's all she has ever been, a source of wealth, a tool for advancement—only, in her case, Ferreras bet on the wrong horse.

> *His life with the Guinness heiress was marked by scandal, particularly during his trips to Paris, where he was seen at several gay nightspots. He was also suspected of abusing his teenage stepson, Tara.*
>
> *During the divorce, Oonagh Guinness's attorneys uncovered the checkered former life of Miguel Ferreras. Confronted with his Nazi past, Ferreras denied being Ozores. Miss Guinness obtained a divorce in 1965.*

That was shortly after he met Flor. She remembers it perfectly; she'd found it flattering at the time, that he'd asked for a divorce so he could marry her. One more lie on a list so long it makes her want to vomit.

* * *

There are times when life punches you right in the gut, and this is one of those times. Flor slumps against the faux leather seat of the booth, nauseated.

She doesn't even bother looking through the rest of the documents: copies of a birth certificate, legal documents, other certificates. There's no point.

It's a monumental let-down, and she has no one to blame but herself. This marriage has never been anything but a minefield. For five years, blinded by a troubled and uncontrollable passion born of loneliness, she's shared her life with an intriguer, a bisexual Spanish petty criminal who also happens to be a Nazi, now turned mediocre fashion designer. A liar, a thief, a swindler, an imposter, a gigolo. Quite a rap sheet. All the clues were there, staring her right in the face, and she chose not to see them, just buried her head in the sand. If T were still around, he'd have a good laugh at her and then administer some sort of punishment. Suddenly Flor is ashamed of herself, so ashamed she can hardly bear it. She really is incapable of having a normal life, even after being freed from T's control. She's still bearing that cross, and she'll bear it forever.

Life is nothing but an endless series of disappointments, peppered with occasional, fleeting bursts of happiness to which people give far too much importance. Flor angrily dashes away the tears trickling down her cheeks. A thunderstorm has begun outside, the pavement gleaming wet. The raindrops mingle with her tears, cold as her heart. She *will* turn this betrayal into a blessing.

She refuses to give in to despair. It only takes a few weeks to obtain her divorce.

She becomes Flor de Oro Trujillo again.

Her eternal curse.

She seeks solace from this latest disillusionment in solitude and alcohol, as she knows so well how to do.

SANTO DOMINGO
OCTOBER 1970

1

1970 is a terrible year.

Flor has no trouble getting a divorce from Ferreras, given the revelations brought to light by the investigation she commissioned. And once the last hopes of obtaining T's inheritance were gone, the pseudo-Cuban had virtually lost interest in her anyway. He agrees to the separation without protest, merely denying the facts in the dossier—though weakly, especially since this is the second time a wife has divorced him because of his troubled past.

Flor has little time to dwell on the whole ugly episode. Her mother is dying. Wracked with anguish, she flies back to the Dominican Republic, hoping to make it in time. The terrible memory of missing her father's funeral plagues her through every moment of the journey.

At the Las Americas airport, the immigration officer glances balefully at her passport.

"Wait a few moments, please, Ms. . . . Trujillo."

He utters the name like it burns his tongue. Lips pressed into a grim line, he disappears into a small room with a sign on the door reading "Immigration." When he comes back, his step is purposeful.

"Follow me, please, Ms. Trujillo."

Flor does, and finds herself facing a high-ranking officer with a face like a bulldog.

"Reason for stay?"

No one with a valid Dominican passport is ever questioned this way. Flor answers readily, despite the humiliation.

"My mother is dying. I received an urgent call from one of my aunts."

"Place of residence during your stay?"

"San Cristóbal."

"Duration of stay?"

Flor's eyes fill with tears. The officer's face remains impassive. He was trained by the Trujillo school: no pity, no empathy.

"I don't know. I told you . . . my mother is dying."

The officer doesn't have enough braid on his uniform to make the decision alone. They make Flor wait while several phone calls are made. It takes time, going all the way to the presidential palace. Balaguer, T's old crony, his puppet president, is now reigning over the island, and, beneath his air of respectability, he's presiding over a dictatorship hardly less bloody than that of his mentor. President Balaguer, who was Flor's uncle by marriage during her union with Lope, asks to speak to Flor. Given the circumstances, and out of the sheer kindness of his heart (or is it to avoid a scandal?), he agrees to allow Flor to travel to San Cristóbal, but she must keep a low profile, and she'll be under surveillance the whole time. Trujillos are no longer welcome on the island. The country has started over with a clean slate and no longer wants anything to do with them.

* * *

Flor crosses Santo Domingo from east to west in a limousine sent by Balaguer. A mark of attention, or a way of keeping an eye on her? She doesn't care either way. She lets herself be distracted from her grief by the view beyond the window, so different from what it used to be. The big town with its single-story homes has become a modern city. Taller buildings, wider streets, more cars. Much more traffic, much more noise, many more voices. Flor no longer even recognizes the city of her youth. It makes her feel wistful, bringing home the extent of the change wrought by the past decade. Hardly more than ten years have transformed the country of her birth, meticulously erasing every trace of El Jefe.

* * *

Flor is at her mother's bedside when she passes away, and it's small consolation. At eighty-two years old, Aminta has been worn down by life, by El Jefe's miserliness, his constant snubs, the humiliation, the isolation. Flor holds her hand, wiping her face with a damp cloth and murmuring in her ear that she loves her. She even gets a weak smile out of Aminta when she talks of their Italian holiday together. And she lies, too, telling her mother that she's just met a nice man, a doctor who will love her and take care of her, and that she's happy, very happy. Aminta closes her eyes, reassured. And then, quietly, she slips away.

Flor has her mother interred at the cemetery in Gazcue. There are only a handful of them following the casket. A simple headstone; Flor can't afford anything else. When it comes time to have the stone engraved, Flor realizes that Aminta's birth certificate is unobtainable and that she no longer remembers the date of her birth. In the end, she has the engraver put only Aminta's death date. October 13, 1970.

The loss of the only person who ever loved her unconditionally, the only one who truly cared about her, is immense, the grief unbearable, beyond anything Flor knew she was capable of feeling. It's a childlike grief, tinged with horror and bottomless fear.

She's alone in the world now.

New York
December 1970

Flor returns to her permanent home, at 325 East 79th Street in Manhattan. An anonymous, fifteen-story brick building on the Upper East Side, an unostentatious, reasonably bourgeois neighborhood.

She reads in the newspaper that María, Angelita, and Radhames—the remnants of the Trujillo clan—have won their case. She hasn't been consulted. T's casket has been discreetly transferred from Paris to the Mingorrubio cemetery in Spain, in the district of El Pardo just outside Madrid. El Jefe now rests beside Ramfis in a sort of miniature Pantheon constructed of columned black marble, its frontage engraved with "Familia Trujillo" in gold letters. The choice of architecture was La Españolita's.

The mausoleum is both sinister and pretentious, Flor decides when she travels to Spain to visit T's last resting place. *Will I be buried here beside you, in the Trujillo crypt?* she wonders. *After all, whatever happens to me, no matter who I marry, I always find myself bearing your name again, like a cross, like a curse.*

Having bid farewell to her mother, Flor de Oro now takes a final leave of her father, El Jefe, the man who orchestrated her entire life.

She will never return to Spain, and she will never see any of the Trujillos again.

Back in New York, Flor retreats into the solitude of her modest apartment, a far cry from the sumptuous residences of her youth. She'll rarely venture out of it again, spending her time reading novels and newspapers, with an occasional trip to the movies. A monotonous, reclusive life. A quiet life.

So many things are buried within her, lost forever. Sometimes, though, in a sudden burst of energy, she renews an old friendship for the duration of a day at the races or an evening at the theater, just to remind herself that she's still alive.

NEW YORK
1974

Flor shifts uncomfortably, half-reclining on a chaise lounge, sunlight filtering weakly through the blinds. She eyes the man with half-lidded eyes sitting across from her in a battered brown leather armchair. He's waiting.

Doubt blossoms in her mind. What the hell is she doing here? But no one *made* her come, of course. She's here of her own free will.

It's a book, *La Confession de Carlos, tueur à Saint-Domingue*,[51] that's brought her to this couch. A book she happened to spot in the window of a bookstore in her neighborhood, whose pages took her back in time to the dark years of the dictatorship. Acts of violence, murders, kidnapping, torture, rapes, terror, repression. Reading the book, Flor collided head-on with the ghost of what the repentant killer calls God, and everything came flooding back.

Exactly three lines in the book are devoted to her. They describe her as T's eldest daughter from his first marriage. As the first wife of Porfirio Rubirosa. And as a collector of husbands. That's all. That is the sum total of her life. She might as well not exist. Has she ever existed?

She'd thought that enough water had flowed under the bridge that none of that would matter anymore. She was wrong. Images and memories have come back to haunt her. And pain. It's been so painful.

---

[51] Gabriel Conesa, *La Confession de Carlos, tueur à Saint-Domingue* (Paris: Éditions Julliard, 1974).

Painful enough to bring her here.

To be fixed. Can what is broken in her be fixed? Can they make it so the past can't hurt her anymore? She's never been able to manage it on her own. With help, though, maybe it will be possible after all.

* * *

Flor closes her eyes. A happy little girl with a bouncing, lopsided gait is there, very near, demanding an explanation. *Why did you betray me?* Flor knows that she lost herself somewhere along the path between child and adult. She'll go back to that little girl now, put her arms around her, explain it. She'll try to make little Flor forgive her. She owes her that much.

She takes a deep breath and plunges in, like the street urchins in Rio who will jump into the ocean from Sugarloaf Mountain for a few reals. The man across from her hasn't moved a muscle. Her first words, emerging in a shaky voice, hang in the air. The words are hesitant, painfully articulated. She feels as if she's stripping herself bare.

"I am . . . the daughter of . . . the Ogre of the Caribbean."

The air thickens between them. A pause.

The Ogre of the Caribbean. It sounds like the beginning of a children's fairy tale. The ogre never wins in those stories, and the hero is always saved in the end.

One of the worst dictators the world has ever known. Cruel, manipulative, evil, bloodthirsty. A murder, a torturer, a rapist. How can I call a man like that my papa? This is what Flor should say. But she can't. El Jefe is her father. Despite everything, he will always be her father.

"People called him the Benefactor of the Fatherland . . . "

How can she sum him up in a few words? They'll never be sufficient.

"He made the Dominican motto out of an acrostic of his name: *Rectitud, Libertad, Trabajo, Moralidad.*"

Silence.

"I could do the same thing," Flor adds. She pauses, then gives a sour little laugh. "Fiasco? Failure? Then Lost, or maybe Laughable . . . or Lonely, that's not bad either. Lots of choices for the 'O': Oppressed, or Orphaned, perhaps? I'd choose Orphaned, I think. And R, for . . . Ruined. Rejected."

"That's how you define yourself?"

Flor sighs bitterly and nods. "Yes. A lost orphan who lived off the regime like a parasite, whose life is a fiasco, a total failure. Lovely picture, isn't it? You've got your work cut out for you, Doc."

"You're very hard on yourself."

Flor shrugs, thinking of El Jefe again.

"It was so complicated, so painful, to be the daughter of a father like that. To try to live without being contaminated by what he was. It still is, even though I'm not his *thing* anymore. I never had the strength to really cut the ties. Sometimes I felt like he was an actor playing a role, mixing hatred, love, evil, greatness, ridiculous extravagance, like . . . a reincarnated pharaoh. In Christian tradition, a father's sins are visited on three generations that come after him. But I'm barren, thank goodness. My children that never were . . . they won't have to bear the curse."

Flor can't believe she just said all of that out loud. She opens her eyes slightly and observes the doctor. She wants him to look at her, to feel compassion for her, but of course that isn't what he's here for.

And all of a sudden it becomes easier. Flor wrests open the cracked door a bit further and lets the words pour out. She digs deep into her memory. Her father, the compass of her existence. His nasal voice that undermined his dignity. The mustache that would have looked ridiculous on anyone but him. His splendid dress uniforms, his bicorn hat, his perfectly manicured hands, his barked instructions, his scorn. How difficult it was, living with a tyrant. How difficult to swim in his wake without swallowing any water, to absorb the shocks and convulsions of History.

She speaks of her love for her home island, too. The island all but forbidden to her now. The poetic beauty of its landscape. The gentle souls of its people.

It all tumbles out pell-mell, sentence fragments, long silences, deep sighs, misty eyes, real tears.

After forty-five minutes, a discreet bell chimes.

End of session.

* * *

Flor finds herself outside on the New York pavement, the spring sun warming her body and soul. She's astonished to realize that she's walking with a step almost as light as those of other women. She feels strangely buoyant, despite all she didn't manage to say.

The hand clamped around her heart beginning to relax its grip . . . the pent-up words spilling out of her . . . the overflowing emotion . . . the unexpected absence of shame . . . it's a revelation. Dizzying. The deep unhappiness emanating from every pore when she stepped into the psychiatrist's office has lifted. What a relief it is to talk, even if you don't say very much, or say it very well. Flor, who has never been able to open her heart to anyone without being betrayed, makes her decision.

She'll be back.

Dr. David Wetzner, Park Avenue and 92nd Street.

The little girl with the lopsided gait winks at her and smiles.

* * *

Flor comes to know the office décor like the back of her hand. The heavy curtains, squashy sofa, battered old armchair. The little bowl of cinnamon sticks and citrus peel that does little to mask the odor of stale tobacco.

Here, the slow work of self-examination begins. There are childhood wounds that have never healed over. The unconditional love for her father, endlessly struck down by his indifference. His disappearance from the San Cristóbal household. The pain of her banishment to France with only a rag doll for company. Her report cards that were never good enough. Her mother, forbidden from attending her wedding.

There is Porfirio. The boundless hope engendered in her by their love. The days of sweetness and laughter, the bad days, the slaps. There's the unreliable Ramón, the kind and devoted Maurice. And then all the others. The eternal pattern of illusion, manipulation, humiliation, disappointment.

Sometimes her frustration and anger explode into bitterness, everything she's held inside for so long gushing out in long bursts of sobs and rage and anguish, violent as a hurricane, sweeping aside everything in their path. Then, once the wave has passed, she finds herself on the shore again, drained and peaceful.

* * *

"What's your first name?" the psychoanalyst asks, his voice calm.

"Flor."

"Flor?"

"Flor de Oro Anacaona."

"Anacaona?"

"It was the name of a female Taino tribal chief. It means Flower of Gold. My father chose it as a tribute to my country. But people just call me Flor."

Flor de Oro. Flower of Gold.

"Anacaona was a *cacica*, a powerful woman, a warrior who courageously fought the Spanish invaders."

Her father had chosen the name, but it's so pretentious. Has she always seen herself as some rare and precious object, even as a very little girl? This is what she's trying so hard to untangle in her mind.

She speaks of Julia, that perfect baby, the sister who passed away before she was born. Was the die cast even before Flor's own birth? Was she ever anything but the replacement child?

She tells the doctor about washing her father's belt in the river in return for a handful of pesos. About the episode with the puppy. Her whole life has only ever been made up of her father's choices. A beginning that wrecks a person from the inside. Did her ever-present feeling of being different, separate from the rest of the world, of living on the margins of her life, stem from that? When did she first feel as if she were disappearing, dissolving? When did she become a mere shadow, a nothing, existing for no one?

* * *

"Why do you keep getting married?" her friend Idalina had asked Flor the day after her seventh wedding. Flor has never wanted to think too deeply about the question, but it has a simple answer.

Because El Jefe forced me to.

Was she simply a living windfall for men? A gold mine? There was a tribute to be rendered to El Jefe. A price to pay. And she was the price.

Thanks to the hours spent wandering the alleys and byways of her mind, Flor realizes, now, that it was neither her morals nor a bourgeois concern for decorum that drove her to marry so many times. It wasn't that *she* got married; it was that men married *her*. On El Jefe's orders. And the difference is immense.

"My father didn't want me to be one of those women who men slept with and then discarded a few hours later—like the women who ended up in his own bed, or Porfirio's. I'm not that type. I'm the kind of girl you marry."

"Is that you speaking, or your father?" asks the doctor.

Flor considers the question. T made her a prisoner from the moment of her birth. The marriages were his way of keeping her under his thumb, of subjugating the men who became interested in her, bending them to his will, forcing them to acknowledge the value of his Flor de Oro.

She submitted to these marriages because, beyond being pressed into them, beyond wanting to please her father, they were also her way of getting revenge on Porfirio, of proving to him beyond the shadow of a doubt that she was worth more than all his mistresses put together.

"And I should mention money. Money was my father's only way of expressing affection. He bought everything: people, land, industries, my husbands. I benefited from his power, his fortune, his omnipotence, but I was gullible and optimistic. He never told me directly when he was angry with me; he always sent a messenger to do that. Is that how a father speaks to his daughter? I would have been ashamed to complain or admit I was ill. That would have been offensive, given my position. But I was never free. And in the end they all abandoned me. My father, my husbands, my uncles, my brother. My whole life has been nothing but separations and abandonments. There was only my mother."

"Your mother?"

"My mother, poor Aminta, God rest her soul. She hardly existed. She was a deeply religious woman with simple tastes. She was completely devoid of ambition. She'd defied her parents by marrying my father, and that was the only act of bravery in her whole life. And it was a huge mistake. My mother loved me, but she couldn't really give me any guidance. She didn't understand my father's moods or desires, and she was afraid her advice would only make him angrier. He erased her from his life very early on. She was always afraid of him—like me. Never had the strength to stand up to him. I was a slave to my love for him, my fear of him. For years I had no freedom whatsoever. But even so, there were always two people inside me.

The one that bowed to his authority, and the rebel. The rebel found unhealthy ways of defying him, and the submissive one suffered the consequences."

"It's long past time for you to rid yourself of this neurotic fixation on your father and to make peace with yourself, because you have nothing to feel guilty about," the doctor says at the end of one session. "You have to stop carrying around the weight of mistakes that aren't your own, of the identity you've had to bear. Your name is not a life sentence."

* * *

Once she's started down the path, Flor's journey is so rapid that it startles the psychoanalyst. And little by little, the burden of guilt lifts. She's been like a fly, she realizes, hurling itself futilely against a closed window, when the one next to it is wide open.

She tells everything. There are episodes she'd like to skip past, like her most recent marriage, a hell of a mistake that El Jefe had nothing to do with forcing her into, but she summons her courage and faces it all.

"Which of your husbands did you truly love?"

"All of them. I loved them all, each in a different way, though sometimes very briefly."

She admits her loneliness. "After my father died, I was like some odious thing. I became persona non grata in my own country, and I found myself totally alone. I've always been a woman caught between two worlds, a foreigner wherever I go. Even now, I'm living far from home."

And so, bit by bit, Flor shrugs off everything that's been weighing her down. Her anger, her frustration, her sorrow. She admits that, above everything else, she remains her father's daughter, marked forever, indelibly. The stark sense that she is two people at once, a woman and El Jefe's daughter, a feeling that has almost driven her mad many times, softens and fades. If she can't escape her identity, even by changing her name, as she's sometimes thought, she can still free herself from the paralysis rooted so deeply within her, the hopeless malaise that has ravaged her to the core.

Looking back over her life, Flor sees that she's never actually built anything solid. On the contrary, it's been nothing but a series of failures, a field of rubble, a tragic, dramatic, chaotic whirl driven by the search for love, for some unattainable peace. She doesn't want to be a mere spectator anymore. She's tired of the questions, persistent as a swarm of yellowjackets, of the dark thoughts she has to push away every morning on waking. She wants to be part of the world outside herself at last, to really live, for and by herself, as much as she possibly can. She has to accept herself for who she is; she can take it. The important thing is to keep moving forward, seizing along the way those small happinesses that do so much to soothe the soul.

There's still the matter of her addictions to deal with, fully and permanently, and she knows that won't be easy.

And there's also the inexorable slide toward old age, the increasing vulnerability she'll have to gain mastery over. Sometimes she imagines what's to come. The isolation. The decline.

* * *

She scrutinizes her face in the mirror for long moments. It's more serious now. Her cheekbones stand out sharply in her gaunt face. Little fans of fine wrinkles have appeared at the corners of her eyes, and two vertical lines frame her mouth. She forces herself to smile. Strangely, despite everything she's been through, her expression hasn't hardened. In fact, if anything, her eyes seem softer. She can even see a spark of the old impishness in them, a trace of the child she once was. She decides that she likes this new face. It's been a few months now, and she feels ready.

Her life from now on will steer firmly clear of anything that reminds her of the spoiled, frivolous, neurotic woman she was. Solitude becomes the essential component of this strategy, and she feels able to face it.

She stops frequenting the places favored by Dominican exiles. Once, on the street, she runs into Manolito, El Cojo,[52] Manuel Hernandez, once a jailer in the torture center of La Nueve. Her stomach drops. She squares her shoulders, drops her gaze, and crosses the street with her eyes fixed firmly on the asphalt.

She remembers how much she used to love reading, especially French novels. She starts volunteering in a reading room for the elderly, recording books that she reads aloud in Spanish for the blind.

She gives up on her lawsuits against Angelita and Radhames for good.

She forgets about Lina's children.

As for men, she draws a line under them.

And gradually, the wide, confident smile returns to her lips.

---

[52] *El Cojo*: "The Gimp."

New York
1975

Flor is fast approaching sixty. Time to take stock of her life? The accumulated years, wear and tear, and a host of bad habits have all gotten the better of her. Apathy, fading desires. It's as if all her energy has simply drained away.

Is a woman old at sixty? Her childhood and youth feel so close she could almost touch them.

But her worn-out body tells a different story.

Rubi did well to avoid reaching this age.

T lived another ten years beyond it. At age sixty he was still sharp and well-dressed, his grip firm on the country's tiller.

The thought of ending it all doesn't occur to Flor. It never really has, or not for more than an instant.

So. In looking back over her life, Flor sees . . .

She sees it all, the whole thing, and it's a vast tragicomic saga with her at the center, its tiny heroine.

She is the little girl battling her dead sister's ghost, struggling to restore her mother's vanished smile.

She is the child wrenched from her island and exiled to the other side of the world for a European education.

She is the adolescent growing up with a permanent sense of not being good enough. Who trembles all over as she holds her school report card out to her father.

She is the young woman enthralled by a lieutenant in a white uniform, married with great pomp in front of her country's elite.

She is the wife reluctantly raising her arm in the official Nazi box at the Olympic Games.

She is the idealist who has forever dreamed of unwavering

love, who believed in it every time, and who, every time, was proven wrong.

She is the resigned woman admitting to herself that youthful dreams are nothing but dreams that don't come true.

She's been all those things, Flor de Oro, and so many more.

In the twilight of her life, as the sun sinks over Manhattan, melancholy sweeps over her, and she wonders what it has all added up to.

But the time for dwelling on her sorrows—that time, too—has passed.

New York
1977

Emerging from her solitary nest one day, Flor ends up proving the Arab palm reader from Paris right.

Despite the scars on her heart from so many failed marriages, her body and soul are aching for love.

She marries for the ninth time on the day after her sixtieth birthday. A gift for her old age? A new promise of happiness?

George Farquar is an engineering salesman, a job that often takes him away from home. Flor has virtually no interest in what he does for a living, but he's a kind and decent man who will be able to provide her with a comfortable lifestyle.

And he, at least, isn't marrying the Ogre's daughter, because the Ogre is no more.

At best, Flor hopes the marriage will mean peaceful companionship.

At worst, another divorce.

But Flor is calm.

Her strength has been ebbing recently.

There isn't much left keeping her in this chaotic world.

Her health is fading.

The doctors have found a lesion on her lung.

The tumor is malignant. The cancer is in an advanced stage.

George Farquar has come along at exactly the right time.

New York
Early February 1978

In a room at Beth Israel Hospital in Manhattan, a woman—still young, still lovely—is fighting her last battle. Her hardest one. The enemy is vicious, relentless, savaging her lungs, consuming her body from the inside. The fire burning within her is aggressive, brutal, deadly.

Flor de Oro slowly turns her head to look at the photo of George on the bedside table, her only companion.

She lifts her eyes to the window, her body quivering as pain runs from her neck down to the small of her back. Outside, a leaden late-winter sky. Weak sunlight illuminates the room with a faint gleam of hope. Flor feels the warmth of it on her face. She can tell, from the softness of the caress, that the day is drawing to a close.

She shuts her eyes.

Everything is telling her that this is the end. Sometimes you have to know when to let go, she thinks. Strength doesn't last forever, and hers has run out.

Her mind wanders, her thoughts drift.

To men. They were her perdition, keeping her forever trapped in their shadow.

Her father.

Porfirio, her true love.

George, her husband. The last one. Her man of resignation.

Where is George? Flor presses the button by her bed. A few minutes tick by. An eternity. The disagreeable sound of rubber squeaking against linoleum. A nurse enters the room.

"Where is George? I need him."

To loosen the knot of anxiety gripping her throat, Flor breathes in deeply. Once, twice, the way Maurice taught her. She relaxes, and waits.

It's time to give up the fight.

New York
February 14, 1978

Flor rests quietly.

She thinks of what was, of what could have been. Of the years that have flown past like fine sand.

She thinks of her shortcomings. What she did, what she didn't do. That weakness at her core, that inability to *be*, to protect herself. The men she couldn't love. The man she loved too much.

She's known so many men, lived in so many countries, experienced honor and disgrace, extreme wealth and poverty, rubbed elbows with the bohemian and the upper crust.

She's been courted, desired, brandished like a trophy, jealously coveted, betrayed, rejected, neglected, humiliated, abandoned, forgotten.

Was she ever loved? Even a little?

Despite all the uncertainties in her life, she is sure of one thing. She *loved*. Despite them. Despite herself. Beyond reason.

To love is all that matters.

How will people remember her? Will anyone remember her? No one will remember anything. She will have spent her time on the earth like a marionette, always with someone else pulling the strings, forever bound by a vow of silence.

What is a life unlived? A life lived by proxy, squeezing into the tiny spaces allowed her, a life lived like an act of vengeance, from man to man, country to country, a mad race against time, against existence itself?

Why was she never strong enough to assert herself, to break free from the weight of sins not her own?

Now, Flor. It's too late for questions. Too late for regrets.

A slight tugging sensation makes her open her eyes. She sighs, looking at the tube connecting her thin arm to the morphine pump.

Her gaze drifts to the window. The February sky is gray, but something in the light hints at the spring creeping closer.

February, the month of lovers.

Flor de Oro closes her eyes. Faces appear behind her eyelids, moving in a slow ballet. The faces of men. Men, her eternal curse.

T. Her beloved father. Her loathed father. El Jefe.

Porfirio, her great, her true, her only love.

The others.

And somewhere among them, her mother, smiling gently. The unloved, neglected Aminta.

In the drawer of her bedside table, her wedding ring. She's taken it off because she kept losing it; her fingers have grown so thin.

A polished seashell she could never bring herself to throw away, with a porcelain-smooth surface and serrated lips, that made a promise and failed to keep it.

Two photographs.

In the first, Flor is sitting on a rattan sofa next to her father. The picture was taken on her first visit home from Bouffémont. She's eleven or twelve years old, wearing a pretty dress in some pale color. Two thin little arms poke out from the dress's puffy sleeves. A wide smile reveals all her teeth, her face lit up with childish happiness. Her father is elegantly dressed in a civilian suit, the corners of his mouth quirking into what's almost a smile. Flor is sitting very straight, looking directly at the photographer. It's the only picture where she's alone with her father, the only one he ever sat for with her, one of the few photos from that time when she believed in life and happiness.

The other photo is a tattered snapshot, once torn into four

pieces and then taped back together, the tape yellowed now into a dirty cross. It's a photo from her wedding. She's so *young*. She stands there in her communion-like dress, radiant on the arm of her suave, handsome husband, confident in the brilliance of their future. *It can't be any other way*, her smile of pure joy says. So many illusions shattered. And yet the photograph is still around. It's survived all these years, accompanied her through the ups and downs of her life all the way to this hospital bed.

Two men, a father and a husband. Two toxic loves.

Responsible, together, for snuffing out the bright hopes of her youth.

The men who made her. Shaped her. Sacrificed her to their folly and ambition.

Who made her the woman she has been.

A monster.

A monster in the most literal sense of the word, the original Latin sense: *monstrum*, a being set apart. A stranger in the world. One born under an unlucky star.

How cruel fate can be.

The ballet behind her eyelids is more beautiful now.
A little white dog with brown-spotted paws.
A rag doll with yarn hair.
Her mother's rounded cheeks and tender expression.
Her man, her only love. Rubi.
Her father, her original sin. Papi.

The words of a love song Lope wrote for her resonate in her mind: *You're the gentle dawn after my sorrowful nights.*
The plaintive melody goes on.
She dances.
Her father is calling her. "Flor de Oro, *mi'jita!*"
Porfirio is reaching out for her. "Fleur, *mi amor!*"
Flor twirls, from one man's arms to the other's.

Then she pulls away, turns her back on them. Frees herself. Jettisons everything that crippled her spirit.

Feels, anew, forgotten sensations. The pure, caramel-scented air of the San Cristóbal fields of her childhood. The taste of salt on her lips. The coolness of river water on her skin. The deep rumble of thunder before a storm breaks. The burning caress of the sun on the back of her neck.

It's an epiphany.

She waltzes alone, whirling, slowly at first, then faster and faster. Flor de Oro is released, infinitely light, free as she has never been.

She's ready.

Papi, Rubi, it's me. Flor de Oro. Flor. Fleur.
I'm leaving you. Farewell. I'm free. At last.

It's February 14. Valentine's Day.

How sardonic death is.

Flor de Oro dies on the holiday dedicated to lovers.

* * *

In accordance with his wife's wishes, George Farquar has her body flown to the Dominican Republic. There, she's watched over by a handful of friends in the chapel of La Paz in the Blandino funeral home in Santo Domingo, then buried in the national cemetery on the Avenida Máximo Gómez.

* * *

Somewhere in the heart of Santo Domingo, a city that once bore her father's name, anonymous and forgotten, Flor de Oro rests.

She's the only one of the Trujillos to be buried on Dominican soil.

The gray marble tablet marking her grave, damp-spotted, is half-buried beneath vegetation, endlessly subjected to the relentless onslaught of sun and rain. It says simply: *Flor de Oro Trujillo de Farquar, July 7, 1915–February 14, 1978.*

In keeping with Dominican tradition, the names of her father and her last husband are affixed to her first name.

Next to Flor's grave marker is its twin. *Aminta Ledesma, October 13, 1970.* There is no date of birth.

From time to time, an unknown Good Samaritan clears away the weeds.

* * *

The grave of Flor de Oro Trujillo as it looks today,
Avenida Máximo Gómez cemetery.
The grave on the right is that of her mother, Aminta Ledesma.

IMAGE SECTION

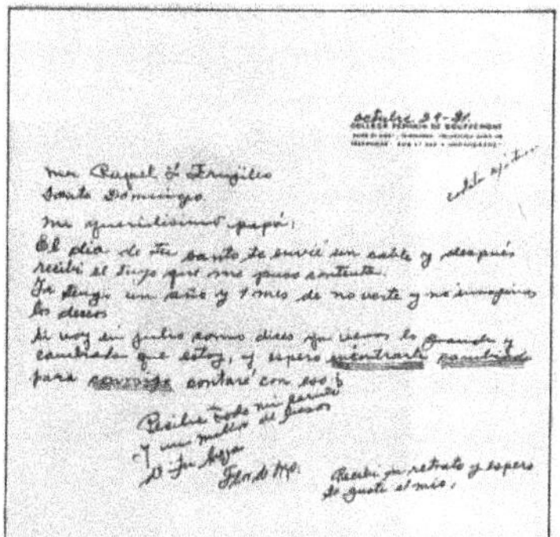

octubre 29-31.

Mr. Rafael L. Trujillo
Santo Domingo

Mi queridísimo papá:

El día de tu santo te envié un cable y después recibí el tuyo que me puso contenta.
Ya tengo un año y 1 mes de no verte y no imaginas los deseos
Si voy en julio como dices ya veras lo grande y cambiada que estoy, y espero [illegible] [illegible] para [illegible] contaré con eso.

Recibe todo mi cariño
y un millón de besos
de tu hija
Flor de Oro.

Recibí tu retrato y espero te guste el mío.

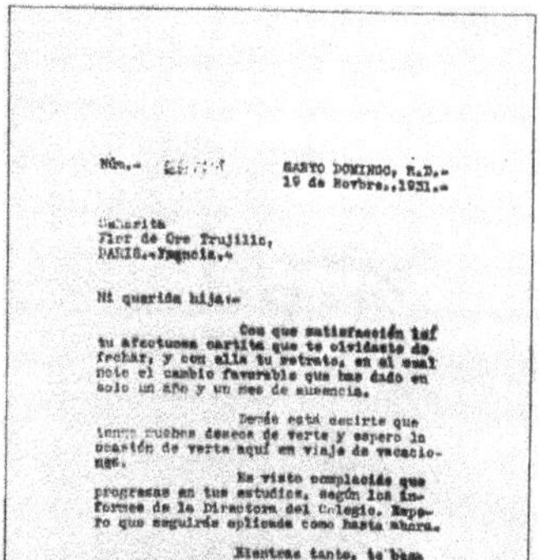

Núm.- [illegible] SANTO DOMINGO, R.D.-
19 de Novbre.,1931.-

Señorita
Flor de Oro Trujillo,
PARIS.-Francia.-

Mi querida hija:-

Con que satisfacción leí tu afectuosa cartita que te olvidaste de fechar, y con ella tu retrato, en el cual noté el cambio favorable que has dado en solo un año y un mes de ausencia.

Demás está decirte que tengo muchos deseos de verte y espero la ocasión de verte aquí en viaje de vacaciones.

He visto complacido que progresas en tus estudios, según los informes de la Directora del Colegio. Espero que seguirás aplicada como hasta ahora.

Mientras tanto, te besa y abraza tu padre,

RAFAEL L. TRUJILLO.

rej-
ep.-

Source: Bernardo Vega, *Los Trujillo se escriben*,
Santo Domingo: Fundación Cultural Dominicana, 1987.

Marriage of Flor de Oro and Porfirio Rubirosa, December 3, 1932. © DR

Flor de Oro with her father and her half-brother Ramfis, 1933. © DR

Flor de Oro and her father, New York, 1940/1941. © DR

Flor de Oro, 1944/1945. © DR

Flor de Oro returning to the
Dominican Republic
for her father's funeral, June 1961. © DR

Behind the Scenes of
The Ogre's Daughter

Back in the 1990s, I wrote a travel guide to the Dominican Republic, then a little-known destination. The "Famous Natives" section didn't have very much in it. "Don't forget Rubirosa, the polo player," my father said. "He was married to Danielle Darrieux." The top French star of the era.

That was how I came to learn about this legendary international playboy with the checkered past, half-gigolo, half-diplomat/spy, whose life ended at the wheel of a Ferrari that smashed into a tree in the Bois de Boulogne in the early hours of a Paris morning. His first marriage had been to Flor de Oro, the eldest daughter of Trujillo, the dictator who ruled the Dominican Republic from 1930 to 1961.

I found all kinds of information about Rubirosa: his scandalous exploits, his female conquests, his marriages, the legend that he was the inspiration for Ian Fleming's James Bond. Plenty of material for a life story.

But of his first wife, Flor de Oro Trujillo, there was almost no trace.

She intrigued me, with that unique first name of hers. Flower of Gold.

What kind of person was she?

What was her childhood like? Her youth? Her life as a grown woman?

Had she been spoiled as a child?

Had she turned a blind eye to the atrocities committed by her father, one of the world's cruelest dictators, a killer, a rapist, a power-mad megalomaniac?

How had she dealt with her appalling parentage?

How did she choose to live her life? Defiantly, in spite of everything? Did she try to fly under the radar? To disappear?

Was she lovable, this daughter of a father so far from lovable himself?

How did she manage?

Did she only just manage?

So many questions that demanded answers.

I read *Enfants de dictateurs*.[53] No mention of Flor de Oro. Who cared about a dictator who ruled a small Caribbean island more than half a century ago, much less his daughter? You would have had to be really interested, or particularly attached to that country.

I was particularly attached to that country.

So I began to search.

In the Dominican National Archives, in the newspapers of the time, in the few books published on Trujillo's dictatorship.

I unearthed photographs of Flor de Oro, and I thought she was beautiful. What struck me most of all was her dazzling, irrepressible smile.

One person who knew her near the end of her life told me, "Flor was vibrant, cultivated, intelligent, joyous, even buoyant . . . and also ill, alcoholic, manic depressive. That's what was rumored, anyway."

I wanted to know what lay behind that smile.

One by one, and not without difficulty, I found her nine husbands.

Nine husbands? A Bluebeard in a dress?

Gradually, as my investigation wore on, I learned the turbulent life story of Flor de Oro. A life story worthy of a novel. One thing is certain; even the most creative writer would have trouble making up a story like Flor's.

---

[53] Christophe Brisard and Claude Quétel, *Enfants de dictateurs*, Paris: First, 2014.

So I decided to tell it. To try to understand her neglected childhood, her relationships with her father and other men, her hunger for freedom, her wasted life.

Flor de Oro's story is a story of abuse, of a life mishandled and poorly lived. It's the journey of a woman turned monster in the most literal sense, a being set apart from the rest of humanity, a woman who dreamed of freedom and made one mistake after another. It's also, in its context, the story of an implacable dictatorship that did unspeakable damage to the Dominican Republic for three full decades.

"The novel is a device invented by humans to understand reality in all its complexity."—Louis Aragon.

Acknowledgments

I received the support of many people while writing this book. I'm endlessly grateful to them all.

Special thanks to:

Sylvie Murelli, always there, unshakably loyal, from the earliest days of my writing career.

Brice Homs, for his encouragement upon reading what was then only the outline of a novel.

Albane Helbert for her careful reading and extremely helpful comments.

Jean-Luc Thorel for having traced archival documents all the way to university libraries on the other side of the Atlantic.

Bernardo Vega for having shared his memories and giving me access to his publications and to the archives of the Dominican History Society.

Frank Burgos and José Manuel Díaz from the National Archives in Santo Domingo, who responded quickly and kindly to all my requests, providing me with rare and precious documents.

Caroline Laurent, my editor, whose enthusiasm and guidance are priceless.

Sarah Rigaud, who watched over the development of this book with patience and care.

The amazing team at Les Escales, who have been with me since the beginning: Marguerite Mignon-Quibel, Anne Laborier, Caroline de Maublanc, and Héloïse Vincent, and last but not least, Vincent Barbare.

Contact me at lafilledelogre@yahoo.com.

Bibliography

Conesa, Gabriel. *La confession de Carlos, tueur à Saint Domingue*. Paris: Éditions Julliard, 1974.
de Galíndez, Jesús., *The Era of Trujillo: Dominican Dictator*, edited by Russell H. Fitzgibbon. Tucson: University of Arizona Press, 1973.
Rubirosa, Porfirio. *Mi vida como play boy*. Santo Domingo: Letra gráfica, 2008.
Trujillo, Flor de Oro. "My Tormented Life As Trujillo's Daughter," interview with Laura Bergquist, *Look* 29, no. 12 (June 15, 1965) and "My Life As Trujillo's Prisoner," interview with Laura Bergquist, *Look* 29, no. 13 (June 29, 1965).
Vega, Bernardo. *Los Trujillo se escriben*. Santo Domingo: Fundación Cultural Dominicana, 1987.
Vega, Bernardo. *Nazismo, Fascismo y Falangismo en la Republica Dominicana*. Santo Domingo: Fundación Cultural Dominicana, 1985.
Vega, Bernardo. *Trujillo en la intimidad según su hija Flor*. Santo Domingo: Fundación Cultural Dominicana, 2009.

Further Reading

Alvarez, Julia. *In the Time of the Butterflies*. Chapel Hill: Algonquin, 1994.
Vargas Llosa, Mario. *The Feast of the Goat*. Translated by Edith Grossman. London: Picador, 2002.
Vázquez Montalbán, Manuel. *Galíndez*. Translated by Carol and Thomas Christensen. New York: Atheneum, 1992.

About the Author

Catherine Bardon is a French writer who divides her time between France and the Dominican Republic. She is the author of *Les Deracines*, which has sold over 600,000 copies and won numerous awards. *The Ogre's Daughter* is her first novel to be translated into English.